On Turtle Beach

Lynne Fisher

For Sheilah, Jean and Dennis

ISBN-13: 978-1545417003
ISBN-10: 1545417008 ISBN

Edition 2017

Cover design by DRF
Images courtesy of pixabay.com

On Turtle Beach

'You can kid the world, but not your sister'

Charlotte Gray

Prologue

December 2009

George Allen sighed. He didn't want to die, but he was resigned to it. He didn't have any energy left to play host to the parasite that had invaded his body over the last two years.

It was just a matter of a few days now, just long enough for him to sort out his affairs, rather than spend the time working out how he felt about dying. His body was taking over anyway, telling him he'd had enough. The most that could be said by the hospital staff was that he had been 'made comfortable'.

This afternoon he was more cheerful than of late. Not because the pain had subsided for a while. The morphine had eased that. No. He smiled and sighed again - in relief.

Both his daughters were by his bedside, both of them at the same time, one on each side of him. This was a major accomplishment for which he was very grateful. The sun slanted through the window blind onto his bedclothes to cast its vote of approval.

'I want you to make an effort to get along,' he murmured. 'Promise me, after I've gone, you'll try.'

'Don't, Dad...don't worry yourself,' said Rhea, the eldest. 'You're looking more tired today.'

'No, I mean it, love. You'll only have each other, you know. Auntie Kathy's well out of the picture in Sydney now. You're going to have to make an effort. You barely ever see each other.'

'You're right, Dad. But I've tried lots of times to suggest a visit...' Lucy replied, her voice tailing off as she saw George's expression.

'That may be true, kiddo,' he said. 'But I want you *both*

to make a fresh start. You're more like each other than you realise. I'm sure you'll find some common ground. I don't want you to be estranged. That's what happened to me and my brothers over the years. It's not healthy, you hear me? It's not right.' George's voice struggled to rise. 'And you've got your kids to think of, they need to know their cousins.'

Rhea and Lucy looked hard at each other, then at their father. They both managed to say, 'Okay, Dad,' almost in unison, but not quite.

'Promise?'

'Yes!' They managed some emphasis.

'Now, Lucy, tell me what you've been painting lately, and Rhea, tell me what's happening at the store.'

Taking it in turns, the two sisters chatted away to George on their favourite topics, while he nodded, smiled and asked questions, the challenge forgotten for the moment, normal modes resumed. But after a while, Rhea fell into a silence.

'You okay, love?' George asked her.

'Oh yes, fine, Dad.'

She paused and glanced at George's water jug on the side cabinet. It was only a third full. She looked at Lucy and smiled. 'Can you go and get Dad some fresh water?' she said, handing it across to her.

'Oh, okay,' Lucy said. Then she frowned. 'You're not trying to get rid of me, are you?'

'No, of course not. Please Lucy.'

'Oh, alright then.' She cast Rhea a look of suspicion as she left the room.

Rhea waited until Lucy had left, until her footsteps disappeared down the corridor. George's room had just one other occupant, a hulk of a man dozing in the corner bed, with his head arched right back on his pillow, confirming his unconscious state by a gaping mouth and an occasional snort.

'Dad,' she said hesitatingly, leaning forward towards

George. 'Dad. Can I tell her if I have to?'

'What?' George was confused.

'You know what,' Rhea said with a sharp look of despair.

A moment of realisation hit George, square in the forehead. His brow crumpled. 'Oh, Rhea, it's been over thirty years. Such a long time. Do you really think it would do any good to tell her?'

'I don't know, Dad. I really don't. But I need to know if it's okay with you,' she pleaded.

George closed his eyes and sighed.

PART ONE

1

Caretta caretta

This was going to be it. What Lucy had been yearning for the last two months, since she and Rhea planned this holiday together, even longer subconsciously, she felt, once she found out about them. Maybe her whole life, she'd been waiting. To see the Caretta caretta. Even their name sounded like a mantra for spiritual renewal, their very being a surviving source of ancient wisdom, according to legend. And Lucy needed to see them. She wanted something from them.

She'd chanted their name softly and rhythmically under her breath on the flight there, while she gazed down at the white wilderness of cloud that looked like a blanket of icing sugar stirred into mountains and valleys, peaks and troughs extending to the horizon and far beyond, while she searched for the occasional glimpse of ocean sparkle below - while Rhea dozed in the adjacent seat, much to Lucy's ever so familiar annoyance.

Nothing changed there then, she reflected. Rhea had always been able to do this: in the back seat of the car on family holidays where there was nothing to see for hours except high hedges or dry stone walls; within half an hour of laying her head on the pillow when they shared a bedroom; *even* when later on as a teenager she'd got bored with attempted late night conversations on the meaning of life. As a light sleeper, easily tipped into insomnia by insistently thumping thoughts caged in her mind, Lucy found the spectacle of such easy unconsciousness as insulting as a slap in the face.

So, urged by the sheer beauty of the scene below, and determined to make an effort, she nudged Rhea awake with a dig in the ribs, to show her the view through the scratched plastic. She received a measure of muttered approval, with a little turn of the neck and swift glance from Rhea, that had to keep Lucy satisfied.

And here they were now on their way to see the Caretta, the giant loggerhead sea turtles that inhabited the Dalyan river delta in South Turkey. It was around 6am on the first morning of their two week holiday, and the sisters had managed to catch the sunrise as they'd waited on the jetty - low embers of red firing to gold behind a backdrop of purple peaks, veil upon hazy veil melting into the dawn.

'Wonderful, isn't it?' Lucy had said, gazing at length.

'Mmm,' said Rhea, rooting around in her handbag. 'I must make sure I've got my camera.'

Arriving late last night, they'd merely had about two hours sleep, and were now on the only pre-booked trip they'd made. Lucy had insisted upon it. She'd been assured by the brochure it was the best time and the only way to see the Caretta, when the turtles were tempted to cast their privacy aside and allow themselves to be lured to the sides of boats for early morning feeds for the delight of the tourists. All other trips were to be decided upon when they got here. The sisters would bargain and barter for them, tit for tat, like they'd done when they were little girls. Lucy was now one down, and she suspected the penalty might be a mud bath, a Turkish massage, or a whole day's shopping.

But for now she was happy. She sat at the back of the boat, away from the main cluster of visitors. Straightening her back, and tucking her legs under her seat, she reached behind her head and removed the hair band holding her hair in its usual scrunched ponytail. She slipped the band over her wrist and directed her face into the cool sea breeze, feeling the wind buffet her hair, and tasting sea salt on her lips. She couldn't reach down far enough to trail her hand in the water, but otherwise it was just perfect. It was a forty minute trip and she was determined

8

to savour every sight, every sound, on her way to seeing the turtles.

The chugging vibrations of the river boat's engine and the lapping waves induced in Lucy an imagined sense of old world exploration and discovery, going where no man or woman had gone before, up the Amazon into dark dense forests festooned in wet mists, or down the Nile passing bleached deserts, scurrying with scorpions, magnified under a burning sun. From the reed bed delta, the slow beating wings of some grey herons, roused from their private meditations of one legged stances amongst the reeds, and the rustling and whispering of bulrushes and pampas, provided the perfect sound accompaniment to Lucy's reverie.

As the boat meandered its way through this maze of islands of tall reed beds, twisting and turning from one channel into another, she remembered the Dalyan delta was a location where *The African Queen* had reputedly been filmed. Perfect setting, she thought, peering into the reeds. The boat had got mired in the mud of the reed beds, in the sluggish green water, while Katherine Hepburn and Humphrey Bogart, or Rosie and Charlie, now on first name terms after their ordeals, had sweated and swatted flies and mosquitoes, then collapsed into exhaustion as torrents of rain pelted the muddy water with pins and needles in an agitated frenzy. Lucy loved that film, she loved struggles against nature, struggles for survival. It all appealed to her romanticising nature. In fact she would have loved to be in a film of her own. Dunes or jungle, she couldn't quite make up her mind. She noticed the mud bases of the reed beds, roots and mud sucked by the river into pitted sculpted forms reminiscent of gargoyles - her artist's eye always drawn to the power of the visual. But then she spotted some dark-grey moving blobs emerging from this sinister camouflage.

'Terrapins!' called out the tour guide, Seda, swiftly interpreting Lucy's enquiring glance. 'We'll soon be there to see the Caretta though.'

I can wait, Lucy thought. There's so much to see on the way. It's all part of the suspense.

As the boat entered a wide channel, Lucy scrutinised the motion picture landscape, to see if she could spot the promised landmarks along the way, these landmarks also of interest to the other early birds on the trip, who were switching on their cameras weighted around their necks and shifting around in their shorts. Rhea was sitting on the opposite side of the boat from Lucy, a little slumped, head down.

'Rhea!' Lucy called over to her. 'Here, have a look! The rock tombs are up there.'

Rhea roused herself. 'I'm tired, Lucy.'

'Yes, well so am I,' she said. 'But we can't miss this. We'll relax and do nothing later on. Okay?'

Rhea caught hold of her bag and staggered a little as she crossed over to the right side of the boat where Lucy had a great view. Lucy had decided to leave her own camera back at the hotel, as she wanted to see and savour the experience through her own eyes and not the objectifying lens of a camera. She wanted the images to burn into her memory.

Some of the male tourists, having gone through various permutations of twisting and leaning in their seats, were now on their feet armed with their cameras, clicking, snipping and snapping at the cliff-sides, as if their very lives depended on grasping proof of their whereabouts - to show off to, and undoubtedly bore, friends and relatives at home. Some fashioned themselves on those journalist photographers they'd seen in war-zone documentaries, legs spread wide, arms tucked in, for *the* best shot. Others were like a Jack Russell at the heels of a postman making a hasty exit down a garden path, as they chased their quarry down the length of the boat for a panoramic series of snapshots. A couple of ladies got their cameras out and quietly took one or two pictures, hardly moving an inch, but satisfied with their efforts, they tucked their cameras away again.

Lucy sat transfixed by the tombs. She stared at the frowning façades carved into the rock which shaded the coal-black chambers within. She'd read about them when she booked the holiday - some writer waxing lyrical about them in a brochure. The tombs overlooked the labyrinth of the estuary to where the Aegean and Mediterranean seas coalesced, whilst their dark interiors were open to the shifting seasons and were explored only by the scanning rays of the sun and the moon. So haunting, Lucy mused, gazing at them. They seemed to be ordering the living never to forget the dead. That's how it should be, she decided, and she thought of her father. He would have found them fascinating, he'd have wanted to meet a local historian for a good long chat.

Seda's voice broke in upon her reflections. 'They were carved 2000 years ago, in the Lycian period,' she said, addressing her captive audience, 'for Greek nobles and later on the Romans from the ancient city of Kaunos, which you can see there to the left. You can just make out the ruined citadel from here, high up on the rock - you see? It's the highest point in the estuary. Note the classical temple portico entrances to the tombs. The unfinished Ionic one shows the methods of hand-carving they used. As you can see, they stopped the detailed carving a third of the way down.'

'Awesome!' enthused a lofty American, gazing through his telescopic binoculars. 'But how did they get up there?'

'The...the...masons, is that the right word? They were lowered down on ropes from the top and worked at different levels on the ropes. The whole point was they wanted the tombs to be in a difficult place, so they could not be looted - see?'

'Awesome!' a collective echo sprang up.

Rhea started taking some photos, with enough motivation to complain about the movement of the boat.

'Don't bother, Rhea! Just look at them! You can't capture the atmosphere on film,' Lucy urged. 'Look, there are some lions facing each other in that one,' she said, pointing up. 'Dad would have loved them, wouldn't he?'

'Yes, he would. But I *do* want to take some pictures, Lucy.'

'Gee, aren't they neat,' a crouching American said loudly in Lucy's left ear, knocking her shoulder as he twisted himself close to her for a different shot.

For goodness' sake, Lucy thought, squirming away from him, whilst giving him one of her especially cultivated irritated scowls and hoping that all this energetic enthusiasm wasn't going to spoil the turtle watch.

She turned her head away from the rock tombs to find something else to look at - for *her* eyes only. She'd always had an aversion to being part of the crowd, but there was no escape on a boat. She found herself searching the swells and ripples of the river water, wanting to see turtles.

Still sitting beside Lucy, Rhea drew a Dalyan brochure out of her bag for a read.

The boat lapsed back into silence as it meandered further down-stream, past the blurring feathered rushes, whilst the heat from the morning sun began to caress the visitors, promising another scorching day in this late June.

But soon there was a commotion up ahead, raised voices and waving arms. The boat slowed up at an opening between two station posts with tall wooden pylons.

'The fish gates have to be raised to let us through,' Seda called out. 'Dalyan has always been a fishing town,' she reminded them. 'It harvests the fish that swim in the Dalyan river. The river flows between the turtle beach, called Iztuzu beach, and the freshwater of Lake Köyceğiz, where the river ends.'

The gate that kept the fish inside the river was slowly raised. There were creaking sounds with the strain of pulleys, as the underwater gate was lowered to let the boat through. The boat inched forward.

Lucy felt it was as if they were taking their leave of some ancient kingdom. Perhaps they were just one of a whole fleet of boats heading for the open sea to go to war, perhaps never to return. Perhaps any second they would be staring up at a Colossus statue towering over the Dalyan lagoon. Perhaps... Perhaps...

Oh, I must stop doing this, Lucy said to herself. I should have grown out of this by now. But there again, what's so wrong with having an imagination? Artists are supposed to, aren't they?

As they entered the sheltered lagoon behind the golden arc of the beach, Seda got to her feet again. This is it! Lucy thought. Soon I'll see the Caretta. She glanced at Rhea, glad to see an expectant expression on her face, brochure tucked away again, whilst the whole boat waited for Seda's instructions.

Seda cast her long dark plait over her shoulder into the centre of her back with a quick flick of her wrist. 'Okay everyone. We are going to moor alongside that fishing boat - you see? We all have to be quiet while the family try to get the turtles to come. They will be using the blue crab that the Caretta like to eat. I think we are the first visitors here this morning, so we should be in luck.'

'Can yer tell us something about 'em, Seda? The turtles, that is,' asked one of the American ladies. 'They have 'em in Florida you know.'

'Yes, of course I will. We'll just get settled for the watch.'

The boat anchored just a few feet away from the bobbing blue fishing boat. The engine was duly switched off and the water slapped gently against the hull. Everyone's eyes were fixed on the man leaning over the side of the fishing boat. He had a cigarette cocked in the side of his mouth, and was lowering a line with some bits of crab attached. He splashed the water with the back of his hand while the man's wife and little boy chatted to each other with animated gestures as they sorted out the bait into buckets.

As everyone waited, peering over the side of the boat, Seda took centre stage for her monologue.

'The Caretta caretta have been coming to this beach, Iztuzu beach, for hundreds of years to lay their eggs. Between May and October. They lay their eggs in sand on the beach and after sixty days all the little babies hatch and make their way to the sea at night following the light of the moon on the water.'

There was a chant of 'Aw' from the visitors, which Seda paused for with rehearsed ease. Lucy was pleased Rhea didn't join in. She had discovered, only recently, that both of them resisted this kind of emotional programming, and had decided it must be a family trait. The Allens simply didn't suffer fools.

'But only a few make it,' Seda continued, 'maybe about ten from each nest of a hundred eggs. They have many enemies. Sea birds, foxes, big fish in the sea, but also the lights from hotels can lead them in the wrong direction. So, to protect the turtles there can be no building on the beach here in Dalyan, no lights to take them away from the moon, and it can only be used from 8am to 8pm. There is also a strip of protected sand all the way along the beach. Where the eggs are laid. You see?' Not wanting an interjection from the crowd at this point, she carried on quickly. 'The marsh here protects them. They can feed here before leaving for the ocean. They live for over a hundred years -'

'Look! Is that something?' Lucy interrupted, leaning low over the side of the boat, staring deep into the green water and seeing fluttering shadows. Everybody followed her gaze.

'Nope, just some tiddlers, minnows maybe,' said the lofty American, who went back to adjusting some dials on his camera.

'They live for over a hundred years, migrating through the open seas,' Seda carried on, her voice raised now, 'but they return to the same beach where they were born to lay their eggs, swimming thousands of miles. So, they spend their whole lives in the water except when they come to lay eggs where they crawl up the beach to dig hole. They can rest or sleep underwater for many hours, but come up for air before diving. We should see them coming up for air when they come to be fed here. Are there any questions?'

'What do they feed on most of the time?' asked Rhea.

'They have good heavy jaw and can feed on clams, conch, crabs, mussels, but also eat jellyfish and sea grass. Their shells can be up to 49 inches long and they can weigh 300 to 400 pounds,' Seda said, still in practiced monologue mode, while her audience gasped.

'Is there any folklore about them,' asked Lucy, twisting round and looking up at Seda.

'Oh yes! That is nice question. They are held as sacred, an ancient sea creature, that has been on earth for over 150 million years. They are linked to the creation of the world itself, and many myths describe them as protectors of people - I like that. They have such kind-looking faces. You will see.'

'Mmm,' said Lucy. Protectors of people, she thought. What a lovely idea. Then her eyes caught sight of a big shape low in the water. 'Oh, I think I can see.... Oh no, it's just a rock! Can't you keep your eyes peeled too, Rhea? You're not making much of an effort.'

Rhea frowned at her.

Just then the excitement that Lucy had been trying to quell, bubbled right up to the surface, as the fisherman started pointing down into the water, a few feet away, but between the two boats. All the visitors congregated together on the left side, nudging each other to get a good view. Dark rounded shapes were moving under and around the boat, reflecting occasional flashes of golden yellow. The crowd quickly shifted from one side of the boat to the other, following the route of the flashes, Lucy always at the front, Rhea well behind.

Seda glanced down. 'Yes, here they are. Quiet now, they are shy.'

The blurring forms focused and enlarged, closer to the surface. Maybe three or four of them. Lucy leaned right over the side and could make out their heavy bronzed mottled shells, their splayed and paddling limbs. But then they disappeared into the shadows again. The fisherman resumed his efforts, refreshed with a newly-lit cigarette, twitching the blue crab offerings on a few more lines he'd set up.

And then the waiting was finally rewarded.

Just for a few brief moments.

A blunted golden ochre head patched with brown blotches broke the surface of the water - a face with dark eyes, heavy lids, nostrils and a wide curving mouth. It took in some air, then slowly dived back down. But a few moments later, it surfaced again to grasp the blue crab on a line right alongside the fishing boat hull. The little boy smiled, edged next to his father, and reached down to stroke the turtle's brow as it tugged at the line. The turtle accepted this gesture of affection for a second or two, then turning, swam under the boat and didn't come back. The tourists began to return to their seats, following Rhea's lead.

Lucy felt crushed. What's the matter with me? she wondered. She was pleased she had seen a Caretta, but somehow the experience just hadn't been enough. She ached to touch the turtle. She envied the boy. And thinking about it, she envied the family's regular contact with the caretta. How lucky they were. She hadn't thought that was all that would happen. Why hadn't the boat been surrounded by turtles surfacing, with many pairs of kind eyes, that looked as if they could impart ancient wisdom, holding hers in theirs. But she knew it was all over. Why had it been so brief? It just wasn't fair. It wasn't what she'd wanted.

The feeding enticement went on for another ten minutes, to adhere to the allotted time. Then the fisherman signalled it was all over.

'Okay, everyone?' asked Seda.

'We didn't see a lot,' said the lofty American, who had been trying to film the turtles with little success.

'Sometimes that happens if there has been another boat here first. Sometimes they are not hungry. You can always come out again. I'm sorry if you are disappointed. There was a sighting....'

'It's okay, Seda. We did see them,' said Rhea. Then she scowled across at Lucy.

'Yes, Seda, don't worry. It was fine,' Lucy said, trying to twist her mouth into a smile.

As the boat returned through the delta maze to Dalyan's river harbour, they all sipped some hot apple tea, provided in dainty plastic cups. Lucy contemplated the steamed droplets breaking into tiny runnels down the inside of her cup, turning it around and around in her hand.

'What's the matter?' asked Rhea, edging closer to her, well out of earshot of the others.

'Oh, I just wanted to see more of them. There's so many close-up photos of them in the brochures.'

'Yes, but what exactly did you expect? To go swimming with them? Up close and personal, like with dolphins, I suppose?'

'Well yes, that would have been nice,' Lucy said sarcastically, as she hadn't liked Rhea's tone.

'Oh, Lucy. That's just typical of you. Everything's got to be so perfect for you, hasn't it?'

Lucy said nothing.

'Why's it so important?' Rhea persisted.

'You wouldn't understand,' replied Lucy, her eyes

fixed on the river cliffs.

Rhea lapsed into silence.

Maybe it had been a stupid idea, Lucy thought, but she certainly wasn't going to explain it to Rhea. Rhea had never understood her anyway. She found herself fighting back some tears that were scalding her eyes. She forced them back down to that painful place they wanted to escape from, to fester some more for another day.

She looked into her lap at the embroidered daisies blurring in and out of focus on her skirt. She'd bought the skirt just before the holiday, because the white daisies reminded her of their mother. Her mother used to put a jug of ox-eye daisies and grasses in the middle of the kitchen table in the summer, and those little black beetles used to crawl out of the yellow middles. She remembered Rhea flicking them out of the way with her finger tips, her mouth sneering with disgust. At least Mum died in her prime, Lucy thought, albeit tragically, at least she didn't live long enough to become disappointed with life. She'd been happy. And their dad, well, he'd never seemed to understand Lucy either. *You're so like your mother,* he used to say, when he couldn't see her point. She slipped the band from her wrist and tied her hair back again, as she always felt more responsible like that. Tougher. It would be so humiliating to cry in public. She was in her mid-forties for goodness' sake. She sighed. The turtles really had been a stupid idea.

2

Sisters

The sisters' hotel was just five minutes from the riverside, so after the early morning turtle watch, Rhea was much relieved to discover they were still in time for breakfast. It was served on a leafy roof terrace, festooned with pink and white bougainvilleas, and they had it all to themselves. The whole day was ahead and it was going to be hot.

'Very hot yesterday and same today, looks like. About thirty degrees. Hot, yes?' replied the hotel owner to Rhea's enquiry concerning the temperature, wiping his brow with the back of his hand.

She read it as an exaggerated gesture, deliberately designed to elicit grins and bobbing heads from them both, as he set down their coffee cups. They obliged him. She remembered he'd checked them in on arrival in the early hours of the morning, when they were dazed and disorientated after a swerving, bumping, thumping ride over pot holes on the right side of the road in a minibus from the airport, driven by a local lad.

'You need sunhats and tan cream all through Dalyan summer,' the hotel owner added.

She noted he had a particularly attractive smile.

As they ate their Turkish breakfast of boiled eggs, sliced sausage, cucumber, olives and tomato, with bread and honey, and as they poured their coffees out, there was little conversation between herself and Lucy. A few perfunctory questions surfaced concerning one sugar or two, milk or no milk, with retorts such as 'Don't you know *yet*?' adding to the tension she'd felt between them since the boat trip. They established that Lucy took milk, no sugar, and she herself took milk and one sweetener. She extracted her sweetener supply from a side pocket in her holiday tote bag, which she'd picked for its superlative range of compartments.

The hotel owner's dog was irritating her. It was acting like a sentinel at their table, shifting from herself to Lucy, examining their every move and facial expression with twitching brow and tilt of the head, pleading for scraps with its dark liquid eyes. Lucy, predictably enough, indulged it, stroking its black wiry scalp flecked with silver, when it finally stationed itself on her side, after she dropped a few bits of bread and sausage. She was trying to do this surreptitiously under the tablecloth, but Rhea was perfectly aware of her activities. And she disapproved. It would be a few stray skinny cats prowling around next, she reflected, like she'd seen in Spain and Portugal.

She began to leaf through a Dalyan trips guide, her pen poised in her neatly manicured right hand. The ring on her third finger kept flashing when it caught the light. It was a recent acquisition, that for some reason she hadn't been able to leave at home: an oval-cut, prong set, pink kunzite and diamond yellow gold ring - 8.6ct. She'd bought it from 'Rocks and Gems', an auction shopping channel, the *best* jewellery shopping channel in Rhea's opinion, classy and select; she didn't bother with the others. The ring had claimed her attention as the price went lower and lower, as the multiple facets of the gemstone sparkled closer and closer on the finger of her favourite presenter, Gemma, captivating, persuading, as she angled it in front of the camera to show off the breathtaking shimmer of this kunzite, to find traces of violet in the delicate pink, to be seen in natural daylight to be truly appreciated. 'Oh, the colour! The clarity! The brilliance!' exclaimed the tanned Gemma, sculpted tightly into a satin evening dress like a Lladro figurine. The ring was a bargain at just £200. 'Last chance!' Gemma announced.

So Rhea had overcome her inner critic, who'd lamely reminded her she had no need of another ring. But she'd argued that she'd been depressed lately since the death of her father, that she needed a treat to cheer herself up - a bit of retail therapy. And she'd only bought about five in all, since she'd first discovered a dormant passion for gemstones a few years ago. So she'd picked up the phone and ordered it. And right now, it looked perfect against her spray tan. But she knew she'd have to be careful not to wear it on the beach, as the gemstone was reputed to fade in strong sunlight; the information card that came with the ring had been quite specific about this. It also said that kunzite had some spiritual properties, bestowing inner peace and joy on the wearer. Well, she didn't believe in any of that nonsense, but she'd keep it in their hotel safe deposit box during the day, and mostly wear it in the evenings. And as she ticked the things in the trips guide that she *might* want to do, this ring flashed intermittently, like a full beam headlight signalling in the dark and telling her to proceed with caution.

And she did feel worry nibbling at her core of coolness.

Now and again she twisted the ring around and around on her finger. She felt that at the moment Lucy wasn't being the Lucy she knew. She wasn't doing her usual chattering: chattering that asked lots of questions or pointed things out, probing, pushing, squeezing; chattering that had made the young Lucy the fanned flame when aunts and uncles visited, all that fluttering round her, all that laughing and teasing; that very same chattering that stung Rhea deep inside a tender part of herself she didn't like very much, when it had made Lucy their mother's favourite. She remembered when she and Lucy were arguing up in their bedroom, she'd often told Lucy that she *wittered on* too much, that people got tired of it, the older sister giving 'guidance' to the younger. Lucy had sometimes gone quiet after that, but not for long of course. And Rhea realised now, it was as if she was trying to snuff Lucy's candle out.

And earlier, on the boat, when Lucy had been leaning so far forward and looking into the water, she'd actually felt like shoving her over the side. This compulsion had appalled her. Where had it come from after all this time? It was in terrible taste, considering their own mother had died by drowning all those years ago - something she'd been trying not to dwell on since her father died. *A tragedy*, people said of her mother's death, *just like Edith Holden...you know...The Country Diary of an Edwardian Lady... reaching for those chestnut buds down at the Thames.*

After it happened, Rhea had never been able to push anyone into the pool at the swimming baths during school lessons, or even during their 'family fun' times. Their dad had insisted they go swimming together as a family - *Swimming's great,* he said to them. *I don't want you to miss out because of what happened to your mother. It's best to deal with it now. Water's nothing to be afraid of.* And he'd made them duck down in the deep end holding their noses, then float to the top, and he'd made them practice taking a deep breath, going under to hold it for as long as possible, then start to slow-release silver bubbles through their nostrils. He did all these exercises with them to demonstrate correct technique. He wanted to equip his girls with the necessary skills to enjoy the water and never be afraid of drowning. He meant well. But Rhea had hated these underwater tests. She'd kept imagining her mother. She only did them to keep her dad happy. And ever since these 'family fun' times, she'd always preferred to swim with her head well out of the water.

So why did I feel like pushing Lucy out of the boat? she wondered, searching for a logical answer. Well, she's always so full of herself, she thought. It's always about her. Always was. All that chattering, all that wittering. All that admiration. *It's just because she's the youngest,* her dad explained all those years ago. But it didn't cut any ice.

In the end though, Rhea discovered a distinct

advantage for herself. On family visits, Lucy's wittering meant that she, Rhea, could keep herself to herself. *A bit of a dark horse* those relatives said about her, slow to get any answers from their desperately dredged up questions of *And what do you want to be when you grow up, Rhea?* and even worse, *How's school?*

There was a lot to be said for privacy, Rhea thought, a certain freedom in it. Because of Lucy's chatter, she'd never had to think of much to talk to her about in their later years; and actually, she had to admit that the adult Lucy had provided a reasonably interesting pick and mix of subjects, so there was usually one that she felt to be palatable. And that was how she liked it. But right now, Lucy wasn't talking, ever since the turtle watch, and Rhea felt uneasy. She'd tried to find out what was wrong with her, hadn't she? She'd made an effort. This holidaying together was going to be harder than she thought. In fact, she'd given it *little* thought. And why was that? she pondered. Well, whatever the reason, she should have.

She turned another page of the brochure. 'There's so much to choose from,' she said, casting the booklet down on the table and glancing at Lucy. 'Here, you'd better have a look. Hopefully they'll be some things we both want to do.'

As Lucy examined the brochure, Rhea sipped her coffee, stirring it occasionally to keep the flavour consistent. She found this action soothing and it always aided her thinking.

This holiday had actually seemed a reasonable idea six months ago, just after their Dad's funeral. They'd taken on board his specifically asking them to make an effort to get along, now that they were only going to have each other - as he'd put it. He'd even reminded them about it in his will.

Of course this request had come as a bit of a shock. It had made the two sisters' unwritten and unspoken

23

contract of mutually agreed avoidance just a little too real, as if something fuzzy like snow had been frozen and sharpened into a blade of ice - to prod and accuse them both with the irrefutable fact that they were really lousy sisters. And George had never let them forget about it over the years. Christmas times had been the worst, very difficult to avoid each other then.

Of course he hadn't made any legally binding stipulations in his will, such as forcing them to visit each other to get their share of the inheritance (which had of course been split down the middle). No, that wasn't his style. That would have been inviting too much of the Hollywood drama, a bit too Joan Crawford and Bette Davis, all arched eyebrows, pursed lips and grotesquely played parts. No, he'd been cleverer than that, and he'd been a gentle-natured man. He'd simply appealed to their reason and suggested they should want to do it for themselves. And a holiday had been Lucy's idea, proposed as a good way to get to know each other properly, with no family or work distractions, with no way to avoid being together - just the two of them.

So after a market research-style consultation with each other on what they both liked, which reassuringly for their relationship (they decided at the time) didn't hold too many surprises, Lucy had found out about Dalyan in Turkey.

Dalyan was a fishing village river resort in the Muğla province of Turkey on the south coast, just half an hour's ride from the airport. It had access to a protected beach for turtles, where no water sports or speed boats were allowed, so it was perfect for sunbathing and swimming. There were ancient sites to visit and trips could be arranged further afield.

A major advantage was that it didn't offer the kind of fun, frolics and readymade 'entertainment' catered for in the larger resorts, for easily bored kids or fly and flop adults. No vast multi-storey hotel complexes, no drunken nightspots and bars, no chained-together herds of rowdy rebel rousers hoofing it down the streets. Dalyan was relatively quiet, and a safe bet for couples and more mature people, shall we say, who didn't want children around, or boozing young 'adults' who couldn't hold their drink, swearing their heads off in the early hours, then vomiting up semi-digested kebabs in shop doorways. No, in this respect, Dalyan was a veritable haven. Rhea and Lucy had agreed it ticked all the boxes and booked it.

But really! Rhea thought. What was I thinking of? Going on holiday together? I must have been mad. Of course, it was straight after the funeral and she'd felt they *did* have to find a way of getting along better, so she'd agreed to the holiday. But the fact was, they'd never got on and they never would. They were just too different. And what was so awful about that anyway? It wasn't so unusual in families. Clare, her secretary, hadn't spoken to her brother for fifteen years and she'd heard of other similar cases, although they generally kept it quiet of course. You had to whittle it out of them, like a shameful secret. You tended to hear more from the supposedly inseparable siblings, gushing on about how close they were to their sister or brother, always visiting, distance no object, wouldn't be without them *for all the world*. But was that really the case?

No, she reminded herself, she and Lucy were doing this holidaying together for their father, and she did intend to try. Really, she did. But two weeks! And they were sharing a room together - she just couldn't think about that yet. Why had she agreed to *that*? Last night she'd been so tired, just collapsing into bed around 3am, no time or energy for realising the ramifications. If sharing hadn't worked when they were girls, what made them think it would work now? And this was only the first day. What was she letting herself in for? She drained her coffee cup and contemplated the dregs.

'Come on, then,' she sighed, eventually looking up at

Lucy, giving her the short tight smile she'd cultivated during her early years of customer service. 'Let's go and sit over there, pick our trips, then go and find the rep and book them. Okay?'

'Okay,' said Lucy.

They moved from under the shady awnings to the edge of the terrace, where there were two leather sofas on either side of a coffee table, all dappled in sunlight.

The dog went with them. It jumped onto the shaded end of its favourite sofa and curled up for a snooze with a snorted sigh. It couldn't be assigned to a particular breed, but it was slimly built, with the floppy ears and long nose of a collie. Lucy sat next to the dog, Rhea opposite her, and they ordered more coffee.

'Are you still tired,' Lucy asked her.

'Well yes, aren't you?'

'Yeah, I am now.'

'Okay then. After the rep, shall we just get a feel for the place, just relax, like you said earlier?'

'Yes, fine. Your choice now. Oh God, Rhea!' Lucy exclaimed, her face brightening. 'Look at the view!'

They both got up and leaned on the terrace wall, resting their arms on the cool white marble.

Adjacent roof terraces jostled for attention, their vine-scrambled canopies sheltering tight compositions of potted palms, banana plants and red geraniums with check-clothed tables, chairs and hammocks, so that every inch of space could be used to bask in the heat and the view. Craggy mountains stippled with pines surrounded the town on all sides, a town of pan tile roofs and satellite dishes pointing to the heavens, a town still guarded by the spirits of ancestors in the river cliff temple tombs. And piercing the sky, reaching for Allah, was the minaret of the mosque in the central square.

'It's so beautiful,' Lucy sighed.

'Yes, it is. It reminds me of Spain in a way,' Rhea said.

'You've travelled a lot haven't you? Charlie and me

have always gone on walking holidays mostly, you know the Western Isles, or the Devon coast. We sent you a postcard sometimes, do you remember? I could do with a bit more of this though. I've always thought travelling to different landscapes could inspire my painting.'

'Well maybe now Poppy's at Uni, you can do that,' said Rhea, trying hard to remember Lucy's postcards *or* her paintings. Their father had some of Lucy's paintings on his walls at home, but Rhea realised she'd never really looked at them properly. She knew they were landscapes and that was about it. She might have looked at them properly after the funeral, but when they were staying at the house to sort out the contents, Lucy had already taken them away. As for Poppy, she was Lucy's daughter. Just like her mother, Rhea thought, another artist-type, flaky and unpredictable. And of course their own mother had been like that, which is where they must have got it from - but she pushed the thought away. Rhea had always been quite fond of Poppy though, when she'd seen her on the occasional visit. She'd always wanted a daughter. But Rob, her son, he'd turned out all right, she reflected. He was kind-hearted, reliable, practical, and she'd made sure he could look after himself. He could make a Spaghetti Bolognese and do his own washing and ironing. She'd made sure he could be either independent or make a good husband.

Not at all like his father, her slippery slug of a husband, who left a slime trail for her to clean up behind him, wherever he'd been slithering, wherever he'd happened to have paused for a few seconds: a knife oozing with butter, a seed scatter of breadcrumbs on the floor, tea bag stains on the worktop, cupboard doors wide open, and that was just the kitchen. No matter how firm she'd tried to be with him over the years, it had made no difference. So much for thinking she could change his habits. Thank God he stayed in his so called 'den' most of the time now.

This contemplative moment was broken by the hotel

owner setting down their coffees on the table behind them.

'Sadik, he bothering you, no?' he said, gesturing to the curled up sleeper, who opened one eye.

Lucy smiled. 'Oh, no. He's fine. What does Sadik mean?'

'Sadik? I think it mean...faithful, in English.'

They all looked at Sadik and he cocked the other eye at them.

'You two sisters, yes?' asked the hotel owner.

Lucy and Rhea looked sharply at each other. Rhea wondered how he'd picked up on that. They'd never mentioned it when they'd checked in. She could never understand how people could see a likeness. She'd never thought they looked like each other at all. She was blonde and curvy (a bit too curvy for her liking at the moment), and Lucy was dark and annoyingly slim of course, as slim as a pencil with the paint stripped off. Anyway, they certainly didn't act like sisters.

'How can you tell?' asked Lucy, frowning.

'Same noses, same mouths,' he said, grinning. They both stared at each other, straining to find the likeness, like they had done on countless other unresolved occasions scattered across the years like bits of broken glass they might step on, sharp and potentially harmful. The hotelier broke the silence that seemed to be stretching out, taut like a rubber band about to snap and cause an injury. 'But otherwise, of course, you very different, I'm sure. I'm Hasim,' he said. They shook his hand and introduced themselves, first Lucy, then Rhea.

Hasim was tall, lean, and well toned for his age, Rhea decided, with none of that spare belly flesh that swelled out like dough left to rise, over the trouser belt of an overweight man - like Chris, her husband. Hasim's aquiline features seemed to bestow him with the look of an Arab - these features enhanced by his short wavy hair and designer stubble. Only the greying hair around the temples betrayed the fact that he was probably in his late forties. She was convinced he held her own hand for longer than Lucy's - she felt his long strong fingers, their firm grip. She noticed his arched black eyebrows, the easy relaxed look in his dark eyes as he held her gaze. It was as if he knew her already, as if he could see into that soft part of herself she didn't like very much, as if he wanted her, as if he'd been waiting - just for her.

Then she caught hold of herself. I'm getting carried away, she thought, all these Turks must be the same, they've probably all got these come-to-bed eyes. But why hadn't she noticed him when he checked them in? But there again, she and Lucy had been so tired, like drooping vines propping themselves up at the reception desk, desperate for refreshment.

She spotted the seating arrangements behind him in the centre of the terrace. Low bed recliners and cushion arrangements around a low table, for traditional Turkish relaxation time: maybe smoking some tobacco the conventional way through one of those water pipes; maybe eating Turkish Delight, all sweet, soft and languorous, like in a Turkish harem, semi-naked, draped in translucent muslin clinging to soft flesh in the vaporous heat, feeling the grazing of dark stubble from an insistent jaw, the opening into a probing kiss, making love seraglio-style - and she stared back into Hasim's eyes.

Lucy cleared her throat and Rhea managed to take the hint. Get a grip, she said to herself, grateful for Lucy's interjection, though she doubted its helpful intent. She jolted herself out of the throbbing circuit of attraction by breaking eye contact with Hasim and sat down at the table, now scattered with brochures from Lucy's bag.

'Come on, Lucy,' she said sharply, 'we'd better get on with this.'

'I have good book on Dalyan,' Hasim said. 'I get for you.'

And much to Rhea's relief he went off and started

searching behind the bar.

Sadik raised his head, looking over to where the rummaging thumps were coming from, then gave a long yawn before resting his head down on his paws again. He glanced at Lucy, who smiled at him, then he closed his eyes.

Rhea and Lucy started discussing their choices. The priority was what to book up for, as some of the trips were on set days. Rhea pulled out a notebook from her bag and started drawing up a holiday time chart to fill in for the two weeks, starting from their first day, which was a Sunday.

Lucy scowled. 'Do we really have to do it this way?'

'Well, it's better to be organised.'

'Not much room for spontaneity though, is there?'

Rhea frowned, staring down at all the mornings and afternoons to fill. 'Okay, we can leave optional spaces for deciding as we go. But at least we can plan the time better with this.

'Okay - I suppose so.'

The time had finally come. They could no longer put off the decision making, so they started to state their preferences, leafing through the booklets and showing each other the glossy pictures and seductive descriptions.

'I really want to go snorkelling,' Lucy said eagerly. 'I've been practicing going under water again at the swimming baths, like Dad used to make us do. I've found I really enjoy it now. I borrowed a friend's set of fins and snorkelling gear to practice in the pool and it's really easy, Rhea! It's wonderful! You might like it too. It's quite safe, you know. Especially with a valve at the top to stop the water coming into your mouth. I might like to try some scuba diving as well, actually.'

Rhea was dismayed. Lucy's degree of motivational planning made her feel uncomfortable again - pricking her into thinking that she too should have been thinking of personal challenges. But wasn't this holiday challenge enough? Record levels of sunbathing was what she'd had in mind. She just *might* be able to cope with the snorkelling. She could probably put her face in the water for that. But scuba diving? Being trapped fathoms down in murky dark water, totally reliant on breathing equipment, and what if it was faulty anyway? And then there was the having to jump into deep water from the boat - a huge jump, a frenzy of bubbles, struggling to get back to the light - or even worse, being expected to roll backwards into it - plip, plop, just like that. Finding yourself in God knows what position, with your bottom sticking out of the water. Well, no way. Lucy really had to be joking.

'Well, the snorkelling might be fine,' she said in a measured tone, 'if it's true you don't have to worry about getting water in your mouth. There's a twelve island sailing boat trip here that I've marked. It sounds good. You can sunbath, swim and snorkel while they stop at a few bays, and you get lunch provided. It's on a Friday.'

'Yes, I saw that one, it looks great.' That trip was duly agreed upon and Rhea penned it onto the plan.

'But what about the scuba diving?' Lucy asked.

Oh my God, she's not going to let it drop, thought Rhea, sinking into herself to dredge up an answer. 'Well, it's bit adventurous, isn't it?' she said, wanting to scream at her – No way!

Lucy paused. 'Well yes, I suppose that's the point. Being adventurous. I think Dad sometimes wanted to be a bit more adventurous. Like the time that friend of his offered him a motorbike. Mum was up for it, but Dad told her it was probably a bit too dangerous. But he did take a while to decide. I think he was tempted,' Lucy went on. 'They might have loved it, something for them to do together, like you and Chris - Chris used to have a bike, didn't he? Anyway, did you ever see them doing anything together? I remember seeing Dad looking at the bike in the drive, circling round it, he even sat on it. Mum got all excited, but he wouldn't take it on. She was very disappointed and -'

'Yes, I think I remember,' Rhea cut in. But she didn't want to remember. Those days were gone, and she wanted them kept that way. 'He was generally cautious though, and he did have the two of us to think of. He kept us safe after she died, it was his main priority.'

'Oh, I know that. But he might have got more out of life if he'd - oh, I don't know, all I was meaning was, maybe deep down, he would approve of us having a go at diving. Life's too short and all that.'

'Maybe. But I don't want to do it, Lucy. And thinking about this. Do we have to do everything together?'

Lucy stared at Rhea, her mouth gaping open. 'What?' she exclaimed. 'You're kidding! But that's why we're here! Doesn't separating off rather go against the spirit of that?' she said exasperatedly. 'I can't believe you've said that! *Why* have you said that?'

Rhea was silent, staring down at the holiday plan, then she dragged her eyes out over the rooftops to the sky, where she spotted a bird with a large wing span. With her gaze, she followed its outstretched wings and gliding flight path. It circled overhead, then it angled itself towards the horizon, slowly becoming a speck, and then nothing. She wished she could follow it. But Lucy was still waiting for a reply and she had to make it a good one. She turned and looked at her.

'Well, it's only ...' she began - already finding it difficult to hold eye contact.

Just then, Hasim came over with the book he'd been hunting for. 'Maybe it help a little, yes?' he said, looking from one of them to the other, his brow creased in concern, as he handed it out to them, as it hovered in the air, as he waited for one of them to take it. It had the fluffy worn edges and comfortably creased cover of a book well thumbed, either a sign of it being an out-dated irrelevancy or a venerable tome of reference. 'But maybe you not - '

'Thanks, Hasim,' Lucy said quickly, grabbing hold of it. She had a look at the title: *Dalyan: The Land, The Sea, The People*, and it was in English. She started flicking through it. 'Oh, this looks really interesting! Thanks. Is it okay if I borrow it…for reading later in our room?'

'Yes, yes. That is fine, no problem.' He turned and made a swift retreat down the marble staircase, two steps at a time, his wavy head of hair disappearing out of view. Rhea and Lucy were alone with their coffee and it had gone cold.

'Well?' Lucy said, thumping the book down and waiting for a response from Rhea.

Rhea tried again. 'Look, Lucy, we have to be realistic.' She squared up to Lucy's stinging stare. 'It's impossible for us to do all the same things. I want to go to Ephesus, you said you didn't. I want a Turkish massage or maybe the mud baths, you're not bothered. I want to do some serious shopping, you don't. You want to go scuba diving, I don't. I know we have to be together most of the time, and I want that to work too. But why spoil a good holiday in a lovely place feeling deprived. Do you see the problem?'

Lucy frowned. 'Well, I suppose so. But it seems very defeatist.'

'Well, we'll see what we can both do with some compromises, but allow for a few separate days on our own. After all, we'll have all the evenings together,' Rhea sighed.

Lucy thought for a moment. 'Okay, I can see what you're getting at, I suppose it makes sense - in a *way*.'

After more discussion, they found they could agree to do the following activities together: riverboat or bus trips to the turtle beach; going over to the ruins of Kaunos and maybe seeing if they could climb up the slope to the rock tombs; relaxing by the hotel poolside; local shopping; booking a trip to the nearby town of Fethiye for shopping, which also included visiting a ruined city and the Blue Lagoon; going on a Turkish entertainment night; and of course they'd be having their meals together in the cafe bars. Lucy made it clear these joint activities sounded only just adequate, but to Rhea's mind they were more than enough.

Individually, Lucy was to have her scuba diving day and an 'authentic village life' excursion to see the 'real' rural Turkey, whilst Rhea was to have her day trip to Ephesus and a Turkish bath and massage day. But this was all providing the trips were running on schedule. Rhea was praying that this would be the case and intended to be firm about it.

Then another thought occurred to her. 'What about the turtles though?' she asked Lucy. 'Do you want to try another turtle watch?' She tried to say it casually, knowing that not getting a closer view of the turtles had upset Lucy. God knows why, she thought, some crackpot idea of hers, but she didn't fancy being with Lucy for two whole weeks if she was going to be pining for them all the time.

'No, I don't think so,' Lucy replied, looking into her lap.

Rhea leaned forward. 'You know, Seda told me there was a turtle sanctuary on the beach. You'd already marched off the boat when she told me.'

Lucy looked up. 'Oh, right. I didn't know about that. What do they do there?'

'Well, Seda said they look after some of the injured ones. They have big tubs of water that they keep them in.'

'Injured ones? That's awful! What injures them?'

'She said they get caught in fishing nets. But also the boat trips can...you know, the boat propellers. Ironic, really. It's partly the tourist industry - more tourists, more boat trips, more injuries -'

'Oh my God! That's awful! Just awful!' Lucy jumped to her feet and started pacing around, her hand glued to her forehead. 'If I'd known, I'd never have wanted to go on a turtle watch. Never!'

Sadik awoke, jumped off the sofa, and followed at Lucy's heels, turning when she turned, stopping when she stopped. Ready to be commanded, his face scrutinised hers - just like a dog at Crufts going through its paces.

'Well, we weren't to know, were we? Sit down, will you! You're upsetting the dog. Anyway, do you want to see them in the sanctuary or not?'

Lucy stopped her pacing and looked at Rhea, her face ashen. In that moment Rhea realised her mistake, groaned inwardly and braced herself.

'What?' Lucy shrieked. 'No! Are you kidding? See them maimed, missing a leg or two? Broken shells? No way!' Sadik seemed prompted to take his cue and he barked deeply.

'Will you please sit down, there's no need for all this,' Rhea said despairingly.

This is just like the old Lucy, she thought, all fired up about something and showing herself up. But thankfully there was no-one around on this occasion to witness Lucy's performance. She'd done her best to show Lucy some consideration, hadn't she? And look at the reaction. Was it worth the effort? The expression 'overreacting' came to the tip of her tongue, she rolled it around like a marble, probing it, examining it, feeling the compulsion to spit it out at Lucy. But she thought better of it and swallowed it back down. She'd often accused Lucy of this when they were girls, and she knew it would only make her react even more. No, she'd vowed to herself, she was going to be careful. After the last few difficult months, she was determined to find a way to somehow enjoy this holiday. For that to happen, things had to go smoothly, which meant Lucy had to enjoy it too. There was no other way. And they both owed it to their father. They were adults now, they were sisters, they only had each other. Her father's words replayed in her mind like they had on the flight out: *I want you to make an effort to get along, promise me, after I've gone, you'll try.* She was trying to hold onto these words, to have them ring loud in her ears, to convince herself through their volume and force. But right now, they'd faded to a tinkle. And this was only the first day.

Still pacing, Lucy looked at her. She stopped, went over to Rhea, sat down next to her and sighed.

'Look, Rhea. I'm sorry. I know you don't like it when I rant on, I just can't help it sometimes. Some things get to me more than you, you know? I'm suppose I'm more sensitive than you.'

Rhea felt her own temper rising, but decided to let the comment pass while Lucy continued.

'I know you're just trying to help. But, no. I couldn't bear the sanctuary. Just forget about the turtles. Okay? Just forget about them,' she said with emphasis.

Then she put her arm around Rhea's shoulders to give her a hug.

Rhea stiffened, but she let herself be squeezed and she managed to crack a grimacing smile at Lucy. Oh no, she winced inwardly, not the hugging thing. They'd somehow ended up hugging now and again when they'd been sorting things out after the funeral. Lucy had started it. But that was then, when they hadn't been themselves. Surely they didn't have to carry on? After all, they'd never been demonstrative with each other. It was a bit hypocritical to start now.

Lucy resumed her seat opposite her, much to Rhea's relief. 'Come on, here you go,' she said to Sadik, patting his place on the sofa. 'Alright then?' she asked Rhea.

'Yes. Fine.'

Rhea was glad both the outburst and the demonstration of affection were over.

'Is there anything else you want to do, then?' she asked Lucy, wanting to move her on from turtles.

'Well actually, there's one thing left we haven't talked about.'

Rhea raised her eyebrows. 'What?'

'Hiring a car for the day. A jeep to be more precise.'

'A car?' Rhea said incredulously.

'Well, a jeep. Open top would be much nicer, don't you think?' She placed a brochure in front of Rhea and pointed at a picture. 'Like that one.'

Rhea stared at the white jeep in the picture: a four wheel drive, all-terrain vehicle, chunky bodywork, antiroll bars, spare wheel on the rear, open to all weather seats, and back seats you had to climb into, just a shallow front windscreen to keep kamikaze flies from bombarding your face. She imagined herself and Lucy sitting in it. Together. A whole day. No escape. But she tried to wriggle a way out.

'Have you brought your license? I haven't got mine.'

'Yes, I've got mine. So, I'd have to do all the driving, then. But you know, I did mention it when we decided to come here. You said 'maybe'. I thought you might have brought it just in case.'

'Oh, yes. Sorry.'

Rhea vaguely remembered Lucy talking about it, but she'd been *wittering on* about so much, as usual, that Rhea tended to tune out, as usual. And she didn't think she'd been serious. But she was beginning to realise she'd been underestimating Lucy. She tried some more wriggling.

'But they drive on the right here.'

'Yes, but that's okay. I've always wanted to have a go at driving on the right.'

'Yes, but it's more difficult than you think. I've only done it in France and it took some practice - I only really felt I'd got used to it by the end of the week. Anyway, they don't exactly seem to follow the rules here, weaving around all over the place - it might be a bit dangerous.'

'But that just makes it more exciting. It's adventurous. And I want to be more adventurous. Anyway, I'm used to handling a land rover, so that should help. Of course you'll have to do the map reading.'

'Well that's another thing, we don't have a decent road map.'

'We can probably get one.'

'What about insurance?'

'It's included in the price.'

'What is the price, isn't it expensive?'

'No, actually. It seems to be about 80 lire a day. Plus the petrol of course. Anyway this holiday isn't about stinting ourselves, is it?'

'What if we break down?'

'Oh, come on, that's not likely to happen! Anyway there's a call out service apparently.'

Rhea slumped her shoulders, feeling like a hammered-down nail. 'Where will we go?'

'We can ask the rep for some advice. But the map in this brochure shows a road that goes all the way around the lake, and maybe there's a beach we can go to. It would be great to see some of the surrounding countryside, don't you think? I'm only thinking for one day.'

Rhea couldn't think of any more excuses. Lucy would just have to find out for herself. It wasn't easy driving on the right. If they had an accident, then so be it.

'Okay,' she said tersely. 'We'll do it. But later on in the second week.'

'Great! That's fine. Thanks, Rhea, it means a lot.'

Rhea looked at her watch. 'It's half eleven already. Come on, we'd better go and find the rep.'

As she stood up, she realised the waistband of her linen shorts had been cutting into her waist all morning, like a ligature squeezing that inch of spare flesh that she hadn't been able to get rid of at the gym before the holiday. These shorts suited her curvy figure perfectly, when that inch of spare flab wasn't there. They flattered her shape by showing off her slim waist, and she'd kept them for years because of this, tucked at the bottom of a pile of looser fitting ones. Shorts were like trousers, so difficult to find a good fit, so she'd felt she had to bring these with her. They were fine for walking around in, but she'd been doing a lot of sitting and was feeling the pinch.

'I'm just going to change first,' she said to Lucy who was gathering the brochures together.

'Why? You look fine,' Lucy said, casting her eye over Rhea.

'I won't be long, okay? You can wait for me in reception.'

'Yes, but why do you have to change?'

'Well I need to…. Look, I just do! Okay?' she said, with an edge to her voice.

'Alright, alright! Just don't be long.'

Lucy grasped hold of Hasim's book and handed it to Rhea. 'Here, pop this in the room, will you?'

Despite her aching calves, Rhea somehow found the energy to stamp through the interior courtyard with its stately potted palms and upstairs to their room. She thrust the key into the lock, flounced inside and slammed the door. Flinging the book onto Lucy's bed by the balcony window, she started rummaging in her luggage bag for another pair of shorts, finding the ones that she designated as easy-fit. They had a low slung waistline and wider legs, quite unflattering she felt, but roomy to wear. A long loose cheesecloth top was chosen to look floaty and hide her hips. After she changed, she felt a bit calmer and ready to go back down. Lucy was waiting and was probably already getting impatient.

But she was struck by a thought. She hadn't had her morning cigarette. It was the one cigarette of the day that she never missed at home. And right now, she decided she needed it. She felt she had to take this opportunity, as she never smoked in public places, and it would be hours before she'd get another chance. She smoked in secrecy these days, not being able to endure the detrimental judgments upon her character, even though she kept it to five a day. She took out her Marlboro Lights and lighter from the bedside table drawer, grabbed hold of the chunk of glass provided on the dressing table, and went out onto the balcony to light up. She gazed down at the pool. It really did look beautiful - a lake of turquoise tranquillity, its calm water kissing its marble shoreline. She could look forward to that later on in the afternoon. As she took her third deep drag, the urgency to quickly get through her cigarette vanished in a puff of smoke. She decided she'd take her time as she felt manipulated over the car hire day. She slowly exhaled. Lucy could wait.

3

At The Pomegranate Cafe

As they both stepped onto the pavement, a pressing heat wrapped around them like a blanket of balm, soaking into their pores and acting as a general anaesthetic on their frayed nerves. At least for the time being. It was simply going to be too hot to be tense, too hot to be in disagreement, and they were here to try to enjoy themselves. The heat might even serve as an ally in promoting a climate of compromise between them - through stupefying their senses and sensibilities. Lucy had promised Rhea they would spend the day 'chilling out', and she herself wanted to get a personal feel for Dalyan. The two aims could surely not be found mutually exclusive.

They stood there for a moment, disorientated in the glare of the overhead sun, then fished in their bags for their sunglasses. Rhea's were tinted dark grey, Lucy's brown; so Dalyan was to be seen through two different filters. As they appraised one another, this came as no surprise whatsoever after a lifetime of different tastes. If they'd found something in common it would have caused a good degree of consternation and self-examination, rather than a warm glow of sisterly alliance.

To their left, the narrow pedestrianised street led to the riverside and a bobbing fringe of bright boats, Turkish flags flapping in a gentle river breeze, waiting to welcome passengers. But this was presently a dead end for the sisters' purposes, so they turned to their right to where they could just make out an intersection of streets. The location of the holiday representative's office was indicated as a squashed spider splattered in biro on the map of Dalyan that Rhea was clutching.

But progress was slow.

First, a moped bore down on them, manoeuvring around them with a clearance of only a few inches from Rhea's arm, making them both halt and stare after it. It proceeded down the road, which was brimming with shops and restaurants, buzzing and meandering through the general flow of holiday makers, like a bee that wasn't quite sure where the nectar was, only that it was surely towards the centre of Dalyan. They followed the bee.

The next impediment was that the restaurants had started touting for lunch customers, so strategically placed waiters were at their designated posts outside the entrances to pull in the punters.

'See the menu, ladies?' A well-dressed young man, wearing an endearing smile, came forward into their path from a restaurant called the Tamarisk. 'Fresh fish, sea bass, caught today. Just 15 lire. Good, yes?'

Rhea muttered to Lucy under her breath, 'Just ignore him. Don't make eye contact. Don't stop walking.'

But it was too late. Lucy had stopped and smiled back, so Rhea had to do the same, and they were both forced to listen to the young Turk list all the specials, the prices, with a stream of information punctuated in final emphasis by the pulling out of a chair at a table in the shade and a flourish of his hand.

'No, sorry. Maybe later,' said Rhea. 'Come on, Lucy, we have to go.'

'Yes, sorry,' Lucy said earnestly, casting her head around her shoulder to throw back another smile as they strolled off. The young man put his hand to his heart, a conscience pricking gesture, designed to convey he was sorely aggrieved at being deprived of their custom, as if he'd meet no-one else like them ever again. Never. 'Should we go there this evening, then?' she asked Rhea.

Rhea was adamant. 'No! We haven't decided what we're doing yet. You're going to have to learn to ignore them when we're not interested. Look, here's another one now. Just walk on. Don't stop.'

'Yes, but it feels so rude,' Lucy said, struggling to walk straight past another waiter addressing her. 'There must be another way.'

Rhea glared at Lucy. 'There isn't! Trust me.'

'Okay, I get it, alright? Anyway, what makes you such an expert?'

'More holidays in hot places than you. Now come on, we've got to get to the office.'

The heat redoubled its efforts, and as the sisters used their map to orientate themselves in the right direction, they were soon ambling through the streets of Dalyan in a manner more befitting a holiday - pausing to inspect the wealth of shop displays set up on the pavements, and without engaging in conversations with keen proprietors, lured from their Aladdin's cave interiors by the flickering cast shadows of potential trade outside.

The sisters even managed to turn the odd head as they passed by. This was a nice bonus considering they were in their mid forties, although the fact that they were aiming for the ten years younger look, so vital to western taste these days, made them a little more expectant. Their idling curiosity couldn't help but wonder which one of them was receiving the most attention.

Lucy was the tallest at five foot seven, and her narrow face and delicate features suited her size ten figure, which the years had done little to alter. She was wearing a short-sleeved white linen shirt and a pale blue cotton skirt embroidered with white daisies. Her long dark hair hung loose down her back, beneath a softly brimmed straw sunhat, decorated with a cluster of pink roses. Behind her brown tinted shades, a pale complexion highlighted her grey-green eyes and small mouth. Her Auntie Kathy, fond of making golden age movie star comparisons when they were growing up, told her she had a touch of the Audrey Hepburn about her. *You've got that delicate elfin look, just like Audrey in Breakfast at Tiffany's*, she'd say to Lucy. The leather strap sandals Lucy was wearing were cushioned for comfort, as she'd come prepared to do a lot of walking, and she'd rubbed factor 50 suntan lotion over her neck and arms, more concerned about burning than building up a tan. A languid gliding with a slight slouch of her shoulders was her characteristic walk, although these days she was paying more attention to her posture. She didn't think a slouch befitted a 43 year old, so periodically she'd straighten up by an inch.

At five foot three, Rhea had suffered the fate of many elder sisters by being outgrown by the younger. But she made up for this lack with a more curvaceous figure, an hourglass with a nipped in waist. *Just like Lana Turner*, Auntie Kathy used to say, *a great sweater girl*. Rhea had enjoyed these 'pin-up girl' assets until she hit her forties, when even furiously thrusting aerobics and weight training sessions at the gym had made little impact upon the touches of middle-age spread on her hips, thighs and bottom, which meant now, at the age of 47, she was only just holding onto her size fourteen figure. Her facial features were certainly different to Lucy's. She had a rounder face, with blue eyes behind the grey shades and a fuller mouth, framed by blonde hair, currently cut in the style of a shoulder length bob. Her professional spray tan gave her a healthy glow, in contrast to Lucy's typically western, plucked chicken pallor. But it was their long noses that were similar, and perhaps more tellingly, a certain shared creased expression around the eyes when they were thinking about something and staring off into the distance. Rhea was wearing a long white cheesecloth top over her comfortable green khaki shorts, her hair worn in a short ponytail drawn neatly through the back of a green combat cap. A bit of extra height and elegance were strategically achieved by a pair of backless wedge sandals, Rhea's intention being certainly not to be doing any significant walking today. Her quicker walking pace kept her nicely in line with Lucy's longer legged stride, and she'd always held herself straight-backed as she needed all the height she could get.

They slowed up a little as they approached shop fronts that attracted them: leather bags, belts, purses; rugs and embroidered textiles; long flowing cotton sundresses for Lucy; beach tops for Rhea; ceramic balls decorated with birds and flowers; caretta turtle fridge magnets and bottle openers, regarding which no comment was made; blue and white evil eye amulets, boxes of Turkish Delight in rainbows of powdery pastels; dazzling bowls and plates swarming with a kaleidoscope of intricate designs. And of course nearly everything was supposed to be bartered for.

'These will make good presents, if we can get them home in one piece,' Rhea said, stopping to handle a large orange-glazed platter, but putting it down with haste as she sensed approaching feet.

'For crying out loud, Rhea, we've only just got here. There's plenty of time to think about presents. Honestly-'

'Okay! There's nothing wrong with getting ideas, is there? You're going to have to ease up a bit, Lucy, if this is going to work, you know. Just not be so intense.' She angled some emphasis at Lucy over the top of her sunglasses, then cast the same look at the hovering shop owner, who swiftly retreated.

'Yes, alright, I know. Sorry. I'm just excited.'

They picked up their pace and passed the local junior school's playground, just some scratches of weeds straggling in what was otherwise a dustbowl of concrete, with all the children at home as it was Sunday. They passed an ATM machine and the post office where they could get their UK currency exchanged for Turkish Lire, as marked on their map. Then they found themselves in the main square, which extended down to the riverside.

This square was the hub of Dalyan. This was where the mosque called for prayer; where a bronze figure of Ataturk stood, father of the Republic, never to be forgotten by the people; where the restaurateurs didn't have to work quite so hard for customers, as the open sunny space and a flock of umbrellas hovering over tables and chairs invited a sit down before a waiter was even spotted; this was where the tourist companies had their offices and advertised their trips; where the local minibuses picked up passengers to the far end of the turtle beach and beyond. And this was where the main roads of Dalyan intersected at a small roundabout, a memorable place if one managed, somewhat inconceivably, to get lost in this small resort town.

Rhea and Lucy needed to find a side street from here, that led to the Go Turkey office. But they halted, dazed in the heat, as they caught sight of something unexpected. There was a stone creature in the centre of the roundabout. It was suspended in the air on a scroll of foam, being sprinkled all around with ribbon jets of silver beaded bubbles thrusting upwards to bathe the creature's body - a bronze-blotched body, swimming, a wrinkled eye, a sad smile, and baby creatures by its side.

This was such a strange sight that Rhea and Lucy were both drawn to it, dodging the passing cars, which were dodging each other. The creature came into focus. It was a painted sculpture of a caretta turtle with its babies, the wise looking after the young. It was a special mascot, an honoured animal, the protector of people, the people of Dalyan. An iconic reminder that the turtle was vital to their livelihood. In the very centre of the square's roundabout, cars and mopeds orbited around it like satellites.

Lucy and Rhea stared at it.

'Oh well,' Lucy said finally. 'I guess this is one way of getting 'up close and personal.'

Trish, the local rep, was waiting for them as arranged at the Go Turkey office. It was right next door to a coffee shop and gallery called the Nar Galerie Kafe, its painted graphic on the black sign depicting a juicy pomegranate. Trish's burnished bronzed tan gave them a warm welcome, and she suggested they take some refreshment at the cafe while they book their trips.

'Just pick yourselves a table,' she said with a sticky strawberry jam smile, 'I'll just go and print off some more booking forms. It's been a busy morning.'

Rhea and Lucy gazed at the cafe tables, trying to decide where to go. Separated from the road by a low wall, its lush garden area promised some shade. It was a cool haven of shabby chic, turquoise painted furniture, chair legs resting in bleached pebbles. Overhead, the leaf margins of green canopies of rubber and banana trees framed brilliant patches of blue. A large striped hammock slung between two pomegranate trees invited a reclining snooze to those of lesser inhibitions, while at the entrance, the trailing leaves of an arching shrub and its fanned flowers of pink and cream tendrils feathered the sisters' elbows as they brushed past.

'I hope I can get a book on the plants of Dalyan. There's so much I don't recognise here,' Lucy said stopping to finger the feathery flowers.

They headed for a table outside a ground floor window, just by the entrance to the gallery. Wispy smoke trails of freshly ground coffee wafted from the adjacent kitchen. Through the shadowy door opening they could just make out that the building housed an upstairs and downstairs gallery and shop, with a spiral staircase giving access to the second floor. Externally, there was a tiny balcony on the second floor, just large enough to seat two people at a table. Lucy said it was just perfect for lovers. Rhea made no comment.

After settling themselves, Rhea ordered a banana milkshake, Lucy, a homemade lemonade. Trish presently joined them, cradling a clipboard to her chest, and ordering an espresso by calling through the serving hatch.

'Keeps me going,' she said, manoeuvring her bottom

into the back of a chair and plaiting her tanned legs tightly around each other with practised ease. She was wearing a tight turquoise sweatshirt over a pair of shorts, both emblazoned with the Go Turkey logo of the crescent moon of the Turkish flag, with the profile of a jet heading towards its centre - right where the star would normally be. Her long face was elongated further by shoulder length red hair, straightened into thin tails. Her fleshy toes, with fine creases and wrinkles, betrayed her advancing years and were squashed into glittering gold strap stilettos. Her red painted toenails completed her uniform of the holiday rep working on location - glossy, immaculate, with a requisite relaxed style to persuade visitors to do just that - Relax! Everything's so cool here!

'But it's a Sunday,' said Lucy, commenting on Trish's inference of a heavy workload. 'Surely things slow down a bit on a Sunday.'

'Yeah, but Dalyan's a seasonal place. Everywhere is open for the visitor trade. Anyway, you two, did you enjoy the turtle watch?'

'It was fine. Yes.' Lucy looked away towards another table, where an older couple had just sat down.

'You sure? You saw enough turtles, did you?'

Rhea replied, 'Well, since you're asking, for visitor feedback purposes, it was a bit-'

'It was fine!' Lucy said. 'Just leave it!' She scowled at Rhea.

Trish looked from Lucy to Rhea in turn, her tanned face now crumpled like a walnut shell.

'Sorry Trish, just carry on. Let's book the trips,' Lucy said.

Trish crossed her legs over to the opposite position, clamped them together and reached for her pen. 'Okay, shoot! Don't worry, we'll soon have you both sooo chilled!' she smiled, her facial contours temporarily restored.

Rhea pulled out her notebook with the timetable in it.

She opened it and pressed it down flat. Her kunzite ring flashed as it caught Trish's eye. 'Oh wow! That's beautiful! What's the stone?'

Trish's gushing outburst caused the heads of the older couple at the other table to swivel around in a synchronised fashion, like two basking lizards checking out some prey.

'Kunzite,' replied Rhea in a worried tone. 'I forgot to put it in the hotel safe,' she said to Lucy. 'Remind me when we get back, will you? It's not supposed to be worn in bright light.'

'Oh, that's weird! What happens then?' Trish asked.

'It fades.' An unfamiliar voice spoke over their shoulders. Then a face peered down at the ring, a face framed with short, tight frizzy curls, hair that had been over-permed and over-bleached, rendering that certain 'look' that only very regular salon visits could ever hope to achieve. 'Hope you don't mind me having a peek, pet.'

It was the woman from the other table.

Her husband had remained seated but waved a greeting. 'Can't keep her away from the jewellery,' he called across. 'Costs us a fortune with all those bleedin shopping channels.'

'Oh, it's you, Mrs Walker. June isn't it?' Trish said. 'I didn't see you there. Here, let me introduce you to Lucy and Rhea. June and her hubbie are staying at the Onur, like you,' she said to the sisters. 'Came in on the flight just after yours and they're staying for the same length of time too. What a coincidence, eh?'

Lucy and Rhea took a good look at Mrs Walker. Her eyebrows were plucked into fine pencil lines arching over her small flinty eyes. She sniffed her snub nose and her tight mouth went up at the corners into the fixed smile of a puppet. Her brown neck was stringy and adorned with three or four gold linked chains, the kind that for all their inherent value, you'd have to view with a magnifier in the vain hope of finding any decorative interest. But her hands, one of which was caressing her chains at this moment, were sporting a collection of flashing rings, captured colours of the rainbow with diverse settings.

'Nice to meet yer, dears, you must have been late to breakfast. But mind you, Brian and me are early risers. Yes, that's a cracker of a ring, pet. Good choice that. You know it's meant to give the owner some peace, that kind of thing. Now, what else can I remember about kunzite? It's a bit of a hobby of mine, you know, the qualities of gems...' She paused as she surveyed the ring from different angles, as if to divine its esoteric properties.

'Well, thank you for your interest, June,' Rhea said, 'but I'm not sure I believe in that kind of thing.' She slipped off the ring and put it into the front zipped flap of her bag. 'Nice to meet you, but we're wanting to book our trips right now, if that's all right with you.'

'But lovely to meet you, June,' added Lucy hurriedly.

'Oh, of course pets, no bother! I'll let you get on with it, then. Brian and me have booked ours already, early risers, you see.' She sidled off back to her table, her nose in the air, until she resumed her seat, then she leaned forward and started whispering to Brian.

'Right, girls,' Trish said. 'Let's have a look at this timetable of yours.' Trish's head dipped down over Rhea's notebook, with the booking forms waiting on standby.

In the ensuing silence, Rhea sat back and sipped her milkshake.

After a few minutes the Walkers left, calling a 'see you later' to the girls. Lucy waved in reply, then she sat forward propped up on her elbows. She started twisting a length of her hair around and around in her fingers until it tightened into a coil, then releasing it, she started over again - coil, release, coil, release. As she read the menu card on the table and then a promotional leaflet about the gallery, its paintings, artists and artefacts, she raised her eyebrows now and again and tutted to herself, coiling her hair tighter. Rhea stirred her shake, slowly, around and around, both sisters harmonising in their reverie - after a fashion.

'Okay! You're quite lucky,' exclaimed Trish. 'Must say, it's not often a visitor presents me with a timetable! But, it's actually quite good, I might suggest this to other visitors. Okay, here's how it stands.'

Just then there was a faint sound that started up in the tree canopies above them - a high pitched hissing that steadily rose in volume, louder and louder into a full continuous chorus.

Rhea groaned. 'Oh, no!'

Lucy looked hard into the branches but could see nothing. 'What? What is that?'

'Cicadas,' Rhea and Trish said in unison.

'What's that?'

'A kind of beetle,' replied Trish. 'Seda's told me all about them. Seda's the guide that did your turtle watch.'

'Yes,' Lucy nodded. 'Lovely girl.'

'Yes, she is, isn't she? Always wanted to be a guide, you know, loves the job, ever so good with people, and of course it's only seasonal, finds it harder to get work in the winter months, it rains a lot then, you know-'

'What about the beetles?' Lucy interrupted.

'Oh yes, well...let's see, what can I remember. I did some research, you know, because people do ask. This will be a good test,' she giggled. 'Right. It's a male mating call and after they've shed their skins, they sing in trees on sunny days, feeding on the sap, they just love the heat! Well, don't we all? You hear them a lot at night. Everywhere! They don't bite or sting, it's difficult to see them, even though they're one or two inches long. Can you believe that? Apparently each species has its own song that they sing together. Oh, and they're sacred to Apollo, the sun god. Now what else?' She paused. 'Oh, yes...they're a symbol of resurrection, ecstasy and - '

'They get on your wick,' Rhea said.

'Oh, don't you like them, then?' asked Trish, her face beginning to crease into its walnut shell. 'You kind of get used to them after a while, you know.'

Rhea didn't reply.

'I like them,' Lucy said to Trish. Then she saw the look on Rhea's face. 'Come on, back to the trips. Sorry I interrupted.'

'Well, you're actually lucky,' Trish said. 'It's quiet at the moment, late June can be like that. So trips are usually discounted and the operators don't mind small groups. We can accommodate pretty much all of what you're wanting to do. But it's certainly easier with you being here for two weeks.'

Lucy and Rhea nodded.

'So, let's go through the activities. Let's see... You can go to the turtle beach any day you like, you can get on a boat by the riverside, they go all the time, takes about forty minutes, same route as the turtle watch. Or, you can go by bus approaching from the landside. The beach is a four and a half kilometre sandbank, connected to the mainland at one end, open to the sea at the other. You can walk all the way along if you want to, bus to one end, catch the boat back to Dalyan at the other. You catch the bus from the square, where the mosque is, you know? They're called dolmus's. But you have to leave the beach by 8pm, for the turtles.'

Rhea started scribbling in her notebook while Trish was just doing her warm up.

'Going over to the Roman ruins of Kaunos. Well, the easiest way is to be rowed across the river by a lady who does it everyday, from the riverside just near your hotel. It only takes five minutes and there's a cafe on the other side. Then you can walk along to Kaunos, takes about half an hour. You go past the base of some of the rock tombs too, and you can get up to them, but it's a bit of a scramble. After you've come back along the path from Kaunos, you *must* cross back over the river by six o'clock, because that's the last crossing time to return, otherwise you'll be stranded. There are refreshments at the site itself, but fairly basic. It's best to go over in the morning or late afternoon, as it can be very hot there, okay?'

Lucy and Rhea both nodded again.

'So, allow about a couple of hours and take plenty of water with you. There is some shade here and there, but I wouldn't spend the whole day there, it's just so hot, okay? Right, what else have you got?' Trish continued. 'Poolside and local shopping. Well, whenever you like basically, though the shops can be shut in the afternoon - they have a rest before the evening. The evenings are when everyone goes out for a meal or to shop, because it's so much cooler then. Mind, they expect you to haggle. And then there's the market here, that's on a Saturday. For the hotel pool, you're best to bag your recliner in the morning, otherwise they can stay occupied all day, same for other resorts, but I expect you're familiar with poolside etiquette,' she tittered.

'Yes,' Rhea replied, 'that's what towels and books are for.'

'What do you mean?' Lucy enquired.

'You'll see. Let Trish get on, will you?' Rhea said, with a look of irritation.

'Right,' Trish continued. 'Well, I've got a booklet for you here which you can read later, some customs to observe, how to avoid mozzie bites. You'd better get yourselves some repellent as soon as possible, Sin Kov, otherwise known as Dalyan perfume,' she said with another high-pitched giggle. 'Oh, and don't forget to drink bottled water to be on the safe side. Also there's information about the hotel loos, that kind of thing.' She paused as she placed the booklet down in front of them. 'But it's the trips next. Some together, some separate. Well, you can't both like the same things, can you?' She tittered again. 'Perfectly understandable, that is. But generally, you'll be picked up from the hotel by a coach, and brought back the same way.

'Right then, the Turkish night. Two of you for that. Well, they go on all the time, but your hotel is having one in the second week on the Thursday. It's quite nice to leave the Turkish night for towards the end of your stay. Bit of letting your hair down before you go back! Does that sound alright, instead of the day you've got here? We do that for 35 lire each. At the door they charge a lot more. And that includes your meal and unlimited wine.'

Rhea and Lucy exchanged a few words and glances.

'Yes, that sounds fine, Trish, thanks,' Rhea said. 'Just enter it on the timetable will you, and I'll rewrite it later.'

'Great!' Trish said, amending Rhea's timetable with flourishes of her pen. 'Now the shopping trip to Fethiye and the market, with the ruins of Kayakö and lunch, then the Blue Lagoon. 45 lire each. That can be this Wednesday, as you've got marked here. Mind you, they call at a gold centre before the market, posh place, it is. I expect June will be going in there.'

'What? You mean the Walkers are going on the same trip?' Rhea asked sharply.

'Yes, why? Is it a problem? You could leave it until the second week.'

Rhea thought hard for a moment. 'No, leave it as it is. It'll get it over with. The socialising thing, I mean, with them. Same hotel and all that.'

'Get it over with? Well, you're supposed to be enjoying yourself, you know! Or is it June you don't like? Well, to be honest, just between you and me, I'm not fond of her myself, she was very demanding this morning-'

'Let's get on,' Lucy interrupted, seeing Rhea's screwed up face.

'Okay,' Trish said. 'Now the Göcek twelve island cruise by sailing boat. You've chosen the right one there, much better than the double-decker boat cruise. Oh, you'll love it, absolutely love it! Everybody does. Sheer luxury. And you can take a dip or snorkel at any of the island stops.

Lunch is included. We're doing that for just 60 each at the moment. That's on a Friday, and you can go this week, as you've got here. Okay?'

Rhea and Lucy nodded again.

'Hmm, the jeep hire day. Well, that can be the day you've got marked here too - next Tuesday. It can be any day of the week. 80 lire plus petrol. Mind, the petrol is expensive round here, okay? I'll just make a note here about you specifically wanting a jeep. You've got a licence with you?'

'Yes, I have. I'll be the driver,' Lucy said. 'And I really want an open top jeep, if that's possible, Trish. And have you got any ideas where to go? One of the brochures mentioned a beach?'

'Well yes, there's a lovely quiet one south of Dalyan, bit of a rugged winding road, but that's part of the fun, isn't it?' Trish chuckled. 'It's called Asi Bay. You'll see some of the real Turkey on that route too. Plenty of wild goats, steep slopes and the oleanders are out at the moment.'

'Sounds great!' Lucy enthused. 'What do the oleanders look like?'

'Oh, well you'll see it everywhere just now in the wild. It only survives the goats because its poisonous to them. The flowers can be white or pink.'

'Yes, I've seen it before,' Rhea commented, 'in Portugal, I think. It's nice. But is there anywhere else we could go in the jeep?'

'Well, yes. Some people like to take the road that skirts around Lake Köyceğiz. They have lunch in town, and then stop off at some hot springs by the lake that the locals use. Or, you could maybe go into Muğla, the capital. There's an Ottoman style bazaar there, or you could wander down the old quarter, visit a tea garden -'

'Goodness, Trish, you really know your stuff, don't you?' said Lucy, looking impressed.

'Should do, this is my fourth season, I absolutely love it here!'

'Well, I must say that sounds better than the winding hill roads,' Rhea said.

'Well, we'll have to *discuss* it, won't we?' Lucy said.

'Can't wait,' Rhea replied curtly.

'Maps are hard to get of the local area, mind, so don't bother looking, okay?' said Trish. 'I'll make a copy of a favourite one of mine that I've got back in my flat and leave it at the hotel reception for you. Just in case you decide to go off the main roads. You'll need it for the bay, if you choose that route.'

'Thanks, Trish! That would be great.' Lucy beamed at her.

The discussions went on, with Trish adjusting Rhea's timetable here and there and forms being filled in. Luckily, there was no necessity for Rhea to be firm about any discrepancies, as Trish negotiated the timetable with the same care as an elderly person wearing stilettos and stepping onto slithery stones to cross a stream in full spate - giving each stone equal measure in significance to survival.

Lucy's scuba diving day had to be on a Thursday, so Lucy chose the first Thursday of their stay and since the local Hamam was open any day, any time, Rhea decided she could be having her foam massage then, after some time by the pool. The authentic village life trip for Lucy was booked for the second Wednesday, while Rhea could go to Ephesus - a particularly masterful stroke from Trish.

'So, Lucy, you'll be going up into the Taurus mountains to visit a farm, maybe even get to ride a donkey, while Rhea, you'll be wandering through the best preserved classical city in the Eastern Med! Long day for you, mind, Rhea, lots of sitting on a bus, but well worth it. Not to be missed! *And*…June Walker hasn't booked for that,' Trish said finally, with a wink.

Trish totted up the bill, which Rhea and Lucy insisted upon splitting down the middle as they proffered their credit cards. It seemed excellent value for money, with a favourable exchange rate, coming out at around £140 each.

'Okay, I'll love you and leave you now,' said Trish as she gave them their receipts. 'But I'll be visiting your hotel during your stay, times on the reception notice board, if you need anything else - okay?'

'Cheers, Trish, you've been great,' Lucy said, giving her a broad smile.

'Yes, really excellent,' added Rhea. 'We'll look out for you, then.'

As Trish strutted back to her office, Rhea and Lucy decided to order some lunch. The cicada song had stopped and the only ambient sounds were the low murmurings of some new visitors placing their orders.

'I'm glad that's all sorted out,' Rhea said, after returning from the ladies toilet. 'We can start to relax now.'

'Yes, me too. Good value for money, isn't it?' Lucy said, slurping the dregs of her lemonade through the straw.

'Oh, yes. Unbelievable.'

'Dad would approve, wouldn't he?'

Rhea paused. 'Of course he would.'

'We're not been too extravagant then?'

'Of course not! He'd want us to enjoy ourselves.'

'We're doing enough things together?'

'Yes! We've been through this already. Compromise is fine. Come on, Lucy, we're allowed to enjoy ourselves. Dad would be okay with that. You know he would. It's been tough lately.'

'Yes, hasn't it? Just awful. Do you know, I feel like there's a big gaping hole where he used to be. But also, I feel like he's still around somewhere. I sometimes see a man in the street from a distance and for a second I think it's him - the same way of standing a little hunched, the same tilt of the head, same profile. I get a split second of relief inside, then I realise, and get this ache instead. You know?' Lucy looked searchingly at Rhea. 'I know you and he were very close, but I really miss him too. I wish he was still here.' She sniffed and rooted around in her tote bag, eventually digging out an old fluffy tissue from its cavernous depths.

'Well, that's understandable,' Rhea replied. 'He was our father. Look, I don't really want to get into this right now. We'll talk about it later, after we've settled into the holiday.'

'Oh, alright,' Lucy sighed. 'But we really should talk, you know. You're not supposed to bottle these things up. I think I'm a bit tired anyway,' Lucy said, blowing her nose.

'Well, the food's coming now, so tuck in. You probably just need some sugar,' Rhea said as the waitress placed their dishes on the table.

Lucy started picking at her plate of mozzarella cheese, sun-dried tomatoes, olives and rocket on a thin crispy bread base, while Rhea got stuck into her chicken and rice with meat balls, while further examining the menu card.

'Will you have some cake, do you think?' she asked. 'I fancy the lemon drizzle.'

'God no! Maybe I'll have a dessert with our evening meal. But it's far too heavy for now, don't you think?'

Rhea's expression darkened. 'I suppose you're right. Mind you, you've got nothing to worry about.'

'Maybe. But it's a matter of healthy eating too. Not just body weight.'

Rhea flung the menu onto the adjacent table.

'What are we going to do next, anyway?' Lucy asked, draining her lemonade glass of its final drop of fizz.

Rhea hesitated, while she chewed a mouthful of food. 'Well, I want to go back to the hotel and be by the pool.'

'Oh. I thought we would have a look around the town together.'

'No, Lucy, I want to chill by the pool. Wandering around in the heat might be your idea of chilling, but it's not mine - and it's my turn, isn't it? After the turtle watch?'

Lucy groaned. 'Yes, I suppose so. But I'm itching to get a feel for the place.'

'Well, why don't you go off and do that, then meet me later by the pool? You could start off in the gallery here, having a look at the artwork.'

'Maybe.' Lucy glanced towards the open door of the gallery. 'Don't you fancy a look too?'

'Oh, there's plenty of time for that. We could use this as a regular base, okay? You don't get any hassle here.'

'So, we're going our separate ways already, then?' Lucy scowled. 'And I'm to start with bloody paintings.'

Rhea looked puzzled. 'I thought you liked art. You're a painter, aren't you?'

'Yes. But I don't necessarily want to look at other people's art.'

'Why not? What's the problem?'

'Oh, it's too complicated,' Lucy groaned. 'You wouldn't understand.'

'Oh, come on! Why not? I'm sure it would be within my grasp,' Rhea said sarcastically.

'Oh, there are so many issues, I wouldn't know where to start. It's hard to explain these things to someone who isn't in the arts.'

'Well, if we're supposed to be getting to know each other, you should try, shouldn't you?' Rhea said in a huffed tone, as she straightened her back.

'Yes,' Lucy said. 'And you're going to have to open up too, aren't you? Tell me what's been happening to you in the last twenty years.'

Whilst they tidied up the dishes onto the serving tray, the only communication between them was the chink, clink and clatter of cutlery on ceramic.

'Oh, look,' Lucy said eventually. 'Let's not bicker already. I'll do what you say. I'll have a look in here, have a mooch around the town, then see you back at the pool.'

'Right. That sounds good. A nice compromise. You know, Lucy, you don't have to look around the gallery. Nothing's forcing you. If you don't want to, you don't want to.' Rhea shrugged her shoulders.

'Yeah, I know. But I think I will - see what the local style is. Off you go, I'll pay the bill. See you later.'

Rhea put on her sunglasses, slung her bag over her shoulder, then stretched her arms up and yawned. 'See you later, then,' she said as she moved away, edging carefully around a few tables towards the exit.

'Oh, hang on!' Lucy rushed over to Rhea and grabbed hold of her shoulder.

Rhea flinched and struggled to back away, almost tripping over her heels. 'What the hell-'

'Don't forget to put your ring in the safe,' Lucy whispered in her ear.

'Oh! Rhea's mouth dropped open. 'Yes…I'd forgotten about that. Thanks!'

4

In The Gallery

As Lucy stepped over the threshold into the gallery, she was hit by a sudden coolness that nibbled at her bare skin, making her wish she was wearing a cardigan to clutch close around her and pull the sleeves down over her wrists to stop the cold getting in. The withdrawal of heat made her senses more alert, which wasn't necessarily a good thing.

She threw a crooked smile at the silhouette by the desk as she ventured further in. 'Just having a quick look around,' she mumbled to the female figure, whose head was bent over a book.

Lucy took off her sunhat and shades, unable to identify any of the shadowy shapes in the dim interior. But she knew from the leaflet on the cafe table, that she'd analysed and read in some depth, that it was meant to house a cross section of paintings, ceramics, textiles, jewellery, and also included some traditional Turkish illuminated manuscripts. Perhaps, she might find one that her husband, Charlie, would like, she wondered. So, the gallery didn't just house paintings, there was plenty of craft to look at. A critical factor. And as for the paintings? Well, they might very well be of alternative styles and subjects, in a totally different country, they might be of no harm at all. But Lucy still felt goose bumps prickle her arms.

There was a weighted silence in the air as her eyes adjusted. The coolness from the white-washed stone walls, together with shafts of light glancing across the concrete floor from some narrow windows, made Lucy feel as if she'd just walked into a church. She was pressed upon by an urge to be reverent, and with some disgust tried to shake it off - unsuccessfully. It was a quasi-religious awe, collective in its effects like mass hypnosis, and culturally induced in most law-abiding members of the public when visiting art galleries. And the artists themselves were no exception. Indeed the very fact that they were artists at all demanded that they collude in this placing of art on a pedestal, work done by 'creatives', the 'gifted', or far worse than this, work done by a so-called 'genius' - a term historically applied only to men, and therefore inherently objectionable to Lucy's mind.

So, the simple hanging of paintings in a gallery setting, seemed strategically designed to demand these responses. And although Lucy was well aware of the artifice in this, she fell for it every time. Sometimes the fall was slight and she could pick herself up, see the light by regaining her perspective. But other times it was bruising, leaving its mark upon her as she fell into a kind of hell, losing her faith altogether. It really did depend upon the artworks on display.

Right now, she felt the old familiar dread starting to creep inside her, like a rank mould seeking to stifle and make stale her own creative impulses, and ultimately destroy her passion for painting.

As she stood in the shadows, she felt her eyes seeking out the paintings. She tried to shift her gaze, to seek out the crafts instead, crafts to be admired and valued for their skill, their processes, materials and function, for the honest handiwork of the crafter. These hand-made qualities were usually reflected in the prices, a simple relationship between cost of making and net profit. This was unlike within the art market which operated on a completely different and highly questionable basis. The higher the prices, the higher the supposed aesthetic value. Time and effort were dirty words. It was about the concept, the inspiration, the expression. And Lucy knew what the viewing of any paintings was going to do to her - she'd compare them with her own, and she felt doomed to suffer her own torments even before she'd begun.

'There's more upstairs.' The voice at the desk called over, an English accent, pleasant enough, but the words laced with threat to Lucy.

'Thanks,' she replied. 'You've got some lovely things here.' The same old routine, same old comments, Lucy thought, the same old shit.

As she found her eyes being dragged towards the paintings, she felt a sickly amalgam of forced attraction and repulsion, like oil and water in constant agitation in a glass, never allowed to settle their differences. She wanted to look, she needed to look, but she hated to look. This was how it was these days. She decided, just now, she would look at the paintings first, to get it over with, leaving the viewing of the craft as a reward at the end. She would feed her compulsion to view other artists' work and so engage once more with her inner 'issues' - even though it was bad for her, even though it was like not being able to stop picking at a bleeding scab, instead of leaving it alone to heal. Considering the self discipline this took, she was very relieved Rhea wasn't here. Her earlier look of scathing miscomprehension had been very galling.

Come on then, Lucy told herself, let's get on with it.

The paintings were displayed on white rough textured walls, a lovely backdrop, she thought, but she knew she was procrastinating. She told herself firmly again - *get on with it* - and started to slowly peruse the paintings, with a practiced saunter, hands behind her back, a stance designed to mask her tensions.

Her usual routine was to move in close to examine technique, then out again to judge, from a wider perspective, the effect of the whole. On occasional visits to London, when she'd dragged Charlie to the National Gallery, she'd frequently been given suspicious looks by security staff, when making her close inspections of some marvellous medieval paintings, much to her inner indignation. *What* did they think she was going to do?

Didn't they know how much she admired them, that she would never lay a finger on them? That in this case they had earned her full respect, paintings from a time when painting was a craft based on the development of skills. No. She was gestured at with a beckoning hand to move away from them, with no recognition by the staff of her harmless intent, her love of the work. She would feel insulted, but try to look completely unaffected; she wouldn't give them the satisfaction. And the cause of this treatment? Well it was all that reverence for the canon of art, based on the belief, Lucy felt, that similar skills were irrelevant today.

After all, the contemporary art world had moved on. And how. These days she could barely tolerate looking around art galleries, only the historical ones were safe ground. And her own daughter, Poppy, had been resolute in going to university to study contemporary fine art of today. She was in her second year now, and Lucy had tried hard not to engage in any serious discussion with her about each other's artwork, so that they wouldn't upset each other. Poppy was still developing her own style and it was only fair that she should be left uncontaminated by her own mother's demons.

But today, in Dalyan, something was different. The paintings in the Nar Galerie actually took her by surprise. What was different was their vivid colour, and some of them were quite realistic. Not all abstracts, which is what she was expecting.

There were scenes of village life, men and women at work in the orchards, picking oranges, or resting outside their homes in dappled light. There were scenes of the riverside and the bright colours of the boats, a view of the rock tombs against a cloudless plate blue sky - all local artists, Lucy presumed. There were also artists from further afield exhibiting cityscapes of the minaret towers and Byzantine domes of Istanbul, even international artists with a connection of some kind to the area showing Turkish townscapes and seascapes.

And gazing at them at length, Lucy felt strangely numb. She didn't really like anything, as such. Stylistically, they were still too loosely painted for her own taste. But she was really affected by the colour. Garish at first sight, but certainly reflecting this saturated land of the sun. And why not? she said to herself. Why not full colour?

She cast a glance towards the woman at the desk who was now sipping at a cup and reading something on her computer screen. She was safely occupied, so Lucy could start to relax, and as she stared at the frothing foam of a wave on canvas, she contemplated her own pathway into art.

She first discovered painting, after becoming disillusioned with the fashion designing she'd been doing from home. She'd studied textiles at Newcastle, not far from where she and Rhea were brought up, and it was where she first met Charlie, who was studying sculpture and ceramics. After she graduated and settled down with Charlie, she hadn't wanted to use her training to work in the industry as a buyer, or design fabrics, which seemed too technical. And she'd found herself pregnant with Poppy. So, for the first few years, her time was taken up with motherhood and renovating the cottage she and Charlie bought near Corbridge. She loved rural living, and came to like the idea of being self-employed. So, she started her own fashion design business to sell direct to the public, which dovetailed with family life.

But increasingly, over the years, she found it too repetitive: the sourcing of fabrics, the pattern cutting, the tailoring, the finishing, and finding selling outlets. It was also very time consuming with hours spent slumped over her overlocker. She remembered how much she'd enjoyed drawing and painting in the first year of her degree, and she dragged out some old sketches of seedheads she'd done. One of her favourites was of some honesty. She remembered how her mother had been before she died - all those paintings and drawings she did, one after the other - she'd particularly liked life drawing and did quite a few family portraits. Lucy had been around nine then, and saw how passionate her mother got, how inspired she seemed, clenching one brush between her teeth, whilst working with another, stroking or stabbing at the canvas with the latest fast-drying acrylics. Whenever Lucy got back from school she would find her mum in her 'studio', formerly known as the conservatory. *Just a second Lu, I just need to do this. Can you lay the table? Sorry, it's fish fingers again.*

So, it seemed entirely appropriate to Lucy that she try painting for a new direction in her life. Maybe it was in the blood? And she felt it would be a more liberating pursuit. She did some local courses to learn about the use of media, and also found herself interested in the history of art, so a new library of art books started elbowing out of the way the dressmaking books on her shelves. Charlie's old ceramic studio at the end of their drive became hers, refitted to suit her needs. Lucy had become a painter.

Oil paint was her favourite medium. She loved the creamy consistency, the smell of the turpentine, the working up from dark shadows to bright highlights, the soft and finely graded blending one could achieve, the stippled dabs of the brush to bring textures into sharp focus. And she learned her craft well. Of course, it was still part time, since she had to look after Poppy and help out in the garden centre that she and Charlie ran together for his parents - the family business. But she was able to exhibit her paintings there, so it was reasonably convenient.

Subject-wise, she'd started with the textures of the Northumberland landscapes that she relished. And once she had tapped into the visual, she was like a bubbling stream – there were always new ideas, always derived from nature.

The ideas came when she was driving the car, when she'd have her camera by her side, ready to freeze-frame the moving panoramas of the farming countryside - that confluence of field boundaries, that neatly trimmed hedge, that rustic gate fringed with sweet cicely, that brooding sky. They presented themselves when she was jogging along her local farm tracks, where the music in her head from her player coloured the views with ecstasy or sorrow according to the track she was listening to, feeling the sublime in nature, just like those Romantic painters she'd read about. The ideas came when she was washing up, where she'd shift her focus from the suds, to the fields beyond the back garden, where soot black cattle grazed on rippling grass. The ideas came in the night as glowing after-images imprinted on her retina: the feathered tipped edging of dark pine plantations riding the peaks and troughs of the land; the clotted earth of a recent ploughing; the graphic contours incised by the harvesters like the burin marks of an old woodcut; the fine spray of oil seed rape flowers flushing through the green, ripening from lemon yellow to golden gamboge; the stippling of mosses and lichens on dry stone walls with all those crevices in-between; the light filtering through trees; the restless shadows of clouds shifting across the land; and a rare find these days - the bright blush of vermillion poppies in a creamy corn field. The pictures were endless.

And realism was Lucy's passion. Each painting was a journey which she wanted to savour: the building up of glazes; the tonal variations to render form; the visual recession through the use of more blue tones near the horizon; the fine details of foreground grasses, wildflowers or the addition of some wildlife such as the jaunty strutting of a jet black rook amongst the spiky stubble of a harvested field. So the visions would form in her mind, and she would take delight in deciding which techniques to choose to render the subject, to make them real, to make them breath. Not to make them *pulsate with some kind of inner energy of their own creation* like some contemporary artists would avow, or to *give form to profound personal visions developed through experience*, but in Lucy's case, to simply and honestly capture nature.

And if she ran into problems, she'd solve them, because she never gave up on a painting. She didn't cast it aside, proclaiming it *a disaster*, like other artists she knew these days who seemed to be continually experimenting and suffering from self-imposed angst. No, if she ran into problems, she would simply *make it work*. Making it work was the penultimate part of the journey, the point at which you've climbed a steep hill, then emerge victorious onto the summit and see the view clearly for the first time. There would be that sense of accomplishment and the joy of creating something unique.

More reluctantly, she sometimes painted specific places, such as Hadrian's wall, or coastal landmarks such as Dunstanburgh Castle or Lindisfarne. These paintings did sell well, so Charlie suggested that since people were obviously drawn to places they knew, she might as well concentrate on those. But Lucy wasn't keen. They felt too clichéd, too hackneyed, and in order to stay true to herself, she preferred to paint more generalised places, *distilled essences* of her north country land, you might say, if you were forced to employ artspeak. She usually worked small, the largest pieces being around fourteen inches square, with two to three weeks spent on each, if she counted up the hours. This was all due to her love of detail.

But there was the rub, the cause of her torment.

A voice intruded and made Lucy jump. 'Are you okay there?' the lady at the desk called over. Her tone sounded irritated.

'Yes, fine. Just browsing,' Lucy snapped, moving on to view another painting. She wanted to resume her recapping. She needed to. She was determined to get it out of her system, then forget about it for the holiday, in case it dragged her down.

These days it seemed that most people, including many artists themselves, expected paintings to be loosely painted - either using wispy suggestive bands of colour, or more 'immediate' in the use of thick dabs of paint straight from the tube. All done quickly, without a small brush in sight.

So, when Lucy approached local galleries, the owners would be a little confused to see her detail, a little lost for words, except to suggest she try something 'simpler', and they usually only offered her limited wall space for say three of four, for what they perceived as a niche market. Although no-one said it to her face, she knew what they thought about those who painted as she did. She'd overheard comments at previews: *Isn't it a bit overworked?* they'd say, and *You might as well take a photograph.* And sometimes other painters would say *maybe they should try being freer now,* as if detail were a lower rung on the ladder of painterly progress. And did those earnest souls who loved detail, cry out in defence at the looser style painters, that *their* work was *unresolved, too ill defined?* No, of course not. But they knew it was a battle they couldn't win, as loose somehow meant 'creative', and that was that.

So, they took it on the chin and went on working in their own way, heartened by a few fellow lovers of detail. At least Lucy used oil, it was what the professionals were supposed to use. Oil paint *was* fine art. So that was a bonus, and she had a reasonable degree of success in the first two years, selling a good number of her paintings and building a reputation.

But then she struck a serious problem, and inevitably it was an extension of the old.

Abstract art exploded into fashion, landscapes in particular. Supported by enigmatic artists' statements (the more conceptualised and indecipherable, the seemingly more effective), they flooded the local market: ill-defined blocks of colour fuzzy around the edges, swirling shapes, unnatural colours barely hinting at any subject matter, wax textures dribbled, scraped and scratched into the foregrounds to render whatever the viewer imagines they see. Descriptions didn't help either: *a synthesis of natural and social processes in the landscape; a dialogue with the natural world and the inherent elements of unpredictability; an exploration of the lyrical and the sensory.* People would stare at them, determined to ascribe a location to a painting they just couldn't recognise. Lucy overheard snatches of conversation: *Where is that supposed to be? What does the title say?* Lucy felt convinced that it had to be a temporary trend.

But it wasn't.

After three years it was firmly established and the public had been persuaded of their value. They became admiring. They became buyers. They felt the mood, the atmosphere, they felt the 'message', the 'meaning', they felt the artist in their work, felt their originality, their talent. The bigger the pieces, the more worthy, and accordingly the more pricy. The smaller pieces were seen as far less significant, so afforded far lower prices. That was the expectation. So, it would seem that size mattered, regardless of the content.

And Lucy felt betrayed, outraged. Some artists plundered the triptych form of medieval altarpieces to imbue the panels with a spiritual power, to move art and religion that bit closer together again. Many artists started to be 'inspired by', 'emulate', or just plain copy (depending on one's interpretation) these styles. But Lucy didn't. And she warned Poppy to go with her heart. And she did - she too followed the abstract approaches. *You don't understand, Mum, it's not what you think,* she said. But Lucy stuck to her realism, and she stuck to her small canvases, telling herself that personal integrity was the most important thing. So her sales fell. *Maybe you should move on?* a couple of her artist friends said - they never knew how much they hurt her.

And as Lucy remembered these comments, right now in the gallery, tears stung her eyes and rolled down her cheeks. For God's sake, she said to herself, get a grip. She groped in her bag for a tissue and pretended to blow her nose whilst she mopped her face.

'There's more upstairs,' the desk voice called over again.

So she climbed the spiral staircase, throwing grateful glances at the hand-woven rugs, as she brushed against them. Functional, beautiful. What was wrong with that?

Dappled light shed warmth into the upper floor through the open balcony doors, which were framed by leafy branches.

She sat down at the small table on the balcony and looked down over the railing into the cafe area. Trish was there, clipboard in hand, talking to another couple. She happened to glance up, recognised Lucy, and gave her a wave. Lucy smiled and waved back, then she leaned forward on the table, chin cupped in her hands, staring blankly ahead, finally registering she was looking at a newly built villa across the street - fresh peach plasterwork and gleaming chrome balcony, with a 'For Sale' sign already in place.

Just imagine escaping here to Dalyan, she reflected.

But her thoughts marched back into the same old groove, the same track of self analysis with a brick wall at the end.

In the face of the popularity of abstract styles and the denigration of detail, she hit that wall. She couldn't bring herself to paint anything, it felt so mechanical, like she was just going through the motions. *Just see it as taking a break*, said Charlie, and she explained it in these terms to Poppy. But the truth was she was desperate in herself, frustrated, furious deep down, seeing that the time and process that went into her work had become completely irrelevant, and even worse was seen as unenlightened.

She would wander into her studio about once a week. She'd water the row of spider plants, finger the baby off-shoots wilting on their pendant stems, and smell the scented geraniums on the windowsill in front of her painting table. She'd cast her eye over the pots of brushes, turpentine, linseed oil and mediums, the scraped-clean palette board. She'd make sure the caps on her tubes of oil paint were still easily removable - that Prussian blue, one of her favourite pigments, was always sticking hard. She'd stroke her brushes, the hogs hair, the sables, aching to use them again. She didn't want to paint only for her own pleasure, she wanted others to enjoy her paintings. That was the paradox of being an artist, any kind of artist - self expression, but also needing some degree of appreciation. That over-used adage and fodder for comedic sketches - *I just want to be taken seriously as an artist*, had much to answer for. And Lucy sometimes felt as if her studio was a stage-set room in a museum, all her tools and materials like relics of a former life, revered, yet unused.

As she stood there in the light from her studio window, she imagined dragging herself out of her Slough of Despond. She'd remember her Granda Allen's saying - *don't let the bastards get you down*, which for Lucy could bend itself to fit a wide variety of personal slights, and which she'd employed on many occasions. She imagined grabbing hold of a canvas, perching it on her easel, pulling up her wooden stool and starting to sketch a hedge in charcoal, ready to paint. She imagined that familiar relaxed state of absorption wrap around her, as she mixed her colours and applied them to the canvas with her favourite brush. The hours would sink beneath the surface of the day, as they always had. Then Charlie would poke his head around the door, saying *what should we have for tea?*, and she'd resurface and go over to the house with him to evaluate the contents of their fridge together. This routine was what she craved. To be back doing what she was meant to do - her art.

But now, she made sure things got in the way. An extra shift in the garden centre, more runs in the fields for Laddie, their border collie. Or she'd vacuum, or even do the ironing. She'd check her emails too often, or ring her friend, Jeanie, who she knew would never stop talking for an hour or more. She was all too aware that she was finding these excuses.

Why? Because it was important to have a tidy house before she could work? A sleeping dog? Ironed socks, before her muse could enter? Logical for some, but not for Lucy, as she preferred the lived-in look. No, it was simply that a resistance born from disillusionment had set in. Disillusionment with art. She couldn't even view her own daughter's art with any pleasure. And all this meant she had lost that lightness of being that comes from feeling *everything is as it should be, and everything's all right with the world*. And this state of disillusionment is how it had been just before her father's death and for the last six months. And now, together with her artist's block, she was feeling the added burdens of being 'forty something', and parentless. Where had the meaning in her life gone?

And here she was in Dalyan, not having properly seen a caretta turtle close up. Certainly not the way she'd imagined from the pictures she'd seen. Oh, she knew it was ridiculous, and she'd never have talked to anyone about it, not even Charlie - but somehow the turtles had acquired some kind of symbolic meaning. The ways things sometimes do when we want something badly, feel hard done to, or want a fresh start: a full silver moon shining in the night sky heralds a new phase in our lives; if that struggling apple tree in the garden produces one measly apple this year, it will bring some good luck; if we throw out that old jumper that we've worn like a second skin, then maybe we'll be rejuvenated.

73

So, Lucy had decided if she could see the caretta up close, if she could look into their eyes, then somehow it would heal her. Heal her and her creativity. And what had led to this notion? Simply seeing some pictures of their faces close up in a holiday brochure and finding some kind of beneficent wisdom projected in the gaze from their slanted eyes, wide mouths and blunted noses. Like some kind of spiritual being. And there was something amazing about these huge creatures who lived for over a hundred years and navigated their way through the open seas. And she'd been delighted to learn from Seda, that they were protectors of people. The folklore fitted her feelings perfectly. But Lucy had been hurt at the end of the turtle watch. It hadn't been the right way to see them.

Do I still stand a chance? she wondered.

And of course, she hadn't been able to tell Rhea. Rhea would never understand. They were very different sisters. They'd battled their way into their teens, with the classic hair pulling of early years, progressing to bruising thumps and the slamming of bedroom doors, culminating in the teenage sophistication of vicious tongue lashings over the kitchen table. They'd been able to live in a kind of stalemate after Rhea went to college in Manchester. But after that, Rhea had lived down south with Chris, so Lucy had never seen her on a regular basis - just occasionally at Christmas time. Of course, they'd spoken on the phone now and again, prompted by George, but it was all distinctly forced.

So, after he died, Lucy had decided that he was probably right, that it was time to get to know Rhea properly. And she was curious. Something had made their relationship worse after their mother died, when she had been eleven and Rhea, fifteen. Rhea had avoided her and had barely spoken to her, unless nudged to do so by their dad, and even then the sarcasm had been thinly veiled. *She's just got a lot on her mind, love*, George would say, *O levels coming up.* But it was more than that, Lucy was sure of it. And since their dad died, she had been thinking more about this phase in their lives after the death of their mother. A dark painful time. And she wanted to know what had gone wrong; and that was why she was here in Dalyan with Rhea, and without Charlie. It was going to be tough being without him, but what better opportunity?

Remembering Charlie, and deciding she had passed her self-imposed test in viewing the paintings and leaving the crafts until last, Lucy moved on to the artefacts, displayed on white painted shelving and bleached wooden tables. There was a lovely display of rings, cabochons of semi-precious stones and evil eye designs, and an arrangement of beaded necklaces and amulets. She felt very tempted to buy something for herself, and wondered if Rhea might like this kind of traditional Turkish jewellery. But she reminded herself she was looking for Charlie.

She found a portfolio of Whirling Dervishes doing their spinning dances on gold-painted grounds. They wore tall hats, full circular skirts, and were posed with outstretched arms. The card on the side explained one hand pointed to the heavens, the other to the earth, so spreading the love of God. But she didn't think Charlie would be interested.

She moved over to some brass cups, wooden bowls, strange pots with spiral handles in green glazes, handling them and putting them back down. There were some bowls, plates and jugs labelled Iznik pottery, decorated with geometrical arabesques of flowers and animals, rendered in deep blue and turquoise, with red accents on a white ground. Lucy recognised tulips and carnations. And there were Iznik tiles too. They might be just the thing for Charlie, she thought. Although he'd never done this kind of ceramic work himself, she was sure he would appreciate them. I'll buy him a set, and he can display them any way he likes, she thought. They can go in my hand luggage to keep them safe. But then she reined herself in. Hadn't she criticised Rhea just this morning for already thinking of shopping?

Someone's heels started clacking up the metal spiral staircase behind her, with pauses and the odd 'tut' thrown into the intermittent ascent. Lucy found her shoulders tensing and her thoughts flying. Was it the woman at the desk - the owner perhaps? She didn't want to get into any conversation with a gallery owner, she was on holiday, she was here to try to enjoy herself, to try to sort out things with Rhea. Not to face her own devils right now. To try -

The footsteps came to a stop behind her.

'That staircase is lethal with these heels! I think I've bent one.'

The voice was friendly. The voice was familiar. Lucy breathed a sigh of relief and she turned to see Trish holding up one of her stiletto sandals, scrutinising its profile, and balancing on the other red toe-nailed foot.

'Hi, Trish.' Lucy was surprised that her own voice actually sounded normal.' Are you finished with work now?'

'Yes, my last customers for the day. Thought I'd just come and see what you're up to. I was keeping an eye out for you. You've been in here for ages! It's a lovely gallery, isn't it? Have you seen anything you like?'

'Well, I like these tiles.' She gestured to the tiles, inwardly vowing not to talk about paintings.

'Oh, you'll see lots of tiles everywhere. Plenty of choice for you, although those are bigger than average and the quality will be spot on in here. Gill sources her crafts really well, and the paintings of course, some of them are international, you know.'

'Gill?'

'The owner. She's just downstairs actually.'

Time to get out of here, Lucy decided, and a sense of urgency spilled over inside her. She wanted to feel the sun on her face. 'Oh well, I'd better be off. I told Rhea I'd join her by the pool.'

'Oh, okay...actually the reason why I popped up to see

you was…well…I noticed you and Rhea seemed not to have enjoyed the turtle watch. And - '

'No, it was fine,' Lucy interrupted. 'Really!' she said with emphasis, feeling her heart quickening, and wanting to forget all about turtles now. She wanted to get out of the gallery, right now.

'Well, the thing is, it can be very brief - the viewing, I mean. A matter of luck sometimes. I was just going to say that you're both welcome to go on tomorrow's 6am trip free of charge…just if you want, as a gesture of good will.'

For a fraction of a second Lucy's heart leapt at the offer. But she controlled herself by remembering the contrived nature of the viewing, something she had been silly not to have foreseen. Inevitable, on reflection, but not natural. Natural it had to be, or not at all.

'No really, Trish, it's fine. I'd rather see one as I'm swimming or snorkelling on my own maybe - you know, naturally.

'Yes, I understand. That's what visitors like the idea of best - those interested in the turtles, of course. But I can tell you, no-one seems to manage it. The caretta are very elusive, you know. The Nile turtles are much easier to spot along the river.'

Yet another ray of hope dashed then, Lucy said to herself. Nile turtles were not the caretta. 'Well even so, just forget it. Right?'

'Okay, it was just a thought. Of course there's always the sanctuary, you know about that, don't you?'

'Yes, yes…not my scene, too upsetting…' For God's sake, she felt like screaming, leave it alone, will you! Then she noticed Trish's walnut shell face. 'It was lovely of you to think of us though,' she said, managing a smile. 'Right, I've really got to go now.'

She edged around Trish towards the staircase. Trish followed her down, hot on her heels, after rapidly removing both her shoes for a safer descent. They crossed the gallery floor, were both almost at the desk, practically arm to arm, almost out of the door, when just then, the owner looked up and Trish stopped in front of her.

Don't stop! Lucy yelled internally at Trish. If Trish lingered to talk, then she would have to linger too. It would be too rude to just carry on marching through the doorway. Defeated, Lucy halted by the desk with Trish and looked at the owner. She was a lady in her fifties, dark hair, dark eyes, dark jacket, dark demeanour. Her skin was so pale, it looked as if she never went out in the sun, and even if she did, that she might very well turn to ashes.

'You off now, Trish? Business done for the day, is it?'

Her tone was controlled, and Lucy was sure she could detect an edge of derision.

'Yes, another day, another dollar! Oh actually, I should introduce Lucy here. Lucy and her sister, Rhea, are visiting from the UK. She likes the tiles you have upstairs. Lucy, this is Gill, she owns the gallery. She's an expat. Been here for ten years or so.'

Lucy felt like running now. The last thing, the very last thing she wanted, was to be introduced to a gallery owner, especially one who looked like a vampire ready to suck the life out of you. She willed her feet to stay glued to the floor. 'Nice to meet you,' she murmured, just giving Gill a swift glance.

'You too. Have you seen any paintings you like? You were studying them for quite some time.'

Lucy cringed - here we go again. But the sarcasm in Gill's voice as she said, 'some time', rallied Lucy to play the game. 'Well yes, I particularly like the seascapes, and the colours are so vibrant in general.'

'Not gaudy, then? Some people find them a bit lurid, you know.'

'No, not at all - the colours fit the subjects. Don't you think?'

'Maybe we can tempt you later on, then?' Gill smiled, her expression becoming marginally lighter.

'Well actually, I paint myself - professionally, I mean.

78

Oils mostly. So I tend to have my own on display at home.' She searched Gill's eyes, to register any changes, given this kind of information that she couldn't have been expecting. But Lucy found her inscrutable - not a twitch, not a flicker.

'Wow!' Trish exclaimed. 'Why didn't you say?' She nudged Lucy's shoulder affectionately.

'What subjects do you paint?' Gill asked.

Lucy hesitated. Was she really interested, being challenging, or just being polite? She couldn't decide. 'Landscapes, nature, that kind of thing,' Lucy said, holding Gill's gaze.

'Oooh, Gill! You'll have to have a look at Lucy's work. See if you might want it in the gallery. Wouldn't that be lovely? Just perfect,' Trish gushed.

'Of course. Glad to take a look,' Gill replied in her even tone. 'Have you got a card you can leave me?'

Gill now appeared plainly disinterested, with a vague faraway look in her eyes, as if she was returning to wherever she had come from, perhaps some craggy peaks with ragged rooks circling overhead. In any event, she was just following procedure.

Rooting around in her bag, Lucy managed to find a business card in her purse where she usually kept them. Annoyed with herself, she discovered it was creased, but handed it to Gill, fighting back the urge to apologise.

'You can check my website - details are on there. Thanks for your interest,' Lucy said.

Then she stalked out through the doorway, with Trish scrabbling to put on her shoes and hobbling after her.

The heat sank into Lucy's limbs and burned her eyes. She reached into her bag for her sunhat and shades as she made her way through the cafe garden. She didn't feel free until she was well beyond the entrance wall and standing in the street. But Trish caught up to her.

'Wouldn't that be great, if she took some of your

paintings?' Trish enthused.

Here we go again, Lucy thought. Same old, same old. 'Maybe, but she might not like my style.' Lucy felt annoyed at having to respond to Trish's innocent enthusiasm and her defensiveness kicked in. She pulled down her shades and adjusted her hat so the roses were on the left side, where she liked them best. She reached into her bag again, pulled out a bottle of water and took some deep gulps.

'Oh, well, yes, maybe, I suppose.' Trish paused. 'But she needs some new stuff, you know.' She hesitated again. 'Actually, between you and me,' she said, lowering her voice and glancing over her shoulder towards the gallery, 'she's practically ready to sell up.'

'What? Why?' Lucy was shocked. It was the last thing she was expecting to hear.

'Oh well, it's the recession I think. And visitors just aren't buying paintings. She's just not making much with the gallery, it's the cafe that makes the money. And she's hankering to go back to the UK too. She comes from Gloucestershire. Her husband's still there. He was supposed to follow her out, but he never did. Stayed behind to look after their sick dog. Well, the dog died, and he still didn't come out. Can you believe it?'

'Well…it's a bit odd.'

'And she's not fitted in very well with the expat community here. Bit too stiff for them, I think. Tries to organise other people a bit too much. They told her they didn't want another WI out here, or any other women's group for that matter.'

That's it, Lucy thought. Things had gone too far. Here she was listening to gossip in the street about a woman she didn't even know. She could do that at home. Even more bizarrely, she was actually starting to feel sorry for the woman.

She gave herself a shake and checked her watch. It was around 3pm already. 'Sorry Trish, I've just got to go now.

See you soon.'

She turned away, while Trish was opening her mouth to say something else. She wanted to be by herself, she wanted to walk, walk anywhere, so long as it was away from this gallery. She wanted to be absorbed by the heat, and her thoughts melt away into nothing.

Trish's voice trailed to a trickle as Lucy strode away. But with the urgency of making her escape, she found herself proceeding down the street she was in, rather than doubling back the way she and Rhea had come. She also realised that she didn't have the map. Rhea had it. Typical, she thought. But she noted that the hotel was very close to the riverside, so she could always walk along the river to find it.

Trying to relax, and fulfil her afternoon priority of getting a feel for Dalyan, she adopted her usual gliding walk, examining the gardens of local villas facing the street. It was a residential area, perhaps housing some of those expats Trish had mentioned.

She paused at the entrance gate to one of the villas, and mouthed the name 'Villa Vita' scripted on the lacquered sign and dug in her bag for her camera. Now this was what she called *really* getting a feel for Dalyan. By the gate was an urn planted with red hibiscus, and beyond was a creamy marble courtyard shaded by a canopy of grapevine, its delicate new shoots trembling in a warm breeze. Around this courtyard were arranged low sofas covered in an Aztec patterned fabric, and some rattan chairs set around a table draped with a white lacy throw. Some carelessly arranged newspapers served to invite repose, though Lucy felt a few classic novels would have made the scene just perfect. The back door of the villa was reached by a few steps, and the dark stained door was ajar, revealing a dimly lit hall. A shopping bike rested against the wall, as if someone had just returned from getting some supplies and they'd rushed inside the villa to put them away. Terracotta pots graced the doorway and flowed out into the garden, drawing Lucy's eyes to the pool. It was empty, and Lucy was free to gaze at the recliners, the fringed parasol, and the sparkling turquoise water. She imagined lowering herself in. Just heaven. How wonderful it must be to live in a place like this, she mused. And maybe she could do this poolside relaxation after all?

Reluctant to leave, she pacified herself by taking a couple of wide-angle shots to make sure she captured as many of the villa's features as possible, trying not to think about painting subjects. She just wasn't in the mood for inspiration since being in the gallery. Wrenching her eyes away, she moved on.

There were more villas and gardens, some with cars parked in the drives, some just with mopeds or bicycles. There were flowering shrubs she couldn't identify, and some she could - such as orange canna lilies, prickly pear cactuses and blue convolvulus scrambling over the walls. She peered down into the unfamiliar discs of some bright red and yellow daisy flowers, taking some close-ups, her eye drawn to the cluster of tiny inflorescences. Another painting subject possibility she was forced to acknowledge. It felt as if Dalyan was bursting with heat, bursting with colour, and she was mindful of the fact that she'd never actually been to a hot country before. So this is what it's all about, she thought. Good weather practically all year round, and being able to grow these wonderful plants. No frosts to worry about, just plenty of watering, hence all the hoses snaking around the gardens. And she found herself thinking of Charlie, and wishing he could share these sights with her.

Continuing with her Dalyan tour, she determined to be practical, and reasoned if she kept turning left, she should find herself coming to the turtle roundabout off the main square. She passed by other westerners, shuffling through the hot streets, sucking on their ice creams and gawping into shop-fronts. Coming to a minimart, she took the opportunity to get some drinking water and a bottle opener for wine later on. From a pharmacy, she bought the Sin Kov Dalyan perfume Trish had mentioned. A shop that looked as if it had a wide range of books and maps, prove fruitless for local road maps or flora and fauna information - much to Lucy's annoyance. And just as her carrier bags were starting to pull her to the centre of the earth, making her feel stupid for having bought two 2L bottles of water, she emerged onto the roundabout, relieved to see the turtles freeze-framed in their jet streams.

Tramping into the square, she sank onto a wooden bench under a gum tree. She could absorb plenty of sights from here. She noticed the base of the tree trunk was painted white, and scanning the other trees around the square, it was obvious this was common practice, with the exception of the palms. Maybe I can ask Hasim, the hotel owner, about it? she thought, her mind always itching with curiosity. The riverboats were moored close by, and the Dalyan river slid past its rock face on the far side. Turning her head, she saw the entrance to the mosque, and her eyes travelled up to the dome, then to the pinnacle of the white minaret, its turret glittering with iridescent blue. There was a carved balustrade just below the turret, with speakers positioned for the Imam to call the people to prayer. But right now it was silent. But Lucy was stirred into a flutter, as she noticed some men taking off their shoes and disappearing inside. Could she go in too? Could women go in at all? But she stilled herself. It was important to learn the correct custom and there was plenty of time. Two whole weeks.

Happy that she felt she was finally casting off the feelings she'd had in the gallery, like an old patchwork coat that had been dragged through too many bramble hedges too many times, she looked around again and spotted a white minibus pull up at a stand close to the roundabout. A dribble of people started climbing out, then more and more. And soon a crowd were puddled on the pavement getting their bearings, sweaty and slumped. That must be the dolmus, Lucy decided, remembering what Trish had told them. Maybe those people have been at the beach all day? Oh, it's going to be so exciting going to the turtle beach, she thought. I just can't wait! I want to forget all about my art problems for two whole weeks and just enjoy this holiday.

Getting up, she headed for the riverside path, to walk downstream in the direction of the hotel, but first treated herself to a pistachio-stuffed cone from an ice cream seller, savouring the cool melting on her tongue as it slipped down her throat, lick by lick - a well earned reward for going into the gallery. It tasted so creamy, she could see how she and Rhea were going to find it very tough to consider calories on this holiday.

The fleet of riverboats were lined up in their blue and white livery and flying the Turkish flag. Long low boats with stretched shade awnings above the decks, decks strewn with faded kelims. Cushioned seating lured guests to sit and be transported to Dalyan's delights, both up river and down. The boats bobbed and shifted, as the boatmen shouted and gestured to one another, as boats eased out from the jetty with their passengers, or jostled for a gap back in the line up. Lucy got some leaflets about trips to the beach and further afield, so she and Rhea could have a look at them later. Surely Rhea would approve of that?

Reaching the end of the pathway, she saw a sign for the Onur hotel pointing to the right, and felt a rush of relief. The weight of the carrier bags was becoming unbearable. But she noticed some rowing boats moored at a small jetty a little way beyond where the path ended. She trudged over and found a sign saying 'Kaunos 3 lire per person'.

This must be where Trish had told them they could be rowed over the river to walk to Kaunos, she thought, with some excitement. Dumping her bags down, she peered across the river to the olive trees on the opposite bank and up to the tombs etched into the cliff face. A large grouping of around seven tombs were carved into the rock, like canyon pueblo dwellings -- with difficult access, but good protection from invaders. They were in a privileged position in the landscape, she realised, always to be seen and never forgotten - memorials for revered forefathers.

And then she thought of her own father. How fascinated he would have been by the history of these tombs. She had never realised how much she was going to miss him. He'd never really approved of her career change into art, probably something to do with her mother she suspected. *Not an easy road, love,* he said when she first told him. And he would never talk about her mother much at all, much to Lucy's frustration. *It's too difficult for me to talk about your mother,* he'd say, *she was the love of my life, you know. You're a lot like her and so is Poppy. Let's just get on with the present, love.* And then Poppy chose art too. Poor Dad, Lucy thought. But he'd tried to show his support in many ways, helping out with Poppy's course fees, and even going to the end of term exhibitions. Lucy had never told him about her art problem, so he'd been very puzzled as to why she didn't go to the last exhibition herself.

Now, scrutinising the cliff face, she could just make out a few coloured dots around the rock tombs, like the pointillist brush marks depicting people in a Canaletto painting. Some were even right outside the entrances. It was obviously possible for people to get up there, as Trish had said. And she imagined exploring the cool shady caves behind those temple porticos, then sitting on an entrance step and gazing out over Dalyan, and out over the maze of reed beds to the Mediterranean.

'Wonderful,' she murmured. 'This is a wonderful place.'

But don't forget, she reminded herself, the purpose of this holiday is to enjoy it, to have a break from my art issues, but most of all to get to know Rhea. And something had definitely made things worse between them since their mother died. She'd been thinking about it since their dad passed away. Something strange happened. They would never talk about her. And Rhea and Dad were so close - Rhea must hold the key.

5

By The Pool

The fiery glow behind Rhea's eyelids darkened as she lowered her shades and slipped into a light doze on her poolside recliner, lulled by the sounds of gentle splashes and ripples of laughter. The book she was reading fell onto the marble paving, shutting in on itself and losing her place, whilst the resolute hero still grasped the reluctant heroine around her tiny waist on the front cover of *Pride and Passion* - the hero undaunted by Rhea's lapse in concentration.

The pool was at the back of the hotel, discrete and secluded. Visible beyond its low containing walls were pan tile roofs nestling amongst the stately spines of cypresses, and the peaks of craggy hills. Orange globe flowers and white hibiscus shrubs provided lush camouflage in the surrounding flower beds. When Rhea had arrived, there were only a few sun-worshippers scattered around the pool, with a couple of scrawny cats slinking its perimeter to select some available sunbeds to stretch out on, then curl up into defensive balls. She'd chosen a recliner and parasol by a wall tumbling with pink bougainvillea. A very light breeze ruffled the leaves and papery bracts, which cast trembling shadows against the creamy marble. It was a beautiful spot, about half way down the length of the pool. The sky above was an intense blue and the water lapped the rim of the turquoise pool with a gentle slapping sound. The chrome bars of the steps at either end gleamed like polished silver. It was just so inviting. She decided she would have a dip later on, after she'd caught some serious sun.

This is it, she'd said to herself. This is what I need.

She'd lowered the sunbed, taken off her sarong, and

settled herself on her towel in her turquoise bikini. She'd already applied some more sun tan lotion to her existing spray tan, so the sun was able to go to work and woo her into a deep relaxation. No clouds to dim the dancing lights in the pool, or to cause anyone the slightest degree of bodily deprivation by a fleeting drop in temperature by their passing overhead.

Now, as the heat pressed upon her, she willed herself into a blissful abyss…sinking, sinking…almost there…the book fallen from her lap, the splashes and ripples of laughter becoming further away, miles away, above the surface, as she drifted down and down into depths of stillness…depths of silence…depths of oblivion.

All too soon, though, she found herself rising. She struggled and found herself fished to the surface by raised voices at the opposite side of the pool. She propped herself up on her elbows and peered across. There was a middle-aged couple standing by a pair of recliners which had already been taken possession of. They were arguing with the prostrate occupants, whose leathery tans proved they were professional sunbathers and wouldn't be budged. To Rhea's horror she recognised the couple with the grievance. It was June and Brian Walker.

'Well, we'll see about that! Won't we Brian,' June announced to the leathery tans, as she picked up two towels that had been folded and placed on the wall behind, and marched off with Brian in tow.

Rhea lay down again in case she was spotted. There was something about June and Brian she didn't like. A look in June's eyes - too inquisitive, yet inscrutable, and somewhat lizard-like. And with Brian as her mated accomplice.

She tried to relax again, totally disinterested in the poolside dispute going on, especially since it involved June and Brian Walker. But as she sought sun-soaked stillness, a stream of unbidden thoughts started to flood through her mind: her ring was safely tucked away in their room number's deposit box, that's okay…no sign of Hasim at all… I wonder where he is…oh stop it…glad the trips are booked…I hope Lucy doesn't turn up for quite a while…hope she doesn't start talking about Dad, the past…I don't want to share… or 'open up', as she'd put it … what good would it do anyway?

She flicked her eyes open. Oh God! she thought. It had become painfully clear that she was going to have to make an effort to get along with Lucy. There was to be no getting out of it, not if they were to get to the end of the holiday. And she'd promised her father. But why did he have to ask them? And how was she going to do it? She felt like shouting out loud like a five year old: It's Not Fair! And why on holiday? It was all so extreme. Typical of Lucy. Right up her street, this kind of wild idea…just like - but she blocked the thought out. Not going back there, she thought. Stick with the present. Lucy would start probing soon - even though they'd agreed they'd wait until they settle into the holiday before talking about their father. There would be no putting her off; probing was her speciality. When she was a girl, if she got a splinter in her finger, she always managed to get it out herself, sucking on her finger or digging into it with a needle, even if she made her finger bleed. And then, there were her constant questions: *'Yes, but how? Yes, but why? What do you mean exactly?*

Rhea groaned. As a teenager, she'd found it very difficult to keep her private life private. When her boyfriends came round, they'd always been accosted by Lucy's questions, before she could manage to drag them away upstairs to listen to records. *She's cute*, they would say. But she was far from cute to Rhea, more like an itch you could never scratch. *She's just got an inquisitive mind*, George would say. *She doesn't mean any harm.*

Well, whether or not that was true, Rhea decided she could do without Lucy's inquisitive mind on this holiday and under no circumstances did she want to talk to her about their father. She'd had enough of thinking about those last few days of his illness, seeing him weakened, so thin, all the flesh gone from his face, then barely able to talk. Then after the funeral, she'd ended up thinking about the past and all these vivid memories had come back. She'd had no control over them. Things she thought she'd forgotten - faces, words, looks - and they were painful ones. She hadn't been able to concentrate at work, so she'd been prescribed Prozac for a couple of months - *just to get you over the worst*, her GP said. And he seemed to have been right. She'd come off the tablets three months ago and certainly felt a lot better. Back in control.

But every day she wished she could talk to George, see his wry grin as he always managed to suggest just the right thing when she told him her troubles on a visit, or asked his advice over the phone. And if he didn't know what to say, he'd resort to his precious pearl of wisdom - *play it by ear, kiddo*. And he'd always been right. It was just at the end, when he was dying, that he couldn't give her an answer. All her life, he'd been the only person she ever talked to properly. The only one. She never talked to her husband, Chris, any more. He was a waste of space these days. So, who could she talk to now that her dad was gone? Certainly not Lucy.

A sudden ache stabbed into her heart, bringing tears to her eyes. This pain was something she'd found quite scary the first time it happened. She'd never felt it before, didn't understand it. But she'd been getting used to it since her father died. No, she decided. She couldn't get into anything heavy with Lucy. She had to look after herself. She had to keep it light, just little bits and pieces about the last twenty years or so, maybe talk about her work, and maybe - just maybe, about Chris. They could still get to know each other more, find out more about each other's lives. But not stuff about their dad. And really, what was there to talk about anyway? They both missed their father.

There was nothing else to say.

A dark shadow leaned over her, blocking her view of the sky and making her shudder.

'Hello again, pet. Enjoying some sun, then? Hope you've got that ring put away.'

Rhea propped herself up and took off her shades. It was June Walker. She'd changed into a chiffon cover-up, patterned with overblown roses and was still wearing her rings and gold chains. Brian was standing alongside in some tight swimming shorts under his distended belly, with a thick gold curb necklace cutting into the flesh of his double chin neck. His arms were full of towels, robes and a beach bag. Rhea noticed that his forearms were tattooed with an inky tangle of serpents wrestling for space on his skin.

'Lovely pool, isn't it, pet?' June said, with some insistence in her tone that Rhea felt repulsed by. June's mouth went up at the corners into its fixed, sinister smile, that reminded Rhea of a ventriloquist's dummy.

'Yes, great,' she replied.

'Your sister not around, then? Lovely girl. Friendly manner,' June said, the words squeezed out from behind her frozen smile.

'She'll be along later, she's exploring Dalyan a bit.'

'Oh well, hope to see her later, then.'

'You look nice and relaxed there,' Brian grinned, as his eyes hungrily explored up and down Rhea's body.

She sat up and pulled her sarong over her thighs.

'Lovely borjonvilla that, isn't it?' said June, gesturing to Rhea's flowery backdrop.

'Mmm,' she said, deciding it best not to correct June's pronunciation at this point.

'We've had some bother you know, with that German couple over there,' June said, throwing them a dirty look over her shoulder. 'Pinched our sunbeds, they did, moved our towels off. Did you know you can't leave your towels on the sunbeds for longer than two hours? That's what they told us, and we've just checked with reception. It's ridiculous! Mind you, trust the ruddy Germans. Do you know, they sometimes book the loungers before they've even arrived at their hotel. Bloody cheek, that is!'

Rhea's book caught June's eye. She picked it up, scrutinising the cover, then handed it to her. 'Here you go, love, looks a cracker that. Maybe I could borrow it when you've finished?' I love a good romance, don't I Brian?' She scanned the poolside with her flinty eyes. 'Oh well, we'd better find ourselves a spot, hadn't we, luv?' she said to Brian. 'See you later, then.' Her eyes glinted in the sun, and her smile vanished, and they slid away to some free recliners in a far corner of the poolside.

Rhea shuddered again. She felt invaded. Brian had been staring at her breasts, and she'd felt too aware of some cellulite on her thighs. I've got to stop being silly, she said to herself, it's not as if *they* are specimens of physical perfection. Far from it. June was a wrinkled prune on sticks and balding Brian, with his bloated beer belly, was reminiscent of a walrus minus the tusks.

She looked across to see what they were doing. Seated together on their towels, Brian was smearing tanning cream onto June's back, whilst June directed the operation, her permed head nodding and shaking at intervals. Then she snatched the bottle from him and started on her arms.

Rhea decided they were not worthy of any more attention. She threw her book into her bag, having developed a sudden distaste for it and cast aside her sarong. She'd selected the bikini she was wearing for just this function, poolside posing - and nothing was going to stop her trying to enjoy wearing it. Pulling out her mobile from a particularly discrete zipped compartment in her bag, she started checking her messages again. She'd promised Lucy not to bring it, but at the last minute when she was packing, she'd decided it was ridiculous to leave it behind. What about emergencies? Lucy wouldn't have thought of that. Well, what Lucy didn't know wouldn't hurt her.

There were no messages from work. That was a surprise. Neal's was always busy in the summer months. There were usually always a couple of queries about customer complaints, or messages from head office being passed on to her, as she preferred to deal with these things straight away. Were they getting on well without her, then? But there again, her new assistant manager, Kevin, was extremely efficient. She'd helped interview him herself. Very likeable, not too pushy. Good background in sales in some prestigious stores such as Lewis's and Frasers. Maybe he was holding the fort well. Then the thought crossed her mind - maybe he was holding the fort too well? Taking it over perhaps. Orchestrating a coup. *Just have a great time*, he'd said. *Don't worry about the store. You've had so much on your plate, lately* - another allusion to the loss of her father. After a little reflection, she decided she didn't need to worry about Kevin. If he was up to anything, she was more than capable of sorting him out when she got back.

There was a text message from her son, Rob: 'Hope you're having a good time. Dad's behaving. Say hi to Auntie Lucy for me. XXX'

She felt an urge to ring him, to hear his voice. It would be around 1pm back home, maybe he'd be on his lunch break. He'd just started an apprenticeship as a mechanic at a local garage, but he'd told her that he and the other two lads tended to just grab a sandwich and carry on working. That seems to be the way of it, these days, she mused - employees not taking their allocated breaks, too much pressure, too scared of losing their jobs. Well, not in her department store. Never. Everyone had rights to breaks, and she made sure her staff took them, as she did herself. But she decided not to phone Rob, as principles aside, she didn't want to get him into any trouble.

There was also a message from her husband, Chris: 'Ring me back please, got a good deal for you. Take care

XX'

That was it, nothing else.

She felt warmed by Rob's message, but chilled by Chris's.

She and Chris had not been getting on very well lately. Actually, that was putting it mildly. Things hadn't been right for a few years now. But it had become worse since she inherited her share of her father's estate, around £200,000. She'd opened up a separate account for it, in her own name, keeping the security password hidden from Chris, not including it on her household management spreadsheet, which he could easily access.

That's how it has to be these days, she sighed - Chris and his dodgy deals. Not the sort of thing insurance brokers, like himself, usually got involved with. I've only just got here on holiday, she thought, and he's pestering me over money. Well he has to learn, I'm not interested in his ideas on what I should do with Dad's money. Let him make a mess of his own investments, projects, business avenues, or whatever he chooses to call them. And she inwardly vowed to ignore all his calls on this holiday.

She glanced around the poolside, ignoring the Walkers, and gazed out at the view beyond. A gauzy mist had veiled the hills and the air hung heavy with heat. This really is a perfect place, she said to herself. Maybe we will be able to have a good time if we just keep things light. She went off and got herself a coke from the poolside bar, then settled herself once more with *Pride and Passion*, just getting up now and again to inch the recliner forward, to ensure she received the full spotlight of the sun. Eventually, when she'd read the same paragraph a few times, she fell into a deep sleep.

She was roused this time by the creaking sound of the wooden frame of a sunbed being dragged over marble. She gave a sidewise glance from under her lowered eyelids to see who was disturbing her again.

'Hi. You look so chilled,' said Lucy. 'Mission accomplished, then?'

She stirred herself. 'Mmm? Oh, yes. It's a really lovely pool. Great view too. How about you? How did you get on looking at other people's paintings in the gallery?'

She realised she'd blurted out this badly phrased question, without taking into consideration Lucy's hidden issues hinted at earlier. She bit her lip. Keeping things light was only going to work if she kept her own curiosity in check.

Lucy paused for a moment. 'Oh, well - it wasn't too bad, actually, apart from the owner - a dark dour woman. But there's some good work there, local artists mostly. Lots of colour. Some very nice tiles there too. Actually, Trish told me the owner's wanting to sell up and get back to the UK. There's a bit of a slump in the art market apparently.'

'Oh, really,' Rhea murmured, wanting to go back to sleep now.

'Yes. Odd, isn't it?'

'I suppose.'

'Anyway, enough of galleries and paintings. Then I walked back towards the square, saw some amazing houses on the way. Spotted the dolmus minibus Trish told us about. Bought an ice cream. Actually I was lost at first because *you* had the map.' Lucy's tone was faintly accusing.

Rhea felt a defensive surge well up inside her and she wanted to spit out a few pointed words. But instead, she grimaced, as she chanted to herself - keep things light, light as air, light as a feather, light as -

'But it was fine,' Lucy continued. 'In the end I worked my way along the riverside to find the hotel. There are some amazing restaurants, you know. Anyway, it was quite nice getting lost. Gave me a chance to spot places, like the local minimarts where we can pick things up. I got a bottle opener for when we want to share a bottle of wine, and there's a bakery or two - you know, if we decide to stay in our room for a bite to eat, where we can talk. Got us some repellent too, so that's sorted for now, and some bottled water.'

Rhea tried to nod in an approving manner. Repellent, yes, water, yes. But talking in the bedroom, no.

'Some great little shops,' Lucy went on, 'though I found nothing on garden plants or animals of the area. There's so many shrubs I don't recognise. It's so frustrating. Anyway, I took some pictures and I'll try to identify them when we get back home. Some of them are just amazing. You know, structurally. And the colours! They just glow! Like those orange verbena things,' she said, pointing over to the flower beds.

'Oh, is that what they are?' Rhea said, squinting across. She had been drawn to them just before she chose her spot. Tiny tubular frilled flowers arranged into pompoms and paired on the stems - colours flushing from peach to pink, through to orange and crimson. 'Can you get them back home?' she asked.

'No, I don't think so. They're probably a tender variety. But I'll check when I get back. You never know, we might be able to get some for the garden centre.'

'Well if you do, I'll have some.'

Rhea felt taken aback by her own response. It bordered on the sisterly. Maybe this was an example of the approach she could take?

'Didn't know you were into plants, Ree,' Lucy responded, gazing at the pool.

The use of the old family nickname made Rhea flinch. Her mother and Lucy had called her this, but George had never joined in. Chris had tried it in the early days, but she'd told him she hated it. Her face dropped now, and she was silent.

'Oh, sorry,' Lucy said. 'I don't know where that came from, after all this time. Do you mind?'

'Yes, actually, Lu!' Lucy's old nickname stung Rhea as

she spoke it out loud. It swallowed her straight back into the past, making the effort to be retaliatory totally counter-productive.

Lucy smiled. 'Fair enough. Mind you, sometimes Charlie calls me that. I don't really mind. But it's no to Ree, then.' She paused. 'So, how do you do this?'

What?' Rhea wondered what was coming next.

'The pool thing. You know. Poolside etiquette, Trish called it. I've never done it before. Charlie and me have never been on these kinds of holidays, like you and Chris.'

Rhea felt relieved to be back on safe ground. 'Oh well, there's not much to it really.'

She glanced at Lucy, peeking over her sunglasses to appraise her. Lucy was wearing a one piece swimsuit, black with a pink trim, with her pink roses hat. Her white skin stood out conspicuously enough to prove the point she had never tried sunbathing before. But Rhea noted with annoyance, that her body was very well toned for a woman in her forties. Her size ten figure, and her long limbs, gave her the natural elegance of a catwalk model, and Rhea discovered a familiar irritation still festering within her since their teenage years. By the time Lucy reached fourteen, it was pretty clear she was going to be taller and slimmer than Rhea. Rhea noticed that Lucy had her beach bag with her, with an orange sarong spilling out of it. Her mood was unreadable behind her brown tinted shades. Only her tone of voice was available for Rhea to work with.

'Okay, pool etiquette,' Rhea said. 'Well, the first thing you have to do is put some tanning lotion on, but put a towel down on the lounger first to protect it, see? Hotels don't like the punters staining the beds. Or, you could put it on before you come down to the pool. But you have to remember to top it up after you go for a swim.'

'What? Every time?'

'Yes. Because the pool washes it off. And you're so fair, you have to be careful.'

'Okay, seems a right palaver, mind. What else?'

'Well, you can lay your towel and perhaps a book on a sun lounger for say an hour, to kind of unofficially reserve it for later on. But if time runs over a couple of hours, the towel can be removed, and your lounger can be taken by somebody else. In other words, you can't expect to reserve it all day. That's what happened to the Walkers over there,' Rhea said tossing her head in June and Brian's direction. 'They assumed they could 'book' a couple of recliners all through breakfast and lunch by the sound of it.'

Lucy stared across. 'June and Brian. Really! Oh yes, there they are.'

'Yes. And they made quite a scene about it - some Germans took their loungers, who were quite within their rights of course.'

Lucy put her hand up to wave, but Rhea grasped her wrist and yanked it back down.

'Don't attract their attention, they've already been pestering me!'

'Oh, but they seem harmless enough,' Lucy said in surprise, rubbing her wrist.

'I don't know about that!' Rhea paused. 'Look that's enough poolside protocol for now. Why don't you try topping up your lotion and sunbathing for a while?'

'Oh God, no! I've got to have a swim first. The water looks amazing! Have you been in yet?'

'No, not yet.'

'Why not? I don't know how you can resist it! It'll cool you off too.'

Rhea felt annoyed at Lucy's enthusing and questioning. Why did she have to be so pushy? And the last remark sounded like Lucy was inferring she, Rhea, needed to chill out more. 'Look Lucy, you do your thing, I'll do mine. I'll take a dip later on, okay?'

'Alright, sorry. It's just it would be nice to do it together, that's all.'

As Lucy reached into her beach bag for a pair of goggles, and stepped over to the poolside, Rhea rolled onto her tummy to toast her back. She clamped her eyes shut in an effort to relax again. There was a squeal from Lucy as she plunged into the water, then the sound of splashing.

'Oh, Rhea, it's gorgeous!'

Rhea groaned. She turned around and looked across the pool to see if the Walkers had noticed Lucy's arrival. But they were laid out like two basking iguanas on their bellies, their toughened hides, complete with gold chains, baked by the sun. For once, they seemed oblivious to their prey. Remaining on the other loungers, there were about three couples and two young women chatting together while they sunbathed.

Rhea pushed her sunglasses over her forehead. The shadows of the recliners had lengthened since she arrived, like oil slicks slanting across the marble. It was obviously quite late in the afternoon. As she squinted at the silver stipples of light shimmering in the pool, she changed her mind, and decided to join Lucy. After all, it might fit with her new approach on being 'sisterly'.

'Just coming!' she called out.

As she padded over the scorching tiles to the edge of the pool, and stepped backwards down the chrome steps, inching her way into the cool water, she felt particularly self-conscious of the backs of her thighs and her bottom. This moment of discomfort passed as soon as she was up to her waist, only to be superseded by the next challenge - the shock of the cool water coming up over her breasts. But by the time she was fully immersed up to her neck, she felt much more composed with no squeal having passed her lips. Her inner resolve saw to that.

Lucy was wearing her goggles and ducking down into the pool, trying to swim underwater, but could only manage about half a width before she bobbed to the surface. Rhea decided Lucy was happily occupied like a child at play, so she started to do a sedate breaststroke down the length of the pool. She swam with her head well out of the water and was wearing her shades. Her ponytail just trailed the water by half an inch.

And it did feel heavenly. Two dragonflies flitted over the surface of the water in front of her, then rose and disappeared in a dance of iridescent green and blue sparkles. As she parted the water with her strong arms and kicked deeply out to the sides, heels leading, she brought her legs swiftly together again, to achieve a long slow glide. In short, she had good form, and knew it. However, she had never been able to progress to putting her head in the water to make it one hundred percent perfect.

After completing about two lengths she studied the other occupants of the pool. There was another woman doing the same kind of breaststroke as herself. They glided past each other like ships in the night, with minimal wake disturbance. There was also an older man, with a shiny bald head, which gave him minimum resistance for his professional front crawl. Lucy stopped practising her aquatic skills to watch him from the side of the pool.

Just then, two teenage boys arrived. They grunted across to a couple on recliners, who must have been their parents, then grabbed a beach ball, and dive bombed into the pool like greedy seagulls. Their splash water stopped Rhea in her tracks, drenching her hair and making her eyes smart. She was furious. She noticed the spray had reached as far as the recumbent iguanas - June and Brian - who raised their heads in synchronised curiosity to locate the source of the disturbance. June gave a dirty look to the two youths and muttered something to Brian. Then she caught sight of Rhea, glanced around and spotted Lucy.

Oh no, Rhea thought. Here we go.

'Yoo hoo!' June called out, waving her arms at Lucy. 'Yoo hoo!'

Lucy looked puzzled, but swam over to their side of the pool. Rhea tried to catch the conversation, but the two lads were making so much noise, throwing the ball to each other, and doing the occasional handstand, right in front of the two young women. Just like performing seals, Rhea thought. Before they started balancing balls on their noses, she decided it was time to get out. She elegantly mounted the steps, once more becoming self-conscious of her bottom and thighs, and tried not to hurry as she made her way back to her sunbed, pulling her bikini briefs back into position to cover her bottom - as much as practically possible.

As she started towelling her hair, Lucy came back and flopped down onto her bed. 'That was great, wasn't it?'

'Yes, apart from those lads fooling around. What did that woman want?'

What, June? Just saying maybe we should all meet at breakfast. They come from Morpeth, you know. That's where Mum came from, isn't it?'

'Yes. But what did you say?' Rhea stopped drying her hair and looked hard at Lucy.

'Oh, well, we don't want to be pinned down like that, do we? Anyway, she's a bit weird, friendly enough, though. Brian seems to be under her thumb, doesn't he?'

'He ogled me earlier. I really don't like the two of them at all. I'm glad you didn't accept the invitation. I think we should steer well clear of them.'

'Really? She asked what we were doing tomorrow.'

Rhea groaned. 'Oh, for goodness' sake, what's with the woman? Why is she trying to latch onto us?'

'Oh, well, we'll try to avoid them. But honestly Rhea, they're probably harmless.'

Rhea raised her eyebrows and vigorously carried on towelling her hair.

After June and Brian retired from their stake out, and as the shadows lengthened, Rhea and Lucy sipped a coke and engaged in some people watching.

The two young women, who had ignored the performing seals, had sunbathed, then had a swim. As they moved around the poolside, they kept pulling their bikini briefs back into position to cover their bottoms, which Rhea recognised as a self-conscious act that had become a poolside convention - you have to do it with style, as if you don't really care. Yet the girls didn't have an ounce of cellulite to conceal. Their smooth tanned skin showed no spots, moles or insect bites, as if any blemishes they may have once possessed had been airbrushed from their fashion magazine bodies. But whenever they left to get something from their room, they tugged on their sundresses to cover themselves up.

'Oh, to look something like that again,' said Rhea. 'But they don't seem to appreciate what they've got, do they?'

'I suppose not. But then not everyone wants to strut their stuff,' Lucy replied, as she monitored the girls.

Rhea sensed that Lucy, as usual, was looking for what *she* would call a discussion, but which was really trying to start an argument.

'Well, I think you might as well enjoy it when you've got it. There are people around this pool that are strutting their stuff, when they've got no stuff to strut, in fact they could do with some camouflage.'

'Did you strut your stuff when you were their age?'

Here we go, Rhea thought. 'Well, a bit, I suppose. But maybe when you're younger, you're more self-conscious, just when you shouldn't be.'

Just then, an older couple passed straight by them, then another - all returning to their sunbeds. Rhea gazed after them. The women had sagging gravity-dragged flesh with doughy pouches spilling over their bikini briefs, while old operation scars formed dimpled crevices on their chests and stomachs. Varicose veins swelled out on their legs like trapped noodles. And the tan that they'd burned onto their skin with religious zeal over countless beach holidays, simply served to accentuate their age, with the wrinkles marking time like the xylem rings of a tree trunk. So overall, their flesh bore the marks and morphed forms of eating a western diet, while at the same time benefiting from the dogged determination of a national health care system determined to keep them alive at all costs. And noticing all this, Rhea found it depressing.

One of the men was thin and creased in the middle with shrunken muscles, chest hair going Brillo pad grey. But at least he was lean, Rhea thought, and probably reasonably fit for his age. The other lumbered ahead, his fat belly bloating over his tight trunks. He eased himself down onto a lounger, reached for a fag, lit up, then rested his hands on his distended pride and joy. It was as if he'd grown it on purpose, feeding it regularly with fermented malt and hops.

'The older people just don't seem to care, do they?' she said to Lucy who was watching them too.

'No. I suppose they're past caring what they look like.'

'Or maybe they just don't see it anymore?'

'Bit of both, maybe. Something to watch out for there. Mind, in some ways, you have to admire them for not giving a damn.'

'I suppose so,' Rhea agreed. 'And they obviously love being in the sun.'

As she continued to scrutinise the group (easily achieved with apparent nonchalance when done behind sunglasses), Rhea decided she wasn't in bad shape after all. She determined right there and then, to hang on to what she had, to try to get herself down to a neat size twelve before the menopause hit - a damage limitation strategy. She'd probably have to cut down on her cigarettes and wine intake. Not an easy matter. But perhaps she could take up jogging, like Lucy? But there again, maybe not. Not with all that bouncing around and people staring and thinking 'now there's someone who overeats trying to get fit'. It was fine for the tall, lithe sprinting types like Lucy, who looked like gazelles out for a warm up, rather than a hippopotamus thudding heavily down the road.

It was around 5pm now, and as the shadows had advanced, a spell of serenity seemed to have been cast over the poolside and its occupants. Low murmurs and light splashes from the pool massaged away tensions, while the sun started its descent towards the horizon, bathing the pan tile roofs and hills of Dalyan in a melting butter glow. Both the sisters fell asleep on their recliners.

But soon, a new sound woke them up. The call of the Imam was being chanted from the mosque in the square. It was a haunting call, broadcast high from the minaret, a resonant mesmerising call, reaching far out over the town and mountain peaks, a call intended to pierce the heart and stir the soul to prayer. It lasted for about ten seconds, but it seemed to echo into infinity. Lucy and Rhea both listened with suspended breath.

When it was over, Lucy sighed, 'Wow! That was powerful.'

But Rhea couldn't speak. She felt as if the Imam had reached deep into her and found what was hidden there, what she wanted to forget and wanted no one to find out. She didn't trust herself to say anything at this moment, but she knew Lucy, with her romantic inclinations, would insist on a response.

'Well! What do you think?' Lucy enquired, right on cue.

Rhea's mouth had gone dry, but she worked her tongue around the inside of her lips and managed to find some words. 'Yes, very atmospheric…effective…amazing.' Her tone had become more forced with each word and she couldn't carry on. For the second time today, her eyes brimmed with tears. She turned her face away from Lucy and started gathering up her things.

'Yes, time to go and change, I reckon,' said Lucy, following suit, 'and think about where we're going to eat.

I'm really hungry now.'

It took them about an hour to shower and change for dinner. Lucy tried on two outfits, Rhea tried on four. They both asked of the other 'What do you think?' Their respective responses of nodding approval were kind, constructive and reasonably sisterly, Rhea thought. A quick touch up of make-up and they were ready. They both decided to wear their hair loose, and had done some frantic straightening with their tongs.

Lucy was wearing a patchwork maxi skirt, of vintage-style patterns of peaches and pinks, with a fitted brown t-shirt. Around her neck a planetarium of selected beads jostled for space. Flat strap sandals completed her hippie ethnic artist look.

Rhea chose a long black and white printed chiffon dress, nipped in at the waist to show off her bust, the neckline dipping down into her cleavage and adorned with a diamante sparkling pendant. Some black slip-on wedge sandals gave her the requisite height. Contemporary fashion was Rhea's speciality.

They then exited their room and descended the turns of the staircase with measured steps and an occasional flick of their hair, like two glamorous celebrities preparing to meet the flash of the paparazzi and their adoring fans.

When they entered reception they found Hasim on duty, staring at a computer screen behind the desk, his eyebrows drawn tightly together. Rhea tried not to look him in the eye as she said hello, and asked for the key to their security box.

'Hello! Rhea and Lucy, room 23, yes?' he asked, looking at Rhea.

She had to meet his gaze. The way he pronounced her name was different. He rolled the 'r' and lingered on the 'a', stretching it out into an 'ah'. It sounded exotic. *And* he'd remembered their room number.

'Yes,' she said, giving him a small smile.

As she went into the backroom just off reception and took her ring from the deposit box, Lucy chatted to Hasim, asking him why the bases of some of the trees were painted white. Questions, always questions, Rhea sighed to herself, as she slid the ring onto the third finger of her right hand, where it felt most comfortable, and (it has to be said) more prominent.

Hasim's answer was impressively thorough. 'It's whitewash killer for the pests, stops them crawling up from ground and making holes in the tree - also protects the tree bark from sunburn - see?'

'Oh yes…that's fascinating!' Lucy replied, absorbing the information by creasing up her eyes. 'Isn't it, Rhea?'

'Yes,' Rhea said, as she came back to the desk, trying not to look at Hasim. 'But we'd better get going.'

Just then, there was a low rumbling noise in the street outside. The sisters turned to peer through the open doorway, and a chemical smell wafted towards them, slightly sweet, slightly sickly. What looked like some kind of tractor trundled past in the direction of the river, spraying fine jets of a liquid in its wake. They both turned and stared at Hasim.

'Mosquito spray,' he replied, laughing. 'It is bad time for them, down by the river where we are, and all the restaurants want to keep their customers. You should both always have Sin Kov with you, Dalyan perfume we call it here. Do you want me to suggest restaurant for you?'

'Yes please,' Rhea replied. 'It's so hard to make a choice and everyone pushes for business so hard.'

Hasim paused for a moment, then knitted his dark brows together again. 'Yes. Work here is very seasonal, you see. Lots of waiters come from the north just for season, so they have to try hard, you see? They don't make much money the rest of the year.'

Yes, yes of course,' said Lucy hurriedly. 'Totally understandable.'

'Absolutely,' Rhea added, feeling guilty now. She

smiled apologetically at Hasim. 'Where would you recommend then, please?'

'The river restaurants have nice mood, but you have to keep an eye on the mozzies. My favourite is the Calypso. Turn right when you get to end of this road, then along to the bend in the river. The Calypso is just after that. Okay?'

'Right,' Lucy said, and then asked, 'What does it feel like to be bitten by a mozzie?'

Rhea groaned with embarrassment. 'For goodness' sake, Lucy!' she said under her breath. Questions, always questions, she thought - *witter, witter, witter.*

Hasim laughed. 'What can I say? Like little tickles,' he said. 'Or maybe...' he paused and looked at them both, 'as we say here - little kisses in the night.'

It was a lovely spot on the jetty of the Calypso, and the table they selected was right by the riverside. Darkness set in fast and the waiters had lit the red glass candle holders on the tables, so flickering flames added to the romance of the setting.

The lights from the dock flooded the river with an intense viridian green blurring into the inky blackness of the opposite bank. Fringing the jetty were reeds and grasses, whispering in a gentle breeze. The Dalyan river slid past in its channel, and from it could be heard the low squawking of paddling ducks and the fading tinkles of light laughter from the fairy-lit river boats that chugged past, cutting through the silence. From the cliff bank opposite, bells clunked as goats scrambled their way through the incline's rocks and spiny undergrowth. A shoal of fish were feeding alongside Rhea and Lucy's table, as bits of bread were flicked into the water by some of the other diners - concentric rings blurring in and out of focus, stippled with tiny splashes and open mouths.

After taking the precaution of spraying themselves liberally with Dalyan perfume, the sisters were sharing a bottle of red wine, rather than partake of the local raki, an aniseed flavoured spirit, which they decided would be asking for trouble. Although the menu consummately catered for the tastes of all nations, the sisters agreed to order traditional Turkish cuisine for the first evening meal of their holiday.

Deciding not to go with the meze starters, Rhea chose a dish called Karniyarik, which consisted of eggplant filled with onion, garlic, black pepper, tomatoes and ground meat. She ordered some rice on the side. Lucy, who declared she was ravenous now, ordered Levrek pilakisi, which was a kind of sea bass stew, simmered with potatoes, carrots, tomatoes, onions and garlic. They sipped their wine and nibbled on some Pide breads while they waited for their meal. Dessert was to be Baklava, a sweet pastry made of layers of filo, filled with chopped nuts and soaked in a honey syrup, served with ice cream. Rhea decided that perhaps her diet could wait until she got home.

They found the food delicious and ordered coffee to finish, then asked the waiter for the bill. An immaculately dressed Turk appeared from the shadows wearing a black suit and snow white shirt. He introduced himself as he gave them the bill.

'I'm Ahmet, the owner,' he said. Hasim is friend of mine, you Rhea and Lucy, staying at the Onur, yes?'

Rhea and Lucy both nodded.

'How did you know?' Lucy asked.

'Oh, Hasim, he gave me little ring, to say you coming. Two beautiful women, no? You get ten percent discount off bill. Okay?'

'Oh, thank you! That's very nice of you!' Lucy said.

'Yes, very considerate,' Rhea added.

Left alone again, after Rhea paid the bill (to balance the day's spending between them), Lucy leaned forward and whispered, 'What was that about?'

Rhea leaned forward. 'Hasim and Ahmet probably have an arrangement, where Hasim sends his guests here, and maybe gets some commission. The discount was probably genuine though. I can't think of any reason why it wouldn't be. The arrangement would be pretty pointless otherwise.'

Oh, right,' said Lucy. Then she stiffened. 'I just felt some tickles round my ankles. I didn't spray myself there.'

Both sisters got out their Sin Kov and sprayed their lower legs. Then they slowly savoured their coffee, secure in the belief they were both mosquito-controlled zones. They'd been offered Nescafe as an alternative to traditional Turkish coffee, which they suspected would be far too strong for them.

There was an easy slumped silence between them, relations mellowed and nurtured by sated appetites and a full-bodied wine.

Lucy was the first to break the mood. 'We haven't decided what we're doing tomorrow, have we?' she said brightly.

'No, we haven't,' replied Rhea, slowly, cautiously, wondering what was coming next.

'Well, let's do the turtle beach in the morning, then maybe walk to Kaunos in the afternoon,' Lucy said.

Rhea drained the last drop from her wine glass. 'Hmm…that sounds okay.' Sun, sea and sand, and a walk amongst some ruins on the shores of the Med. Pretty idyllic, she decided.

'The beach will be perfect for having a good talk. After all, we're settled into the holiday now, haven't we?' Lucy insisted.

Rhea stared at the wobbling candle flame in front of her, seeking guidance. 'Well yes, I suppose so… but talk about what in particular?' She could have bitten back the words as soon as she spoke them. Why did I ask that? she scolded herself. Here we go again. Stupid. Stupid!

'Well, Dad. You know. We shouldn't bottle things up. And well…the last twenty years. Everything really.'

'Well, that'll take some bloody doing!' Rhea felt a hot flush through her chest and arms, right up to her neck. Under the table, she scrunched up her paper napkin in the sweaty palms of her hands and couldn't seem to let go of it. Keep it light, she reminded herself, kneading the napkin in her lap. Don't rise to it. Keep it as light as air, as light as a feather, light and frothy, like cappuccino foam, like fairy liquid bubbles…

'Well, we can make a start, anyway, start chipping away at it. That's why we're here, isn't it?' Lucy looked earnestly at Rhea, waiting for a response.

Rhea strove to find some kind of qualifying reply. 'Well, it's to get to know each other more. So, yes - in part.' She dragged her eyes from the flame to the dark green river sliding past, impenetrable.

That night, Lucy managed to get off to sleep first, much to Rhea's annoyance. Her soft regular breathing was barely audible, but Rhea couldn't sleep. She got up, feeling the urge to smoke two cigarettes out on the balcony, and managed not to wake Lucy, by tiptoeing around the two beds - the last thing she wanted were more questions. Then she lay in the humid heat of the bedroom, flinging the cotton bed sheet off herself, then pulling it around her again. One word kept reverberating through her tired skull. *Everything*. That was what Lucy had said. They could talk about everything. Chip away at it. Well, Lucy had another thing coming.

6

On Turtle Beach

Borne on warm air currents, from the serrated spine of a mountain range, a white-tailed eagle glided along the path of the Dalyan river, which twisted and turned beneath like a satin ribbon catching and losing light. Past the river cliffs it flew, past the rock tombs where man had carved his mark, its wings outstretched over the scattered mosaic of reed beds and the blue and white canopies of the river boats leaving fanned out tails of white in their wakes. Past the hill top citadel of Kaunos, and out to the delta where the Aegean melted into the Mediterranean sea. The eagle turned and headed south east along the 4.5 km narrow crescent of sun-bleached sand that formed Iztuzu beach. The beach's west end was open to the sea and its passage of sailing boats, the eastern end hipped to a pine-clad mountain of the mainland, and cradling behind it the mirrored reflections floating in Sulungur Lake. The tidal ocean surf crested into wide arcs of foam below, advancing and retreating upon the shoreline in a daily diurnal rhythm, governed by the moon. The shadow of the eagle skimmed over the surface of the water. This was where the Caretta came. And this was where the eagle sought its prey.

The sun filtered through the latticework of the woven cane parasol, casting shadowy spider webs onto Lucy and Rhea as they lay propped up on their recliners. They had just arrived on Turtle Beach by river boat, and were trying to relax, after agreeing on a nice spot for the morning, with easy access to the toilets and changing huts and near a small beach cafe. It was very hot again. One of the male passengers on the boat, wearing a white panama hat, had announced with great authority that it was 35 degrees Celsius in the shade, for the apparent benefit of everyone else on board, and to the obvious embarrassment of his wife, who riveted her eyes to the bow of the boat as it ploughed through the river.

The sand on the beach was blistering hot, and Lucy and Rhea, who had changed into their swimwear in one of the huts, had to hop and hobble over it on their bare feet, as if it were scattered with burning ash. But now they were settled and facing the ocean - just pure ocean - no boats, no jet skies, no paragliders. It was a protected beach of pure sand, with only a moderate number of sunbeds restricted to each end of the beach. This meant the hoards, hungry for a tan, were happier to stay in Marmaris, a large coastal resort 28 miles away, and not venture here. The far horizon lay misted in a steaming heat, whilst warm salty breezes drifted into shore.

The sisters had started their sojourn by fingering the swollen red mosquito bites around their ankles, acquired from the previous evening, deciding they'd got off rather lightly, but vowing to repel any further uninvited *little kisses in the night*. Lucy was quite proud of the fact that she had earned her first ever mozzie bites. She reminded Rhea that Dalyan was a malaria free geographical zone, so they had nothing to worry about. Now all she wanted was to see exactly what the bloodsuckers looked like. Rhea remained unimpressed by her enthusiasm in this matter.

As the heat pressed heavy upon them, and the ocean swelled and contracted upon the shore, Rhea and Lucy fell under the beach's enchantment.

'It's a wonderful beach, isn't it?' said Lucy. 'I can't wait to get in the sea. Can't even remember the last time I actually swam in the sea. Must have been on those family holidays down south when we were kids. Cornwall, wasn't it? Do you remember?'

'Yes, I remember a bit - it was Cornwall,' Rhea said. 'And this is an excellent beach. Haven't been on one better. It's so natural. So quiet. They're usually lined by a Legoland of hotels crowded with balconies and bodies.'

'Maybe we should walk all the way along it and get the bus back,' Lucy said eagerly.

'I don't know, it's a long way, you know.' Rhea hesitated. 'Anyway I think the turtle sanctuary is at that end.'

Lucy stared into her lap.

Rhea turned her head to look at her. 'What is it with you and the turtles? It's not going to cause us too much tension, is it?'

'Oh, I really don't think you'd get it.' Lucy paused, then her brow crinkled into furrows. 'But…maybe we could start sharing now, getting to know more about each other. If I tell you why I wanted to see the turtles -'

'You did technically see them.'

'Yes, but not the way I wanted! You know that. So if I tell you, then you have to tell me something of importance to you, and that can get the ball rolling.'

Rhea pondered for a moment. 'Okay,' she said slowly. 'It sounds a bit childish, but fair, I suppose.'

Lucy gazed into the blue ocean from beneath the parasol. 'Well, I've been having a difficult time lately with my painting, for nearly a year now. I've been finding the art world very false, very fashion driven and very up itself really, and I feel, well…poisoned by it, in a nut shell.'

Lucy went on to tell Rhea what hurt her about it: the galleries been 'the judge' of her work, the abstracts taking over, the way some artists deliberately followed the trends at the expense of their integrity, how the buying public seemed to be very influenced by current fashion, that people who painted or liked realism were in the minority and considered to be behind the times. And ultimately, that for the last eight months or so, she hadn't been able to paint at all. She sniffed now and again, while Rhea handed her a tissue from her beach bag. Lucy only stopped talking to blow her nose periodically, which helped to punctuate her delivery of this information with some dramatic pauses.

Rhea gazed through the spider's web of woven light in the parasol, listening carefully and nodding at intervals, not saying a word, until Lucy stopped talking and stopped blowing her nose.

'Okay, I think I see,' she said. 'And I can see how you feel poisoned. But don't you just have to keep plugging away regardless? Isn't that what artists have to do?'

'I have been! But it feels like I'm flogging a dead horse. If I can't get any enjoyment from it, what's the bloody point?'

'Well then, maybe you should do something else - give up art.'

'And let them beat me?' Lucy cried, sitting right up on the edge of her recliner and glaring at Rhea.

'Well, you can't have it both ways, can you?' Rhea said, turning away.

'But it's my vocation, what I was meant to do in life - like Mum. She would have understood.'

'I don't know. I remember her being a bit flighty about it, a lot of bad life drawings and some strange still -'

'How can you say that? She was consumed by it!'

'Yes, well, maybe she was too consumed by it. She never seemed to make time for us.'

'How can you say that about her? You shouldn't speak of her that way!' Lucy exclaimed. 'When we found her work in Dad's attic, when we were clearing the house, it was the first time I had seen it for years. And I like it! Why didn't he get anything framed? And he told me Auntie Kathy had taken it all after Mum died. So, why was it all hidden away like that?'

Rhea sighed. 'Look we're getting way off track here. It sounds as if you approach it more professionally - that's *all* I meant. Okay? That's all! Now where do the turtles come in?'

'Oh yes, back to the turtles,' Lucy said, taking a deep

114

breath. 'Fair enough.'

While she watched the surf wax and wane upon the shore, Lucy explained to Rhea about the idea, the feeling, that she'd got from looking at some caretta pictures in the brochures after she booked the holiday. How they seemed like such astonishing creatures, living for so long in the earth's oceans, how their faces seemed to symbolise ancient wisdom of some sort, some kind of spirituality. How she felt a connection. Upon saying this, she turned to examine Rhea.

'Don't you give me that look,' she said to Rhea sharply.

'What do you mean?'

'That intolerant disapproving look of yours, that raised eyebrow look, like you think someone is talking absolute crap.'

Rhea looked shocked. 'Sorry! I didn't know I was. Go on, carry on,' she added impatiently.

'Well, that's it really,' Lucy continued in a defensive tone. 'I thought seeing a caretta properly, being able to touch one, could maybe heal me somehow, heal my creativity. And Seda said they were protectors of people. I like that idea.'

Rhea was quiet for a moment. 'Yes, but don't you think that it's all a bit, well... fanciful?'

'Fanciful! Oh, that's so typical of you. Just the sort of response I would have expected. You and Dad always thought I was on another planet. People can believe in all sorts of things, Rhea: faith healing, karma, spirits, all sorts of things that can't be necessarily proven. We can't be all as straight and conventional as you.'

'Oh, so I'm conventional, am I? What are you? Alternative, I suppose, more enlightened perhaps, a higher being?'

They lapsed into silence, while some gulls screeched and circled above.

Lucy lay back on her lounger and twisted a strand of her hair into a coil, released it, then started again – coil, release, coil, release. After a few minutes, she sighed and scrunched her hair into the band that she always kept on her wrist, twisting it into an escaping bun at the nape of her neck.

'Well,' she said. 'It's your turn now. You have to share something as equally significant with me.'

Rhea was quiet, fidgeting with the edge of the beach towel she was lying on. 'What kind of thing?'

'Well, recent stuff I suppose, just to start with, like mine. Let's see…how are you and Chris getting along? You seemed a bit distant from each other at Dad's funeral, hardly spoke to each other, he seemed restless too. It'll be 21 years, same as Charlie and me, with both of us getting married in the same year.'

Rhea reached for her suntan lotion and began applying it to her arms, starting with the shoulder area and working her way down to her wrists.

'Okay. I suppose I can talk about Chris,' she said. 'Well…no…we're not really getting on anymore, actually. He's just not the man he used to be. In the old days he was exciting, unpredictable. I quite liked that. He's certainly still unpredictable, but I don't find him exciting anymore. And he was in good shape then, but that's long since gone,' she said. 'A slow decline since Rob was born. Now he's basically just a slug with a beer gut. I have to do everything around the house, he just acts helpless, or he gets stressed because he's got to be dashing off somewhere to close a deal of some sort. He was sulking at the funeral, because I insisted he leave his mobile at home. You see, since he started working for a different insurance firm, all he's bothered about is shuffling money around, playing the stock market, and getting involved in dodgy deals. There's a couple of associates at work that seem to dabble in it on the side and they taught him the trade, so they call it a partnership. Anyway, he spends most of the time on his mobile, pacing around like a demented cat and yelling or cajoling down the phone. I keep half expecting him to get arrested for fraud or something. Though he says everything they do is quite legitimate.'

'Seems weird for someone in insurance to be taking risks with money.'

'Yes, I know. The irony hasn't escaped me. And he loses most of the time anyway, and he's lost money I've given him too, or money he transferred from my account against my knowledge! That was a real betrayal, the last straw. I don't give him any money to *invest* now. I don't trust him. I've put Dad's money in an account he can't access.'

'Oh God, Rhea, that sounds serious! How do you cope with him, then?' Lucy asked, her eyes wide.

'Well, he's got his own room which we call his den, he works in there and plays in there. His 'cave' - as that book *Men are from Mars, Women are from Venus* would call it - not that I could get him to read beyond the cave chapter in the book, of course. Just typical. I kept checking every week to see if he'd moved the bookmarker further on. But oh no, he'd received sanction to be a cave dweller, hadn't he? Didn't want to read beyond that. So then I changed things. He could be a cave dweller, but he had to get his own meals or starve. I just cook for Rob and me now, and he gets take-out. So basically, we avoid each other. I moved myself into the spare bedroom too - for me to have a cave. He says he doesn't want to split up, *says* he still loves me. But it doesn't feel like it and he doesn't show it.'

Lucy looked concerned. 'Do *you* still love *him* though?'

Rhea started smearing lotion onto her thighs and calves. 'Oh, I don't know, Lucy. It doesn't sound like it, does it? What's love anyway?'

'Oh come on, you know what love is. The all consuming nature of it, the passion, the closeness -'

'Infatuation you mean. That's probably all falling in love is. Attraction, then infatuation, sex and procreation of the species. That's all it's for. After 21 years, how the hell can it be still like that? No. It wears thin, it wears out, and then you just tolerate each other.'

'Oh, that's so grim, Rhea. A very black view. Charlie and me work, we're still in love,' Lucy said.

'Well, bully for you - you would be, wouldn't you?' Rhea retorted.

'Sorry, I didn't mean to sound smug. It still needs working at, we've had our difficult patches over the years. You have to talk it through. But, you know, at the end of the day, we're basically soul mates,' Lucy said wistfully.

'Oh, of course! Soul mates.' Rhea said. 'Two halves of the same heart beating as one. 'Islands in the Stream' with Dolly and Kenny and all that. Don't you see that it's just wishful thinking?'

'No, it's real! Just because your marriage has gone off the boil, doesn't have to make you cynical about love.'

'Yes, but you've said you and Charlie have had rough patches. It can't still really be all white picket fence and roses around the door.'

Rhea put her lotion away and resumed a recumbent pose.

Lucy was quiet for a moment. 'Well, the only issue really is that he hasn't been all that tolerant of my artist's block lately. Thinks it's a bit of a luxury - which it isn't! It hurts. You see, he compromised his own art by giving up his ceramics business and managing the garden centre instead.'

'Yes, and why did he do that?'

'Well, because he wasn't making a living at the ceramics. Said he had to face reality.'

'Exactly! Reality. In other words he gave it up for you and Poppy, to make sure the bills were paid.'

'Alright! I know what you're driving at. I do understand, you know, and I do my share, but yes, he made the change so that I could still do what I wanted. But it *is* what we both went to college for in the first place. A career in art and design. One of us should stick at it.'

'I like Charlie, wish there were more like him around.

You're very lucky to have him you know, Lucy.'

'I know,' Lucy said. Then she hesitated, 'Do you still make love though? Or should I say have sex? I mean Chris's still got that wild panther, twisting shifting body language thing going on, hasn't he? You know - all that pent up energy.'

Rhea turned to stare at Lucy. 'Do we still have sex? Well, that's a very personal question!' she exclaimed. 'For God's sake, Lucy. I'm not going to tell you. Mind your own bloody business. And as for the wild panther thing, I know what you mean, but somehow it hasn't translated very well into middle age. He's more of a slippery eel these days, always wanting to wriggle out of things, rather than pounce.'

A few moments passed, the waves now advanced and retreated like an indecisive army, while a swarm of thoughts and feelings buzzed and probed around the two sisters like bees around a hive, their stings at the ready. Rhea put her arms behind her head, while Lucy extracted a strand from her scrunched hair and resumed coiling.

'Well,' Lucy said at last. 'I guess we should go on with our sharing. It's my turn again to spill. What do you want to ask me next?'

Rhea was quiet. With her lips pressed tightly together, she twisted her mouth around as if trying, with her tongue, to find a piece of food stuck between her teeth.

'Well...come on,' Lucy insisted. 'There should be masses of things you want to know.'

'Well, it's not that easy,' Rhea squirmed.

Well, honestly!' Lucy scowled at her. 'That's actually quite insulting, you know, I mean for –'

'Okay! I've got one,' Rhea blurted out. 'Right. Continuing with your current issue with art, what have you told Poppy? - considering she's studying art at university. How are you handling that?'

Lucy looked deflated, like a child opening a Christmas box to find nothing inside. 'Oh. It's back to art again, is it?'

She paused. 'Well, I haven't told Poppy how I feel. I don't want her to be affected. She's naturally enough attracted to the current fashion, she uses a of lot sand, resin and wax for textures, so I really avoid talking to her about it, and avoid visiting any exhibitions too. I've just told her I'm taking a break to recharge my batteries. I never told Dad either, just pretended things were fine.'

Rhea looked astonished. 'That must have been very hard for you - not talking to Poppy or Dad. You usually talk about anything and everything.'

'Yes, it's been very difficult. Only Charlie knows, and now you, of course. Mind you, I think Poppy's suspicious. But I didn't want her and Dad worrying, you see. Anyway, the more people know something like that, the worse it gets. Like being on a stage in the spotlight with the audience waiting you to perform.'

'Hmm,' Rhea said slowly. 'I can see that. Well, hopefully you'll solve the problem soon, but if you don't, you'll have to talk to her, won't you? Otherwise, she'll think you're not interested in what she's doing.'

'Yes, I know that,' Lucy sighed, continuing to coil her strand of hair. Then she stopped. 'Well it's my turn again to ask, isn't it?'

'Yes, you know it is.'

'Well...' Lucy said, hesitating. 'It's about you and me really.' She cast Rhea a swift sideways glance. 'When we were kids, we always used to fight and argue. But after Mum died, you ignored me a lot. I would say our relationship got much worse. Of course you were fifteen then, a teenager, I was only eleven. But you and Dad got on so well, I used to feel shut out a lot of the time. You and Dad wouldn't talk much about Mum either, which really didn't help. It was tough not being able to talk about her. And now Dad's gone too,' Lucy said, sniffing again and blowing her nose into a scrunched up tissue that had hardened in the heat.

Rhea didn't move. She froze into her pose on her

sunbed like a reclining marble figure, mouth slightly parted.

'Well?' Lucy asked.

Rhea slowly came back to life. 'What are you asking exactly?'

'Well, basically, why did you and I stop being proper sisters after Mum died.'

'We didn't stop being sisters! That's a bit dramatic isn't it - just typical of you!'

'No, you can't deny it. It's true! What happened? Why did it happen after Mum died?'

'That's just ridiculous, Lucy. We were all changed by Mum's death. We all have different ways of handling things, you know.'

'And now, you put off talking about Dad too - it's only been six months since he died and –'

'I *don't* need the reminder, thank you. I feel it just the same as you do. I miss him every day. I think of him all the time. You don't have the monopoly on grieving you know!'

'I know that, and we can talk about Dad later. But what about us?' Lucy said.

'I don't know what you're talking about. You've got some idea into your head. You always get ideas into your head. But there's nothing to it. We're just very different, that's all!'

***

After a few swollen moments of pained silence, after the swarm of bees had delivered their stings, Lucy jumped to her feet. She flashed a look of fury at Rhea and snatched her swimming goggles from her beach bag. She ran over to the water's edge, over the dry sand to the firm amber wetness of the shore. Taking some deep breaths, she vowed to herself that Rhea was not going to spoil her first dip in this ocean.

A film of lacy bubbles crept up and nibbled her toes, then withdrew, sucking them down deeper. She started to feel calmer, the bubbles reminding her of long soaks in a relaxing bath. She stepped in the seawater up to her ankles to test the temperature. The shock of the cold against her heat-soaked body made her gasp, but she waded further in, right up to her waist. Then with more gasps, she felt compelled to let her body cool down inch by inch, though she wished she could just run into the waves like a seasoned beach swimmer - splash, splash, forward thrust and away you go.

As she waded in deeper, she felt the motion of the incoming waves, swelling and subsiding. Warm and cold currents snaked around her legs, and underfoot the sand rippled in ridges. She discovered that the beach shelved very gradually into the sea, so she would have to go quite far out to tread water. Putting on her goggles, she put her face down into the seawater. It was so clear, she could see the sand dune patterns underfoot, shaped by a tidal ebb and flow. She squatted down a little and immersed herself fully up to her neck, then swam out to a depth where she could just touch the sea bed with her toes. The fullness of the cool on her skin felt heavenly.

As Lucy looked back at the beach to get her bearings, she couldn't see Rhea at all. And the land seemed so small and insignificant compared to the ocean that held her in its swell. How long is it, she wondered, since I swam in the sea? It felt only vaguely familiar. She remembered some pictures in the albums of beach holidays in Cornwall - before her mum died. There was a picture of herself, aged six, running towards the shore, flowery dress tucked up into her knickers, hair whipped by a strong breeze. One with her and her mother kneeling down and gazing into a rock pool. One of Rhea, aged ten, on her tummy in the sand, examining some shells she'd collected. One of their dad by a cliff-side, pointing to an striated rock pattern. And finally, a group shot, which a stranger must have taken, with the whole family sitting on their towels, arms tangled around each other and bursting with smiles. Those were the days, she thought. All of us happy.

She remembered her father teaching her to float on her back, remembering his arms supporting her waist, then letting go. *If you can swim on your back,* he said, *you'll always survive a ship wreck, because you can bob around like a cork for hours.* She used to love seeing herself as a cork, bobbing about and changing direction at the whim of the tide. She pushed up her goggles, smiled, and tipped herself onto her back. The sky was cloudless and she stared up into the blue - cobalt blue, she mused, straight from the tube. She felt as if she was floating in shifting swathes of silk, noticing she had to do very few leg kicks or sculling with her arms to hold her position. Must be the salt, she thought. Increased buoyancy. Very different feel to a swimming pool. Wearing fins would be amazing - she could swim for miles.

She flipped onto her front, and keeping her goggles up on her forehead and head above water, she started some breaststroke, going further out from the shore. The sea was breathtaking, as the glittering rays of the sun reflected silver sparkles of light, dancing at eye level, flashing her, blinding her. She swam out further. This is wonderful, she said to herself, I'm swimming in the ocean shimmer. I want to follow the sparkles all the way to the horizon. I want to find out what's there. I want to merge with the sea. I want to be a sea nymph, who swims with the caretta turtles and dwells in a silvery cave in the deep salt sea. She'd been reading a book on Greek mythology before the holiday, and had been captivated by the stories of the sea spirit sisters who rescued sailors in perilous storms. And now I feel like one, she thought, a sea sister. She turned around, and treading water, gazed at the shoreline. It looked really far away now. A gulf of ocean between herself and civilisation. She couldn't make out any people, just a thin line of land. And as she rocked with the ocean, as she rocked with the world, the mainland looked like a different reality to which she didn't belong, she belonged instead to the sea. She could swim out further and when she got tired she could float on her back and let the ocean take her. To oblivion.

She drifted on, daydreaming of swimming with the caretta, diving down into wafting green seagrass depths, seeing rainbow fish...finding conch shells...Ursula Andress striding out of the sea, singing about moons and mango trees, throwing her shells onto the sand.

Then a warning bell finally sounded. A loud siren. She turned and sought land. It was barely visible. A sickly rising panic swept through her - I've swam out too far, she thought. All this stupid daydreaming, I'm being so irresponsible! I've got to get back. Get back to Rhea. Our mother drowned. I can't be another family casualty. *What a waste, so tragic*, Auntie Kathy would say.

She wrenched her goggles over her eyes, flipped over and began to do a front crawl, but she kept getting water up her nose and a mouthful of seawater. So, she resorted to a slower, more consistent breaststroke back towards the shore. It was harder than she thought, took longer than she thought, as the beach only slowly advanced back into view, tilting and wobbling through her goggles. But at last, she tried touching the sea bed with her toes and felt sand. She was safe. Tragedy averted. What a relief! But there again, she decided, she'd have been okay really. Dad had shown herself and Rhea so many techniques, she was sure she could have survived an emergency.

As she swam further in, she was born on the tidal waves surging towards the shore. And she could see the turquoise and pink dots of Rhea's bikini and sarong perched on the sand. As the surf swirled around Lucy, she turned, and with firm ripples of sand underfoot, she faced the surging waves, letting them crash over her - breasting the force and resisting their power. This was a new experience, and she found it exhilarating. She thrilled to see the next wave advance, rolling its momentum towards her, gathering speed, forming a white charger, a frothing frenzy of foam. She remembered the acrylic on canvas of sea spray at the Nar Galerie back in Dalyan. Hmm, she thought, they got it right. The movement, the energy. Maybe I should have a go at seascapes? That's if I can get over my artist's block.

Deciding to tread water again, to see how it would be in the surf, she discovered something else new to her. She was held in an easy up and down motion, no resistance was necessary as a wave took her with it in its swell, lifting her up and then down. No struggle was needed to keep her head above water, there was no submergence, and that surprised her. She couldn't decide which she liked best - braving the waves, where there was an addictive compulsion to face another, and then another, or going with the flow, just letting the waves take control. It's a metaphor for life, she said to herself - struggle, or go with the flow. And in a way, it related to her art problem. Should she face the struggle, tackle it head on, force herself to paint, force herself to approach galleries, force herself to toughen up? Or should she give up the struggle, stop flogging the dead horse, and see where life took her instead? Give up the art, as Rhea had suggested, do something else. What would Dad have told me to do? she wondered. But she knew already - *not an easy road*, he'd said, and he'd been right. But then, her mother had been happy painting, she'd seemed successful. But I don't really know, do I? Lucy thought. I was too young to know. And Dad and Rhea never talked about her. But I need to know now.

Feeling tired, she returned to mess about in the shallows, seeing what it was like to float up onto the beach on her tummy, elbowing her way through the sand. The friend whose snorkelling gear she'd borrowed back home, told her that's what you did if you went snorkelling in the sea. And this floating to land on her tummy was also a new experience. She felt her weight being pushed and pulled by the tide, as it slowly nudged her up, as it beached her. Like a piece of driftwood. It felt primeval somehow, like a primitive marine creature being persuaded to move onto land, grow legs and evolve. She tried to imagine this, feeling the full heat of the sun on her back.

After her reverie finally drained away, she turned and sat in the shallows, then waved over to Rhea, who she realised was now within hailing distance. Maybe she and Rhea could have a splash about, and then she'd try asking more questions.

'Come on in!' she called over to her.

***

When Lucy had stormed off to have her swim, Rhea had felt like a disturbed ants nest, thoughts and feelings scuttling in all directions - her father, her mother, the past. She didn't want to think about the past. Why did improving their relationship have to drag up the past? She couldn't afford to remember it, because she'd promised George to try to get on with Lucy, and focusing on the past wasn't going to help that at all.

She wasn't comfortable staying on her sunbed any longer, so she began gathering her things together. She noticed Lucy's beach bag, slumped heavily in the sand, knowing it contained Lucy's new digital SLR camera. Oh, for crying out loud, she thought, I'm presumably expected to stay here and look after the thing. She looked across to see Lucy up to her waist in the sea, splashing about. Lucy, the irresponsible younger sister. *You're the sensible one*, her mother used to tell Rhea. *You're the oldest. You need to look after her sometimes*. Well, not now! Rhea fumed. Lucy had no right to badger her the way she'd been doing, and she had no right to expect her to look after her camera.

She tied her pink sarong around her hips, gathered up

her things, and made her way up to the beach cafe. She had to put on her flip flops so her feet didn't get scorched, but it was slow and clumsy progress, having to shift her weight around in the sand. She also felt a little overwhelmed by the heat. It stifled her breathing. As she reached the boardwalk, she was able to straighten up and resume her customary poised and controlled walking style, although being on a beach meant that a more nonchalant pace and a swing of her hips were deemed necessary.

The cafe looked cool and inviting with the raffia fringing overhanging the roof and casting flickering shadows. It was also surprisingly quiet for around lunch time. And Rhea was hungry. After a visit to a toilet hut, which was surprisingly clean for a hole in the floor, she bought herself a salad baguette and treated herself to a gin and tonic, sitting at one of the wooden picnic tables in the shade. As she glanced out at the ocean, munching on her baguette, she remembered that Lucy was out there somewhere. And all of a sudden, she felt uneasy and nearly bit her tongue. Wings fluttered in her chest. But Lucy is a grown woman now, she thought, she can take care of herself. And she's a good swimmer. She was always happy to have a go at everything Dad taught her.

As the gin and tonic took effect, she felt herself relaxing, feeling some sea air breathe in through the raffia fringing, flapping her sarong gently against her legs. She took out her mobile from the zipped compartment in her bag and checked her messages.

There were three from Chris: 'Where are you???' Followed by - 'You have missed the chance of a lifetime!! - share values rocketing now'. So the deal has timed out, thought Rhea. Good. Then the final message: 'Let me know you are ok'. Right, she said to herself. At last some note of concern. Although she'd resolved to ignore his messages for the duration of the holiday, she decided to send him at least one message back, so she wrote 'I'm fine.

Having a fab time, say love to Rob for me. X.' She decided to concede one X, to let him think all was well, but as she stared at it, she was struck by the fact it could just as easily be read as some kind of prohibitive symbol of danger, rather than one of affection.

She looked back out to the beach and remembered Lucy's bag. She felt guilty now. A few hundred quid's worth of camera in a beach bag left unattended. But I've only been twenty minutes or so, she said to herself. Nevertheless, she slung her bag over her shoulder and hurried back to the sunbeds. Lucy's bag was still there, and the camera was still inside. That's lucky, she thought, feeling relieved. Then her thought twisted around. Trust *her* to be lucky. Why her? It was just so typical!

She peered out to sea, remembering that Lucy hadn't swam in the ocean since she was a girl. But their sunbeds were too far away from the shoreline to make anyone out, so she picked up her towel and their two bags, and selected a spot close to the water's edge. She scrutinised the horizon, but a sprinkle of bobbing heads was all she could see.

It's only been about half an hour, she reasoned to herself, there's no need to worry. And there aren't supposed to be any dangerous currents here.

Deciding she could do with a dip herself, to cool off, she weighted down the towel with the bags and stepped over to the water's edge. Dipping her silver polished toes into it, she decided it was acceptably warm, and slowly waded in. There was nothing underfoot to harm her - no protruding stones to bruise her ankles, or arrowhead shingles to cut the soles of her feet. She felt the water's mass coolly advance up to her chest, then up to her neck. That's far enough, she decided, she didn't want to get out of her depth. Lovely, she sighed. She performed her sedate breaststroke, swimming parallel to the shore. It was blissful. So quiet, she could easily imagine the shore as hers alone, her own private beach. She could imagine she was a Roman lady cleansing herself, detoxifying herself in the healing salt water. She floated on her back for a while, getting her hair wet, to more fully immerse herself in her very own salt spa. Then tipping herself upright, she stared towards the distant land masses, veils of purple in the vaporous heat. This really is a special place, she thought. She was forced to admit, that Lucy had done well to pick it. She waded back to the shore as elegantly as possible, feeling like Venus emerging from the sea on the island of Cyprus, with warm breezes to blow her dry.

Tying her sarong back around her hips, she settled herself again on the towel, her legs tucked to one side. Still no sign of Lucy though, as she stared out into the waves.

And a creeping dread started to finger its way up her spine. What if she didn't come back? *You're the sensible one*, her mother said, *you need to look after her sometimes*. Her fear took her by surprise, and it reminded her of how she used to feel on those beach holidays in Cornwall. Her dad always used to swim so far out she couldn't see him anymore, and she would worry. *He's fine*, her mother would say. *He knows what he's doing.* But Rhea would be left fretting on the shore, alone, collecting shells to distract herself from the feeling that she'd never see her dad again, collecting shells she could show him when he came back, collecting shells would make him come back, while Lucy and their mother paddled around silly rock pools, sticking their fingers in gunk, oblivious to the fact that some day, a strong current could drag their father away forever. And now, it could happen to Lucy, and she, Rhea, would be all alone then. Distract yourself, she told herself, think of other things - that's all you can do. That's all you could ever do.

She noticed a small crab on the sand close to her. She'd been sitting so still it seemed oblivious to her presence. It scuttled to one side, then froze, as if to detect movement, then advanced, then scuttled again to the other side, and froze again - it seemed like some kind of cloak and dagger ritual to ensure it'd make it safely to the water's edge, though it looked comically indecisive. She looked across to the glittering wet sand and saw more tiny crabs, running hither and thither, like scuttling spiders, dancing in formation with the water's edge, but not wanting to be caught in the tide. Foraging for food, she decided. But she sat, mesmerised. They were shifting, evasive, and tactical. And that's what I've got to be with Lucy, she said to herself. Tactical.

But where the hell *was* Lucy? She looked out to sea again. Nothing. Panic started beating in her chest. What if she'd drowned? Drowned like their father might have drowned, drowned like - Oh God, don't go there. Don't think about that. What about Lucy's point – sisters - 'Why did we stop being sisters after Mum died?' Oh, it was all so messy. Yes, after their mother died, things were different. Yes, she got on with her father best. No surprise there, after what happened. But there were reasons for that. Messy reasons. Murky reasons best left in the past - unless Lucy was determined to force things to get nasty. Yes, Lucy would have felt left out. But she'd had frequent Sunday visits to Auntie Kathy's over in Ponteland and Auntie Kathy doted on Lucy. So *like your mother,* she'd say to her. *I miss her, Lu! What a waste, so tragic,* and she'd cry and hold onto Lucy, tugging her back for another hug in the hallway, when her father and Rhea went to pick her up to return to the family home in Hexham. *Bring her back soon, George!* she'd call out every time, waving a handkerchief from the doorway, as they clambered into the green Ford, fish and chips to be bought on the way home. Rhea used to wish they could leave Lucy with Auntie Kathy for much longer. Like forever maybe?

She stiffened. She didn't want to think about then. Didn't want to look for likenesses between Lucy and their mother. Both were flaky, irresponsible, selfish. That was plenty, that was enough. But where was Lucy? What if she'd drowned too? *I want you to make an effort to get along, promise me, after I've gone, you'll try*, her Dad had said. How was she supposed to do that, if Lucy died, drowning like their mother. It was unthinkable. Rhea broke out in a cold sweat and her breath dragged itself in and out of her lungs. Her mouth felt like sandpaper. This just couldn't be happening. It must not happen. This can't be happening! she screamed inside, as she got to her feet and ran to and fro over the water's edge, scanning the ocean.

Just then, she managed to make out one of the bobbing heads that seemed to be making a direct line for shore. She went rigid, she waited. It came closer. Closer. And finally she recognised the ponytail, the goggles, and as the figure became more visible, she recognised Lucy. 'For God's sake,' she rasped out loud. 'Just typical, just bloody typical!'

A young man and woman passed by, hand in hand, staring at her. Rhea burned bright, acutely aware of how strange she must seem, running around, ranting, so she took some deep breaths, and went back and resumed her sitting position on her towel. She looked to where the crabs had been, but unsurprisingly - they'd gone.

It was some moments before she could even bring herself to look where Lucy was now. There she was, mucking about in the surf having a great time. So selfish, so thoughtless, she fumed. It's always about her! It always was. Mum's favourite, who has to be protected at all costs. Pandered to. No cares. No worries. One minute all steamed up and angry about something, the next all exuberant, with cares cast off like mucky clothes flung into the laundry basket. Erratic, that's what she is, like a spoilt child. Well, I'm not like that, she said to herself. It's more of a slow wind up with me, and she's wound me up really tight already. Only the second day of the holiday and she's dragging up the past. Well, I'm not having it.

***

'Come on in! Come on! It's really warm, when you get used to it!' Lucy shouted.

'I've been in, actually!' Rhea replied, staying stuck to her spot like a limpet on a rock.

The wind on the beach was slowly picking up now, and Rhea's sarong was buffeting her legs.

Lucy stepped out from the shallows and stalked over to Rhea. 'I thought we could go in together for a while.'

'I've been in, thank you!' She looked hard at Lucy. 'Where the hell were you anyway? You were out there for over an hour.'

'Really? I had no idea. It was absolutely brilliant though, Rhea. First time in the sea after all these years.'

'You went out too far. You don't even know what the currents are like. I couldn't even see you. And while you were doing your mermaid act, you just expected me to look after your camera, didn't you?'

Lucy was silent for a moment. 'Well, I wouldn't call it a mermaid act. Though I wish I could have a pair of gills.' She paused when she saw the look on Rhea's face. 'Oh look, I'm sorry, Rhea. I didn't think,' she said, shielding her eyes from flurries of sand grains which were being whipped down the beach by the wind. 'It was a bit selfish of me. I'm sorry. And I know I went out too far, I did think of you, and about Mum, when I realised. And then I came straight back.'

'Well, that's something to be grateful for, I suppose.'

Lucy sat down next to Rhea, twisting water out of her hair. 'I'm sure the winds will die down in a minute. Why don't we carry on our chat? I'm sorry I stormed off before, it was a bit childish. Look, I really want to talk about Mum and Dad - the old days.'

'Well I don't, Lucy.'

'What? Never?' Lucy asked incredulously.

'It's too soon.'

'But that's why we're here!'

'We're here to get to know each other more, like we

promised Dad. That's fine - but we don't have to drag up the past to do that,' Rhea said, looking straight at Lucy.

'But I think we have to, Rhea - I think we need to!'

'Well, I don't need to and I don't want to.'

'But we've got to share how we feel about Dad dying and there's so much more,' Lucy insisted.

'No!'

Lucy jerked to her feet. 'You can't do that! You promised you would! I need to, Rhea. There are things that might help me, things about Mum!'

Rhea's eyes narrowed and she sprang to her feet facing Lucy. 'It's always about you, isn't it?' she shouted at her. 'Everything's always about how you feel, what you think, what you need to solve, what's bothering *you*!'

Lucy looked shocked at Rhea and grasped for some retaliatory ground. 'Well, maybe if you talked about your feelings more, *shared* a little bit more, it could be about you as well. It's easy enough to say it's all about me, when you don't do any talking!'

Rhea turned her back and picked up her beach bag. Just then her mobile phone rang. A vintage telephone bell chimed out louder and louder.

'What the hell is that?' Lucy screamed at her. 'You brought your phone? I don't believe it! You promised not to! No distractions, we said! We agreed!'

'No, you agreed! Anyway, I thought better of it, in case of emergencies,' Rhea said, turning the phone off.

'You've been using it, then!'

'Just to check messages, not to make calls, that would be too expensive,' Rhea replied.

'Oh, ever the pragmatist, then,' Lucy said, wrinkling her nose. Then her mood changed again. 'You've broken our trust now, bringing that!' she wailed, pacing about, as the wind intensified, sandblasting her face and tugging at her loose hair.

'Don't be ridiculous. And don't be so dramatic. Look at you! I've had enough of this, and the wind isn't dying down, so I'm going back to the hotel,' Rhea said. 'Here's your bag.'

She turned and started running back to their sunbeds, shielding her eyes, Lucy close on her tail.

'You can't do this!' Lucy shouted. 'It's not what we agreed!' She caught hold of Rhea's arm.

'Tough!' Rhea replied, shaking off Lucy's grip. 'I'm going. I've had enough. You can do what you like, you usually do! You've got some money for transport back. It's no big deal,' she said, slapping on her sunglasses, and struggling into her shorts.

Lucy watched Rhea stumble through the sand, she watched her make her way past the cafe, then to the boardwalk, and then to the other side of the beach where the boats docked. She watched Rhea until she became a dot and disappeared.

7

In Need Of A Man

As Rhea sat on the boat weaving her way back through the reed beds to Dalyan, she was determined to stay in control. Before returning to the hotel she'd planned to take a shower in one of the huts on the beach, but circumstances had dictated otherwise. So now she felt like a tattered and torn wreck. The seawater had matted her blonde hair into coarse straw, with the wind drying it at all angles, so that a bird would have been quite happy to nest in it. Salt and sand lay scratchy on her skin. Over her bikini top she'd put on the white linen shirt that she'd worn on her way to the beach. It was now badly crumpled from having being stuffed into her bag, and for some reason it felt too tight all of a sudden, with the buttons straining across her chest as if she'd swollen in the heat. Feeling thirsty, she swallowed down all of her remaining water supply, being careful not to suck air out of the plastic bottle as she drank, so it wouldn't contract and then snap noisily back into shape and thus make an exhibition of her.

She didn't feel like talking or even making eye contact with any fellow passengers, so resorting to a socially acceptable means of withdrawal, and to soften the feelings of isolation, she reached into her bag for her mobile. But it wasn't in its compartment. Anxiously, she dug around, then tipped out all the contents to find her phone was actually missing. She felt a sick heaving in her stomach.

I must have dropped it on the beach, she thought. Tears began to smart in her eyes, well hidden behind her shades. Well, I'm not going back, she vowed. I'll just have to do without it. It's all Lucy's fault! She just can't leave things alone. Always probing, pushing, squeezing.

She tried hard to feel numb. Numbness worked best. Anodyne, opium, morphine, drop by drop, cotton wool clouds, billowing sterile sheets filling with air and becoming balloons, floating up through the clouds, up into space, then darkness, then nothing.

But it didn't work. And the time passed sluggishly as the boat twisted and turned past bulrush beds and pampas, as the occasional boat full of passengers chugged by in the opposite direction, its occupants waggling their hands at her. But Rhea couldn't respond.

At last the boat came into the river harbour and bumped against the pier. She was the first off and stalked in the direction of the hotel. She wanted a shower, and to just sit on the balcony, smoking a cigarette and getting her head together. She and Lucy were supposed to be going over to Kaunos now. Well, that's off! she ranted to herself, and Lucy could take as long as she liked getting back from the beach too. The longer she took the better. In fact if Lucy carried on like this, dragging up the past, she was going to go home. The tears that she'd battled back on the boat started stinging again.

As she turned into the forecourt at the front of the Onur, what she saw next made her stop in her tracks. She pushed up her shades and blinked hard.

Hasim was sitting astride a motorbike, examining the controls, the denim of his jeans stretched tight across his thighs. When he looked up and saw Rhea, he grinned. 'I just got my bike back, it lacked power on throttle. Now all tuned up and ready to go.'

Rhea stepped across to have a good look. She recognised the bike clearly as a Suzuki Gsx 1100. It was black with a red trim. Chris had wanted one in the Eighties, but hadn't being able to afford one. It had now earned the status of a classic bike. It was majestic. And Hasim looked just perfect on it.

'I recognise the make,' she said. 'It's a classic.'

'1984,' Hasim said. 'You know about bikes?'

'A little. My husband always used to have one when we were younger. We used to go for lots of rides.'

'Has he still got one?'

'God, no. He thinks they're too dangerous now.'

'What about you? Are you afraid?'

'Well no, I don't think so. But it's a long time since I was on one.'

Rhea felt more tears stabbing. Yes, it felt like a lifetime ago. That was when she and Chris were going out together, when they were both at college in Manchester. And talking about Chris to Lucy had unsettled her. What had happened to that cheeky sexy laddishness of his? All oil slick lean in his biking leathers as he pulled up at the kerb, the spiked mullet hair, short at the sides, long at the back, the Paul Newman crystal blue eyes. She thought he was gorgeous. At the time, they thought they were in love. And although they saw themselves as rebels, following the punk scene together, they were both doing business studies with a sensibly planned, financially secure future ahead of them. But were they really in love? Or had they just fitted each other's blueprint of the ideal mate? Sex and security seemed to just about sum it up. The earth had never actually moved. And Lucy had reminded her of all this, and now…the bike…and Hasim.

'You cry?' Hasim asked, getting off the bike and looking into her eyes.

As Rhea looked back into his, she felt her defences collapsing like a castle under siege. He'd battered down the entrance door and found that soft part of herself again, the part that wanted to surrender and dissolve in his arms.

'No… no, I'll be all right in a second. Just feeling tired,' she muttered. 'I had an argument with Lucy on the beach.'

'You come for a ride,' he said. 'It will cheer you up.' He moved closer to her and touched her arm.

'No, I can't. I look a sight,' she replied, looking away, acutely aware of her scarecrow hair and dishevelled shirt

137

and shorts.

'No. You look beautiful. Like the wind has danced with you. But you probably think I lie or just flatter,' he said, looking concerned at Rhea's wide-eyed expression.

She couldn't find a reply. She was certain that he was just flattering her, but she wanted to believe him. She yearned to believe him.

'Look, I not mean anything. We just ride on the bike, no talk, just enjoy the bike, then back we come. A couple of hours maybe. You just have to trust me. Okay? Then we have a nice time. I am experienced biker. I have helmet for you. Yes?'

'No talk?'

'No talk, just ride. We can go around the lake.'

'Okay. That sounds good.' Her words sounded alien to her, like they were coming from behind her, from another Rhea who had been programmed differently and was now taking over. Oh, my God, she thought, I'm being adventurous.

The next few minutes felt like a slowed up sequence of blurred camera shots: as she let Hasim take her bag and go and lock it in his office, as he emerged with a helmet for her, then helped her fasten it under her chin, as he mounted the bike without one, as she straddled the seat behind him, as she put her arms around his waist to hold herself steady, as the engine roared, as they took an exit off the caretta turtle roundabout and left Dalyan behind.

***

Back on turtle beach, as Lucy watched the boat disappear with Rhea on it, she felt abandoned. Betrayed. This was not how this holiday was supposed to be. She and Rhea had never argued since they were teenagers, years apart had seen to that. The argument had left Lucy shaken up, like a dice thrown from a cup, but not knowing what the score was.

Looking at the ground in front of her she saw Rhea's mobile resting in the sand. Picking it up, she marched back to the sunbeds and collapsed into a hunched figure, resting her elbow on her thigh, and her chin on the back of her hand. She stared down at the sand, thoughts and feelings piling up inside her into a long queue. An image of Rodin's *The Thinker*, flashed into her mind - a pensive brooding bronze of a man battling with a powerful internal conflict, eyebrows drawn together, body straining with tensed muscles and tendons. She realised she'd adopted the same pose, and was doing a pretty good imitation for a woman. Reading all those art history books has certainly had an effect, she thought, but not much use to me, as usual. She turned her attention to the restless queue of thoughts. One at a time, she said to herself. Please. The waves on the shore became more ruffled and choppy as the wind picked up, as she sat there thinking.

What had she asked Rhea that was so bad? Why would her father and Rhea never talk about the past? What had gone wrong after their mother died? What? How? When? But the answers didn't come. One thing was clear, Rhea did not want to talk about the old days, and she did. Rhea did not think it was relevant, and she did. It was like facing a proverbial brick wall. As soon as she managed to knock out a brick, Rhea had the cement ready to plug the gap. If this was how it was going to be, it would be exhausting. She shifted from her thinking pose, and noticed she was still clutching Rhea's mobile in her hand. I suppose I'll have to look after it, she thought, but right now, I feel like flinging it in the sea.

She felt a gnawing in her stomach and realised she hadn't eaten anything since breakfast. As the breezes gusted, she caught hold of her towel, and shook it in the direction of the wind, to make sure grains of sand didn't go into her bag with her camera in it. She knotted her orange sarong into a halter dress with some difficulty, as the force of the wind kept flapping the edges out of her grip. Stuffing her towel and goggles into her beach bag she headed up to the cafe.

Chewing some kind of spicy mince bread, she felt a little guilty as she didn't generally eat red meat. But for some reason she couldn't resist and was now wolfing it down with some Diet Coke. Seated at one of the tables, she was reasonably sheltered from the wind that was now dust storming the beach. Rhea's mobile was set down in front of her.

But her feelings had slipped out of her grasp and intensified. It was as if she was on a merry go round of fury, frustration, betrayal, revenge. Faster and faster, she kept spinning. She felt she'd never be able to get off and make the dizziness stop. She'd revealed something so deeply personal to Rhea about her artist's block and the turtles, so deeply personal, and although Rhea had told her about Chris, she didn't feel it was of equal weight at all. It wasn't the same. Typical, she thought. Why is it always me that has to give the most? And where do we go from here? The way things were going, Rhea would probably be booking an early flight back. And then what about their promise to their dad?

She stared at the numbers on Rhea's mobile in front of her and an idea popped into her head. She managed to remember the dialling code from Turkey to the UK from one of the brochures Trish had given them. Charlie answered straight away.

'Hello,' Lucy said. 'It's me.'

'Hello you! How are you doing?' Charlie's voice sounded so incredibly close, like she could turn around in her seat and he'd be there. Like he could fold her in his arms.

'Okay…but I miss you.'

'Well, I miss you too, Lu! How's it going with Rhea? You two getting along?'

'No, not really,' Lucy sighed. We just had a terrible argument. She just marched off and left me on the beach.

140

She won't talk about our childhood, Mum or Dad. And we're supposed to be making an effort. I wanted to resolve some things, you know, that have been bugging me since Dad died.'

'Yes, I know, we've talked about it. And you're right. But you know she's not as open as you. And you have only just arrived.'

'Yes, I know. But Charlie, I don't think it's going to work.'

'Oh, come on, Lu. Knowing you, you've probably pushed her too far too soon. You're like a dog with a bone, you know, once you get started. And you've told me before, she's very stubborn.'

'Hmm…I suppose so. Listen, I'm using her mobile, so I can't really talk for much longer. What should I do?'

'Well… try leaving the bone alone, cut her some slack. Maybe just focus on the holiday for now. Try being just like a couple of girlfriends. Do you think you can do that?'

Lucy paused. 'Yes…I'll try. We can be like that - sometimes.'

'And then you can enjoy the holiday more. And later on, you can try again, when you're getting on better. Maybe she'll be able to talk then. You know, kind of time it.'

'Hmm…that sounds like a good idea.'

'Okay. So you have a plan now. What's it like there anyway?'

'Oh, it's gorgeous, Charlie! The beach is perfect. I've just had a wonderful swim.'

'Great. Well, make the most of it. Can you get back alright from where you are?'

'Oh yes, don't worry about me. I'd better go now. Is Poppy okay?'

'Yeah, she called the other day. Sounds fine. Another course project on the go, theme to do with the frequencies of radio waves.'

'Hmm. Okay, better go.'

'Right. Take care, then. Love you.'

'Me too.'

Lucy switched off the mobile and dropped it into in her bag. Talking to Charlie was just what she'd needed. The merry go round of emotions had stopped and she'd clambered off. She glanced out from under the raffia overhang and decided the sea looked a little calmer, so she'd walk all the way along the beach to the other end and get the bus back. That would mean she could explore most of the beach, and see more of Dalyan's scenery on the way back to town. She wouldn't visit the turtle sanctuary and hoped she didn't even have to see it in the distance. So, she put on her walking sandals, shouldered her beach bag, and made her way back over to the water's edge, starting to walk south along the 4.5 km spit of crescent sand that formed Iztuzu beach.

***

After coming to a junction at a rock face outside Dalyan, Hasim and Rhea took a left to Köyceğiz, indicated in hand-daubed paint on the rock. They flashed past a few homesteads with whitewashed walls and pan tile roofs, doorways cluttered with bikes, Coca Cola signs, vines and red geraniums scrambling in and out of old petrol cans. Sounding his horn three times in rapid succession, they were waved at by the local residents resting from their labours and the heat of the sun in dark doorways, Hasim deftly dodging the odd chicken and goat straying into the road, while donkeys looked on from their cool posts under the shade of fruit trees.

Under the sun, the bike sliced through the heat like a blade, with the air cooling them as it rushed past. Riding pillion meant that Rhea was necessarily wedged in tightly behind Hasim, her chest pressed up against his back. Although she had realised it would be a squeeze, and knew from memories with Chris that it was an intimate experience, she hadn't being totally honest with herself about the effects it would be likely to have now. With her arms around him, fingers spread wide, she could feel the rise and fall of his rib cage, the tightness of his muscles, the feel of his skin beneath the thin cotton t-shirt, the stretch of his leather belt over his hips. She could see the stray curls of his dark hair, lifting in the breeze against the nape of his neck. She watched his hands on the handle bars, the right hand pulling back the throttle to accelerate, the tangle of dark hairs on his wrists, the reflective glint of his steel watch. When he turned his head a little, on a long stretch of road, to give her his easy smile, she knew she was in trouble. And she didn't care about the waistband of her shorts digging into her, or the fact that the top button of her blouse was hanging on by a thread.

Hasim detoured to the left, bumping down a single track into the shadows of a pine forest. She felt the coolness on her skin and she smelled the tangy scent of sap stir in the air, as they brushed past pendant clusters of needles weighted with cones. Hasim negotiated the rough track with practiced ease as he twisted and turned the bike to avoid fallen branches, proving that this was his home turf.

They came to rest in a clearing, and Lake Köyceğiz lay before them, the spot where Hasim parked the bike being right by the lakeside. He helped Rhea dismount, then he grinned and put his finger over his mouth to remind her there was to be no talking. She smiled back at him, nodded, and took off her helmet. They stood in silence gazing at the lake.

It was a wide mirror of metallic blues and greys, steely in its stillness and heavy with heat, framed by recumbent hills. The only movement visible in the lake were the smoke trails of cirrus clouds from overhead and the flickering green tips and fringes of stands of rushes and sedges. Blue and green damsel flies hovered low over the surface, like miniature helicopters, and further out a few reed warblers fluttered in and out of their basket nests suspended in the tall reed beds.

As they walked around a little to stretch their legs amongst the bronzed grasses and shrubs freckled with yellow flowers, the heat expanded with the stereo sound of hundreds of invisible beetles and crickets. Rhea's previous numbness had dissolved in the thrill of the bike ride, and now, an open-mouthed sense of wonder overcame her as she gazed around. The cricket song intensified her feeling.

Hasim paused at a huge pile of red earth and started inspecting it. He waved Rhea over to have a look. As she bent in closely, she could see a labyrinth of tunnelled holes. Out of some of the entrances, the heads of insects peeped out, their antennae twitching at all angles, investigating Hasim and herself in turn.

'Ants,' Hasim said. 'Clever animals.' He turned to look at her. 'We go on now? Past Köyceğiz, to the other side of the lake?'

Rhea nodded and put her helmet back on. Now, she didn't want this bike ride to ever end, or to think about anything else. She simply wanted *now* to go on forever.

They hit the road again in a blur of tarmac and the full blaze of the sun, passing petrol stations, business premises, new build offices, gleaming with glass and chrome, approaching the town of Köyceğiz. Hasim took a left through the town and out towards the open road again.

Heading south west, flat fields of orchards came into view, rows of dark green glossy leaved fruit trees growing in red earth, with plastic hoses meandering in-between. Homesteads with vegetable gardens, some alive with green in the inhabited ones, some shrivelled and brown in the abandoned ones. As Hasim slowed down to pass the dwellings, some children ran along near the bike, calling and waving. Hasim shouted back greetings. They sped past tractors ambling to and from the fields, with women seated at the rear, their long black skirts and headscarves fluttering with flowers, their hands and faces toughened by labouring in a hot climate.

Soon, they were on the other side of the lake. The road hugged the contours in a series of hairpin bends, with sheer cliffs on their right, and steep scree slopes on their left, lush with pines and plunging to the lakeside. The heat stretched across the road like a sheet of shimmering cellophane as they cut through it. Rhea could tell that Hasim was in his element, as he eased on and off the throttle to take the bends, as he leaned the bike deep into the turns. He's good, Rhea thought. Easily as good as Chris was all those years ago. But where had *that* Chris gone? He'd sold the bike to put a deposit on their first car - *More practical*, he said. *But don't you mind?* she'd asked. *No*, he'd said, *It's served its purpose, hasn't it?* What did that mean? Anyway, there were no more bike rides after that. And then Rob came along. Well, you didn't go gallivanting off on a bike when you had a small son to take care of.

Rhea's thoughts were interrupted by Hasim slowing up and coming to a halt in a parking area littered with cones.

'Speak now?' he asked, grinning.

'Yes, fine,' she laughed.

He handed her a bottle of water from the saddlebag and she took some deep gulps. The plastic popped and snapped, but she didn't care.

'Nice view here. See?'

Rhea gazed out over the tops of young conifers, florescent green against the backdrop of the blue lake, and blotched with clusters of cones bobbing in a warm breeze. The view beyond was spectacular. Islands, stippled with pines, floated in the lake, casting their dark feathered reflections into the blue, while misted hills lay on the horizon like overlapping wings. Under her feet she could feel a soft bed of pine needles, and the crunch of a cone or two, as she stepped through the undergrowth to find a rock to sit on and take in the view.

Hasim squatted down beside her.

'You feel better now,' Hasim said, looking directly at her.

'Yes.' She returned his gaze. His eyes were so brown, framed by dark lashes. So compelling.

'Family stuff. Yes?'

'Yes. Lucy and I have never got on very well. But we came here to make a go of it.'

'I see. Well, you must try. No argue,' he said. 'You know, here in Turkey, family is everything. It is the most important thing,' he smiled. 'We go back now, okay? It gets late, I'll be needed at the hotel.'

'Yes, fine, Hasim, It's been wonderful. Thank you.' She felt the urge to touch his thigh, the urge to kiss his cheek and feel the graze of his stubble. No, she thought. It would instantly lead to more. She knew it would. She'd be done for. She had enough complications to think about right now with Lucy. Keep it cool, polite and friendly. No kissing. Lucy's earlier question about her sex life had made her remember she hadn't had any decent lovemaking for years. Just a perfunctory release of frustration for her and Chris now and again, out of mutual need. No strategic foreplay, no peak of perfection, no warm afterglow - instead a rather sordid animalistic feeling.

Just then, Hasim reached down and picked something up. 'Yours?' he asked.

Rhea gave a sharp intake of breath as she recognised the button of her blouse sitting in the palm of his hand. Her blouse had finally burst apart and the button had fallen off. She glanced down to see her very visible cleavage squeezed into her bikini top. She put the button into her pocket and tied the front bottom corners of her blouse into a knot - the kind of look she associated with 1950's Hollywood films when a woman starlet is out on safari - Ava Gardner, or Grace Kelly perhaps. Anyway, it was all she could contrive to tidy herself up.

'Looks good,' Hasim said, getting up.

Rhea was astonished. In no way had she noticed him looking at her chest while they'd been sitting here talking. But why hadn't he? What was wrong with it? It was one of her best assets. She felt offended for a moment. Wasn't he interested, then? Had she read the signals wrong? No, that was unlikely, she wasn't that rusty. Well, she reasoned, if he had stared, he would have come across as lecherous, and that's the last thing he would want her to think he was. She found herself impressed with the way he seemed to be operating. He appeared to know exactly what he was doing.

As they rode back to Dalyan, Rhea thought about what Hasim had said. *Family is everything*. Then other reminders marched in: *I want you to make an effort to get along, promise me, after I've gone, you'll try. You'll only have each other, you know.*

Oh God, she thought. This was only the second day of their holiday and look at the mess they were making of it. It was appalling. The second day! How were they going to make it through? Well, they wouldn't if Lucy insisted on dragging up the past, and kept losing her temper. And it just wasn't up for discussion and that was that. She wondered what Lucy was doing right now. She must have gone ballistic back on the beach. Damn, she thought, I'll have to apologise for going off like that. But in no way did she agree that *family is everything*. And these words sounded in her mind like a spent echo in a deserted canyon.

***

Back on turtle beach, Lucy was finding that the hillside hipped to the east end of the beach was taking far longer

147

than she thought to come any closer. She picked up her pace, striding along the firm wet sand. The wind had died down and the sun soaked into her pores, so she searched in her bag for her straw sunhat with the pink roses on, pulling it well down over her brow, and took some swallows of water from her water bottle. Under the brim of her hat, she stared out at the ocean. It was glittering with sequins and spangles and she felt the urge to go swimming again, to swim into the dancing lights. It's so inspiring here, she reflected, being on this beach. When I'm not thinking about Rhea, of course.

But now she had a basic plan in place, she felt more relaxed, and began to imagine where else in the world she could be. Making her way back to her hut on an Indonesian island perhaps, to eat her rice from a banana-leaf? Being on a retreat in the Maldives - islands like stepping stones covered in palms, with long jetties into the sea. But wait, that didn't fit. The Maldives would be Rhea's thing. So would strolling towards a cocktail bar in the Bahamas. Where else for me? she thought. Washed onto the shore from a shipwreck and stranded on an unknown deserted island in the Indian ocean, with a tangle of jungle to explore, wielding a machete. That was better. And diving for fish in the sea, with a handmade knife clenched between her teeth, and diving for conches and giant clams to decorate her camp - no wait, she'd already done Ursula Andress for today. Anyway, come to think of it, being stranded alone sounded just a little too dangerous.

So, what else? Walking along my own private beach, she thought. Yes, that's better. My villa is up on the hill, with a rock-strewn path winding its way up through scratchy seedheads. The villa has a veranda overlooking the ocean, where I can sit with a lemonade in a squeaky swing seat, reading tales of adventure. And Grecian urns, planted with bird of paradise, provide splashes of colour against the bleached boards of the veranda and the blue haze of the sea. Maybe Charlie is out there in the bay on his boat? - the white sails catching the wind. There's a garden of course, and a study, and a computer for contact with Poppy and the outside world. There's an open-top jeep parked behind a screen of pines, to take the ten mile journey to the nearest town, my hair streaming out behind me as I bump over earth tracks to a main road, stirring up a trail of dust.

Would there be a studio in the villa? she wondered. But the image didn't come.

Her meditations were interrupted as she spotted some pebbles underfoot, the first she'd come across. As she stared ahead towards the end of the beach, she could see more of them like studs hammered into the sand. She slowed her pace and scanned the stones, bending over to inspect some, then moving on. The ones that caught her eye were white ones embellished with charcoal coloured threads and knots, and grey ones threaded with white. They complemented each other, so she selected one of each. They could go on the veranda of the villa, she thought, if only it existed. In the meantime, surely Dalyan wouldn't mind her having a couple of souvenirs? She'd add them to her glass globe of collected pebbles, that she and Charlie had in their bathroom. The Dalyan ones would be exotically different from those from Bamburgh, the Western Isles, or Devon. But taking back two would have to be the limit; if everyone did it there would be no pebbles left! She suffered a pang of guilt, but got her camera out and took shots of others that attracted her.

Finally, the crescent of sand came to an end, with an enclosure of some land on her left, instead of the open maze of reed marsh. There was a planting of palm trees, and another cafe, a toilet and changing block, and a sun bed area. She ignored a sign to the turtle sanctuary, which indicated a path that wound out of sight further inland and she was relieved at not being confronted with structures housing them or visitors milling around, which she would have found very difficult to ignore. Out of sight had to mean out of mind on this occasion. She ambled around to find where the bus stop was, at the back of some outbuildings and noted from the sign that they came on the hour and every half hour until 7pm. There was no bus there now, so after delving around in her bag to find her watch, and discovering the time was just after 4pm, she decided to find some shade until the next bus came.

Glancing around, she noticed a small lake on the land side, beyond some windblown trees, wispy in their leanings. Beside the lakeside she saw other trees, flowering shrubs and tufts of golden grasses. It looked like a peaceful place, so she made her way over and found an old pine to rest in, perching herself on one of its low gnarled branches. Alongside her, tall stems thrust upwards, bearing rhododendron-like leaves and pink flowers with five petals and ragged centres. She took a close-up of one of the flowers, wondering if it was the oleander Trish had mentioned. She drank some more water and peered out from under the feathered overhang of the pine needles, out to the rugged hillside and the ocean beyond. Since she still had sight of the parking area, she could get to the bus as soon as it arrived.

Sitting here, she determined to get her head straight before returning to Dalyan. Now that she'd decided to bide her time with Rhea, she felt happier. All we have to do, she thought, is try to make up for today. That's the most urgent thing. I'll apologise again for swimming too far out, and for pushing her with questions, and for ranting of course. That should do the trick. Then promise to try to get along as girlfriends. That should be easy enough.

Of course, she reasoned, Rhea wasn't the kind of person, she'd normally be friends with. Far from it. She was too strait-laced, reserved, conventional, you just couldn't get close, a bit like a cactus, not so much for its prickles (she acted too cool for that), but its thick outer skin. And she was driven by her career. Well, there wasn't anything wrong with that, but it seemed to have led to her being quite materialistic, what with buying genuine gemstone rings. It had been impossible trying to buy each other Christmas presents over the years, as they had no idea what each other liked. They'd mutually agreed not to bother. Just cards at Christmas and birthdays, with the minimum of greetings had to suffice. And even then, they sometimes forgot. No news updates either, they got those from George.

They were such opposites. Lucy had a border collie called Laddie, who could never do enough running about in the fields. Rhea had a long haired, creamy Persian cat called Suki, who was kept indoors because of her delicate nature and pedigree breed. That just about summed it up. And when they were at school, Rhea was in the girl guides, then the tennis club, while Lucy would tread the boards in the drama club. They shared mealtimes, evening television occasionally, and family outings. They only managed to share a bedroom for about a year, before they came to blows, screaming at each other and tipping each other's clothes out of their drawers all over the floor or flinging them down the stairs. Then later on, after their mother died, Rhea barely spoke to her. *Of course she loves you*, George used to say, *she's your sister*. But he knew things weren't right. Lucy could tell.

So what about now? Could they get along now? Well, they were both in their forties, both female, and they'd grown up together. That had to count for something. But nothing seemed to excite Rhea, and she made Lucy feel stupid for being enthusiastic or passionate about anything, as if she was making an exhibition of herself. It really was quite hurtful. They never seemed to relate to the same things. But what could they both enjoy? She racked her brains. Okay, she thought. There's food, wine…clothes, and maybe a bit of interior design, a bit of music, old Hollywood films - different tastes of course, in all respects.

And a very long time ago, they used to dance together with their mother to pop songs - Suzi Quatro's 'Devil Gate Drive' was always a favourite. Well, she could hardly hope for dancing now, but the rest might do.

By the time she was sitting on the crowded minibus, she felt more resolved. Things might actually work out. She craned her neck to look down at the views through the window, as the bus heaved its way up a hill, leaving the coast and winding down the other side, hugging the edge of Sulungur Lake. The road twisted and turned past pine forests and oleanders, past villas, hotels and balconies, back into town.

**

When Rhea finally got back to the hotel room, Lucy was there, lying on her bed and reading the book Hasim had lent them.

Lucy gave Rhea a wry smile. 'You look a real sight,' she said. 'All windblown. What have you been doing?'

Rhea sat down on her own bed and faced Lucy. 'Look, Lucy, I'm sorry I left the beach like that. Did you get back okay?'

'Yes, I got the bus back. Very nice views.' Lucy hesitated. 'I'm sorry too,' she said, putting the book down. 'I did go too far out and I was a pain, pushing you to share like that. I was being selfish, just like you said.'

'I find talking about the past difficult. Like Dad did. And I can't share my feelings as easily as you. You know that,' Rhea said.

'Yes, I know, it's okay, and it's probably too soon anyway.'

'Yes it is. It really is.'

'Well, how about we just try to get along in the now so to speak, like we would with a girlfriend? Dad would approve of that, wouldn't he?'

'Yes, that sounds fine. And if you do ask me something

about the past, I'll try to answer it, but if I can't, I can't. Okay?'

'That's fine. I'll try not to though.'

Lucy reached into her bedside cabinet drawer and handed over Rhea's mobile to her. 'Here,' she said. 'But before you thank me, I've got a confession to make. I made a call home to Charlie. I was very confused on the beach, you see. I needed to hear his voice. I'll pay for the call.'

Rhea drew a deep breath. 'Oh, never mind about that. It's good to know you found it and kept it for me, rather than stamp all over it.'

'Well, I'm not that bad, you know!' Lucy sat up and gave Rhea a gentle nudge on the arm. 'What have you been doing though?'

'Well, actually, I went for a bike ride with Hasim.'

'You what?' Lucy cried. 'Really?'

'He just asked, and I went. Right there and then, when I got back off the boat. I didn't even change first.'

'Oh my God! I don't believe it. That's so unlike you. Wild! How was it? Where did you go?' Lucy asked, doing a sitting bounce on the bed like a teenager. 'I *knew* you liked him.'

'Well, more or less around the lake, you know, Köyceğiz lake? You'd like it. Lovely pine trees. The lake is huge. It's actually quite beautiful.'

'But that's a long way, by the sound of it.'

'Yes, it was. I'm a bit saddle sore actually. I'd forgotten about that after all these years. But it was a lovely ride. And Hasim was…well…it was so easy being with him.'

'Oh my God. You're in trouble.'

'Don't be silly.'

'You're smitten. You are. I thought there was a connection when he held your hand the other day. I can't say I blame you, with Chris behaving the way he is - you know, with the way things are between you. And Hasim is very good looking.'

'No, I'm not *smitten*,' Rhea said, sitting down at the

dressing table and yanking her hairbrush through her tangles, wincing with every tug. Then she looked sideways at Lucy. 'But he is nice, isn't he? Don't worry, it's nothing serious. Actually he was very good company. There's something about him, I can't explain it, he's so...'

'There you go again! Trouble! And your eyes are shining.'

'No, they are not! It was just a bike ride. For goodness' sake, Lucy,' Rhea said, the shine in her eyes dimming. 'Cut it out. He's just a friend. I expect he tries to have a holiday romance every season - like in *Shirley Valentine*. Well, I'm not going to be the latest in a long line-up of blonde ex's. Not really my style, is it?'

'Okay. Okay! But it might not be the same as *Shirley Valentine*. Anyway, we'll leave it there for the time being. Now, what should we do tomorrow? The coach trip isn't until Wednesday.'

'Well, we were supposed to go to Kaunos today. So, tomorrow, why don't we have lunch somewhere and then go over to the ruins in the late afternoon, like Trish said, to avoid getting roasted.'

'That sounds perfect!' Lucy replied. 'Just the thing.'

And after sharing another meal and a bottle of wine at the Calypso, Lucy and Rhea both slept soundly that night.

PART TWO

8

The Coach Trip

'Do you want the window seat on the way there, or on the way back?' Lucy asked Rhea, as they sat at a cafe table at the front of the Onur, waiting for the tour bus. Lucy was facing down the street so she would spot it first.

'I'll have it coming back,' Rhea replied.

'Sure?'

'Yes, that'll suit me.'

'Should be a good day. The gold centre sounds right up your street and the market will be interesting. It's supposed to be huge, so I bet we spend a bit there. Are you into abandoned towns though? Of course the blue lagoon should be good, but there again, it's a big attraction,' Lucy said.

'Well, all of it sounds fine really. Though I can't see how we can have much time to spend in each place. I bet there's no time for a swim in the lagoon.'

'Oh, there must be! You could hardly go there and not be able to swim. They must allow for that. Surely?'

'Well, we'll have to see, won't we.'

Just then, June and Brian Walker emerged from reception and advanced upon the forecourt. June's permed frizzy curls nodded and shook as she trotted towards them; Brian's bulk trailed behind.

'Oh no,' Rhea muttered.

'What?'

'I'd forgotten they were coming,' she said. 'Funny, they didn't say anything at breakfast.'

'Oh, they're all right really.'

Lucy managed to squeeze in her reply, just before June scraped another couple of chairs over the marble floor to join them.

'Morning, you two. I bet you forgot we were coming,' June said, waggling her hand at Brian to get him to sit down. 'I told you, didn't I, Brian. I said, I bet they've forgotten we're coming.'

'Aye, you did, Juju,' Brian replied, squashing his weight into the frame of a chair. He plonked June's large canvas bag on his lap. 'I hope it's not long now, mind. I can't stand hanging about, like.'

'I think you've caught some sun,' June said to Lucy. 'Delicate complexions like ours have to be taken care of, you know.' She swivelled her head to look at Rhea. 'Oooh, Rhea, you're wearing your Kunzite ring!' She leaned over towards her, stretching her neck.

Rhea placed her hands in her lap, well under the table.

'It's coming!' Lucy jumped to her feet, and Rhea followed her quickly to the edge of the pavement.

'Hey, let *them* get on first,' Rhea hissed in Lucy's ear.

'What? I can't hear you,' Lucy said as the bus stopped. The door opened, and Seda, the tour guide, welcomed them on.

Lucy clambered up the steps. 'Come on,' she said over her shoulder.

Rhea sighed and followed.

Lucy chose a pair of seats for them at the very front of the bus on the right hand side. She slid over to the window seat, stuffing her bag at her feet. Rhea settled herself into the aisle seat and looked around. The bus was about half full.

June and Brian pushed their way on after the sisters. June jerked her head around as if it was on strings, checking out the empty seats, then selected ones right behind the sisters. 'We can have a chin wag,' she said to them, shifting herself next to the window and popping her head between the backs of their seats.

Brian eased himself down. 'Bit of a squeeze again, Juju. Jesus - I could swear they make them for midgets these days.'

'Oh God, no,' Rhea said under her breath and leaned towards Lucy. 'You should have let them get on first. I tried to tell you!'

'Stop stressing, for crying out loud. It'll be fine,' Lucy muttered.

The tour bus lurched its way on to all the pick-up points, ending with a couple of newly built hotels in a large unfinished complex on the outskirts of town. The presence of concrete mixers sitting in the dust and the absence of any greenery confirmed the area was a work in progress. The coach slowly filled up to the maximum, wheezing escaping air, and sinking under the weight every time it stopped to take on bodies, while Seda collected the receipts for the trip from all the passengers.

As the coach turned right to Fethiye at the rock face junction, Seda took up her position at the very front, adjacent to the driver. After introducing him as Ediz to the passengers, she announced they were on their way. Flicking her glossy dark plait over her shoulder, she gave everyone a reminder of the itinerary and approximate timings, saying she would give them some more information when they were approaching the first stop. As the passengers resumed their murmurings, she turned around in her seat to talk to the sisters.

'You enjoying your stay so far? Yes?' she smiled, with her thin legs crossed, her dark eyes shining.

'Oh, yes, Rhea said. 'It's a beautiful place.'

'Yes, it's amazing,' added Lucy.

'What did you do yesterday?' Seda asked.

'We went to Kaunos,' Lucy and Rhea said in unison.

'An old lady rowed you across?'

'Well, she didn't seem that old, actually. But yes,' said Lucy. 'We had a lovely time, didn't we, Rhea? The ruins seem so untouched, and the views are to die for! A very romantic place.'

'Mmm. It took more than half an hour to walk there, though,' Rhea said, 'and it was hard going in the heat, even though we left it until later in the afternoon.' Then she saw Lucy's face. 'But it was good. We stayed for a couple of hours.'

'Lots of wildlife too,' Lucy said. 'Buzzing with insects and beetles, so many types, I tried to take a few close-ups. And there were goats clambering around and sheep in the bathhouse ruins, just like an Arcadian wilderness. We even saw a snake, a long brown one, didn't we, Rhea, down by the marsh?'

'Hmm, can't say that was a highlight,' Rhea smiled at Seda.

'Did you see wild tortoises?' Seda asked.

'Tortoises!' Lucy's eyes widened. 'What? Just wandering around?'

'Yes. Little ones though. Next time you go, you see.'

'*We* saw some tortoises. Big ones. Didn't we, Brian,' June said loudly from her window seat, pushing her snub nose between Rhea and Lucy. 'When we went on the 'Dalyan Classic' trip.'

'Oh, really,' Lucy turned around to talk to June, 'Where was -'

Rhea elbowed Lucy in the ribs and frowned at her.

'That's nice, June, very nice,' Lucy said to June, then turned back to Rhea, scowling at her.

Seda caught sight of Rhea's ring. 'Oh, that is a beautiful ring. May I look? she asked hesitatingly.

'Of course you can,' Rhea took the ring off her finger and handed it to her.

Seda examined it, turning it in her slender fingers so that it caught the light.

'Kunzite,' she said. 'Good cut and good colour. Lots of purple in the pink means better value, I think. You know it gives the owner understanding and peace. Also in ancient time it belonged to planets Pluto and Venus.'

'I think you'll find that last bit out of date now, dear,' June's voice rang out from behind. 'The main point is, as I said the other day, if you want to keep the value, you shouldn't wear it in bright light because it fades,' June said with emphasis.

'Of course, that too. I was going to say,' replied Seda, her face reddening under June's flinty stare.

'It's okay, Seda, I already know that,' Rhea said, ignoring June. 'I'm taking care of it. You really know about gemstones, don't you?'

'So does June. Remember?' Lucy whispered, nudging Rhea. She'd twisted her neck around to see June sitting back in her seat, her puppet mouth drawn into a sharp line, her stick arms crossed. Lucy gave her a smile.

Seda turned to face forward again and started chatting to Ediz.

As the coach picked up speed on a main road, the evil eye talisman, suspended on a chain from the rear view mirror, swung to and fro, scanning the coach's occupants to detect bad spirits. The passengers, finally finished with their fidgeting, were lulled into quiet contemplation.

***

Rhea couldn't help reflecting on the previous day. On the whole, she felt it had gone reasonably well. She and Lucy had a nice lie-in and missed breakfast, so they had a decent lunch by the riverside. She had treated herself to cheese omelette and chips, one of her favourite meals, while Lucy had a chicken salad. Well, she would, wouldn't she? Rhea thought. It was as if she did it on purpose, just to make a point about calories. She could swear she saw her arch her eyebrows when the waiter brought her plate and set it down.

Lucy asked her about her work, so she'd said how she'd been getting on after her promotion to store manager at Neal's in Leicester two years ago. How the main challenges were motivating staff during sales and promotions, especially when high street competition was pretty ruthless, and how the perks of the job were designer fashions with a fifty percent discount. She'd been able to furnish her home using the staff discount too. But when she started explaining about sales figure analysis, Lucy started glancing about and twisting a strand of hair around and around, like she did when she was bored or stressed. So, Rhea racked her brains to think of something to ask Lucy about that didn't encroach on art, which was obviously a sensitive subject these days. So she asked about the garden centre, and Lucy told her how many long hours Charlie put in, how they were under pressure to go down the gifts route, in addition to the cafe area, when all Charlie really enjoyed was the plant care and consulting parts of his job, and how he would rather be part-time, so he could pick up his ceramics again. Rhea suggested maybe the centre needed a part-time manager who would free up some time for him, but Lucy said that would be tricky as they tried to keep the business strictly within the family.

By the time they were plodding along the baking hot concrete to the classical ruins of Kaunos, after they'd passed beneath the rock tombs and the back yards of a few local dwellings, their conversation had naturally enough fizzled out. It was then that Lucy started being annoying again.

As they trekked past prickly grasses, hissing with crickets, and flowering shrubs bordering the path, Lucy kept stopping to peer at the branches on which strange beetles and insects were balanced. She took endless close-ups of them with her new camera. 'Oh, just look at this one Rhea...and this one!' she kept saying over and over again. 'Come on!'

So with the new agreement to forge sisterly bonds in the here and now, Rhea had felt obliged to be jerked along behind Lucy like a toy dog on wheels at the end of a pull cord, subject to the whims of a wayward toddler. And she had to look properly. Lucy could tell if she just glanced at the bugs. There was a particularly disturbing one with a grey body, red wings and orange eyes, that made Rhea shiver as it swivelled its head and stared right into her. Funny, she thought, she hadn't minded looking at the ants with Hasim. And come to think of it, where had he been yesterday? A young lad had been manning reception when they left the hotel.

When they finally trudged up the rocky incline to the ruins, they were both wilting like bedding plants on a hot day. So they sat down outside the refreshment van and ate some ice creams, which melted faster than they could lick away the drips.

After they checked out the Roman Bathhouse and Byzantine church ruins, they descended the steep hillside to see the Temple of Zeus, surrounded by toppled columns and capitals. It was a relaxing place, Rhea felt, where you could just soak up the sun. But Lucy had difficulty staying in the same place for more than five minutes, and had wanted them to get as close to the marsh as possible, down near the fountain ruins. Why this urge? Lucy wouldn't or couldn't explain. But it was a boggy area and infested with fat waspy bugs, with red bodies and yellow bottoms flapping around the sisters and hovering over fetid water puddles.

As the sisters made their escape onto a grassy pathway - that was when they saw the snake. A bronzy brown one with fishnet stocking scales, its body over a metre long, slowly unwinding itself through some reeds and making straight for them. As Lucy clutched Rhea's arm, insisting they stand their ground, the tension mounted as the snake kept on advancing, coiling and uncoiling, like a lasso, until it stiffened its body a couple of feet away, raised its head, and regarded them with its beady jet eyes. They just knew that in the next moment its forked tongue would slither out of its mouth, then it would hiss, spit, and then strike. So they both shrieked, clutched at each other and stumbled backwards. They ran back to the temple area and beat a calf-aching retreat back up the hillside. At the top they panted in the glare of the sun, wiping the trickles of sweat from their faces and gulping down water. Only when they felt composed did they move on.

They found the amphitheatre next, which Rhea decided, had to be the highlight of Kaunos - a stepped arena looking far out over the lagoon of marshes. They looked around it in silence, which Rhea felt was a comfortable kind of silence - for a change. But then Lucy got a second wind, and started clambering all over the place, taking pictures. When the deep clanging of bells heralded the arrival of a small herd of goats which trotted swiftly past them, Lucy decided to follow them down the winding pathways. 'To see where they're going!' she shouted back to Rhea, leaving Rhea quite alone.

For crying out loud, Rhea thought, this was just so typical of Lucy. Where did she think they were going? Did she think they would lead her to a special place? A cave of treasure? A golden fleece?

She sighed now, thinking about it on the coach, thinking of Lucy's silly notions, as she continued examining the back of Seda's neatly plaited head.

So, she had stayed in the amphitheatre alone, sitting about halfway up, on a cool seat in the shadow of an olive tree which was rooted into the stone. It was a beautiful spot, overlooking the Mediterranean. She started reading *Pride and Passion* again, which she'd shoved into her bag just before they left the hotel room. It was set on the high seas in the Caribbean during the colonial era. The reluctant heroine, Madelaine, was now feeling better disposed towards Jacques, her kidnapper, the pirate ship's captain, after he'd forced a kiss upon her on the quarterdeck. Not that she was going to let him know of her changing inclinations of course - it was far too soon in the plot for that. He had to be driven demented with lust first. While Rhea sat immersed in the story, Lucy had returned about half an hour later, telling her how amazing the winding paths were, how she thought she saw some locusts. Then after sitting quietly together for a while, they decided to go back to Dalyan.

Yes. On the whole, yesterday had been reasonably successful, Rhea thought, as she twisted the pink kunzite ring around on her middle finger. Well, at least they hadn't had any arguments.

***

Lucy felt a bit differently. As she gazed out of the coach window at the olive groves and orchards, the garages and building sites, with breeze blocks piled in the dust along the roadside, she hoped today would be an improvement on yesterday. Lunch had gone quite well, and she hadn't realised what a high-powered job Rhea had. She obviously had a huge amount of responsibility - a level of responsibility that Lucy just couldn't imagine. She'd done very well for herself. Worked very hard. She'd made an amazing success of herself in her chosen field. And Lucy felt cords of jealousy tightening inside her, then snapping and pinging in all directions. As Rhea went on explaining, the wayward cords tied themselves into a tight hard knot in the pit of her stomach - a feeling she was only too familiar with. But, she reminded herself, Rhea's job was in a city, and she lived on a modern estate, with all the houses built to the same formula. Of course, it was an up-market estate. What else for Rhea? But too sterile for Lucy's tastes. No, she preferred old stone walls, an open fire, birds nesting in the eaves, old furniture she could strip back and put her stamp on. Of course, there were the patches of rising damp you could never get rid of, the daily dust, which Rhea would never be able to tolerate, but that was part of the charm of living in a cottage in the country. No, she wasn't jealous of Rhea for her lifestyle. And Rhea was obviously entrenched in, and motivated by a consumer-driven world. How could she stand it? Lucy wondered, and only just managed to stop herself from asking. She'd been careful with her reactions, and had tried to look as interested as possible. I actually did quite well there, she thought.

But on the way to Kaunos, their chatting had become a sluggish stream in a drought. Rhea had been sulky, taking little interest in the wildlife or the backs of local gardens. She'd just wanted to get to the ruins and wasn't interested in the insects or the plants. And there had been so much to look at! It was so exciting seeing all the strange insects. 'We'll get too hot,' Rhea kept saying, 'dawdling along like this.' She seemed to be the sort of person who always poured cold water on things - a killjoy, a glass half empty sort of person. It was such a shame, she was missing out on so much. Of course, the incident with the snake had been a bit over the top. Good to look back on though, she giggled to herself. But of course, ever so predictably, Rhea had blamed her for that. 'You and your wanting to get as close to the marsh as possible. What for, anyway?' she'd said, rolling her eyes.

Well, after that, Lucy decided that Rhea wasn't going to spoil her fun, so the highlight of Kaunos for her had been following the goats, not knowing where the paths were going to lead. There weren't any people around, so she was deliciously alone. Alone in a pastoral wilderness. Perhaps shepherds might wander into view wearing classical robes and bearing wooden staffs. Perhaps she might accompany them, and then they could all discover a tomb. A tomb with an enigmatic inscription on, that the art world could puzzle over for centuries to come. She realised she was thinking of Poussin's painting, *Et in Arcadia ego,* which she'd read about in one of her art history books. It was considered an important painting in the canon of art. She didn't actually like it personally, couldn't see what all the fuss was about, but what did the inscription mean again? She'd racked her brains and it came to her - 'I too, once lived in Arcadia' she chanted to herself, happy to be able to remember. Death in life and all that. And these ruins on this hot rocky hillside, overlooking the Mediterranean, with its sheep and goats, seemed just *the* perfect place for pretending you were in such a wilderness. And she reflected that her dad would have loved it here. And he'd probably have been impressed with her remembering the painting too. *You've got a good brain love*, he used to say, *you just need to channel it a bit more*.

But honestly. Rhea had just wanted to sit reading that novel of hers. Nothing wrong with a bit of escapism of course, she was hardly in a position to criticise her for that. But she could have kept it for the poolside, where there was nothing better to do. It was such a waste, reading a book in the midst of a pastoral idyll. Rhea said she was perfectly happy, that it was a peaceful place for reading, that she was listening to the birds. So, they tried to sit peacefully together in the veil of quiet that hung over the amphitheatre. Lucy spotted a couple of lizards hopping down the stepped seating, and she kept still so she could watch them for as long as possible. One passed right by her. She felt Rhea stiffen. But then the veil of quiet was ripped apart by the yelling and whooping of some teenagers in the hillside above. They sounded like an ancient tribe psyching themselves up to charge into combat.

'They're probably trying to get to the citadel,' Lucy said. 'I don't know why they have to be so noisy about it.' She hesitated. 'Are you sure you don't want to try getting up there?'

'No, Lucy, you can get that out of your head!' Rhea replied. 'We haven't got enough male stupidity laced with testosterone for that! It's not accessible to two women in their forties.'

'Oh, thanks for the reminder. Cheers for that! What about 'you're as young as you feel', then?' snapped Lucy.

The lizards scuttled into some dark holes between the blocks of stone, and the boys kept on hollering in their assault on the summit, so Lucy and Rhea decided to return to Dalyan.

That evening they had another meal by the river, in which they'd commented together on the behaviour and appearance of passing tourists and a group at a nearby table. Then when that started to feel a little low, a little beneath them, they upped their standards and chatted about their favourite books. But it soon became clear to Lucy that they wouldn't be able to read each other's taste in fiction unless they had guns held to their heads. Lucy's favourite novel was Virginia Woolf's *To the Lighthouse*, while Rhea's was Margaret Mitchell's *Gone with the Wind*.

So, overall, Lucy decided, she was disappointed that they hadn't made enough progress. Never mind, she said to herself, today we're going to so many different places. Lots to see and do. That should help.

***

'Right, everyone,' Seda's voice rang out, jolting everybody into the here and now. 'We will be coming to gold centre in a few minutes. There will be a guide to welcome us and sign us in, then you can have a look around, maybe spend some money. Just for your information, Turkey has good gold industry. This one is family business, but with many employees. The work is highly skilled and made on site. If there is something you like, you ask price, and you should get a 30% discount for being on the tour, and no problems at customs. You get a certificate for anything you buy, for insurance, you understand?'

Everyone bobbed they heads.

'All to be back at the coach in exactly one hour.' She checked her watch. 'That's ten minutes past eleven.' She paused. 'Oh, and no photography please, they have to protect copyright of the designs.'

'How am I supposed to do any decent shopping in an hour?' a smart American lady smiled at Seda. 'Oh, just kidding, honey,' she said when she saw Seda bite her lip.

The coach parked up at the front of a modern red stone building, with a columned entrance portico and a central cylinder dome. The passengers eased themselves up and into the aisle. They started shifting and shuffling their feet along, like a huge centipede crawling through a tight tunnel in which there was no possibility of ever going backwards. June and Brian were the first in line, beating Lucy and Rhea to it, which meant the sisters ended up getting off last, by mutual consent. One thing they found they had in common was a distaste for such predictable programming of human behaviour, and that getting off last was just as good as getting off first. It was the pushing and shoving in between that was the problem.

Seda led the coach party into the building of polished marble, Ionic columns, chrome and mirrored walls. After signing in, and a brief introduction, they were left to wander around the glass cabinets which displayed an admirable variation of gold rings, necklaces, earrings and bracelets. Dark wood fixtures, along with swagged burgundy velvet curtains swept back with gold tassels, and matching sofas and chairs, all graced the classical design of authority with a decadence recognised the world over - a show of wealth to convince the affluent that not to spend money here would be absolutely criminal. Lucy peeked at some anterooms where serious purchases were being made over mahogany desks, with coffee being served. She tutted and went to find Rhea.

Rhea was browsing the cabinets, attracting some attention from the staff, who kept asking her if she needed any help. Her salmon pink dress, which flared over her curves, together with her shapely blonde bob, and the sparkle of her kunzite ring in the spotlights, seemed to portray the kind of woman who may well have a serious intent to buy. This was in contrast to Lucy's own daisy-embroidered skirt, white t-shirt, wooden beads, and scrunched ponytail, which seemed to be having quite the opposite effect on the staff; the only thing she had been asked was not lean on the cabinets.

Lucy sauntered up to Rhea. 'You know, you look pretty posh in here. Right in your element aren't you?'

'Is that supposed to be a compliment or an observation?' Rhea asked.

'An observation.' Lucy grinned at her. 'Have you seen anything?'

'Well, yes, everywhere. High quality gold, diamonds, sapphires and so on. Beautiful craftsmanship, but still too pricy for me. And I'm trying not to buy any more rings or necklaces. I never get round to wearing them much, you know. That's why I brought this one on holiday,' she said, waving her hand at Lucy. 'Bit stupid though. With the sunlight problem - I never thought.'

'Well, yes. But if you're careful, it should be okay.'

'I probably shouldn't have brought it with me today though. Will you remind me to keep it out of the light?'

Lucy nodded, 'I'll try.' Then her mouth fell open. 'Look at those two! They're going into one of the private serving rooms!'

Rhea followed Lucy's gaze to see June and Brian sinking down into a couple of leather club chairs, being attended to by an immaculately dressed young Turk.

Rhea raised her eyebrows. 'Oh, it's the prune on sticks and the walrus.'

'What?' Lucy gasped. 'What did you call them?'

Rhea reddened a little. 'Yes, I know, you think it's cruel. That's what you're going to say, isn't it? But it just keeps them in perspective. I think they're creepy.'

The sisters peered over towards the Walkers again.

'Judging from the fact that they drip with gold chains and flashy rings, they just might be serious collectors,' Rhea said. 'I wouldn't be surprised if they insisted on that personal service too.'

After Rhea had trailed her fingers along a few more cabinets, they both decided they'd finished their visit ahead of schedule, and joined their fellow passengers who were waiting for the coach in the shade of the entrance portico. Only June and Brian seemed to be missing.

There were some stiff attempts at making conversation, born from that inherent human need to be accepted into a social group. After all, if you are found to be selfishly stand-offish, you might not get your fair share of the pickings, or the right to have your say, or you might even be cast out, if the group has to survive some kind of life-threatening endangerment. Such extreme scenarios are contrived to supply the life blood and moral education within countless disaster movies. So, Lucy and Rhea joined in the chatting. The trouble was it was all so predictable: *Where do you come from? How long are you staying? Where are you staying? Is this your first time here? Which agent did you book with? What trips have you been on so far?* And then the inevitable comparisons. Someone else's hotel or favourite restaurant is always the best choice, has the best food, is the best value, has the most stunning views. And someone else has been on better trips. And in this case, someone else had seen plenty of turtles on the turtle watch, masses of them in fact, right by the side of the boat. So, Lucy stiffened and looked away.

'You two sisters?' a smart American woman standing next to them asked, wearing cropped chinos and a white linen blouse, which showed off her well-coiffed red hair to perfection.

Once again, Lucy and Rhea stared at each other.

'Well, don't you know?' the American woman asked, laughing.

'Well, er.. yes,' they stammered.

'We just don't think we look like each other. We don't understand how people can tell,' Lucy said.

'Oh, sure! Something about the eyes. Here, let me take your picture. It'll be nice for when you get home. I can email it over to you.' The woman brandished her compact camera. 'Stand here under the pillar, come on.'

'No, no, it's okay, we can...' Rhea said, trailing off as she saw Lucy's face.

Come on. It'll be so cute. Promise. Now, get in closer together...closer, that's it. No, you need to get in closer, maybe put your arms around each other. That's it. Now smile. Both of you. Smile!' The woman clicked the shutter several times. 'Okay, done. That's real nice. You both look real pretty. You'll love it. Now can I have your email?'

Lucy scrabbled around inside her bag, found a pen and a scrap of paper, then carefully wrote her address on it and handed it over.

'I'm Eleanor, by the way. I'm staying at a friend's villa in Dalyan, but I'm on my own, so I've booked quite a few trips,' the woman said, folding up the paper neatly and putting it into a compartment of the Mulberry leather satchel that was draped over her shoulder.

'I'm Lucy. This is Rhea,' replied Lucy. 'It's very thoughtful of you, Eleanor, to take our picture. Thanks very much. I hope you're enjoying your holiday.'

'Yes, thank you Eleanor,' Rhea added.

'Oh, I just love your accents! Where do you both live -'

'Look, the bus is coming,' Rhea said. 'Thanks again, Eleanor.'

When Seda did a head count, two people were missing. Rhea pointed out that it was June and Brian they were all waiting for. Five minutes went by, as everyone kept checking their watches.

'It's so selfish to hold the coach up,' Rhea said to Lucy. 'It's a very tight schedule.'

'Yes, but it's bound to happen sometimes, isn't it?'

'Well, I don't want it to happen to us. Okay?' Rhea glared at Lucy. 'I can see you doing it, the way you get carried away.'

'Okay! I'll be careful!'

Just then June and Brian climbed onto the coach.

'So sorry, luv,' June said to Seda, breathlessly. 'The

paperwork took a while.' She settled herself into her window seat.

Brian handed June their canvas bag and slumped down heavily. 'Bloody hell, Juju. That was a bit of a spend,' he said loudly.

'Shush,' June whispered. 'There's no need to announce it to the ruddy coach.'

When they were back on the main road to Fethiye, Seda explained that they'd be arriving in about half an hour and parking on the seafront, very close to the market. The market was very large and they would have an hour to shop there. There were also plenty of bars on the waterfront if they wanted some refreshment. Then the coach was quiet for a while as the evil eye swung like a pendulum from the rear view mirror.

'Hey, Lucy.' June thrust her face between the sisters seats. 'Do you want to see what we bought?'

Lucy turned around. 'Yes,' she smiled. 'Go on, then,' seeing Rhea roll her eyes.

There was a rustling sound, then June handed a long gold necklace to Lucy. It was smooth, but composed of intricately carved bands woven together. Lucy held it up to examine it.

'It's gorgeous, isn't it? June breathed. 'It's 18 Karat. We just couldn't resist it.'

'It was bloody expensive too, even with the discount,' Brian added.

'Mmm,' Lucy said, as she fingered it. 'It's very nice. It looks like a vintage style. You know, I think I would hang a locket on it.'

'Oh, that's a nice idea, pet,' June said. 'I think I've got one at home that'll suit. An oval one with roses on it.'

Lucy continued to handle the necklace. 'You know, Rhea, this reminds me of one that Mum used to have. Do you remember? She had a oval locket on a thick chain that reminds me of this one. Can you remember?'

Rhea glanced at the necklace.

'No, I don't think so.'

'Come on. You must remember it.'

Rhea looked again, then stared long and hard.

'Well...I...I don't know.' She faltered. 'No, I don't remember,' she said, her voice shaking. She turned her head away.

'Oh, come on! She wore it all the time. You must remember it!'

'No, I don't, Lucy!'

'What? But that's ridiculous! Auntie Kathy ended up with it. I remember her wearing it when we went for our visits. I found it really comforting.'

'Will you just drop it?' Rhea said, with a vicious look.

Lucy stared at her. 'What's the matter?'

'Is your mum dead, then?' June asked, thrusting her chin further between their seats.

Rhea groaned.

'Yes,' Lucy replied, turning around. 'She died when we were girls. 1978 it was. I was eleven and Rhea was fifteen. She was brought up in Morpeth actually, where you and Brian live.'

Rhea stiffened and shot a look of fury at Lucy. 'There's no need to tell our bloody life story,' she rasped, spitting out the words.

'Oh, really! She died. Oh, that's so sad,' June said. 'Girls need their mothers. Isn't that sad Brian. Isn't it?'

Aye, oh aye,' Brian muttered.

'Well, never mind,' Lucy replied slowly, seeing Rhea's face. 'It was a long time ago now. We don't really like to talk about it.'

'Course you don't, pets - only natural that.' June shook her puppet head from side to side. 'And fancy her being brought up in Morpeth, where we live. You told me that at the pool. Where did you tell me you both live now?'

'Oh well, I don't think I said. But Rhea's down in Leicester and I live near Corbridge, close to Hexham, where we were both brought up.'

'Oh, well, isn't that nice! Home ground. Maybe we could visit each other, when we get home. Isn't that lovely Brian?'

'Aye, oh aye.'

Rhea shoved Lucy in the ribs. 'Be careful,' she said in a low voice. 'Cut the personal information.'

Ediz, the driver, happened to switch on a local radio station, so conversation came to an end as pairs of ears at the front of the coach strained to hear the drumbeats and exotically warbling lyrics in the vain hope that they might sound familiar. Rhea adopted a more relaxed pose, uncrossing her legs, closing her eyes, and resting her head back. Lucy returned to gazing out of the window, her forehead wrinkled in thought.

Next stop was the market.

'Right,' Rhea said to Lucy, as they stalked after Eleanor in hot pursuit of her over a bridge, heading straight for Fethiye market. 'We've only got one hour here. We have to stick together, and just browse mostly. You're not to wander off.'

'All right! But I'm not a naughty child, you know.' Lucy paused. 'So you're going to '*browse mostly*', are you?' she giggled. 'Okay, okay!' she said, as Rhea angled some emphasis at her over her shades. 'Tell you what. You can choose where we go, what we look at, I'll stay right by your side, just as if we were handcuffed together.' She hesitated again. 'What was up with you earlier, anyway, why did you get upset over the necklace?'

Rhea hesitated. 'Nothing was up with me.'

'Oh, come on, Rhea!'

'Look, it was nothing. And anyway, remember what we agreed about dragging up the past, and just getting along 'in the now' instead?'

Lucy thought for a moment. 'Yes, okay, fair enough. But we're only talking about a necklace.' She saw Rhea's expression. 'Oh, forget it, then!'

Stepping into the tented interior of the market, they saw Eleanor disappear into the crowds. Her red head became a tiny pixel in the galaxy of infinite forms and colours contained under the stretched canvas. The sisters took some deep breaths and slowed their pace. It was like walking into a botanic garden hothouse: airless, steamy, and dulling to the senses, yet infused with the desire to discover exotic flowers and strange fruits. They were pouring with sweat and licking their lips within seconds. And this time it was Lucy who dutifully followed Rhea around.

They quickly lost their bearings in a labyrinth of walkways, meandering to the left, then right, then right, then left. The layout and the displays of stalls, stands, racks and rails seemed designed to hold captive all who dared to enter. Once beyond the threshold, the entrance sealed itself up and there appeared no way out, and being sucked into a humming babble of people chatting and haggling, increased their sense of disorientation. Lucy kept close to Rhea and said they should have tied a ball of string to the coach. Rhea said that they'd carry on with their browsing, then when it was time to leave, they could always find their way back by working their way around the perimeter from the outside. Lucy said she thought that would be cheating.

Passing through the food section, the bountiful harvest of locally grown fruit and vegetables, piled high on tables and spilling from crates, were an assault on the senses. Lucy declared that there were all the colours she could possibly mix. And the constellation of textures was infinite: waxy, shiny, furry, dimpled, crinkled, pitted, patterned with veins. Shapes were full, round and bursting, or stretched or fingered or clustered or lobed - forms all subject to the play of an inspired creator. Lucy admitted to Rhea she didn't have a clue what half of the produce was, despite her attempts at home to cultivate a more creative diet. She took some pictures of the fruits, and bought Rhea and herself a ripe peach each. 'For later,' she said, dropping them like bombs into her beach bag.

When they passed by the spices, Lucy was enthused again. 'It's just like looking at ground pigments,' she said to Rhea, making her stop to look. 'Light red, yellow ochre, burnt sienna, burnt umber, raw umber, raw sienna, gamboge yellow, vermillion, terre verte ...' she pointed and chanted out the names like an incantation. 'Aren't they beautiful?'

'Stop showing off, Lucy,' Rhea remarked.

'But aren't they beautiful? So earthy, so sun-baked looking. And the smells!'

'Well yes, they are,' Rhea said gazing at them too. 'I must admit, I do love colour.'

'Well, there you go. That's something we have in common, then.'

Rhea slowed up in the clothing section, her hands caressing designer leather bags, belts, and scarves. She spotted a good offer and bought three pashminas for the price of two - including one for Lucy. They were a great price at 25 lire, considering they were sixty percent silk, Rhea observed, although they were probably made in China. She was a little disappointed she hadn't been able to haggle though. Her favourite was a purple Paisley pattern, interlaced with gold thread. Lucy chose a Paisley and striped design in dusky pinks, peaches and browns. It would go with her patchwork skirt, she said, as she thanked Rhea.

Next, Rhea tried on a couple of pairs of knee-high suede boots, surveying herself in a mirror, under the watchful eye of the market trader, whose relentless banter she studiously managed to ignore. She told Lucy, somewhat inconceivably, that she was just trying them on to see how they looked.

Lucy was sceptical, but swiftly told her she didn't have the height for them. Then she started leafing through a booklet she'd brought with her, to find the page which listed some common Turkish phrases.

'Hayir tesek - kürler - No thank you - you should be saying to him,' she said to Rhea, who'd sat back down.

'Hmm? What does it say for 'Just looking'?'

'That's not here.'

'Okay. What is it for 'I might come back later'?'

'Oh, for God's sake, Rhea. That's not here either. And it would be a lie.'

'What about, 'Ever so sorry, my sister thinks I'm simply too short to wear boots'?'

'Oh, Rhea!' Lucy hissed, as she saw the stall holder working himself up and waving his hands around. He aimed a few emphatic points at them both in Turkish, which bounced off the sisters like rubber darts. Then he rooted around in other boxes, and stacked some into a pile by Rhea's side.

'Rhea, tell him! Highear tessek curler,' Lucy urged. 'I can't stand much more of this.'

'Lucy, I can't pronounce that. Look he's just doing his job, he's used to people like us. What is it in Turkish for 'How much'?' That might come in handy here.'

Lucy stared at the booklet. 'Ne kadar,' she said. 'That's not too bad.'

'70 lire,' the stall holder said loudly to Rhea, pointing down at the boots she was wearing.

'Oh no! Now he thinks you want to buy them,' Lucy wailed, collapsing into the chair next to Rhea's. 'It's just too hot for all this,' she said, putting her head in her hands.

'Stop it, Lucy. Stop showing us up. What will he think?'

'Me showing us up? You're the one showing us up! Anyway, I don't care what he thinks anymore. It's too hot in here. I can hardly breath. I'm wilting in here!'

'Look, it's not for much longer. Have a drink of water. I just want to check out the fabrics.'

Rhea took off the boots, handed them to the stall holder, giving him one of her neat swift smiles. 'Back another day, okay?' she said. 'Really good leather. I'm sorry, not today.'

'Okay, okay, okay,' he replied, shaking his head. 'You come back soon?'

Rhea tugged Lucy to her feet and they marched away.

'You come back soon, yes?' the trader called after them, his hand on his heart. 'Soon!' he called again, like a persistent echo ricocheting around the walls of a cave.

'I can't take much more of this,' Lucy said, looking paler than usual at Rhea. 'I think I'm going to faint. The heat is just -'

'No, you're not. We're nearly finished. Just hang on. Okay? Just the fabrics, okay?' She searched Lucy's face for agreement.

But first, Rhea came to a halt at a miraculously balanced display of ceramic pots, and began handling bowls and plates teeming with evil eyes and flowers. And then, she stopped at some jewellery stands of artisan and ottoman designs - costume jewellery, heavenly delights. She gasped in admiration as she scrutinised the intricate filigree and enamel work of rings, chandelier earrings and mesh necklaces, dripping with crystals or embossed with semi-precious stones and gems, all with their own esoteric properties. And always the nazar, the evil eye, hiding somewhere within, to guard the spirit of the wearer. Cabochons of amethyst, carnelian, malachite, mother of pearl. There were so many, she couldn't take them all in. And then there was the jewellery for belly dancing - necklaces of cascading coins, weighted with exotic sensuality, and coin belts to jingle and glitter with every hip drop and shimmy.

'It's all so decorative, so lavish,' she murmured.

'Rhea, we've only got twenty minutes left,' Lucy urged, who'd kept her word and not wandered off, despite a few tugs at the handcuffs when she spotted the wool and sewing accessories.

So they asked directions to the textiles from an elderly woman, sitting crooked in her chair by her table of lacework, whose crinkled lived-in skin and sucked-in smile gave her the look of a soothsayer. They followed her pointing knobbly finger, and gulping down their water supply, they made a dazed dash for the fabrics.

Somehow they got there. And slumping against a table, Rhea's mouth fell open as she looked at the display. Bolts and rolls, rolls and bolts, of woven patterns, coloured stripes and kelim geometries; printed cottons of paisleys, batiks, floral arabesques fluttering over the surfaces; embroideries, leafy, fruity, trailing trellis stems and tendrils; or stately medallions, restrained in their regular rows and repeats like the stained glass windows in a mosque. Rich dark colours burning with the mystery of the orient, through to primary brights, bold in their purity, and pastels, cool and airy in their more knowing sophistication.

Rhea was speechless as Lucy pulled her over to the dress fabrics. The more reasonably priced fabrics seemed to be floral cotton prints on black grounds, busy and full of colour. But there was so much more. There were silks, satins and chiffons, shimmering, starred and spangled. There were embroidered fabrics encrusted with seed beads and crystals, flowering, feathering and flowing over the surfaces. There were sequins scattered or poured, silver, gold, bronze. Some long full skirts had been made up in sequined chiffons to show the semi-transparent fabric off to its best. Rhea handled one, letting the fabric slide through her fingers.

'They must be belly dancing skirts,' she said. 'They're gorgeous.'

'It's all too much!' Lucy said. 'I can't take it all in. Look, we'd better get out of here or we'll be done for.' She looked at her watch. 'It's exactly one 'o' clock. We're supposed to be back. Right now! Come on!' She pulled

Rhea's arm.

Just then a red head and a frown appeared in front of them. It was Eleanor, weighed down with some bags. 'I thought it was you two. Come on. We're late. We can be late back together and share the blame.'

'Can you get us out of here?' Lucy asked, looking around in all directions.

'Sure. I've been round a couple of times, checking it out. I want to come again - maybe on the dolmus. Come on!'

She sailed ahead like a well-stoked steamship into a hazy fog, with Lucy and Rhea following close in her wake. Eventually they stumbled into the light, eyes squinting against the midday sun, its heat burning their skin.

Rhea balled her right hand into a fist and pressed it against her waist. 'Protecting the ring,' she said to Lucy, in response to her questioning look. Wriggling through the crowds like a demented snake, the three women crossed the bridge, and gasping for breath, they arrived at where the coaches were parked – many of them.

'Which one is it?' Rhea said to Lucy and Eleanor, her voice rising. 'Which one?'

They stared back at her, shaking their heads. The coaches all looked the same. A red and white stripe and the Go Turkey logo on the sides.

'Hang on, our coach has an evil eye hanging from the driver's mirror,' Lucy said.

They hurried along a row of coaches, scrutinising the windscreens. But all the rear view mirrors had evil eyes.

While Lucy and Eleanor stood still, staring around them, Rhea started pacing around other coaches. With her hand still pressed to her side, she looked as if she had a painful stitch. Then she a spotted a slender girl, with a long glossy plait reaching down to her waist. It was Seda. She was by the door of the coach talking in frantic tones to Ediz, the driver.

'Here!' Rhea waved over to the others.

They followed Rhea, running up to Seda.

'So sorry, so sorry…thanks for waiting,' they muttered, in a jumble of relief and regret, as they climbed up the steps, to be met by the frowns and raised eyes of the tourists in the front rows. Seda followed them on and indicated to Ediz to proceed.

'I nearly had to leave without you,' Seda said to the sisters.

'But we're only about ten minutes late,' said Lucy. 'Is it all really so critical?'

'The times are very tight, and we have rules we have to stick to,' Seda said with a small smile. 'I get in trouble if we get behind. So does Ediz.'

'So sorry, honey,' Eleanor called out from her seat near the back.

'Sorry, Seda,' Rhea said. 'It was my fault. We took too long to get to the textiles. The market has such wonderful things.'

A voice chipped in from behind. 'Yes. Just like the gold centre, eh?' June said, her arms folded tightly across her stomach. 'That's how easy it is, you know.'

'Come on, Eddy man, get us out of here,' Brian called over to Ediz. Ediz's forearm muscles were straining, working the steering wheel all the way round to the right, then all the way to the left, manoeuvring tightly around a couple of coaches that had just arrived, while he shook his head, gave a few blasts of the horn, and threw his hands in the air at the other drivers.

'I thought coach tours were supposed to be relaxing,' Lucy said, watching a row of heads in another coach, slide past her window with inches to spare.

Rhea carried on chatting to Seda, as the bus made its way from the seafront. She told her she just had to go back to the market to buy some fabric and probably some jewellery. Seda said next Wednesday would be best, she could get a dolmus from Dalyan square. Lucy reminded her she'd be going to Ephesus that day. That was on the timetable, and being spontaneous wasn't part of the plan. Didn't she remember? Rhea told her it wasn't very mature to score points, so Lucy gave her one of her irritated scowls.

As the coach finally picked up speed on a main road out of Fethiye, Rhea took off her ring and placed it in the front zipped flap of her tote bag, while Lucy looked on.

'That's right, dear. You look after it.' June's voice came from behind.

Rhea leaned into Lucy. 'Are these seats transparent?' she whispered.

Lucy shrugged her shoulders and chuckled.

By the time the coach had climbed, twisted and turned for about half an hour, passing rooftops and cliffsides, the coach party arrived at the ruined hillside town of Kayuköy, the third stop on the itinerary. It was a site of hundreds of deserted homes, uninhabited since the 1920s, a ghost town with historic monument status. They were all to have lunch in the valley below, close to the coach park, then they'd be free to explore the ruins for exactly one hour. Lucy and Rhea were last off the coach, bringing up the rear of the party.

With dry dust under their feet and the featureless blocks of grey stone dwellings above them, roofless and windowless and scorched by the sun, it was as if the sisters were being led into a noisy, colourful oasis of plenty - an oasis with a distinctly Las Vegas feel. And people were pouring into it in their droves from the surrounding arid landscape. Camels at the entrance to have your picture taken with were just one of the many attractions.

Under the spreading green shade of planted date palms and pomegranate trees, the complex of open air restaurants and bars bustled with waiters, buzzed with music and vibrated with colour, while shuffling queues from the coaches were led in, fed and watered and entertained, then led out again- all these movements finely orchestrated by an invisible conductor, intent upon perfect timing.

A self-service buffet provided plenty of choice to suit all tastes and the sisters shared a little conversation with Eleanor, who kept them a couple of seats as they queued for their food. They strained to hear each other through the general chatter and clatter of plates being collected as soon as someone left their knife, fork or spoon on a plate for longer than a few seconds.

'I can't wait to explore the town,' Lucy said, squinting up at the deserted houses, which looked like tombstones jostling for space in the side of a hillside graveyard.

'I don't know, Lucy. You might not be able to do very much in an hour,' Rhea reminded her. Anyway, just do what you want, I'm going to stay near the coach.'

After lunch, Seda took the coach party over to the entrance of the site and told her captive audience some history - how the houses were built by the former Ottoman Greek residents, how they had to return to Greece after the Turkish war of independence, how it was probably the most best preserved ghost town in Asia minor.

As the coach party dispersed, scattering themselves like seeds into the dry terrain, Lucy suddenly found herself free. Free to wander up winding stepped streets, stumbling over fallen rocks and scratching herself on barbed grasses, higher and higher into the heat, free to explore inside the weed-tattered walls of countless former homes, free to imagine what it must have been like to work and live here. Little old ladies in black, bent over their lace making, donkeys sure-footing their way up and down the slopes, traders calling from their shop entrances, children running and hiding behind walls, and washing lines stretched across the streets like bunting. She was free to imagine, until she came to a perimeter fence blocking further access.

'What's the problem?' she said to a man she recognised from the coach, who was standing reading a sign on the wire.

'You have to pay,' he replied. 'There's a paying point somewhere, must be further down. We don't have enough time.'

Lucy groaned and turned back. She made her way back down to the coach park to find Rhea perched on a wooden seat in the shade of a pomegranate tree, reading her book.

'That was quick,' Rhea said, looking up at Lucy, eyebrows raised.

'Waste of time,' Lucy said, plopping herself down.

'Why?'

'You can only get so far, then you have to pay an entrance fee. And if you do that, you need more time. And we don't have enough time. You could wander for miles up there, anyway. It's deceptive.'

'Well, that's sensible of you. But couldn't you have spent a bit more time, anyway?'

'No. It would have been torture to see more - I'd have wanted to go further. Right up to the top. And see the view from the other side. I could spend a whole day here!'

'Yes, that's the trouble with coach trips, when you find something you really like, you get dragged away - like the market.'

'Dad would have loved it here too, a really important social history site.'

'Yes, he would.'

'I wish he was here,' Lucy said wistfully.

'Yes.'

'And I'm fed up with being blocked by things…by life. You know?'

'Well, you just have to make the best of it, we can't really be free spirits you know, and it doesn't do to think too much.' Rhea sighed and closed her book.

'Well, what about 'I think, therefore I am'? Thinking is vital to human development. Anyway, making the best of

185

it sounds like copping out to me.' Lucy scowled.

'Yes, but to be practical, Lucy…you can't always get what you want.'

'Well, I know that. It's not about *I want, I want*. It's more about being able to follow your heart. We owe it to ourselves to try, otherwise what's the point?'

'Oh, I don't know Lucy. It's too hot for this!'

'Yes, but what's the point? At least Mum followed her heart by being an artist. And even if she died young, she didn't spend her life full of regrets, frustrations. Did she? She was happy, wasn't she?'

'I don't know,' Rhea faltered. 'I think so.'

'What do you mean you think so? Of course she was happy! For goodness' sake, Rhea. Did we have the same childhood or not?' Lucy said, glowering at Rhea, with her voice rising enough to cause some heads in the coach park to turn and stare.

'Remember what we agreed?' Rhea said, in a low tone, noticing the attention they'd attracted.

Lucy flashed her a look of despair. 'Oh, okay! We'll leave it for another time.'

She put her camera back in her bag, rooted around and extracted the two peaches she'd bought in the market. Their snagged skins were now dripping with juice. The bombs had exploded.

'Oh, hell,' she said, dabbing at the inside of her bag with some tissues. 'We'd better get these eaten.'

'I can't eat that,' Rhea said, looking at the peach Lucy was holding out to her,' it's far too big.'

'You have to eat it,' Lucy said, pushing the peach at her. 'It's wasteful not to, someone took great care growing these. Just stick your face into it. We've got fifteen minutes.' She thought for a moment, turning her peach around in her hand and smelling it. 'You see? Blocked again. Here's a luscious sweet fruit, begging to be eaten, but we can't get our jaws around it.'

'Maybe we're meant to cut it up,' Rhea said, trickles of

juice running down her chin into the folded tissue in her cupped hand.

'So, if we had a knife, we've got the choice of cutting it up into manageable bite-sized chunks, eating one bit at a time to be practical, or we can try gobbling it all up in one go, enjoying the juice running down our faces. Is that a metaphor for life, then? If so, then I suppose you tend to live like the first, and me the second.'

'I don't know, Lucy. But will you cut out the analysis!' Rhea said, angling some more emphasis over the top of her shades.

A few minutes later they joined the group of coach party members gathered around the coach door, waiting for Seda and the driver. A conversation was underway and Lucy and Rhea listened in. It was about Trish, the Go Turkey rep.

'Not much of a job though, is it?' a tall man wearing a white panama was saying to June and Brian. 'Nice enough girl, but not exactly a career. Probably doesn't pay into a pension either, and what will she do when she's older? She's getting on as it is, not married either. I mean, she must be at least -'

'Well, at least she's doing what she wants to do,' Lucy said loudly, the man turning around to see who'd interrupted him. 'At least she's seeing something of the world,' Lucy continued. 'Life isn't just about working at a boring job all your life to make sure you get a big fat pension, that you might not be fit enough, or alive enough, to enjoy in the end. It's all a matter of perspective. And it will surprise you to learn that different ones to yours are actually allowed.'

All eyes were trained upon Lucy, including Rhea's, which were wide with horror.

'Well, there's no need to get on your high horse,' the man replied.

'Why not? You're on yours,' said Lucy.

'Well, what do *you* do for a living?'

'I'm an artist.'

'An artist?' he said airily to June and Brian and the woman at his side, who was fidgeting with her handbag strap. 'Well, that isn't exactly a reliable field either, is it?'

'No, but it's what I've chosen, that's the point.' Lucy hesitated. 'It's what I enjoy. Presumably, it's the same for Trish - it's about personal fulfilment.'

The man frowned, then addressed the surrounding faces. 'Well, if we all had that attitude, what state would the world be in? There has to be order, there has to be taking responsibility...' But he trailed off when he saw Seda and Ediz coming.

'Stop it now,' Rhea hissed in Lucy's ear. 'Stop it. You're just showing yourself up.'

Lucy looked at Rhea, her eyes brimming. 'People like that make me bloody well sick. They're so narrow minded. Thinking everyone has to think the same way they do. It's pathetic,' she said, stifling a sob. 'Dad never taught us to think like that.'

'You need to calm down now,' Rhea said to Lucy as they climbed aboard the coach. 'Maybe you can swim it off when we get to the Blue Lagoon.'

Lucy thumped her bag down as she settled herself into her seat.

'Alright, pet?' June's voice came from behind. 'Just for the record like, I agree with you. Don't let him bother you, luv, he's a plonker.'

'Aye. Orses for courses, that's what I always say,' added Brian.

Lucy's face brightened a little, as she turned around. 'Thanks June, Brian. I appreciate that. Nice to have some support,' she said, glowering at Rhea.

By the time the coach arrived at Ölüdeniz, Lucy was nodding off in her window seat, so Rhea shook her awake. 'We've got an hour and a half here. We make for the changing huts at the far end of the lagoon, after paying an

188

entrance fee, Seda says. It's a bit of a walk, but we should manage a dip - okay?'

'Another entrance fee, then,' Lucy said. She paused and looked down at Rhea's right hand. 'Ring still in your bag?'

Rhea nodded. 'But it might be best if I leave it here on the coach in my bag, and put my swimming things in with yours. It might be best if you leave your camera here too.'

'Okay, but make sure you put your flip flops on,' Lucy said, looking down at Rhea's wedge sandals.

Towels flung over their shoulders and speed walking in the roasting heat with a bulging bag, Rhea and Lucy headed down the landscaped pathways alongside the beach to the Blue Lagoon.

This was one of the most photographed beaches in the Mediterranean, the jewel of the Turkish Riviera, with its long crescent beach ending in a blue lagoon in a sandy bay, protected by pine-clad mountains. Hang gliders and paragliders from nearby Mount Babadağ, descended like strange exotic birds and ancient pterodactyls, taking off from a height of 2000 metres, then diving down through a tilting earth, to see Ölüdeniz's ultramarine sea, bleeding like ink into its crystal clear cyan blue shoreline. To twist and turn and angle themselves towards the beach and scatter its bleached white pebbles underfoot as they landed.

Lucy squinted up and noticed the tiny rainbow-coloured wings hovering in the sky. 'Would you ever do that?' she asked Rhea. 'It must be amazing, mustn't it?'

'I suppose so,' Rhea said. 'I can't imagine doing it, can you?'

'Yes, I think I can, actually.'

Rhea arched her eyebrows. 'Yes, I suppose you would.'

After paying their entrance fee to enter the national park area, they found a hut and quickly changed into their swimsuits and sarongs. Then they meandered through the pine trees and shrubs to find the lagoon.

It was a beautiful place, with mountains mirrored in its

still waters. But the sisters found its sandy shore was crowded with families, staking their claim. It was littered with towels, bags, picnic paraphernalia and bodies, lots of them, and kids running and splashing round. It was so different from the turtle beach in Dalyan.

Rhea screwed her nose up. 'I don't fancy it.'

'But you must have been on busy beaches before, in Spain,' Lucy said.

'But there aren't any loungers here.'

'Just sit on a towel then.'

'Look, you go in, I'll just wait here - go on.'

'Are you sure?'

'Yes - go.'

'Okay, if only to say I've swam in the blue lagoon.'

Fifteen minutes later Lucy picked her way through the bodies, back to Rhea. 'It's a little bit muddy, probably because it's so still. Makes you feel as if so many people have been in it. Maybe we should go around to the main beach on the other side.'

'We haven't got much time now – just over half an hour.'

'Oh, we can manage it. Come on!'

But the main beach wasn't really satisfactory either. As they hobbled their way over the scorching pebbles to the water's edge, Rhea turned her nose up again.

'I'm not going in,' she said. 'It's too pebbly for me.'

So Lucy thrashed around in the sea a few metres out, ducking under and bobbing up again to practice her underwater skills, she said, for her scuba diving trip the next day, while Rhea sat on her towel soaking up the sun and watching the tiny coloured birds and pterodactyls twist and turn in the sky.

'What time is it?' Lucy called to her after a little while.

Rhea checked her watch and her stricken look said it all.

'Out!' she cried. 'Out now! Quick. We've just got ten minutes to get back!'

After making a hasty exit from the beach, to find a changing hut, they emerged dishevelled, buttons half done up, fabric caught in zips.

'Hurry!' Rhea said, as they paced along the concrete, Lucy still towelling her hair dry.

'This is your fault. Insisting on going to the pebble beach. It's your fault we're going to be late again,' Rhea remonstrated.

'No, it's not. It's just as much your fault. You were in charge of the time.'

When they got back to the coach, Seda was looking out for them. They were five minutes late and being waited for - again.

With grim faces, Rhea and Lucy got on the coach, with Rhea reminding Lucy they were now swapping seats. Rhea tucked herself into the window seat in front of June. They apologised once again to Seda, who explained to everyone that it meant they wouldn't be able to spend quite as much time at their last stop, an added highlight to the tour that she hoped people would enjoy - a Lokum making establishment. Lokum meant Turkish Delight. There would only be 45 minutes to shop.

Lucy raised her eyebrows at Rhea. 'Shopping again,' she said quietly. 'Mustn't be late for that, must we?'

'Ooo, I just love me Turkish Delight, don't I, Brian?' June said from behind.

As Ediz started the coach engine, Rhea unzipped the front compartment of her bag and pulled out her ring to slide it back onto her middle finger. Pulling out of the car park, Ediz had to brake hard to avoid a collision with another coach, causing everyone to be thrown forward in their seats.

To the sound of mutterings, and indecipherable expletives shouted by Ediz to the other coach driver through his open window, the ring fell out of Rhea's grasp and rolled away under her seat.

'My ring!' she cried. 'I've lost my ring. Seda, I've lost my ring!'

As the coach swung out of the car park, Seda, Lucy and Rhea were bent over feeling about under their seats, hands scurrying like spiders over the floor.

'June, I've dropped my ring! Has it rolled under to your side?' Rhea called out.

June and Brian bent over to look and feel around. 'No luv, sorry,' she said, shaking her curls.

'But it must have!' Rhea cried. 'That's ridiculous!'

'Oy! Steady on, like. Don't you go calling my wife ridiculous,' Brian said.

'Take it easy, Rhea,' Lucy said, throwing a worried look over her shoulder at Brian and June.

'Rhea,' Seda said quietly. 'We can have proper look when we get to the Lokum centre, when everyone gets off the coach.'

'But someone could steal it by then! People like stealing things like rings. Can't we stop somewhere and do a search now?'

'No, I can't! We can't do that. We've got to stick to the schedule.' Tears pooled in Seda's eyes. 'I'm so sorry, it can't be helped. I'll ask the whole coach to have a look for you.'

'No, no! Don't. It's better if they don't know yet,' Rhea said, her eyes darting around the coach.

'I think I have to ask them when we stop, somebody may have it already,' Seda said to Rhea with a pleading look.

'Calm down, Rhea,' Lucy said, touching Rhea's arm. 'She's right. And we can have a proper search if no-one has found it. I'm sure we will find it though. Okay? We'll find it.' Lucy looked into Rhea's ashen face. 'Okay?'

'Okay,' she snapped, 'but stop telling me to calm down.'

She folded her arms tightly across her chest and stared stonily out of the window. And she stayed that way until they pulled into the Turkish Delight centre.

Seda began by giving the passengers some information about Turkish Delight: how its name of 'Lokum' meant contentment of the throat, that a form of it had been made here in Turkey for fifteen centuries. Originally sweetened with honey and molasses, the most common flavours were rosewater, lemon and bitter orange. It became a great delicacy in Britain after being introduced in the nineteenth century. But today, today there were so many flavours: mint, vanilla, vanilla with pistachio, almond, strawberry, passion fruit... She tailed off as she saw Rhea's pained expression.

'Sorry, I get carried away,' she said to the coach passengers. 'Please, before you get out of your seats. Someone has lost a ring. It may be under the seats. Can you all look please, before leaving the coach?'

For the next five minutes there was a bending of bodies and rummaging around with people knocking into each other with their elbows and bottoms. There were grunts and apologies, then a shuffling off the coach, with mutterings of 'sorry, nothing' to Seda. June and Brian were the first off. Rhea followed them with her eyes.

'Is it yours, honey?' Eleanor leaned over towards Rhea. Rhea nodded.

'Aw, that's too bad. I hope you find it.'

'Thanks Eleanor,' she said.

Ediz went off to have a cigarette, after Seda explained the situation to him and they'd discussed it for a few minutes. Then Rhea, Lucy and Seda crawled their way along the aisle on their hands and knees, hunting for the ring, under every seat, and in every crevice.

They found nothing. Nothing but sweet wrappers, trodden crisps and sandwich crumbs.

Hunched in some seats together at the front of the bus, they talked.

'June's got it,' Rhea said. 'I know she has.'

Seda bit her lip.

Lucy frowned. 'You can't go accusing her, Rhea - you just can't. There's no proof.'

'She's been ogling it from day one. It rolled under my seat right into her grasp. I want her searched or something. Can't it be reported to the police?' Rhea said.

Seda's eyes widened. 'Polis? The Jandarma?' She paled. 'I don't think we can get them into this. I think it can just be written down at the office as lost property. We can't go accusing.' Her lip wobbled. 'And it would cause trouble. Please? Do you have to? I'm only just through my training. It will look terrible. This is...this is my dream job, and my brother and I need the money. He's a builder and builders don't work in the summer. Please, I will save somehow and buy you another ring...' She started to cry and Lucy put her arm around her.

'Rhea, it's just a ring. Is it worth all this?' Lucy looked searchingly at her.

But it's important to me,' Rhea said, her eyes watering.

'Why?' Lucy asked.

She and Seda both looked at Rhea. Tears started trickling down her cheeks.

'I don't know...I can't explain. It's special. I bought it after Dad died,' she said, her voice breaking.

'Do you think you will lose inner peace - somehow - you know one of its special gifts?' asked Seda.

'I don't have any bloody inner peace to lose,' Rhea wailed. 'And I don't believe in that kind of thing, anyway!'

'Why don't you have any inner peace?' Lucy asked, frowning. 'Why not?'

'Oh, give it a rest, Lucy! This is about the theft of my ring, nothing else.' She wiped her face. 'Look, I think June should be searched, but I agree not to take it further with the police. And Seda, I don't expect you to replace it. That's out of the question.'

'Oh, that is so good,' breathed Seda. 'Thank you so much. And I will ask for the loss to be written down at head office.'

'But how can you be so sure it's theft?' Lucy asked. 'I just can't see it. June seems harmless.'

'Well, that's typical of you - always thinking the best of people. People do steal, you know. They do it at the store all the time. Especially small things like bits of jewellery, it's easy to hide. And we know that June is a collector. I bet she's done it before.'

'We can't demand it, Rhea,' Lucy said, looking down at her hands. 'Searching her, I mean. We can only ask her if she minds, and it will be very awkward,' she said, looking up, 'Won't it, Seda?'

Seda nodded gravely.

'Who will ask her?' Rhea said. 'She won't take it from me.'

Lucy saw Seda's stricken face and groaned. 'I will,' she said. 'I'll do it.'

'When?' asked Rhea.

'When we get back to the hotel. Otherwise it will be too public. It would be showing us up.'

After two long hours of travelling back to Dalyan, while Lucy and Rhea stared out of the window, watching the orange yolk of the sun float on the horizon, then slowly sink and disappear, everyone on the coach was subdued. Exhausted by such a full schedule, the passengers nodded off until arriving back at their respective hotels, where the bus kept sighing in relief that it was emptying out its load. Thanking Seda and Ediz, the passengers popped some spare change into the tips box and lumbered away with their day's purchases.

Eleanor got off in the square. 'So long for now, girls. Take care,' she said to Lucy and Rhea, who managed a smile.

Rhea and Lucy got off at the forecourt of the Onur with June and Brian. June trotted ahead of them, saying, 'Well, that was a smashing day, wasn't it, Brian?' while Brian trailed after her.

'June, will you hold on please?' Lucy called after them.

June and Brian halted. Their noses wrinkled in the air.

'Can I have a word please?' Lucy said.

'Course, pet,' replied June, her eye's glittering like beads in the twilight, as Lucy and Rhea walked over to them.

As Lucy explained the situation, describing how upset Rhea was over losing her ring, she started to falter. Rhea stood by, silently glowering at June.

'It seems, well...so odd that you didn't find it,' Lucy said. 'It can't have gone very far, and well... it wasn't found. Someone must have taken it.'

'What are you suggesting here, like,' asked Brian, while June's bottom lip started to wobble. 'Are you saying you think we've got it? That Juju here has it?'

June's lip wobbled more, a tear fell from one of her flinty eyes, which she wiped away with a ring-adorned hand.

'Well no...of course not...it's just, it might be helpful, for Rhea's peace of mind, if...' Lucy tailed off, shaking her head. She looked at Rhea.

'I'm sure you've got it,' Rhea said to June, looking her straight in the face. 'You've done nothing but admire it since you first saw it.'

'What?' June's puppet mouth fell open and stayed open as if she had lockjaw. She shook her head.

'Now hang on here,' Brian said. 'I don't know who you think you are, like. But you can't just go accusing people like that.'

'Well, I was going to report it to the police, and I still might. Then, they might conduct an investigation, as I may need to claim on my insurance,' Rhea said.

'Well, for goodness' sake!' June cried. 'If it means so much to you, here, have a look through our bags! Brian - empty your pockets! Go on!'

While Lucy paced around, June and Brian spilled out

the contents of their bags and pockets, piling it all high on a couple of cafe tables, while Rhea searched through everything, including inside the box with the gold necklace. She finished by examining June's fingers.

But she didn't find her ring.

'Satisfied now?' June croaked at her, through a stream of tears.

'No, I'm not,' Rhea replied. 'I know you've got it.'

'That's enough now, Rhea. Please!' Lucy caught Rhea's arm and pulled her away. 'You can't go any further with this,' she hissed in her ear.

As they walked away into reception, Lucy called back over her shoulder, 'So sorry, June.'

'I should bloody well think so!' Brian shouted back.

As the sisters trudged wearily up the staircase to their room, Brian and June packed up their bags. June's curls nodded and shook with every shove and thrust, as she loaded up her stash of swimwear, towels, gold necklace box, Turkish Delight and lace tablecloths, piling the bags onto Brian as if he were her packhorse.

'Well, of all the brass neck!' Brian said holding out his arms to assist the loading. 'It's a bleedin wonder she didn't insist on a body search.'

June pulled out a chain from beneath her blouse, and showed it to him. A pale pink ring dangled from it.

He raised his eyebrows, then smirked. 'Thadda girl!'

9

The Hanged Man

The next morning, as Lucy sat on the boat heading out to sea, scuba diving was the last thing on her mind. Whilst the breezes tugged at her hair, her thoughts were like the foam churned up by the stern - swirling white scribbles disappearing into inky depths.

The night before had been difficult. It had been around 8.30 when they got back, and Rhea had quite understandably not felt like eating out. So, since they both felt physically and emotionally shattered after such a long day, with such an drastic ending, Lucy had gone out and bought some bread, cheese and ham from a minimart, and a much needed bottle of wine. She was especially pleased that the bottle opener she'd bought was now coming in handy.

But Rhea was in a foul mood. She'd smoked four cigarettes on the balcony, telling Lucy it would help ward off the mosquitoes, and had drunk nearly the whole bottle of wine, declaring she didn't want to talk about anything. The loss of the ring hung over them all night, like Rhea's smoke drifting around in an airtight room, then settling into a fog.

And once again, Lucy found questions buzzing in her mind like bees in a bell jar. Why was Rhea so upset at the sight of the necklace June had bought, that looked like their mothers? Why didn't Rhea remember it? And then there was their conversation at Kayuköy, where Rhea had implied that somehow their mother had not been blissfully happy. And why was she so upset over the loss of a ring? It was just a thing, a commodity. Perhaps it had been stolen, but June had proved her innocence. Maybe it would still turn up, she'd suggested to Rhea, who'd shook her head and frowned. And what about her blurting out she didn't have any inner peace - peace of mind in other words. That was a shock, as Rhea had always seemed so self-assured. But what was perfectly clear, was that she lost her cool when asked anything about the past.

Lucy's deliberations were interrupted by her scuba diving instructor, who needed to talk her through the breathing and buoyancy equipment. And very soon, all thoughts of Rhea were pushed from her mind by a build up of nervous anticipation concerning the personal challenge she was about to face. New questions buzzed. What was the pressure gauge for? How tight did she have to hold the mouthpiece between her jaws to stop water getting in? Would she have to step into the sea from the boat with her air cylinder on? How deep would they go? And would she see a caretta turtle?

Her instructor, Ray, who was an expatriate from Scotland, was kind and patient in his answers, and after she'd changed into a wetsuit, which she wore over her swimming costume, and after they'd selected her weight belt, fins and mask, and established the basic underwater hand signals of communication, she sat back and tried to relax. This was a special occasion, and she didn't want it spoilt. Rhea was safely occupied sunbathing by the pool, then she'd be going for her pre-booked Turkish massage in the local hamam, so Lucy saw no reason why she couldn't enjoy this trip.

There was some inner tension in her being the only woman on board, this status exacerbated by her not having a male partner in attendance. But she was in good shape for her age and kept herself fit, so she shouldn't have to rely too much upon male brawn. There was the head diving instructor and skipper of the boat, and a few other Turks, who Ray explained were all about to do different levels of tests on their way to becoming fully qualified Padi divers - divers who could dive anywhere in the world. Lucy would get a certificate to say she'd passed the one day's beginners course, which was a thirty minute dive at around a depth of ten metres.

As Lucy stood up to her waist in the shallows of a rocky shore, she stumbled and slid over the slippery stones underfoot with her fins on, trying to keep her balance like a mermaid with newly acquired legs. While her diving jacket and heavy air cylinder were being strapped on, sleek images of sea nymphs were far from her mind. But as she tipped onto her front, and started kicking gently with her fins, as she started breathing through her regulator, and feeling the cool of the seawater through the skin of her diving suit, as she saw the furry rocks of the seabed through her mask - a sense of wonder overcame her nerves, and she felt she was entering a watery underworld. With Ray accompanying her, and operating her buoyancy controls, they moved out further from the shore, beyond where the boat was anchored, and into the ocean swell. As he gave her the thumbs down signal, and she gave the okay signal, she felt a thrill tingle through her body. She just knew she was going to love this.

They slowly descended into the stillness. Pressure built up in her ears, so she pinched her nose through her mask and blew down her nose to equalise the pressure, as Ray had instructed. She heard her own breathing, the sound of air being squeezed in and out through her lungs, as if it was in short supply, so she told herself to relax and keep it regular - that was the professional thing to do. In no way did she want to hear herself hyperventilating and using up all her oxygen. She found the mouthpiece grip was relatively comfortable - so all in all, it was going well. Now she could look around and decide where she wanted to go, with Ray as her deep sea chaperon.

As they went deeper into the blue, they floated through a shoal of tiny copper-coloured fish, which flickered around them like a thousand flames, twisting and turning to avoid body contact. Beyond the blue, they submerged into grey-green depths, and Lucy became increasingly aware of the mass of water above her. Thinking about the sheer weight of it bothered her. It made her feel strangely claustrophobic, perhaps because there was no quick exit at hand - no quick portal to the sky. How far was it to the surface? She thought it best not to try reading her depth gauge - what she didn't know wouldn't hurt her.

I mustn't panic, she thought. I don't want to have to give Ray the 'thumbs up' signal to surface.

She saw the shadowy figures of some of the Turkish trainees kneeling on the seabed, performing what looked like strange rites of passage. And as she and Ray passed above them, she could see they were taking out their mouthpieces to exchange air supplies. Bubbles rose, higher and higher, a stream of small silver balloons inflating, becoming fatter and fatter to billow and sway, to finally burst on the surface. She put out her hand to touch them, watching them go higher, watching them disappear.

As she and Ray passed over a rippling lawn of seagrass, as they grazed slabs of rock blanketed in woolly fingers and tufts, the shapes of freeform crochet, as they saw a few anaemic yellow fish with sad down-turned mouths, reluctant to be stared at in their underwater canyons, the rock finally gave way to the murkiness of the ocean floor. And suddenly, Lucy wanted to feel grounded, as if she was floating in air and needed some stability. So she gave the thumbs down signal to Ray, and after a few moments, she was able to settle herself on her tummy on the seabed, dragging her hands through the shingle and feeling the grains of sand filter through her fingers like seeds. She felt strangely secure like this. Perhaps there was a reassurance in knowing how far down one could go. More philosophical symbolism there, she thought, but she'd have to think about it later.

All too soon, the time came for them to surface, which they did with a leisurely rhythm of ascent. Lucy savoured every moment. The highlight was when they were suspended in a funnel of converging strobes of sunlight which pointed down into the depths from where they'd come. At that precise moment, it would have been just perfect to see a caretta, to see a blurring shape moving through the rays of light towards her, then a face, then those eyes. Ray had told her how unlikely it was to see one, but she couldn't help hoping.

It took another few minutes before they spotted the shadowy hull of the boat. Clearing the surface through a foaming frenzy of bubbles, and jostled by the ruffles of waves, they took out their mouthpieces, breathing freely at last, and gazed at the clouds above, treading water with their fins. They grinned at each other.

'Thanks, Ray,' she said. 'That was great!'

'You're welcome. Gets to me every time. You did good. We went down about thirteen metres.'

'Thanks, Ray,' was all she could say.

Back in Dalyan, Lucy had her beginner's certificate made out for her at the diving centre office, and thinking of the days ahead, she asked Ray where she could buy some decent snorkelling gear. He escorted her to a nearby sports shop and helped her choose a well-fitting mask, a dry top snorkel with blow off valve, and a pair of dark blue fins, explaining that darker coloured fins were less conspicuous to large fish than brightly coloured ones. 'To avoid attracting the sharks,' he said, winking at her. Lucy bought another snorkel of the same design for Rhea, to use on the twelve island cruise they were going on tomorrow, thinking Rhea would have no excuse not to try snorkelling if it could be guaranteed she wouldn't get water in her mouth. Ray assured her the design was just perfect for that and told her that the cruise boat would have plenty of masks and fins on board. She thanked him for all his help and they shook hands and said goodbye.

'Maybe you will come back again, sometime,' he said.

As she strolled away in the direction of the square, she felt as if she was walking on air. Such a cliché she thought, but now she knew the basis of feeling for it. So light, so buoyant, with a deep sense of harmony - a harmony she hadn't felt for so long.

I did it, she thought, I really did it! I scuba dived!

For a few ecstatic moments she felt anything was possible, even painting again, and she resolved to do as much snorkelling as she could during the rest of the holiday. She would practice doing handstand thrusts, as Ray had suggested, so she could get further below the surface when she wanted. Snorkelling depths were deep enough for her. She'd found there was a slight edginess in going too far down, a kind of excitement mixed with fear, which she'd found a challenge to keep in check.

She glanced down at her purchases, feeling a thrill at the thought that she would get to use her own snorkelling equipment the very next day. And Rhea? Well, she hoped discovering some underwater delights would help her get over losing her ring, then maybe they could get back on track. A moody defensive Rhea would be impossible to question later on. She had to be relaxed and disarmed before Lucy could put her plan into action.

Thinking about Rhea again, she decided to head back to the hotel to see if she was there and to offload her purchases. So, she approached the square, making for the riverside path, and picked up her pace.

But just as she was passing the restaurant on the corner with its red and yellow umbrellas, a voice hailed her.

'Yoo-hoo! Lucy!'

She recognised June's voice well before she turned her head to look. June and Brian were sitting at one of the tables, which was cluttered with an array of empty glasses and straws. June was wearing a tight flowery dress, Brian some huge khaki shorts and bright white trainers.

'Come and join us! Please!' June called over.

Lucy felt the air she was walking on, whipped from

under her feet, bringing her back to earth with a thud. What should she do? How would they be with her, after Rhea had accused June of stealing? How could they just have a harmless chat? And if she did, would it be betraying Rhea? Then, in the midst of this turmoil, she heard her father saying *play it by ear, kiddo*, his favourite advice when facing an uncertain situation. Well, this was certainly one of those times. So, she wandered over, hoping her intuition and some common sense would do the trick.

'Take a seat, pet, please,' June said, her curls nodding towards an empty chair. Her eyes were button bright, her tight puppet mouth drawn up at the corners. A burning cigarette drooped between her ringed fingers. 'Have you had any lunch?'

'Yes. I've just been on a scuba diving trip, my first, actually - but we had something to eat on the boat.'

'Ooo, that sounds exciting! Doesn't it, Brian! Scuba diving.'

Brian nodded, his gold curb necklace tightening like a leash around his fleshy neck. Lucy noticed he was watching a group of skimpily-clad young women sauntering along the riverside, trailing their feet like the model in the Tennis Girl poster, and licking their ice cream cones.

'Men,' June said, following Lucy's gaze, 'always eyeing-up the girls. What can you do with them, eh?' She paused. 'But that was very brave of you, pet, going diving. Mind you, I bet you're an Aquarian.'

Lucy was taken aback. 'Yes, I am actually! How did you guess?' She felt uneasy. How could June have guessed her star sign? It was a bit of a long-shot.

'Oh, I've been studying astrology for years, pet,' June said. 'Aquarians love freedom. They're drawn to the ocean and they like trying out new things. They're trailblazer types. And very mind-driven. They're thinkers, like you. And maybe a bit eccentric? she smiled. 'In a nice way, of course.' Then she paused. 'Very *loyal* too.'

'Loyal...' repeated Lucy, intrigued by June's emphasis. What was she getting at? Where was this going?

'Well you've been very loyal to your sister, haven't you?' June said, stubbing out her cigarette with slow deliberate thrusts.

Lucy faltered. 'Well, yes...I have to be, June. There are many reasons for that, it's just not a matter of sisterly loyalty. But listen,' she said, pausing, 'I'm very sorry you were accused like that. She was very upset, I don't know what got into her. I really don't know what to say to you.' She looked wistfully for a moment at June who was no longer smiling.

Lucy was the first to break eye contact. She felt like a rabbit caught in the headlights of an oncoming car. June's flinty eyes seemed to be burning into her, to find all her secrets: her artist's block, her inner angst, her problems with Rhea, and burning far back into the past.

But when June smiled again, this moment of fear vanished.

'Look, pet,' she said, reaching over and patting Lucy's hand, 'I don't hold grudges. That's bad karma, that. You and me are fine. Okay?'

'Good. Thank you,' Lucy said, surprised at how relieved she felt. What was it about this woman?

'And as for your sister...well, she's obviously got a few problems.'

'Well, I wouldn't go as far as that.' Lucy felt a surge of affection for Rhea. After all, she *was* her sister, and she was very upset over their father's death - that was why she couldn't talk about it. And she was very upset over losing her ring - people could get like that when they lost something important to them.

'Well, let's just say she's got typical Taurean traits.'

'What?'

'Yes, she's Taurus isn't she? Am I right there?'

Lucy found herself speechless. She looked at Brian as if

206

he was a witness to this phenomenon. Having ran out of babes to ogle, he was now listening intently.

'Our Juju's psychic,' he said. 'She can read things about people, like. Sees auras and reads the cards.'

'What? The tarot, you mean?'

'Aye. Always gets it right an-all,' Brian said proudly, draining the last few drops of his pint of lager and sitting back with a loud burp.

Lucy looked at June with a dazed expression.

'Well, is she a Taurus, pet, am I right there?' June repeated.

'Well yes, she is. But how do you -'

'Oh, I can read people for their sun signs easily enough. Of course that's only a very basic aspect of their chart. Just the central character really. There's so much more. Back home, I do natal charts for people. And as for your sister, well she just has the classic character of a Taurean. Feelings run deep below the surface, and they like to stay apart from the crowd. They can be very sensual of course, liking their creature comforts - clothes, jewellery, pampering. But they're very stubborn, and so are Aquarians for that matter. In fact,' June said, leaning further towards Lucy, 'Taureans and Aquarians don't get on very well.'

Lucy found herself giggling at this blatant and deceptively apparent reason why she and Rhea had never got on. Yes, of course, it all makes sense now, she thought. How could they ever hope to get on if they were incompatible sun signs? She stifled her giggles, and pulled herself together.

'Well yes, I think I've read that before, actually. I used to take an interest when I was a teenager. But I don't know if I really believe in it now.'

'Well, *do* you get on?' June asked.

Lucy paused. 'Well no, we don't actually.' It has to be said, she thought.

'Well, there you are then! Taureans are very practical,

down to earth types, classic tastes, and they don't like change. Aquarians are more unconventional and like to challenge things. You beat your own drum, so to speak. So you could both argue over just about anything, drive each other round the flippin bend.'

'Well, that's true enough,' Lucy said, frowning. Where was this going though?

'And then there's your auras. So different you are. Yours is right nice, pet, lots of orange and yellow for being full of life, for being creative - you're an artist, aren't you? And orange for being adventurous - well you've just tried scuba diving - takes guts, that does. And an outgoing nature. And the yellow shows you're brainy. But you're a bit of a perfectionist, you like your details. Am I right?'

Lucy was lost for words again. It all sounded very plausible. 'Can you actually see the colours?'

'Why yes, I've seen auras since I was knee-high. They're like halos of energy around people.' She paused. 'Can Brian go and buy you a drink, luv. You're looking a bit peaky. It's ever so hot again, isn't it?'

Lucy shook her head. 'No, it's okay. I have to go soon.'

Then she felt prickled by curiosity. Against her better judgment, there was an itch she just had to scratch.

'What's Rhea's aura like?' she asked.

'Oh well, it's very different from yours. Of course, if I tell you, you'll have to keep it to yourself. It's not very professional to share it with a third party, you know.'

'Oh, you'd better not, then,' Lucy said, flushing.

'But seeing as it's you - I know I can trust you.' June hesitated. 'Well...it's quite mixed, dear. There's a lot of deep red for strong willpower, and for being a survivor. And that's good. But there's a lot of anger in it an-all. And the grey in it shows she's very guarded, with some blocked energies there. There's like a cloak of black on the outside as well - that shows she's shielding herself, and that there's some deep lack of forgiveness there too.'

'For what?' Lucy blurted out.

'Well, I don't know, pet. But she has some problems there. And maybe you're having problems with her because of it?'

'Well, yes,' Lucy said, nodding and then shaking her head. 'We've never got on at all. This holiday is supposed to be about making a fresh start. We've got the twelve island sailing trip tomorrow and I'm hoping we can snorkel together.'

Lucy sat back and looked over to the riverside, to the vivid blue sky above the cliff bank. It suddenly felt such a relief to be able to talk to somebody. And there did seem to be something to what June was saying. Rhea was very stubborn, held in somehow, especially whenever their childhood was mentioned. From what June was saying, it obviously wasn't doing her any good at all. So, if she could challenge Rhea later on as planned, then it would be for her own benefit. It would help unblock her energies. But how and when to go about it? Slumped in the cafe chair, she shook her head again.

'Look, luv,' why don't I do you a reading - a card reading. You just ask questions inside of yourself and the cards help give you direction. We can go back to the hotel, and be nice and private, like, up in our room. Brian can go and sunbathe by the pool, can't you Brian?'

'Oh aye. Nee bother there.'

'Oh, I don't know,' Lucy said. 'I don't know if I believe in it. That's why I've never done it before.'

'It just takes ten minutes - that's all.' June's tone became wheedling. 'Come on, let me do you a reading, to show no hard feelings. After last night it'll cheer me up too, and maybe it'll help you with your sister.'

Lucy looked into June's eyes. They looked glowing with sincerity now. Maybe there wouldn't be any harm in it? And Rhea *had* upset June by accusing her of stealing. Letting June do a reading might make up for that somehow, to show there was no ill will. Lucy squirmed around in her chair. If I go along with it, she thought, and

Rhea finds out, she'll be furious and might never forgive me - so much for fulfilling Dad's wish then. But if I do have a reading, then I just might get some guidance about her. She's obviously hiding something that stresses her. So, having the reading will be for her benefit, to help unblock her energies. She sighed. On the other hand, it could all be a complete load of rubbish. But the biggest thing she felt was an overwhelming curiosity, inexorable as a wave rolling in to shore and crashing down any obstacles in its path.

'It's just about pointing you in the direction of what you already know, just helps you tap into it, that's all,' said June. 'Nothing to be scared of.'

'Okay,' Lucy replied. 'I'll give it a go. I like to be open minded about these things. I've just got this snorkelling gear to put in our room and check Rhea's off having her Turkish massage.'

'No rush, dear. Just take your time. We're in room 12.'

There. Decision made, thought Lucy, as she gathered her bags together. But as she walked off with June and Brian in the direction of the Onur, she felt nervous again.

***

In the hamam, Rhea sat down and rested her bare back against warm wet marble, while trickles of sweat ran down her forehead and shoulders. She was wearing a cotton pestemal wrap wound around under her arms, and tied at the front over her turquoise bikini. She was impressed by the body wrap, which was a terracotta and cream woven check with fringing, and she'd already decided she must buy one before leaving Dalyan. The sauna was the first stage of the Turkish bath, and she was enjoying the heavy vapid feeling that the heat induced, the slippery sliding texture of her skin, and the occasional sound of water drops hissing on hot coals.

As she closed her eyes and breathed in the stifling

steaming air, steadily drawing it up through her nostrils so they burned a little, she couldn't help thinking about the events of yesterday. Apart from the market, the day had been a disaster: it had been a punishing schedule; they'd been late for the bus twice; Lucy had been doing her philosophising and she'd ranted at a stranger; and then there'd been the loss, or rather the theft, of her ring.

Having her ring stolen had simply brought her to her knees - like a penitent - exhausted and defeated by numerous mental and physical trials, and ready to confess all. She'd made such an exhibition of herself in front of Seda and Lucy, crying like that. It was so embarrassing. Thank God June hadn't seen her like that.

And today? Well, she felt depressed. Helpless somehow, since she'd promised not to pursue her grievance any further for Seda's sake. And Lucy was right - it was only a ring. But it was a special ring. It had such a sparkle to it, so many facets and tints of pink, silver and violet, and the tiny diamonds encircling it set it off so beautifully. And it fitted her finger so well, even though she'd taken a chance with the sizing. It had quite simply felt fated to be hers, superseding the other rings in her collection: the blue sapphire, her mystic topaz, her Columbian emerald, the Madagascan ruby and the blueberry quartz. The kunzite was her favourite, and she keenly felt its loss. Although she didn't really believe in the spiritual properties of gemstones, somewhere inside her she'd liked the idea of the kunzite bestowing peace upon the wearer. She'd felt she needed it when she bought it shortly after her father died. And surely he would have wanted her to be at peace? Just as she hoped he was, after carrying a secret burden for so long.

She opened her eyes and stared at the middle finger of her right hand, rubbing it gently where the ring used to be. Tears brimmed and stung like vinegar. She glanced at the gold band on her left hand. Why couldn't that have been taken instead? These days she often felt the urge to

211

take her wedding ring off, not just when doing the washing up, but permanently. It didn't mean much anymore. Not like the kunzite ring.

She thought of June, and felt such a fury rise from deep inside her gut, the same fury that had led her to search June with such thoroughness last night - a ripping clothes up and smashing plates kind of fury, a cat fighting fury, a baring your teeth and howling at the moon kind of fury. All these feelings she'd kept at bay, like a pack of hounds straining at the leash. And as for the act June had put on. Well, it was unbelievable! Her trembling lip and tears had fooled Lucy, of course, but Rhea had seen these kind of acting skills from shoplifters under questioning at work - the professional ones. June has got my ring, she thought, I just know it. The prune on sticks. It was so frustrating not to have been able to conduct a full body search. Yet there was something about her, you wouldn't want to get too close. Something evil. Like a harpy - whatever they were, but the word fitted. Maybe I can search her room somehow? she thought. Or get access to her safe box? And as for the practicalities, well the ring had been such a bargain, it just wasn't worth claiming on the insurance.

Rhea's thoughts were stemmed by an assistant gesturing for her to follow him under the dome of the hamam. She idled listlessly over and sat on the warm flat belly stone set below the dome. It was like an altar in a church, softly illuminated by the skylights above, and the assistant started scrubbing her arms and neck with an abrasive glove. She was receiving an exfoliating body scrub, so he was quite rough in his actions. As she continued to think about her ring, she felt the pain of its loss in the scrubbing of her skin, as if she was going through another physical trial, being scourged for the sin of covetousness. Once more, she had to fight back tears. There was nothing she could do about the ring. There might be an opportunity later on, but for now she knew she'd have to let it go. If she kept dwelling on it, she'd lose control. And she really needed her composure on this holiday. Composure was critical.

As the assistant scrubbed her legs, a warm tingling crept through her body, and she started to relax. By the time the body scrub was over, she felt purged and pulsing with health.

Finally, she was to have her reward - a foam massage. She lay down on her stomach on the slab of warm marble, pulling down the pestemal wrap around her hips, so more of her body was exposed to the benefits of the olive oil soap. A pair of strong hands started pushing, squeezing and releasing the muscles of her neck and shoulders, edging down her spine and circling her back, down to her hips, repeating and repeating in a persuasive rhythm. With her head resting comfortably on her folded arms, she gazed at the wet mirrored sheen of the marble reflecting the colours of the wall tiles and the stained glass windows of the dome. As she felt the bubbles build around her like clouds of sea foam, as she was pressed into the hard stone, she felt as if she was a Roman lady at her local baths: wet cotton pestemal clinging to her skin, moist tendrils of hair sticking to the back of her neck, her body smoothed and nourished with olive oil - she was one of the languid elite. Or maybe, she was in a harem, she thought, humid with heat, and amongst the chosen ones, chosen for beauty, and much more besides…

Her thoughts drifted on, like a Japanese maple leaf cast into a gently moving stream. The sweet smell of the foam, the balmy atmosphere, urged her to forget all about her ring. Urged her to forget about everything.

Later, when she was rinsing herself at one of the wall faucets, feeling the warm water trickle down her silky skin, she felt rejuvenated. She thought of the next day, and the twelve island sailing trip. It should be good, she thought, the wind in my hair, the warm breezes, the good food and the sun bathing. There'd be Lucy for company, of course. But she was surprised to feel that was actually okay. Lucy had been very supportive over the ring incident; she'd tried to tackle June, which took guts, and later on, she hadn't insisted on talking about everything. She seemed to have got the message. Progress was being made with a new perspective perhaps.

As she was drying off, she looked around at the other hamam customers - there were just a few other women in the section she was in - all shapes and sizes. And she realised she hadn't once thought about how she looked. She hadn't done any visual comparisons like she usually did - looking at the 'trim slims', as she called them, which made her too aware of her middle-age spread, or the heavy 'weebly wobblies', who always made her feel grateful for smaller mercies. But here at the hamam, she'd done no comparing at all. And it felt really liberating. Everyone was here for the same reasons. There was no posing or preening, just a comfortable atmosphere of heat, health and relaxation. I must come here again, she thought. It will keep me centred.

One of the women waved at her. She squinted and recognised Eleanor, who was towel-drying her radiant red hair. Rhea sauntered across to her, smiling.

'You fancy an apple tea?' Eleanor asked.

'Yes, that would be lovely,' she replied. 'Do you know if they sell the pestemal wraps here?'

***

Back at the Onur hotel, after Lucy entered room 12, June drew the voile drapes together and closed off the light from the balcony, causing Lucy to shudder. June's flowery perfume hit the back of her throat, making her cough, and she wished she'd taken the time to change out of the damp swimsuit she was wearing underneath her t-shirt and shorts.

'Now, take a seat, here,' June said, indicating a chair in

front of a low coffee table.

June let the sides of a pink silk bundle slither open to reveal a deck of tarot cards with fluffy worn edges. She smoothed the silk down on the table with her ringed hands, sat on a chair opposite Lucy, and placed the deck in the centre of the cloth.

'One of my oldest sets. I never go anywhere without them. They're a Rider Waite pack. Have a look through them, pet. They're really bonny. You should appreciate the drawings.'

As June lit up a cigarette, Lucy leafed through the cards, seeing blurring flashes of stately enthroned figures, medieval costumes, animals, angels, stars, suns and moons with faces, all displayed with such an order to them, such precisely staged symbols. She felt a fluttering in her stomach. What was she doing?

'Lovely, aren't they?' June said, taking a deep drag on her cigarette, making the tip glow red and blowing the smoke towards the closed balcony doors.

She shuffled the cards and handed them to Lucy to give them a final shuffle, to transfer her essence to the cards, June said. At the same time, Lucy was to think hard of the burning question she wanted answers to, but not to say it out loud.

'Now, remember,' June said, 'the tarot doesn't answer questions about the future, it just points you in the direction of what you already know, somewhere inside you, like. And it's the cards that have the power, not me.'

As Lucy shuffled the cards, she thought hard, questions tumbling around inside her, knocking against each other like stones being polished. She could ask a question about whether she would become a successful artist. Or whether she needed to let it go. But what would she do instead? Something creative still, surely? And then the tumbling stopped. No, this was about Rhea, to help her. Okay, what's the question? Right. Here goes. *Why did our relationship get worse after Mum died?*

She breathed a sigh of relief. 'Done that,' she said to June.

'Right. Good. Well, keep thinking of it, pet, and split the pack into three piles face down on the silk and point to a pile of your choice.'

Lucy did as she was told and pointed to the pile on her left. June turned the pile around to face her, and selected the top five cards, laying them face down out in a kind of cross, chanting 'Present, Past, Future, Reason, Potential.'

She stubbed out her cigarette, then leaned in towards Lucy, propping the backs of her hands on her chin with her fingers splayed like starfish. Lucy stared at all June's rings - glinting sapphires, emeralds, and what looked like diamonds and rubies. Then the gold chains around her neck. Then the glittering beady eyes, the snub nose, the puppet mouth drawn in a line.

This woman is odd, Lucy thought. What is it about her? She's like a female Svengali, or some kind of throwback to Rasputin. Rumpelstiltskin also came to mind - all that spinning straw into gold, she could see June doing that. And what was it with the short curly hair? It was so eighties, so poodle perm, so scarily out of fashion. She decided to avoid too much eye contact with her.

'You've got so many rings,' Lucy said, staring at one after the other - noting that there was no pink kunzite in sight.

'Yes. But I wear them for their special powers, luv - sapphire for opening the mind to beauty and intuition, diamond for removing negative energy and increasing spiritual awareness, emerald for insight into dreams and overall harmony,' June said, wiggling each finger in turn, 'and garnet for warding off evil. They're my special friends,' she smiled. 'And I collect gold for its eternal properties, flexibility and perfection.'

'Well, you're certainly covered, then,' Lucy laughed. She also felt unnerved by June's progression to a more sophisticated language, as if she'd rote learned it from a vital knowledgeable source.

June nodded slowly. 'Shall we begin, pet?'

Lucy felt a tingling in her chest. 'Yes please, I've got to get on actually.' She started winding a loose strand of her hair between her fingers - coil, release, coil, release.

June's right hand hovered over the central card in the cross, then she turned it over, and placed it back down in its position. 'The Hanged Man,' she said. This is your present, pet.'

June's voice lowered and became incantatory, as she interpreted the meaning of the card. It showed a man suspended upside down from his waist on a leafy T-shaped gallows. His hands were tied behind his back and one leg crossed behind the other. Lucy noticed that he was happily alive and looked quite unperturbed by his predicament.

'This is the card of rebirth,' June said, continuing in the same professional language. 'You're feeling blocked, powerless - that's why the hands are tied, life is kind of in suspension, you see? And I'm getting the sense that you're going through a change. Yes, some kind of change. But someone in your life is being very difficult, blocking you.'

Lucy nodded, winding her hair faster. Artist's block, she thought, needing a new direction, yes, it fits, and blocked with Rhea too. Rhea was being very difficult. This was absolutely her present dilemma in all respects.

'So, you need to see things differently to move forward, you need a new outlook, that's why he's hanging upside down.'

'Yes, I get that,' Lucy replied. A bit of lateral thinking, or upside down thinking for that matter, she decided, that's what I'll try to do, imagine myself hanging upside down, like I used to when I was a kid, larking around on field gates. It used to be so interesting seeing the world upside down, with your blood rushing to your head, wondering how long you could stand it for. Then she remembered this was about Rhea. So, it would be trying to see something in her relationship with Rhea in a new way, looking at it from a different angle. But what? Something in the present linked to the past?

June turned over the next card, which was ironically upside down, and Lucy peered at it. It showed a dog and a wolf looking up at a face in the moon, while a lobster-like creature was crawling out of water in the foreground. 'The Moon Reversed is the card in the position relating to your past and past influences still having an effect. And the fact that it's upside down means it symbolises the dark side of the moon.'

Dark side of the moon, Lucy thought, wasn't that a Pink Floyd album? All those haunting and psychedelic electric guitar slides. Mmm, she'd liked those.

'The dog and the wolf show our animal natures, the sea creature, the abyss from whence we came. When the card is reversed it shows secrecy and trickery in the past. It shows illusions and the inability to see things clearly. The realms of the unconscious and dreams. You can move forward spiritually if you trust and act upon your intuitions at this time. It is a healing time for you, pet.'

'Yes, okay. But I don't understand what trickery there can be in the past that's having an effect now?' Lucy was starting to feel itchy in her damp swimsuit. She wanted to get away from June, but felt compelled to stay - like an iron filing stuck to a magnet.

'Well, think of your inner question, dear. That might help. I also get the sense that your mother's watching over you in relation to this. Loved ones often do that once they've passed on.'

'Mum? Well, I have sometimes felt that before, but it's easy to imagine, isn't it? I always thought I took after her. You see, she was an artist too. She was a very passionate person.'

Lucy suddenly frowned. So, if she was going to be open minded about this, then thinking back to her question, something in the past involved trickery, that was still having an effect, and therefore it must have something to do with her and Rhea's relationship having got worse after their mother died. If there was trickery, and Rhea knew what that was, it might explain why she was so reluctant to talk about their childhood. And whenever she did manage to get Rhea talking about it, it was as if she had very different views about it - and about their mother. She certainly seemed to be hiding something. Or maybe she was trying to forget? And that's why she got so upset sometimes - so angry. That would also explain her dark aura, Lucy thought, her eyes widening. *And* it would explain her lack of inner peace. She stared back at June.

'Are we getting somewhere, luv? You know, I noticed on the coach that your sister doesn't seem to like talking about your mother. Could there be something there?'

'Well, she always avoids it, she seems to have completely different views to me, but...' Lucy wavered. She wanted to talk to June, because she really needed to talk to someone. But June felt like a dangerous choice.

'Well, you know siblings can have very different versions of a life. I'll leave that one with you,' June smiled. 'Now, for the next one - the future card.'

She turned the card over to reveal a naked lady posing in the centre of a wreath. 'The World,' she said. 'That's another Major Arcana we've had. This is becoming quite a fate-driven reading, dear, driving towards spiritual awareness. But the world card for your future is a lovely card. It represents accomplishment, the end of a chapter in your life, fulfilment and success.'

'That's lovely, June,' Lucy said. I've been having such a struggle lately. I wonder what I will be doing?'

'I see a circle closing. All will be revealed to you, luv. You're a very sensitive person, an idealist and a clear thinker with good principles - look how you stick up for women, like you did for Trish on the coach tour. You deserve success. I see a circle closing.'

'Yes, you said that,' Lucy said, noticing some

repetitions creeping into June's musings. Not to mention flattery. 'What about the next card?'

June coughed, lit up another cigarette, and snapped over the bottom card in the cross arrangement. It showed a man plunging a stake into the ground, above six other stakes. 'This is the Seven of Wands, otherwise known as the Lord of Valour. And it is in the position of reason - perhaps reason behind your question.'

'Right.' Lucy leaned forward.

'The six staffs are attacking his one staff, but he has the higher position. It is about worldly strife, and he must be determined to succeed by strength of nerve in placing the stake. It shows that with effort, you can succeed in your aims against strong competition.' June paused, glancing at the other cards. 'Now this could relate to the Hanged Man card of the present, the blocking, the difficult person in your life. They could be the competition you have to overcome. And if you don't mind me suggesting, pet, I think this must be about your sister, who has a very darkly guarded aura. Remember?'

'Well yes, that's what you say. I'll admit, there does seem to be some sense to all this.'

'Yes. And of course Taureans are very stubborn. Very determined.' June surveyed the cards again. 'And there's trickery in your past.' She paused. 'I must say the cards are doing very well for you,' she said, arching her thinly plucked eyebrows. 'But of course, it's the cards that have the power.'

'So what is the reason card telling me to do?'

'It's telling you to fight, pet. And deep down you know that already, don't you?'

Lucy felt the hairs on the back of her neck bristle. She had to fight Rhea. In other words she had to take a strong initiative with her to get the answers to her inner question. And of course, she'd known this all along. She had to corner her and strike. But when? And how? All she knew was that it had to be soon, and Rhea mustn't see it coming.

'Right, luv. The final card represents potential - potential in the situation, or the result of taking action.'

Lucy looked at the last card in the spread. It was a crowned lady, sitting in rich robes, and holding a sceptre.

'The Empress,' said June. 'Twelve stars in her crown and the symbol of Venus on the shield near her feet. She is the Earthly Mother, the fruitful mother, goddess of fertility. See? Her gown has pomegranates on it.'

'What does she mean?'

'Well, lots of things really, pet, like beauty...er.. sensuality, creative expression and nurturing. She is the symbol of mother, sister, and wife,' June continued, resuming her chanting tone after a small hiccup. 'She calls on you to connect with your feminine energy. Discover new ways to express yourself through nature. I see one door opening, and another closing. The mother card is a deeply nurturing card. And of course your own mother passed on when you were very young.'

Lucy flinched at the sudden switch of topic. 'Yes, I told you that on the coach. But what's that got to do with anything?'

'Well, she's coming through in this card, pet. Can I ask you how she died? I feel there may be a connection.' June's beady eyes bored holes into Lucy's.

Lucy hesitated. 'Well, she drowned, if you must know. It was awful. She was reaching for some magnolia blossom which was hanging over the pond at the bottom of our garden, and she fell in. She must have got caught in some weeds. Anyway, she drowned,' Lucy said, her voice breaking.

'Oh, luv, that's so sad. But she's watching over you with this card.'

'At least she was doing what she loved. The blossom will have been for a still life painting, I expect.'

'You weren't the one that found her, were you?'

'The one that found her?' Lucy said. The words echoed in her ears, and pictures of her mother's dead body flashed into her mind's eye: white drained skin, staring blue eyes, open mouth, streaming blonde hair, weeds entwined around her, weeds holding her down, inert limbs, lifelessly floating. Then she forced these images away and replaced them one single vision, the one she'd always managed to claw her way to, because her dad had said that her mother had looked very peaceful. It was Millais's painting of Ophelia. Serenely posed, floating on her back amongst the reeds and strewn with flowers. Hamlet's Ophelia was supposed to have fallen from a willow tree while collecting flowers by a river, falling in and drowning - said to be 'incapable of her own distress'. It was a perfect image for Lucy, and she knew her mother had liked this painting. There was no struggle, no pain, and in Lucy's vision of her mother in this pose, her eyes were closed. There, that was better. The right picture was in place and Lucy regained her composure under June's searching gaze.

'No, of course I wasn't the one that found her. That would have been awful. I'd never have got over something like that! Dad found her when he got back from work. Rhea and I were at school, but Dad had finished early that day. That's all I know.'

'That's all you know,' June quietly repeated, looking back at Lucy. 'Well, I'll leave that with you, then.'

'Look,' said Lucy, feeling angry. 'What has this got to do with the Empress card?'

'Well, think of your question - we have the mother, sister, wife card here in the position of potential - potential in your situation, or the result of taking action in your present. Something to do with your mother, perhaps? Your sister? The card encourages you to connect with your feminine energy, find a way to open communication, and to help others grow and meet their potential too.'

Okay, Lucy thought. Her inner question was asking why she and Rhea's relationship got worse after their mother died. And here was the mother card confirming somehow, that her death might be connected. It was a long shot, but if she took the action to tackle Rhea on the same issue, tackle the supposed trickery, as she'd now decided to do, then it would be for both their benefits and personal growth. For the feminine, for sisterhood, even for their mother perhaps. She sat back, feeling exhausted. All this thinking and trying to make links was very hard work.

'Well, dear, that's about it. I hope that's helpful to you,' June said. She'd lit up another cigarette and a dollop of ash was hanging from the end of it, threatening to fall onto the cards. 'It can be like looking through smoked glass, pet. Confusing. But you'll get there.'

Lucy looked at her watch. Ten minutes had stretched into an hour. 'Thanks, June. That was very interesting. Do I owe you anything?'

'Oh, no luv! I don't charge friends.'

'Well, that's very good of you.'

As June opened the drapes, Lucy edged towards the door. 'Well, bye then.' She had her hand on the doorknob, when June replied.

'We'll see you tomorrow, on the twelve island trip,' she said chirpily.

A jolt of electricity flashed through Lucy. 'What? Are you coming to that?'

'Yes. Me and Brian changed our minds, like. We went back to the office and booked it this morning. We're really looking forward to it - cruising the Med, eh?'

Oh my God, Lucy thought. How the hell was Rhea going to handle that? June and Brian on board, with no escape?

'Listen, June. Can I ask you a favour? Not to mention our chat to Rhea. She wouldn't approve.'

'Of course not, pet. I'll be giving her plenty of space from now on, don't you worry.'

As Lucy left, she felt a sense of foreboding. Should she warn Rhea? But knowing Rhea, she'd refuse to go on the trip. No, Lucy decided. She was planning to try to do

223

some more bonding with Rhea, before tackling her about the past in a day or two, when they'd be half way through the holiday. Take the Taurus bull by the horns. So, she would simply try to keep Rhea away from June on the sailing trip. After all, there was the snorkelling for Rhea to try. She'd be sure to love it when she got used to it, and wasn't she supposed to be helping her sister to grow?

***

Rhea lay back in her recliner at the Villa Vita, sipping her tea. It was around 4.30 in the afternoon and the pool shone with silver. She and Eleanor had been chatting for about half an hour.

'This is a beautiful villa, Eleanor. How did you come to be staying here?'

'My friend, Susie, owns it. She wanted a getaway place here in Dalyan. She just loves it here. She got married a couple of years back, but she's always been so independent. We used to run a fashion design business together in New York – 'Diva Designs'. Nice name, huh? That was years ago now. Anyway, she suggested I borrow this villa for a vacation, seeing as Dan and me have been fighting a lot lately and I needed some space. So here I am for a full month!'

'Lovely. Yes, I know what you mean. Chris and I have been married for over twenty years and we've been bickering more and more lately, for about the last two years, actually. Quite frankly, I'm at the end of my tether with him. But we have a son together, Rob, he's nineteen, he's still young.'

'But that's all grown up these days, hon. Is that why you're staying with your husband? For Rob?'

'Yes. I suppose so. That and…well, we've been together so long. It should mean something, shouldn't it?'

'I don't know, honey. Maybe life's too short for just putting up with each other for another twenty years.

Maybe think about what you really want in life. When you get to our age, you have to try and make your dreams come true. Don't you think? You know, kick those red shoes together, like Dorothy in *The Wizard of Oz*.

Rhea grinned at the image. 'If only it were that easy.'

After chatting more about fashion, about retail, about Fethiye market, and about husbands, the shadows of the recliners stretched and both women slipped into a light doze.

Eleanor woke first and roused Rhea, who lengthened her limbs like a cat sunning itself on a warm paving slab.

'Thanks, Eleanor. You know this has been the most relaxing day of my holiday so far. And thanks for not mentioning the ring.' And then a thought occurred to her. And before she'd considered what she was thinking, or had considered Lucy's feelings, the words just popped out. 'Maybe you'd like to join us for dinner. We usually go to the Calypso, down by the riverside.'

'Oh sure, that sounds great,' Eleanor said, beaming. 'What time?'

'Around seven? It's lovely on the jetty, just make sure you've got some mozzie spray.'

As Rhea brushed past a pot of red hibiscus by the entrance gate and began to amble back to the Onur, the sun soaked deep into her and a light breeze lifted her hair. She felt refreshed, easier in herself. The Turkish bath had been very relaxing and talking to Eleanor had been such a tonic. She'd been able to be herself with Eleanor, far more than she could be with Lucy, who always ended up probing her like a biologist doing a dissection under a microscope. No matter how hard Lucy tried to curb her curiosity, her scalpel was always ready to hand and twitching to be used.

And once again Rhea found herself looking forward to the sailing trip - all that lovely sunbathing and a tasty barbeque lunch. There would just be the weekend after that, and they'd be half way through the holiday. Then she'd be back at the store, back in her routine, keeping busy. Just a husband she couldn't trust anymore to decide what to do about. The stealing of her money for a dodgy deal had killed off any remaining love or affection she had for him. And she realised that being away from home had actually helped her see this more clearly. There was still Rob to worry about, but she had gained a new perspective. The holiday would have provided that at least.

As she turned into the reception area of the Onur, she saw Hasim behind the desk. She hadn't seen him since the bike ride. His wavy hair was more tousled than usual.

'Hasim,' she said smiling. 'Everything alright?'

He looked up from the computer and his scowl turned into a grin. 'Hello, Rhea. I haven't seen you for a couple of days.'

There it was again, Rhea thought, that way he had of looking at her, that way he had of saying her name.

He threw his hands in the air at the computer and came towards her. 'Like a drink on the terrace? I've had enough of accounts now.'

Rhea hesitated. How would it be interpreted?

'Come. Just a drink. Tell me what you have been doing in Dalyan.'

As Hasim poured them both a white wine and they sat on the rooftop terrace on one of the sofas together in the late afternoon sun, Rhea found herself tensing up. She was so physically close to him. It was different to how it had been on the bike. It was more personal, like they were more deliberately getting to know each other. She was conscious that their arms and thighs were almost touching. What would she do if he put his arm around her? And would he put his arm around her?

As he explained how he hated doing accounts, even though he'd had some very good training at a hotel in England, she found it difficult to look at him. She didn't want to gaze into his brown eyes, notice his dark lashes, or look at the firmness of his mouth, or the shadow of stubble on his face, or see his easy laugh. She didn't want to notice his strong arms, and the tangle of wrist hairs curling over the glint of his watchstrap, or notice his long fingers that looked like they belonged to a rock musician and the stretch of denim on his thighs. She didn't want to notice the growing attraction she felt for this man or think about where it might lead. Sitting side by side, the only escape from confronting these things was to concentrate on the conversation while looking out over the rooftops of Dalyan. A bird was flying high up, circling, sweeping, as if it was searching for something.

'I lost a ring,' she said, before she'd even realised what she was saying.

'How?' Hasim replied, looking concerned as her eyes finally met his.

So, she told him what she thought had happened, who she thought had taken it.

'But she is staying *here*,' he said. His eyebrows knitted together. 'Have you proof?'

'No, but I'm certain.'

'Have you reported it to the Jandarma? Because with no proof it will be difficult.'

'No, I didn't want Seda, our tour guide, to get in any trouble.'

Hasim was silent for a few moments, then looked deep into her eyes. 'That was nice of you. But I don't think I can help you, Rhea. I can't search her room or her deposit box without the Jandarma.'

Oh, no! I know that, Hasim. I wasn't expecting you to be able to do anything. I don't know why I mentioned it. Really, it's okay. I just got a bit upset about it, that's all. It was special,' she said getting up. 'But it's just a ring. I'd better go and see what Lucy's doing now.'

'Do you have to go?' Hasim rose to his feet.

'Yes, I must.'

'Rhea?'

'What?'

'You're special.'

He gazed down at her. And she knew it was all so toe-curlingly clichéd, he'd be offering to show her his etchings next. But still, she got lost in him. He leaned in towards her, and her hands went around his hips. The kiss was searching, lingering. His lips on hers, his taste, the graze of his stubble, felt so good, so right, and she melted into him.

After a few seconds she pulled away. 'I've got to go. See you later,' she said, hurrying down the stairs. What did she mean by *see you later*? she wondered. What was she getting herself into? Then she tried to shake herself out of it. No, she thought, it's just a kiss, an absolutely perfect kiss, but just a kiss. And that is how it must stay. But a little voice whispered in her ear. *Why?* And she smiled.

When she got back to the hotel room, she found Lucy lying on her bed reading the book on Dalyan that Hasim had lent them.

'Did you enjoy the scuba diving?' Rhea asked.

'Oh yes, it was amazing!'

'Good.' Rhea hesitated. 'I bumped into Eleanor at the hamam. Do you mind if she joins us for dinner?'

'Oh, no, that's fine. It would be nice to get to know her a little and I just love American accents,' Lucy said. She looked at Rhea and smiled. 'You look very serene, that massage must have agreed with you.'

***

That evening, the sisters and Eleanor enjoyed a three course meal at the Calypso, with Ahmet once again giving them a ten percent discount. Lucy waxed lyrical about her scuba diving, while Rhea and Eleanor explained the charms of the Turkish hamam to a puzzled Lucy, which ended in raucous laughter over their wine glasses.

'You can tell you're sisters when you laugh, you know,' Eleanor giggled.

Eventually, Eleanor pushed back her chair, saying she hoped they'd both have a fabulous time tomorrow and that she'd have just loved to come, but she was prone to sea sickness. 'You girls have been real good company,' she said, slinging her Mulberry satchel over her shoulder, 'but I'd better get back to my Villa Vita, otherwise known as the villa life, which I have to say I'm getting used to very easily.'

'The Villa Vita,' Lucy said, frowning for a moment. 'Oh, yes! I saw that place on the way back from the pomegranate gallery. I took some pictures from the gate - hope you don't mind. Oh, it's gorgeous! I love the courtyard bit with the vines. And the bicycle by the door.'

Eleanor laughed. 'Well, I haven't used the bike – it's not my thing. But you can borrow it if you like. You'll have to come over - both of you.'

As Eleanor sauntered away, Lucy and Rhea looked at each other.

'Nice lady,' said Lucy. 'Are you going to try some snorkelling tomorrow? I got you the right kind of snorkel,' she said.

'I'll give it a go,' replied Rhea.

10

The Twelve Island Cruise

When Rhea and Lucy strolled through reception to find June and Brian sitting at one of the cafe tables with their beach bags, Rhea stiffened.

'What are *they* doing here? They're not waiting for the coach? They're not going!' she hissed.

'Oh God - they must be. Trish didn't say anything, did she? Maybe they booked up later on?' Lucy gave Rhea a pleading look. 'Please don't let it spoil things. We can still have a good day. We'll steer clear of them - okay? Okay?' She nudged Rhea forwards.

'How are we supposed to do that on a sailing boat?' Rhea said sharply, sitting down at a table on the opposite side of the forecourt. 'Well, just make sure we're not sitting next to them on the bus this time, or at lunch for that matter!' she said, scowling.

There was no greeting, no communication between the two tables, just eyes panning passing tourists and darting quick glances down the street. When the coach arrived June and Brian scrambled on first, sitting near the front. Lucy and Rhea smiled good morning to Seda and then they noticed Trish was there too.

'What are you doing here?' asked Lucy.

'Can't miss this!' Trish said, with her strawberry jam smile. 'It's one of the perks of the job and I was due a day off.' Then she looked at Rhea and her face crumpled into its walnut shell. 'Seda told me. I'm so sorry, I have recorded it. It's my job to help you if you decide to pursue it further. You've been very understanding. And I'm sorry about them coming, it was a late booking from just yesterday,' she whispered, flicking her hair tails in the direction of June and Brian. 'There was nothing I could do.'

Rhea nodded, and she and Lucy headed down to the back of the bus, Lucy offering the window seat to Rhea. After collecting the other passengers, and about three quarters of an hour later, the coach pulled into Göcek Bay. The Mediterranean stretched out like silk to the hazy horizon and shimmered in the early morning light.

The passengers gathered on the scorching quayside of the marina alongside a polished wood, twin-masted boat, with a balustraded gunwale on its bow. Seda explained that this was the boat chartered for their trip - the Deniz Kizi, meaning the mermaid; it was a gulet boat, made of solid wood and based upon the traditional designs of Aegean sailing boats, which had sailed the Mediterranean seas for centuries.

The Turkish flag on its stern fluttered in the morning breeze as all eyes scanned the masts and rigging, the sleek hull, and most of all the blue recliner cushions and white awnings assembled upon its sun-bleached deck. They would be sailing around the beautiful Gulf of Göcek, Seda continued, which was on the Turkish Riviera, visiting the gulf's archipelago of islands, and they'd also make a stop at Cleopatra's Baths. According to legend, Mark Anthony had given these baths to Cleopatra as a wedding gift. They were built in a bay of clear cyan water, edged with pines. In ancient times there was an underwater hot spring, which was supposed to be good for the skin. These days, Seda smiled, visitors could swim amongst the ruins and maybe come out ten years younger. They would also see Carian rock tombs here and there, and maybe, just maybe, they would see some dolphins and flying fish.

As everyone clambered aboard to bag their spot for these delights, Rhea charged ahead and settled herself on the balustraded bow on top of the galley, where there were some floor-cushion beds lying in full sun, an area designed for those who wanted to doze off and do some serious tanning. She was soon joined by Trish, while Lucy sat cross-legged on a cushion next to Rhea, wearing her straw sunhat with the pink roses on it and craning her neck over towards June and Brian. They had lagged behind, and were sitting in the stern area in the shade. Once Seda had spoken to the captain, and answered some more questions from a few passengers, explaining that chilled drinks were available to buy in the cockpit, she drew her plait over her shoulder and sat below Rhea and Lucy in the shade of the main deck, jotting some notes down on her clipboard. Apart from the crew and the Go Turkey staff, there were only fourteen paying passengers, so there was plenty of room to spread about, plenty of room for private conversations and private contemplations.

After the thudding and coiling of ropes onto the deck, the Deniz Kizi eased itself away from the line up of yachts and schooners, and was soon chugging out of the marina, accompanied by the shrieks of gulls into the ocean sparkle of the bay. With its floating bridge of islands, the bay was framed by coastal mountains with mantles of blue pine forests feathered against a cloudless sky. Only a slight breeze stirred to swell the shade canopies. Lucy scrambled to the pulpit of the bow to watch the midnight-blue velvet sea being sheared into lacy droplets, which danced and chased each other around like snowflake flurries in a blizzard. From a bird's eye view, a fantail of foam trailed behind the stern, fading into the ocean swell.

Rhea took off her shirt and shorts to reveal a white bikini, fashioned with belt, buckles and ties. She put on her shades and a floppy brimmed sunhat and stretched out on a towel on top of her recliner, looking suitably tanned from all her sunbathing efforts and lingering spray tan. She and Lucy had taken the precaution of applying copious amounts of lotion before breakfast, as Hasim had told Rhea that according to the forecast it may reach well into the 30's today. Trish removed her uniform to show off a skimpy red bikini on her bronzed leathery body. The bikini matched her smile, her hair, and her toenails. On her shoulder was a tribal-style tattoo of a heart interlaced with whiplash lines with the name Rick scrolled inside it. Lucy admired the design and asked who Rick was.

'Oh, he's an old flame. I had it done when I was young and stupid in the nineties,' Trish said, lying back on her cushion. 'I've always meant to have it removed, or have a cover-up done with maybe a butterfly there instead.'

Lucy stripped off to a retro-style, dark blue, halter neck one-piece, with ruching across the bodice. What was unusual about the design was that it was cut into men's sports briefs.

'Good God, Lucy! Where did you find that?' Rhea gasped, snatching off her shades.

'Online. It's supposed to be 1940's vintage style,' Lucy said, scowling at her.

'Well, it's certainly that! You're not Esther Williams you know. Remember those synchronised swimming films - all rubber flowers and pointed toes?'

'Yes, well, you're not exactly Ursula Andress for that matter.'

Trish appraised Lucy. 'You suit it, actually. You've got the body length for it. It's quite classy, and vintage is *in* now, isn't it?'

'Thank you, Trish, that's just what I hoped,' Lucy said, cocking her eyebrows at Rhea. Then she got her purse out of her beach bag, smartly stepped down the small ladder onto the main deck close to where Seda was sitting. 'Anyone for a drink?'

As Rhea and Lucy sipped their diet cokes, the toilet cabin door beneath them slammed shut many times before the passengers finally settled down. Then everyone sank into reclining poses, rocked by the rise and fall of the ship as it sailed on between the bridge of islands and the coastline. When they reached the open sea, the skipper ordered the sails to be unfurled, and when these had caught enough wind to billow out and tighten, he switched off the engine.

When the throbbing stopped, all that could be heard was the creaking of guy ropes and rigging, the occasional flap of canvas and the slapping of surf against the hull. The sun beat down upon the sunbathers on the open deck, while those under the canopies directed their faces into a salty breeze.

Seda got up and moved over to the gunwale, her eyes scanning the horizon. 'Just looking to see if there are flying fish about,' she said, smiling at Lucy, who was still sitting cross-legged on her cushion. 'They really look as if they have wings.'

'It's all so exciting. I'd love to see some. Where are we stopping first, by the way?' Lucy asked, as Seda sat down again, crossing one slim leg neatly over the other.

'Cleopatra's Bay. Beautiful water there for swimming.'

'Will you be snorkelling today?'

'Oh yes. Later, when everyone is settled into a routine, though I only learnt how to do it last year. I find nice shells sometimes. Just small ones I take, and put them in my bedroom at home.'

With Lucy's promptings, Seda went on to tell her that she lived with her brother in a flat in Ortaca, the large town that the coach had driven through. He worked through the winter season as a builder, but it was too hot for building in the summer. She worked the summer season as a tour guide, so that way they covered the rent. When Lucy asked why she didn't live in Dalyan, Seda explained that local people couldn't really afford to live there and Ortaca had all the facilities, plenty of shops, supermarkets and a university. Also buildings could be higher than the two storey limit that Dalyan had. Ortaca had a bigger population to build for and foreigners wanted to buy property there too.

Trish stirred herself. 'Everyone back home is wanting a place in the sun these days,' she murmured to Lucy. 'There are villa and flat complexes springing up everywhere here. They're very reasonable you see.'

'How reasonable?' Rhea butted in.

'Oh well, from looking in the estate agents windows in Dalyan, I'd say you could pick up a nice villa for around 55K.'

Rhea and Lucy gaped at each other.

'But let's face it. It's only retired people that can afford to come over here to stay permanently. You know, like Gill, the gallery owner I introduced you to,' Trish said to Lucy.

'Oh, wouldn't that be lovely,' Lucy mused. 'I'd love to live in Dalyan. I just love the delta reed beds, the tombs and the river, and the beach. And I'd be bound to see a turtle eventually. And the nature is wonderful. Charlie and I could grow so many tender varieties of plants, that wouldn't die off in the winter. We could grow exotics. And we could get a boat too.'

'It rains for months in the winter, though,' Trish said.

'What's a bit of rain? I could get back to my painting…' She paused. 'I could read books, I could study something new by open learning. Charlie could go back to his ceramics and build up stock for the tourist trade…'

Rhea joined in. 'I could have a Turkish bath every day, I could swim in my own pool, I could…' She fell silent. 'Oh, what's the point. It's just a fantasy.'

'Well, I get to live here from April to September,' Trish continued. 'This is my fourth season here and I love it. I much prefer it to Spain and Greece, and the people we get coming here are much nicer too. I get on with the two girls I share a villa with, and we have our own pool. Mind you, it's not all rosy, we work very long hours.'

'So, what do you do in the winter?' Lucy asked.

Oh well, you can go home and work in one of the travel offices, but I haven't done that for a few years now. Or you can get work with another travel group in a ski resort and work the seasons back to back. Last year I went to Sauze d'Oulux in the Italian alps. It was great fun.

There were some really dishy skiing instructors too.'

'Don't you ever go home?' Rhea asked.

Trish's face fell. 'Manchester. No, not much. My Dad never approved of my job. I applied for it and left home when I was eighteen. Mum was okay about it and we write to each other, so she lets me know what's going on in the family. I'm an auntie now, my sister's recently had a baby. I just don't know where all the years have gone to.'

'Ever think of settling down?' Rhea said.

Trish grinned. 'Get married, you mean? There have been a couple of nearly serious relationships with other tour reps, but the job makes it difficult. There's no guarantee of getting the same resorts. And there have been plenty of Mr. Wrongs. The local men just tend to want flings, and of course you're not of the same culture. But I love the life. Sometimes I feel I'm getting too old, but as long as you're fit, you can keep going for as long as you like, can't you? In fact, they're encouraging older people to apply these days. They say they have useful life skills.'

'Now there's a thought,' Lucy said.

'Oh here, I nearly forgot. I've got that map you might like to use for your jeep hire day.' Trish rummaged in her beach bag and handed a folded bit of photocopy paper to Lucy. 'Sorry, it's all I've got, but it's accurate. It shows you the route around Köyceğiz lake or you can go south into the hills and down to Asi Bay, like I suggested.'

'Thanks, Trish. That's just great. We'll probably go to Asi Bay, won't we, Rhea? Because Rhea went around the lake on Hasim's motorbike.'

Rhea turned her head and fixed her dark shades upon Lucy, like the compound eyes of a beetle.

'What? He took you for a bike ride?' Trish exclaimed to Rhea.

'Yes,' replied Rhea from behind her shades, not moving an inch.

'He's never taken me for one,' Trish said, with her high-pitched giggle.

237

'And why would he?' asked Rhea slowly.

'Oh, I've always liked him. I get to chat to him about the visitors that are booked in, but he's always managed to avoid taking it any further. You should be careful you know, I don't think he's the type to get serious.'

'Maybe I'm not either.'

'Oh well, I'm just saying. It's really none of my business.'

Rhea raised herself a little and propped her head on her fist. '*Shirley Valentine* - is that what you mean?'

'Well...now you mention it, I suppose so, yes.'

'Well, it can work both ways, can't it?'

As the boat ploughed on, the conversation evaporated like water from a desert canyon creek-bed. The hot sun lay on the deck, and the slumbering bodies basked in the heat like lizards in the Sahara. After more stretching of limbs and more slumbering, the boat slowed up and anchored off the shore of a bay of ruins. The walls were partially submerged in crystal aquamarine waters and lush pines crowded the shoreline, some of their branches bowing over the water under the weight of their hoards of cones.

Seda announced they were at their first stop: Cleopatra's Baths. The fine sand was said to have been brought from Africa by Anthony to prove his love. The existing ruins were actually those of a medieval Greek monastery. Snorkelling gear was available in the stern, or people could simply swim. They should be careful not to graze themselves on the walls and there was a shower hose on the platform on the stern for getting rid of the sea salt afterwards. They had about 45 minutes.

Lucy looked enquiringly at Rhea, who nodded. Tucking their sunglasses inside their hats, and leaving their hats on top of their cushions, they hobbled over the burning boards of the deck to the stern, with Lucy clutching the snorkelling gear. Brian and June brushed by Rhea, headed into the cockpit and rummaged in the drinks cooler. Lucy helped to select a mask for Rhea, and she clipped on the snorkel she had bought for her. She demonstrated to Rhea how to spit on the mask to stop it fogging up and how to breath in through her nose when putting it on to get a good seal. Rhea found some fins that fitted, and Lucy told her she would hand them down to her when she was in the water. Soon they were both ready to descend the ladder.

Rhea lowered herself slowly, inch by inch, into the cool dark water, grimacing, while Lucy waited.

'Come on, Rhea,' she said. 'People are waiting.'

Rhea frowned at her through her mask, her eyes round and staring like a googly-eyed goldfish.

Lucy giggled. 'Here,' she said, handing down the fins.

Rhea struggled to put them on one at a time, holding on to the ladder, first with one hand, then the other. Finally, she was free of the boat, upright and treading water.

Lucy scrambled down the ladder to join her, shrieking at the change in temperature. Soon she was treading water too. Other people were descending, so Lucy and Rhea swam further along the side of the hull, with Rhea doing a strange kind of breaststroke.

'Right,' Lucy said. 'You tip onto your front, arms by the side of your body, and floppy ankle leg motion to move forward. Breath in and out through the tube, not your nose. If water comes down the tube, you'll just feel there is no air to breath, so you rise up a little so the snorkel clears the waterline, then you can get air again. Okay?'

Rhea nodded.

'Oh, and watch out for sea urchins. Don't sit on them or touch them. They look like dark brown spiky blobs on rocks - okay? Ray warned me about them. If you stay in the shallows you'll feel safe enough, and you can always stand on a slab of rock in the water if you need a break.'

'Okay.'

'Oh, and there's no point doing breaststroke legs when

you want to swim, just keep them together and do a long kick, it's called a dolphin kick.'

'Okay.'

'Oh, and look up now and again to get your bearings - I'd stay close to the shore or near the boat if I were you. I'll keep an eye out for you. Okay?

'Okay.'

They plugged in their mouthpieces, and floating on their tummies, they drifted away from each other.

***

Rhea was nervous. Ever since her mother drowned, and ever since those awful swimming lessons with her father, she'd never put her face in the water. But she'd decided to try snorkelling, because you could stay on the surface and you could see where you were going and what was underneath. And so far, she was discovering, it was actually not too bad. So far, so good. At least she was facing her fear; her head was in the water. She was looking down through her mask, into the still blue, bobbing around a little in the swell of the tide with the hush of surf in her ears. She was astonished at how calm it all seemed below the surface. She couldn't see much, just dark blue depths, so she looked up into the blurring ripples at eye-level and spotted a few swimming bodies around the shoreline. She started snorkelling towards them, moving from the indigo blue into the turquoise calm. The sound of her own breathing in and out bothered her. It was as if her oxygen supply was going to be cut off at any minute. But after it wasn't, and after a while, she became accustomed to the sound and she made sure to keep her breathing regular. She started to feel safe; she was breathing air, the snorkel was behaving, and she found that propelling herself through the water was quite easy with the fins. Lucy had given her some good advice, she decided.

As she floated on through the cool and warm currents

240

that spiralled around her, fuzzy shapes became sharper. She saw a few reeds wiggling in the seabed like the tails of strange animals sticking their heads in the sand, and she saw massive boulders dappled with flashes of light, and batches of cylindrical green and yellow jellies glued to the stone. She saw dark crevices and shady niches where she decided that creatures with pincers might be lying in wait. So, she moved away and came to the crumbling walls of the ruins, laid out in grids like an underwater city and spot-lit by rays of sunshine. She was well within her own depth now and felt totally relaxed. Finding a broad section of wall to sit on, she got into a comfortable position, and brought her upper body out of the water. She pushed her mask onto the top of her head, unplugged her mouthpiece and gazed around. The boat looked so far away, but she felt safe because she could see the other swimmers, though she couldn't make out Lucy at all. Maybe she was trying to go right down beneath the surface like she said she was going to do - those handstand dives, as she called them.

She looked up into the branches of an pendant pine close by her, its clutches of needles trailing in the water like fingers, its upper cones parting the sky. She realised how close to the shore she was. And suddenly she heard them.

They were everywhere.

Whistling and fizzing, hissing and sizzling in the heat. Invisible sound. So loud. Cicada beetles. And they pelted Rhea's eardrums like raindrops hammering on a tin roof in a thunderstorm. They echoed louder and louder, mocking her and taunting her, like some kind of grotesque applause. Why do they bother me so much? she wondered frantically. It was unnerving - like the call of the Imam, only far worse. It was a horrible sound. And deep down inside her she felt accused. And the past swelled up. Her mother. Her father. Wouldn't there ever be any peace? And she'd had her ring taken away. She clamped her hands over her ears and gaped at the trees on the rocky shore and the nearby hanging branches. But there was nothing to see, nothing to see for all that sound. She dragged her mask back over her face, the stretch of the rubber strap tugging at her hair and making her wince. She plugged in her mouthpiece and moved off, face down, snorkelling away with her ears submerged, blocking out the chorus of chaos.

A few frantic moments later, she found herself surrounded by legs, kicking around, thrashing around, like shark bait in a *Jaws* film. She moved through them and past them, picking up speed, out of her depth, towards the boat. She needed to get back. She threshed her fins through the water, and her breath wheezed in and out of the snorkel faster and faster. Then there was a sudden thud against her shoulder. It hurt. Someone had bashed into her. Someone wearing a mask and snorkel like herself. Someone with a ponytail of dark streaming seaweed hair. Lucy.

Rhea forced her head up, yanked out her mouthpiece, only to find herself gagging on mouthful of saltwater. She spat it out, spluttering and coughing.

'Sorry,' Lucy said, removing her mouthpiece and beaming at her. Her eyes were magnified through her mask like bottle-bottom lenses. 'How was it? I kept an eye on you. Did you have a good time?'

'It was okay,' Rhea gasped. All she wanted to do was get back to the boat. Get back to her sunbathing. Read her novel. There would be no more snorkelling today. She would tell Lucy that later on.

'Just okay? How can you say it was just okay? You seemed to be getting along very well. Surely you must have found it amazing! I mean, it really is wonderful, don't you think? Did you hear the cicadas? The goats' bells on the shore? It's a beautiful place. Why didn't you enjoy it? Why?'

'It was nice, Lucy. And you explained very well what to do, so I've met the challenge. I've just had enough for now,' she said, furiously treading water. Here we go, she thought. I'm being probed to explain, pressed to justify myself, pressed to spill my guts all over the place and wallow around in pointless feeling, and I'm not even back on the boat.

Lucy looked disappointedly at her. 'Well?'

'Well what?'

'Aren't you going to ask how I got on? I've only really snorkelled at the swimming baths, you know.'

'Can't it wait until we get back?' Then she saw Lucy's mouth tighten. 'Okay, how did you get on?'

Lucy's eyes started to shine. 'Oh, it was amazing, Rhea. I loved it. The colours, the light! I kept practicing plunging my arms down and following with my body, and dolphin kicking, and suddenly I found myself a few metres down. Just like that! I was able to touch the rocks, and some of the sea plants. I followed some fish. You just have to control your breathing. That teaching Dad gave us on breath control has really come in handy after all this time.'

'Good. He'd have been pleased, then. Now let's get back. Look, people are going over to the ladder now and Seda's waving to us.'

Sunbathing, she thought, lunch then sunbathing. It was all she wanted to do now. They swam together, back to the dark hull of the boat, as solid and stationary in the sea to Rhea as a monolith on dry land.

***

Rhea showered on the platform, while Lucy sorted out the gear, having vowed she wasn't going to shower because she wanted to keep the salt of the sea on her skin. Then they made their way to the bow, their noses led by the savoury aroma of meat being grilled in the galley.

But they both halted when they saw the spread of cushions. Their hats and bags were still reserving their beds, but the spare cushions next to them were now occupied.

'Oh God, no,' breathed Lucy, her head swivelling swiftly to examine Rhea.

'The prune on sticks and the walrus.' Rhea glowered, giving them a level stare. 'They've done this on purpose.'

'Oh, not necessarily,' Lucy said, chewing her lip. 'They're entitled to sunbathe.' Then she paused, whilst she and Rhea huddled together on the lower deck. 'What do you want to do?'

Rhea's face tightened. 'Well, I'm not going to move somewhere else. And I don't intend to get into any conversation. I would appreciate it if you didn't either.'

'Okay. I'll try.'

'Try hard, will you?'

Just then, Trish appeared from behind them and gave a sharp intake of breath when she saw June and Brian. 'Are we moving?'

'No,' Rhea and Lucy snapped together.

As she ship sailed on, Rhea and Trish topped up their sun protection and arranged their limbs back into their bathing beauty poses - extended legs, pointed toes, arched backs, being blow-dried by a light breeze.

***

But Lucy felt tense. She made a quick effort to slap some lotion onto her salt-gritted arms, neck and shoulders to avoid burning, then she sat in her half-lotus again. But she discovered that this preferred position of hers was actually difficult to sustain at the age of 43 without getting cramp, and after wearing her fins, a couple of her toes were going into spasm. So she flexed the pain out of them, and decided she'd have to recline too - and be just like everybody else.

But why was everyone being so quiet? And the sea was suddenly so calm. There was hardly any wind. Then an image flashed into her mind and she couldn't help chuckling. It was just like that scene in 'The Rime of the Ancient Mariner', where the sailor kills the albatross and the ship is stuck - *As idle as a painted ship Upon a painted ocean*. She'd always loved that line. And Lucy knew who had put the curse upon the Deniz Kizi. June was lying right beside her.

But so far, so good. Rhea was reading *Pride and Passion*; that seemed safe enough for the moment. Trish appeared to be snoozing behind her shades and Seda was reading some brochures. Lucy looked sideways at June, whose wrinkles were protected a little too late in the day perhaps by her chiffon cover-up of overblown roses, which lifted and flapped around her cinnamon stick legs. She appeared to be sunbathing, but Lucy felt disturbed by the inscrutable smirk on her face, which seemed to hint at some purpose deeper than the superficial calm. Brian was alongside her, looking like a strange species of giant blowfish without the spines. With his arms folded behind his head, he seemed proud of his metamorphosis.

So, with everyone apparently behaving, without June or Rhea making trouble, Lucy lay back on her sunbed and closed her eyes. Reaching for her sunglasses, to tone down the vermillion red behind her eyelids to a crimson glow, she tried to relax. But all she could think about was June. June, who lay right beside her. June the psychic, who had promised not to say anything, who had promised to keep her distance. Well, she wasn't keeping her distance, was she? She turned her head to check on June. She'd broken one promise already. Would she break the other one? Would she say anything about their meeting, about the tarot reading? If Rhea found out, she'd never understand and it would wreck all their progress. They would be doomed like the ship's crew in The Ancient Mariner.

As soon as Seda announced they were approaching the next stop before lunch, Lucy nudged Rhea. 'Fancy another dip to cool off?' If she left Rhea alone with June, who

245

knew what would happen?

'No thanks. I'm staying here. I'm not sure I'll go in again, actually,' Rhea said behind her shades.

'What? But there will be so many stops! And you've got on fine with the snorkelling. You can't be serious!'

'Shhhh,' Rhea hissed, looking sideways at the recumbent June. 'Keep your voice down.' Then she sighed. 'Look, Lucy. I appreciate you teaching me to snorkel. But to be honest, I can't stand the sound of those cicadas on the shore.'

'What!' Lucy gasped. 'But that's so silly…they're so tropical, so atmospheric, so…' she trailed off, as Rhea lowered her shades and shot her a look. 'Well, at least think about doing it this afternoon,' Lucy continued. 'Can't you just swim? You might get very hot if you don't.'

'Okay. I might swim around the boat. Now, you go on and enjoy yourself.'

Lucy lowered her voice to a whisper. 'Will you be alright?' She looked across at June.

'Yes, of course. I can handle *her*. Anyway, I've got my book to read.'

When the swimmers got back on the boat, lunch was ready. It was set out on the lower deck under shade. A long row of tables were assembled together, with canvas strung chairs to sit on. Lucy and Rhea chose some seats nearest the stern, while Trish and Seda sat opposite them. But to Lucy's horror, June pushed past Brian and took the seat right next to her, so she had June on her left and Rhea on her right. Rhea raised her eyebrows at Lucy, then shook her head. June gave Lucy one of her puppet smiles, while Seda and Trish wore worried frowns. And Lucy sat there wondering when the curse of the Deniz Kizi was going to start playing out.

Brian sat opposite June, grinning and rubbing his hands together. 'I'm ready for me grub.'

The crew served the food, which comprised of grilled chicken, wild rice, Turkish meatballs and salad. It looked and smelled delicious, and was served with fruit juice and mineral water. Wine was extra, so Rhea ordered a bottle of white for the four of them to share.

But Brian had a problem. 'There's no chips, Juju,' Brian said, looking perplexed. 'I've got to have me chips. What sort of a meal do you call it without chips?' He sat back, folding his arms across his chest, and flexed his snake tattoos, which wriggled on the rising swell of his stomach. He called across to one of the deck hands, 'Where's the chips, mate?'

'Sorry, sir.' The young sailor shrugged his shoulders.

'Well, I never,' he said to June. 'For crying out bloody loud.'

'Just do without them this once, pet. There's plenty to tuck into.'

'But it's not the same without chips,' Brian said, plunging his fork into a meatball.

Soon everyone was munching and there were sounds of murmured approval from all. Brian had second helpings, then third helpings, and June looked on approvingly, as he shovelled forkful after forkful into his mouth, emitting loud belches, which were presumably intended as compliments to the chef.

'My Brian can eat like a horse,' June said to Lucy. 'I do like a man to have a decent appetite.'

Lucy made no reply. She didn't want to get into conversation with June. Who knew where that would lead? For once she knew she had to keep her mouth shut.

There was plenty of chatting going on between two couples and a family group at the other end of the table, but Lucy, Rhea, Trish and Seda were sitting and eating in silence. Meanwhile, the fruit cocktail was being served.

'Are you enjoying staying at the Onur?' Trish asked eventually, addressing June.

'Oo yes, luv,' June gushed. 'It's one of the best in

247

Turkey we've ever stayed in, isn't it Brian? Ever so clean. The rooms are champion. And the pool views! And that pink and white borjonvilla around the edge and trailing over the balconies – ee, well.'

'It's pronounced bougain-villea, actually,' Rhea said, turning her head to look at June. Lucy saw the sharp look in her sister's eyes stab into June as she made the correction. And she turned to see June's mouth snapping shut and drawing itself into a straight line. Oh God, she groaned inwardly. June was hurt. What would she do now?

'Yes, well, that's great,' Trish said hurriedly to June. 'That's very nice feedback. I'll pass it on,' she said, with her lipstick smile stretched like rubber to its widest limits.

Seda stared into her bowl of fruit, pushing a slice of melon around.

Silence resumed while the group ate their fresh fruit and Rhea decided to have second helpings.

Then it came. June nudged Lucy's elbow. 'See what I mean about Taureans?' She gestured towards Rhea, her snubbed nose in the air. 'They like their food, just like Brian here does. And I told you about her aura, all that red, grey and black, all that anger and blocked energy. It's worse today.'

'*What* did you say?' Rhea asked June.

Oh, my God, here we go, thought Lucy. Please no. June had tossed their secret into the conversation like a hot coal and now it was to burst into flames.

'Are you referring to me?' Rhea said incredulously to June. 'How do you know I'm a Taurus? And what's all this crap about auras?' Then she looked at Lucy, and her mouth fell open. 'Have you actually been talking about me to this woman?'

'Oh dear. I'm ever so sorry, pet,' June said to Lucy. Lucy thought she saw the smirk again. There it was. The curse.

'What have you been talking about? Tell me!' Rhea spat

248

her words out at Lucy, while Trish and Seda shifted around in their seats, exchanging glances.

'Easy luv, calm down,' Brian said. 'You don't half get yourself worked up. First the ring, now this. For crying out loud like. Talk about Mrs Menopause.'

Rhea glared back at him. 'It's got nothing to do with you. And absolutely nothing to do with the menopause, which, by the way, is a highly sexist remark. You should mind your own bloody business.'

Lucy scowled at June. Why had she betrayed her trust? What was she thinking? She looked down into her lap, unable to reply to Rhea. She just couldn't bear to look her in the face.

'There's no need to get all het up, luv,' June said to Rhea. 'I was just having a chat with Lucy, here, yesterday. At home, I do people's charts, I see auras and do tarot readings. I gave your sister a free reading the other day.' She looked beseechingly at Lucy. 'It's all best out in the open, luv, there's a lot of healing needed. Brian pet, pass me a fag, will you?'

'What have you been talking about to this woman?' Rhea asked Lucy again, her voice rising to a high pitch.

But Lucy still couldn't reply. She felt like a naughty child, who had done something so unforgivable, it would never be forgotten, and it would be trotted out for the rest of her life to keep her in line. She needed Charlie, but he wasn't here. She felt like running away, feeling the wind in her hair. But on a boat, there was nowhere to run. She felt tears stinging. How could she explain to Rhea the need to talk to June? The need to try a reading, just in case anything helped, absolutely anything to help her understand what had gone wrong in their childhood. And to help Rhea and herself become better sisters and fulfil their father's wish. Maybe even help herself move on with her art. The cards had seemed to be right in so many respects. And all she could think about now, was what the cards had said, and how she had to be the Lord of Valour, and keep her nerve. She blinked away her tears. She wasn't a naughty child. She was a grown woman with a mind of her own and a right to have her questions answered.

***

As Rhea sat staring at Lucy, a rising heat sweated up through her and into her face. It made her feel so much worse, so self-conscious. She hoped she wasn't actually having a hot flush. That blasted Brian and his comment. She took a few swallows from her wine glass, but the sweating lingered. She felt angry. Betrayed. And embarrassed for causing a scene. Why do my emotions keep getting the better of me on this holiday? she asked herself desperately. Maybe the menopause is on its way? Well, she had her plans to tackle that, to keep the store running efficiently. She made an effort to straighten up and look composed. She had to let the issue drop now, for her own sake, and for Trish and Seda, who kept looking out to sea. But why *had* Lucy been having private conversations with June of all people? June, who had stolen her ring? Where was Lucy's loyalty? Her own sister had betrayed her. And a tarot reading of all things. They were just tricks and kidology. But that was just typical of Lucy and her new age dabblings. Just like their mother. And as for June, she was sitting there smoking her cigarette as if butter wouldn't melt - the prune on sticks, with trickles of butter slithering down her. Her dummy's face was trying to look crestfallen, while spewing out her smoke from between her wrinkled puckered lips. Well, she wasn't fooling anyone. And Rhea suddenly ached for a cigarette herself. She's seen a packet spill out of Trish's bag earlier. Maybe she'd ask her for one. To hell with not smoking in public.

'Well, dears,' June said, stubbing out her cigarette, and pushing back her chair, 'You two have some healing to do.

Siblings often have different versions of a life, you know. And then there was the death of your mother, reaching for magnolia blossom like that - so tragic. But she's watching over you. You'll get there.'

Rhea went rigid. She felt a chill in her bones.

'June, that's enough!' Lucy glared at her.

'I'm sorry, pet, but you'll thank me later on,' June said, patting Lucy's shoulder. 'Come on Brian, we'll go and get our stuff from the bow. It's too hot for us up there. I don't want you catching sunburn.'

Rhea's mind fluttered a little after June and Brian had gone, but she still felt as if the life had been swatted out of her.

'Don't let that awful woman get to you,' Trish said.

'Just stay away from her,' Seda offered, looking upset. 'Don't let her spoil your day.'

Rhea nodded. No more scenes, she inwardly chanted. No more scenes. But she would have to talk to Lucy. Discussing their private business with June wasn't on. Lucy had betrayed her.

Back on the bow, as the ship sailed on, Rhea puffed on a cigarette she had borrowed from Trish, flicking the embers into an ash tray supplied by the captain. She sat sedately with her legs tucked under her, while Lucy sat alongside her fiddling with the rose petals on her hat. Trish and Seda had stayed behind on the stern at one of the dining tables. They said they needed to do some planning for a few trips that were coming up in the next few days, but Rhea knew they were just being considerate.

Lucy broke the silence first. 'Look, Rhea, I'm sorry about talking to June. But I do have a right to talk to whoever I want. Our past isn't something protected by the official secrets act, is it?'

'No. But to her of all people! She took my ring. She's the last person who I would want knowing any of our business, and it seems that, thanks to you, she knows plenty about it now!' Rhea tried to keep her voice from rising. 'How the hell could you?' She glared at Lucy. 'And this must have been yesterday you got together. Did you know she was coming on this trip?' Lucy must have known, she thought, yes, she must have known, yet she'd said nothing. Another betrayal.

'Well yes, she mentioned it after the reading. Oh, don't look at me like that! I didn't see any point in telling you - it would just spoil the day for you. And if there is a battle going on between you and her, then she'd have won a point if you hadn't come, wouldn't she?'

Clever, Rhea decided. Yes, that's a clever argument. A point conceded to Lucy there. 'You still should have told me. I don't feel I can trust you now.' She was surprised to feel a pain pulsing in her breast.

'Yes, I know that's how you must feel. I understand that. But the fact is that I am your sister and you can trust me. But it works both ways you know.' Lucy looked hard at Rhea.

Rhea was struggling again. What did Lucy mean? That Lucy couldn't trust her? Well, there were reasons for that, reasons that she was beginning to question. Was it worth it? Did she care anymore? She'd asked her father in the hospital whether she could tell Lucy everything. But his consent had been unclear and she had been left to fester - on Prozac. Peace perhaps for him, but not for her.

Back to June. That was the point here. 'She'll be a complete charlatan you know.'

'Not necessarily. The card reading did seem to have something to it. Actually it seemed to suggest there's something hidden -'

'Shut up, Lucy. I don't want to know!' She felt like slapping her. If Lucy was going to start spouting rubbish the prune on sticks had come out with, she felt she'd explode. 'She's bound to be a fake. People like her read people's reactions, pick up little clues. They manipulate. They prey on the vulnerable. And she landed you like a fish - you fell right into her hands.'

'Now, hang on a minute! I'm no more vulnerable than you *actually*. And at least I explore my feelings. You just lock yours up. You always did. Well, that's your choice, I suppose. But I've always been curious. And I like to be open minded. There's nothing wrong with that. You're so stubborn, you'd cling to a sinking raft in a storm. Not exactly brave that, is it?' Lucy said sarcastically. 'I can't explore my feelings or the past with you, because you won't talk to me. The mission of this holiday is to get to know each other better, to make up for the past. That does mean we have to work at it, you know!' Lucy glared at Rhea, then fell silent. 'Anyway, she knew your star sign, and she got mine right too. How do you explain that?' Lucy flung her hat down.

Rhea thought hard. 'Well, maybe she saw our dates of birth somehow. Maybe on some paperwork of Trish's? Maybe Brian created a diversion when they were making their booking, so she could root through a pile of paperwork and find us.'

Lucy frowned and shook her head. 'You make them sound like professional spies. It's hardly likely. Anyway, what would their motive be?'

'Well, maybe they get their kicks out of stirring up things between people and they targeted us. I wouldn't put anything past them. You always insist on thinking the best of people. There are lots of weirdos around, you know.'

Just then Seda came up. 'Sorry to bother you,' she said shyly. 'But I thought you would like to know we're having a swim-stop and the crew have set up a diving board on the stern. Then we go on to Tersane Island.'

'Thanks, Seda,' they said.

'The diving board sounds fun,' added Lucy.

They waited for Seda to be out of earshot.

'I don't like the way you always treat me like I'm a silly little idiot,' Lucy said. 'I didn't tell June much at all. And I

253

was wary of her. But you just presumed as usual. She asked how our mother had died and I told her what I knew, which as it turns out isn't much at all. That's it, as far as personal information is concerned. And it's pretty obvious we don't get on very well. I told her that too. She said you had a dark aura, that you were guarding against something and that you have a lack of forgiveness for something.' Lucy sighed. 'Anyway, I've had enough of this. Everyone is going for a swim again. I'm going to see if I can jump in this time.'

Rhea watched Lucy get down off her cushion and stalk over to the stern to where the diving board was. She felt heat simmer through her body again. This time it started steaming and boiling. How dare that woman suggest such things about her aura, about her personality? How dare she? She was evil. And how dare Lucy start telling her what she'd said in the reading? As if she'd ever want to know. Lucy, making out there was no harm in it. All that wittering, pushing and squeezing, all that analysing, all that probing. All that betrayal. And she'd been their mother's favourite. The boiling bubbled over and she stamped over to Lucy. Past Seda and Trish, past June and Brian, past the other holiday makers who were fiddling about with masks and fins.

Lucy was standing at the far end of the diving board, staring down. The board creaked as Rhea mounted it behind her.

Lucy turned around. 'Oh, it's you. You're not going to give it a try too, are you? It looks a bit deep for you.'

Rhea took another couple of steps towards her. The board shuddered under her feet but she didn't care.

Her voice shook and her heart pounded. 'Well, I'll help you find out, shall I? I bet your aura was all bright and glowing, wasn't it? All hunky dory there!' She found herself yelling at Lucy.

And she rushed at Lucy and shoved her hard.

Lucy toppled backwards off the end of the diving

board, limbs flying down into the sea. Such a long way down. There was a loud shriek and a crash, and the sea swallowed her up. She was finally knocked off her perch.

Rhea felt she could breathe again.

But a few comments from onlookers shattered the peaceful silence, though their words were indistinguishable.

Time stretched as she stood at the end of the board, peering down into the dark water, trying to see white arms reaching for the light, or glimpses of a dark blue swimming costume.

But there was nothing. Just a few trails of foam popping their fizz after Lucy's entry. Rhea broke out in a cold sweat this time.

'Oh, my God!' she cried. 'Quick!....Help! Help! she screamed, her cries searing her eardrums. Reality loomed over her now, pointing a fat finger, judging her, accusing her, about to give final sentence: you've just pushed your own sister overboard, your only sister, you've killed her. Precious Lucy, who always had to be protected. *You're the sensible one*, her mother always said, *you need to look after her sometimes*. Well, she had, hadn't she? For so long, in her own way. *Why spread the hurt around?* her father said back then, *she's better off not knowing. She's too young to understand*. And that was over thirty years ago now.

The burly family man hurried up behind Rhea and he peered down. 'She *can* swim, can't she?'

'Of course she can swim! I wouldn't…I'd never have done it otherwise!' Rhea heard herself babbling, tears squeezing themselves out.

'Look,' he said. 'There she is! She's fine. See?' He put his arm around Rhea.

Lucy's head surfaced, her hair slicked down over her face. She pushed it out of her eyes, and sculled with her arms. Her face was alive with wonder. 'Oh, my God, that was amazing!' she exclaimed. 'It's okay,' she said to her audience, after looking at Rhea, 'we're always messing around like this.'

There was a chorus of giggles from the line up of faces leaning over the side of the boat.

But Rhea felt paralysed. Her heart had lifted with relief and now it sank like a rock. It was just so typical. Lucy had actually enjoyed it. And now she'd be jumping off the board all afternoon like a manic lemming throwing itself off the same cliff over and over again. No doubt all the others would join in.

'Rhea.' A female voice alongside her sounded concerned. 'Come into the shade and have apple tea. The boat will empty soon, when we stop at the island. Everyone will go for a look.'

Rhea turned. It was Seda. She gathered herself. 'Good idea. Thanks, Seda. That's a very good idea.'

***

When Lucy had found herself plunging down into the cold shock of the sea, she was afraid. How deep would she go? She had soon found out. It seemed like a long way down and everything became cool, dark, still. Would she be able to get back up? She had no fins to help her. In front of her, she could see her precious breath escaping in a stream of silver balloons. Calm, she said to herself. I've got to stay calm. I've just being pushed into the deep end of the swimming pool, that's all. Remember those lessons with Dad? So she started kicking with her legs, and reaching with her arms, angling her body towards the light she could see flickering far above. She pushed the sea down and away. Again and again. As long as she could get herself moving up and let out as few silver balloons as possible, she'd be just fine. Just like she'd practiced all those years ago.

And it started to work. She was rising into the shafts of sunlight, directed down like torch beams to find her, and she relaxed a little. Rhea had pushed her in and she had learned a new skill. After all, she'd have jumped in anyway, she reasoned. By the time she broke the surface, and saw the sky, she felt exhilarated and wanted to do it all over again.

When she rubbed the salt from her eyes, she saw the faces above. They all looked so serious. She glanced at Rhea, frozen to the spot on the diving board. Her sister, who had pushed her in, because she, Lucy, had pressed one too many of her buttons and had wound her up to a snapping point. She had hurt Rhea, Rhea had retaliated, though she felt shocked at the depth of her anger, the force with which Rhea had pushed her - she wouldn't forget that. And she realised it could have been serious; the fear she felt when she first entered the water had told her that. She noticed Brian gaping at Rhea and shaking his head, and June beside him, nose in the air with a tight smile of triumph. So she called up to reassure those who were concerned, and to save Rhea any further embarrassment, which she felt she owed her. She made out that they were in the sisterly habit of tussles and tantrums, which was the truth in relation to their teenage years, but which had somehow tracked them into their mature adulthood and marched into this holiday. They were simply an example of not acting their age, and therefore an undeniably bad example to the children on board.

***

Rhea's hand trembled as she held her apple tea. Beads of sweat were running down the outside of the plastic cup, making it slip in her grip. She could hear the screams coming from those who had chosen to follow Lucy's example. Of course, the family man's teenagers were making the most of it, competing to see who could make the loudest scream, the biggest splash.

'Are you feeling better now?' Seda asked.

Rhea nodded. She was willing herself to feel better.

Even though she felt like a wrung-out chamois leather left to dry and stiffen in the sun. She decided she'd stay on board when everyone got off at the next island. She'd read her book. That was all she wanted to do now, recuperate with time to think, or perhaps not to think, if she could manage it. *Pride and Passion* would help.

Lucy appeared, towelling her hair.

Seda got up from the chair next to Rhea's saying she was going to have a look and see if she could spot any flying fish. Lucy sat next to Rhea. Lucy reached out her hand, but Rhea saw the gesture and pulled back. No touching, no hugs thank you, and she looked away.

'I'm sorry, Rhea. I know I hurt you by talking to June.'

Rhea felt confused over the apology. She hadn't been expecting it. 'Isn't it me who should be apologising?' She gazed out to sea. No bird this time to take her thoughts away.

Lucy shrugged her shoulders.

Do I feel sorry? Rhea wondered. Yes and no; the same old problem. 'Well, anyway, thanks for making light of it to the others.' She turned to look at Lucy. 'But I don't want to have anything else to do with that woman and her husband on this holiday. And I don't want you telling them any more of our business. Just stay away from them.'

'Of course, I will. Anyway, I think you're right. June's certainly been playing games. I'll stay a little friendly, though. If she's got your ring, it might be useful.'

'I suppose so.' Rhea needed to change the subject and she felt curious. 'What was it like, really? Being pushed in like that?'

'Oh well, scary at first. It felt like a long way down. But once I remembered what Dad taught us, I got on fine after that. You did me a favour really. Something else I can do now, and I enjoyed it. Maybe I'll try diving next.'

Irrepressible, Rhea thought. Always had been. Always seemed to bounce like a rubber ball. Maybe that was why she'd been their mother's favourite? And yet, not quite so bouncy these days, not with her artist's angst. That had come as a surprise. Not so bouncy after all.

'Look, Lucy. I just want to read my book for the rest of the trip now. Okay?'

'Oh well, yes, I suppose so.'

Just then Trish came up to them. 'My goodness. You two know how to put on a show, don't you? Are you both alright?'

They nodded.

'Come!' called Seda, who appeared with a pair of binoculars slung around her neck. 'Come look at some fish flying!'

Guests gathered next to Seda on the bow. The captain came up with another set of binoculars for people to pass around.

Rhea peered through Seda's binoculars at the ocean surf. Silver flashes thrashing their tails through the sea to leap into the air with fan-shaped fins outstretched like wings, leaving wakes of white behind them. Fast gliding, long gliding, they fell, then beating their tails they rose again, and again.

Seda explained they did this to escape predators. They were very lucky to be seeing them.

'Let me see,' Lucy said, trying to take the binoculars from Rhea.

But Rhea held onto them. She found she couldn't take her eyes off the fish, who were turning now like birds in flight. All too soon they were far away on the horizon. They'd escaped. They were free.

The afternoon went quickly for Rhea as the time gaps between the remaining island stops became shorter and shorter, as the count headed towards twelve. She was left to herself, as Lucy made the most of her opportunity for snorkelling, with Seda and Trish joining in. Rhea decided that Lucy was obviously in her element, as she was in hers - sunbathing and reading *Pride and Passion*.

Jacques had become incensed by Madelaine's attitude towards him: she was flouncing her frills around his cabin, when he was trying to study his maps; she was showing him up in front of his crew, who kept warning him it was unlucky to have a woman on board; and she was treating him like a common thug. So he'd lost his temper and felt compelled to reveal he was a privateer, with government sanction, rather than a lawless pirate. He'd been hired by her uncle and guardian (the Governor of Barbados) to take her to Martinique for an arranged marriage to the Comte de Mélac, an unscrupulous villain by all accounts. Her uncle would receive a significant reward, and the count would receive her considerable dowry, whilst gaining political influence. Her life was actually in his own hands. Maybe she should be more grateful? Madelaine retreated to her cabin in shock. He left her to stew.

As Rhea read on, she wondered how she and Lucy were to get through the next few days, which were bound to be awkward after today. But she forced herself back into the plot. With the sea lapping against the hull of the Deniz Kizi, it was a perfect setting to read her novel in, and it shouldn't be wasted in worry.

***

After leaving the boat to explore Tersane island and trip along dusty goat tracks to take pictures of the views, Lucy became despondent. She had so much to think about and couldn't concentrate in the heat. So, she decided to spend the remaining stops just snorkelling around the boat wherever it lay at anchor.

Circling the dark hull felt predatory, as if she was a shark, razor finned with intent. The green stillness, the shadows. It fitted her mood. Rhea had pushed her with such force, there was such anger behind it. Why did Rhea, deep down, seem to hate her so much?

Once again, it seemed to have something to do with

talking about their mother's death. She'd got upset on the coach trip, when June had been asking questions, when she saw the gold chain, the one like their mother had. She never wanted to discuss their mother or her death and their dad hadn't either. And after she died, her and Rhea's relationship had become very bad, yet Rhea had flatly denied this. But Lucy remembered Rhea's scathing remarks from that time, and far worse, being ignored altogether. It had been real. And Rhea had always treated her like a silly little idiot and it was still happening now.

It can't go on like this, she vowed.

She remembered June saying about her mother's death *That's all you know. Well, I'll leave that with you, then.* And it was true, she didn't know much. Just that her father had found her. And she was shocked by the look of horror on Rhea's face when June said their mother was watching over them. What was so wrong with that?

And then there was the tarot reading. Well, June might well be a manipulative poodle-haired Rumpelstiltskin, but the cards had seemed to be hitting the mark. And if they were, there was trickery in the past, Rhea's darkly-guarded aura. The Lord of Valour was needed to fight the competition, open up communication for the Empress of potential, for the feminine, for sisterhood, even for their mother perhaps. And even if June was a total fake, it all still felt so right.

I've got to find a way of pinning her down, she decided. In a place where she can't escape. Just the two of us, stranded somewhere. And she thought of the jeep trip. Into the hills, with Trish's map. The narrow winding road to Asi Bay. And Rhea couldn't refuse, because she'd already been around the lake. Tit for tat, just like always. She'd think of a way to get them stranded somehow, so that Rhea couldn't just drive off. And she'd force Rhea to tell her the truth. All she had to do was make sure that relations between them were kept reasonable until then, so Rhea wouldn't back out. There were three days until the jeep trip on Tuesday. So until then, it was probably best to keep out of each other's way. Three days was plenty of time to come up with a perfect plan.

11

Where Hides Sleep?

That night and the next three days were fraught with escalating tensions.

After the cruise, Lucy and Rhea bickered more than usual, and sharing a room was becoming increasingly difficult. The only thing they managed to agree on was to keep the rumbling air conditioning switched off when trying to go to sleep.

Lucy was feeling the heat and was sunburnt from not being vigilant enough on the cruise. Her back was the worst area from all the snorkelling she'd done. She wanted the balcony door kept open in the vain hope that some cool breezes might drift in, but Rhea wanted it closed to keep the mosquitoes out, and to shut out the sound of cicadas she was certain she could hear. Lucy reluctantly surrendered. But when Rhea lit up her evening cigarette, Lucy insisted she take it outside. Rhea conceded this point and went down to the pool area, relieved to be sharing her musings with what turned out to be only crickets chirping in the shrubs.

By this time in the holiday, they had got used to some of the practicalities of sharing a room and had been negotiating them with great care. Bathroom privacy was the highest priority - at no point, and for any reason, could one sister walk in on the other. They were also not allowed to watch each other changing or shaving their legs. Seeing each other's bodies 'up close and personal' after all this time was simply out of the question.

There was a territorial borderline between their beds, and those which divided the dressing table, drawers and wardrobe in half. Rhea's side of the room was nearest the door and bathroom, and she was keeping it in trim like an Elizabethan knot garden, whilst Lucy's side, next to the balcony, was more Gertrude Jekyll, all luscious growth and full of surprises. They had automatically adopted this approach from their experience of sharing a room when they were girls, an experiment to see how they got along, said George at the time. They had managed, back then, to make it work for about a whole year, before their respective territories were bombed and invaded, when they flung each other's clothes and cuddly toys all over the floor. As a result of numerous fights, Lucy's teddy bear, unsurprisingly called Ted, had needed one of his eyes gluing back on, but the blonde hair of Rhea's Barbie doll could never grow back after Lucy had hacked it short. And so Lucy had to be relegated back to her box room. Shortly afterwards, the family moved to a larger house, where a big bedroom each, meant they could establish an uneasy truce in what was to be the family home for the rest of their teenage years.

Sleeping had always being difficult during that year they shared a room, due to Lucy being a light sleeper. She would be just stretching towards the edge of oblivion when an already fast-asleep Rhea would start making breathing noises. This would snap Lucy back into a coiled spring. Her retaliation would be to ring a small hand bell, a brass lady with a crinoline skirt, that she kept by her bedside, to wake up a furious Rhea, and the precarious process would begin all over again.

And of course nothing had changed on this holiday, except that Lucy, with no bell to hand, had to resort to coughing. They'd both been reading in bed, but Rhea had been falling asleep first and Lucy had been left trying to block out those same sounds. When this happened at home with Charlie, she would drag her weary body into the heavenly silence of the spare room. But there was no escape here.

As Lucy lay in bed now, reading Hasim's book about Dalyan, the events of the day felt as raw as the skin on her back. She wished Charlie was here to talk things over with, as she certainly couldn't talk to Rhea, lying in the adjacent bed. And reading about fishing, fruit growing and farming couldn't hold Lucy's attention long before she was thinking about her shared past with Rhea, their mother and their father, and her need for a plan. But her mind was tired, and as she kept reading the same paragraph over and over again, trying to focus on the words, her limbs felt heavy from all her physical exertions and she started to feel a rocking motion, as if she was still at sea. She gave into it, drifting and floating, just below the surface of consciousness.

The book fell out of her grip and she sank deeper, and soon she was in another place: she was on her way to somewhere, but she didn't know where. All she knew was that there wasn't much time. She carried a large wooden stake on her shoulder. But something was slowing her down as she tried to move forward. Her legs were wading through treacle. No wait - it was more like tar. The effort to take one step after the other was immense, the pulling and dragging of each leg. She longed to free them. Her upper body strained forward but her feet held her back, as heavy as lead. She felt frantic because she was running out of time. It's no good, she thought, I'm not going to make it! Everything was in slow motion, as she became more and more distressed. She woke up with her heart thudding.

She staggered out of bed to get a glass of water, relieved to find she could move her legs again. Rhea was still awake reading *Pride and Passion*.

'You know, you were breathing rather loudly yourself,' Rhea said.

'Yes, well, I don't have to listen to myself, do I?' Lucy retorted, settling her head back on her pillow. 'We haven't talked about how to spend the next three days yet. We've got the jeep trip on Tuesday, but what should we do until then?'

Rhea reached into her bedside drawer for her notebook to consult their timetable. 'Well, the Dalyan Saturday market is on tomorrow. Maybe Eleanor might like to go. We can call on her and see. And as for the rest of the time, I'm quite happy by the pool.'

'Yes, well, that's pretty predictable.'

Then Lucy bit her lip. Careful, she thought. Go easy. It would be best to give each other space to avoid any rows before the jeep trip. 'But whatever you like,' she added. 'And we can invite Eleanor to dinner again. I'll go back to the turtle beach. I love it there.'

She stuffed a pair of ear plugs into her ears, which she had taken to using as a last resort, switched off her reading light, and turned away from Rhea to face the balcony.

'Okay,' Rhea said, yawning. 'That's decided, then.'

***

As Lucy dozed once again, Rhea carried on reading her novel.

Jacques and Madelaine were feigning indifference to one another, but secretly studying each other with sideways glances and surreptitious stares. Madelaine was fighting a passionate attraction for this brooding privateer hired to kidnap her, whilst Jacques was beginning to feel unable to hand her over to the Comte. But what was he to do with this woman, who he felt so stirred by? She was so wilful, so obstinate. And his crew were right, a ship was no place for a woman. Deciding he needed some diversion from his dilemma, he set anchor off the coast of St Vincent and led his men in a little free enterprise on the shore. But in a skirmish with the local Caribs, he received an arrow wound to his chest and was rowed back to the ship by his distraught men.

As the Sea Sprite lay at anchor for a few days, with no air to swell its sails, it was as if the wind was holding its breath for Jacques. His bleeding was stemmed, but the wound became infected and he fell into a fever. His life was in mortal danger. Could the beautiful Madelaine help him? Would she help him?

Rhea put the book down, deciding she'd reached a suitable point in the plot for a break. She turned off her light and strained to see if she could hear any cicada. Mercifully, there was just the sound of some Turkish music coming from a distant house or hotel, its notes rising and falling like those of a snake charmer. Seduced by the sounds of flutes and lutes and the insistent beat of the drums, she imagined herself belly dancing barefoot in a gold spangled skirt she'd seen in Fethiye market, her arms, neckline and hips tinkling with coins. She danced to her own choreography, with a series of hip thrusts, lifts and drops, shimmies and slides. She undulated her arms, hands poised with parted fingers. Encircling the third finger of her right hand was her pink kunzite ring. Then, turning and spinning around and around in a blur of silk and chiffon….she spun herself into a cocoon of sleep.

All too soon, she was somewhere else: she was drifting in water, staring at the seabed. Flickering lights danced on the sand, slabs of smooth rock shelved in from the shore. But suddenly there was a problem. She couldn't breathe. Bubbles of air escaped from her mouth. She couldn't hold them in. She gasped, and her mouth filled with water. Her lungs were expanding, bursting with pain. Then she saw the face of her mother, her blonde hair streaming behind her. Rhea tried to scream, but her mouth was filling with water. Inside she was exploding…she couldn't stand any more. She couldn't face what was to come.

She woke up in a sweat, tears burning like acid, relieved to see the hotel room again.

She flung aside the cotton sheet, but the heat of the

room was suffocating.

I'm not supposed to have that dream any more, she thought. How long is it going to take to get rid of it? It's Lucy's fault, for making me go snorkelling. It's brought it back again. It's just so typical of her to interfere.

But then she remembered what she'd done to Lucy, pushing her into the sea. Such a shocking thing to do. So maybe the dream was linked to the fright she'd given herself. After all, despite their father's attempts, a fear of drowning was hardly surprising after what had happened to their mother. But of course Lucy hadn't been affected. Oh no, and it was just typical. She lay in the dark thinking about the day's events, trying to put everything back into its proper place.

But it was too much of a jumble, so she got up and went into the tiny bathroom, switching on the light and blinking at herself in the wall mirror in the overhead glare. She stared into the mirror as if she hadn't met herself for a while. Did she have a dark aura? Was she still the same Rhea? She peered into it further and felt a surge of relief. There were no poisonous black rays emanating from her. There were just the same even features, the same level gaze, just a little knot of a question mark in her forehead, and that was hardly surprising.

So, she gave herself a mental talking to, trying to undo the knot and sort the jumble. She would somehow get her revenge upon June and get her ring back. Lucy had betrayed her trust by talking about their personal life to June, and she'd probably never forgive her for it, but June was a manipulative woman and Lucy was easily led. Lucy was going to keep June on side to keep the enemy close. Yes, she'd pushed Lucy into the sea, but she was going to jump in anyway, so it was hardly a big deal. On the plus side, she was going to get more time to herself in the next few days. Eleanor had turned out to be great company, despite first impressions, and Lucy had stopped asking questions. Chris was leaving her alone, *and* she and Hasim had kissed. She smiled at herself at the memory. And this time, she did see a glimpse in the mirror of a Rhea she didn't recognise.

***

At around 5am in the morning the sisters were roused by the Imam, sounding the call to prayer which rang out over the rooftops of Dalyan. Rhea clamped her pillow over her head, while Lucy took out her ear plugs and listened with a pensive look on her face. They dozed on until Rhea realised they were in danger of missing breakfast. She bagged the bathroom first, while Lucy got dressed, then they swapped over - a mutually convenient ritual they'd adopted from the first day.

When they got to the terrace restaurant they spotted June and Brian at a centre table, so they selected one by the terrace wall, Rhea sitting with her back to the couple. Hasim was helping with the breakfast and he gave Rhea a smile when he served their coffee.

'Thanks, Hasim,' Rhea said, smiling back at him.

'You're welcome,' he replied. 'Oh, here is Sadik coming to say good morning.'

Lucy turned to see Sadik trotting across. He came to Lucy's side and she gave him a scrap of bread and stroked his brow. He sat and looked up at her with his dreamy eyes.

Do you mind if I take him for a walk in the next couple of days?' she asked Hasim. 'We're not doing anything much until Tuesday.'

'Oh, no. He would like that. Just ask for him at reception.' Then he raised his eyebrows. 'No one has offered this before. It is good of you.'

'Oh, he can keep me company while Rhea's at the pool,' Lucy said. 'I've got some thinking to do.'

'What thinking?' Rhea asked, as Hasim left.

Lucy flushed and started coiling her hair. 'Oh, it's just

269

about my art, you know. What I'm going to do when we get back. I'm still stumped.'

Just then her attention was caught by June waving at her. 'Oh, no,' she muttered to Rhea. 'It's her. I'm going to wave back. Alright?'

Rhea grimaced, but nodded.

As they sipped their coffee, Lucy watched June and Brian from her vantage point opposite them.

'You know, they're not talking to each other at all,' she said. 'They're just sitting there, mechanically eating their breakfast. She tries to chat now and again, but you can tell he's not listening, and then she gives up.'

'Lots of couples can be like that. Not that I relish the comparison with the prune and the walrus, but I know Chris and I have got to that stage. And it always seems to be the woman who makes the effort,' Rhea replied. 'It's pretty typical, I'm afraid.'

'Oh, it's a stage is it? That's scary. I can't imagine Charlie and I getting to that *stage*. We've always got plenty to talk about.'

'Well, I can certainly imagine that *you've* got plenty to talk about,' Rhea said, smirking.

'There's no need for that. I've just got an enquiring mind, that's all.'

'Oh, whatever. Anyway, talk to her if you must. I want my ring back.'

The sisters hurried through the streets of Dalyan to the Villa Vita to see if Eleanor wanted to join them at the Saturday market. She explained she had a hair appointment, otherwise she would have just adored to come. Rhea proposed lunch for them all at the Pomegranate Cafe, but Lucy declined. She would borrow the villa's bike for the afternoon instead of going to the beach, and could practice being on the opposite side of the road for the jeep trip.

Lucy and Rhea worked their way back to the centre of

town, exchanged some currency at the post office and headed for the market, seemingly resigned to being in each other's company for the time being.

The sights, smells, sounds and heat had the spine-tingling familiarity of Fethiye market, so Rhea was in her element. She soon found a cream leather handbag she just had to have, and while she was checking how many compartments it had, Lucy bought some leather belts for Charlie and Poppy at full price, as she was unable to haggle. But Rhea's skills proved supreme. Despite the gesticulated protests of both the vendor and Lucy, and despite her putting down the bag and walking away to feign indifference, she held out for fifty percent of the starting price and won.

'You're robbing him!' Lucy exclaimed loudly, as Rhea handed over the cash. The vendor nodded in agreement, with a downcast face as he counted the money.

Rhea tugged Lucy away. 'Will you stop embarrassing me! It's what you're supposed to do! It's what they expect! Look, you'd better browse around on your own if you're going to behave like this. I can hardly haggle with you tutting and frowning like the sellers.'

'Yes, well, sorry for cramping your style! But it feels wrong. They've got to earn a living and haggling feels mean. I don't like it and I can't do it.'

'Well, is there anything else you actually want?'

'Not at the moment. I'm not in the mood now - funnily enough!'

'Well, will you leave me alone to get on with it, then?'

'Oh well, that's charming! Yes, I'd be happy to leave you to it. I don't want to witness any more of your moral degradation.' She paused. 'I suppose I'll see you at dinner, then. Try and get Eleanor to come, won't you.'

'Yes, I certainly will,' Rhea replied, her eyes already pinned to some masterly imitation of designer jeans.

***

271

While Rhea and Eleanor were having lunch, Lucy grabbed some sandwiches and tried cycling around Dalyan, choosing to have a look at the newly built hotel complexes. But after half an hour of dodging mopeds, with the riders not caring which side of the road they were on, and after she found the seat was set too low for her height, and when the sweat started dripping off her brow so she couldn't even think straight, she returned the bike to the Villa Vita, thumping it back against the wall in disgust and decided that taking Sadik for a walk was a better proposition.

As she sauntered along the riverside path, Sadik made an ideal companion. On the lead, he kept perfectly in step with her stride, just stopping now and again to snuffle by a palm tree to see if he fancied doing any business. Lucy managed to deflect selling attempts from the restaurants and boat companies, with a 'maybe later' response, that surprised her by being reasonably effective. As she followed the river upstream towards the outskirts of the town, the restaurants became sparser, the cricket song denser amongst the straggly vegetation and trees.

Just as she was wondering if the path went all the way to Lake Köyceğiz, she noticed a small square jetty down to the left of the path. It was scattered with cushions and kelims, and the overhanging fringe of its raffia roof stirred in a light breeze. Right on the river, it was framed by overhanging willows, which trailed their leaves in the water like the indolent gesture of a girl being punted down an Oxford river by a besotted admirer. A couple of rowing boats were tethered alongside the jetty in the stands of rushes.

Lucy found she couldn't pass this place by. It was so exotic. It could be anywhere. If she sat there, she could imagine she was in Thailand or Burma, perhaps taking respite from a long river trip, then going on a backpacking expedition into the hills to a meditation retreat, to find some much needed enlightenment. Or maybe she was travelling on the Irrawaddy river to the Bagan plains where hundreds of ancient ruined Buddhist temples and pagodas dotted the horizon for mile upon mile, just waiting to be explored, like in the picture in a travel magazine she'd once torn out and kept. And as these images burned bright in Lucy's imagination, she decided she just had to sit on this jetty, regardless of whether it was allowed or not.

As she and Sadik settled themselves on the cushions, to Lucy's relief a waiter appeared. It seemed this jetty belonged to a hotel hidden through the trees. So she ordered a white wine, and as she watched the green river slide past the cliffside of the opposite bank, she thought hard about the jeep trip into the hills, and how she was going to make sure that they were temporarily stranded – temporarily, being the difficult aspect to solve, as they'd still need to get back to Dalyan. She ran her thoughts past Sadik, who eyed her approvingly, and she stayed on the jetty with him for the rest of the afternoon - totally in her element.

***

Rhea and Eleanor had an indulgent feast at the Pomegranate Cafe. Rhea enjoyed a Mediterranean ploughman's platter, while Eleanor had a dish of tuna fish, roasted peppers and sweetcorn. They progressed to a slice of lemon curd tart and cream. All this was washed down with a couple of lattes.

Rhea's sorrows over being unable to buy the jeans because she couldn't try them on, were quickly soothed by Eleanor's American accent and her topics of conversation, the smooth drawn-out tones somehow conferring convincing assurance upon the content. She talked more about 'Diva Designs', about her flagging marriage, and about her purchases on holiday to date, and how she was just loving the shopping. Rhea told her about Lucy's tarot reading with June.

'That woman gives me the heebie jeebies,' Eleanor said. 'She's always twitching her head around, checking everything out. As for what she gets up to - well nothing would surprise me. Did your sister believe all her hocus pocus? Lucy doesn't strike me as a pushover.'

'Well, sometimes she can be. It would probably depend on whether it suited one of her theories. She drives me nuts sometimes.'

'Oh, well, I guess artists are allowed to be a little zany, huh? Makes 'em interesting.'

Rhea lapsed into silence, while she acknowledged to herself that she had always been determined never to find Lucy interesting.

Eleanor suggested they 'go Dutch' for the meal, then they could take a look around the gallery.

As they entered the cavern of delights, they were both captivated by the internal layout which invited customers into interesting corners, and they both agreed this was an excellent way to display different collections of merchandise. They smiled approvingly at the spiral staircase, sure to lure visitors upstairs.

'Real nice space you have here,' Eleanor said to the lady in black sitting at the desk.

She received only a nod from Gill, the owner.

'What's with her?' Eleanor whispered to Rhea. 'You wouldn't get that in the States.'

'You wouldn't get that at Neal's either,' replied Rhea.

The first thing they examined were the paintings - the seascapes, rock tombs and village scenes that had drawn Lucy's eye, then the cityscapes of Istanbul. Eleanor was attracted by a vista of minarets for 350 lire, painted in soft pastels, compared to those hung elsewhere which were exploding with colour.

'That's real pretty, don't you think? And a good price. I might buy that later on. It would go great in my living room above my white marble fireplace. It would match my decor - I'm not one for garish colours.'

'Mmm,' Rhea replied. 'More cool classic chic, eh?'

'That's me, honey.' She paused. 'What kind of painting does Lucy do? I suppose you buy her work for your place?'

Rhea hesitated, trying to remember what Lucy's art was like. 'She does landscapes,' she said, with a tone intended to end the line of enquiry and so fend off Eleanor discovering she knew very little about Lucy's paintings.

'In what media?'

Rhea groaned inwardly. 'I think she uses a variety.'

'Do you have any of her work?'

Rhea hastily thought of a suitable answer. 'No, actually. Her taste is very different to mine.'

'Oh,' Eleanor's eyes widened. 'Well, can't she paint something to your subject taste, in colours of your choice?'

'Mmm. Well, I don't think it works like that. Doesn't the artist have to be true to themselves, somehow? Their style and subject, their choice of colours?'

'Not in my book, honey. It's customer satisfaction that should count, and market trends of course, if they want to be serious about selling. Commissions should be done to suit the customer.'

Rhea was surprised to feel a twinge of sympathy for Lucy, like a single string of a violin being plucked. These attitudes of Eleanor's were what Lucy had been talking about - do you paint for yourself, or for the market? She pondered further, remembering Lucy's look of frustration and the tears in her eyes, as she'd told her on the turtle beach about her predicament. But Rhea was determined there would be no full violin piece played for Lucy.

She and Eleanor went on to examine the Iznik pottery, which Eleanor had already bought a few choice pieces of in Fethiye market. They both gasped when they came to the jewellery. Their nail-polished fingertips feverishly flickered over the rings, earrings and necklaces. This was high class artisan jewellery of twisted metal wire, beading and precious stones. As they held up item after item, posing the jewellery on their necklines, earlobes and fingers, they consulted each other, and finally settled on one piece each. Eleanor chose a pair of brass wire chandelier earrings, threaded with turquoise and ruby red agate beads. They made a bold and elegant statement against her red hair. Rhea settled on a gold-plated filigree necklace. Its interweaving leaf forms were set with fresh water pearls and rose pink quartz cabochons, the whole assemblage being suspended from a cluster of fine silver chains. She was treating herself, Rhea said, after losing her ring. And, she added inwardly, that if somehow she ever got her ring back, the necklace would make a lovely match.

As they left the gallery with their expensive purchases, finally receiving a curving up of the lips from Gill, they decided they'd meet back at the Villa Vita for poolside reflections.

That evening, Rhea, Lucy, and Eleanor had dinner at the Calyspo restaurant. Rhea noticed that Lucy said very little, as she and Eleanor described the gallery visit and their retail therapy, and she spent most of her time breaking up her bread and scattering it on the water, watching the rings and ripples fade in and out as the fish fed.

Rhea knew Lucy was excluding herself for a reason, but decided to leave her to get on with it. Maybe it was talking about the gallery? But they'd bought jewellery, not paintings.

Then Rhea stiffened as Eleanor asked Lucy about her painting.

'What sort of work do you do? Where do you sell it?'

Lucy scowled. 'I don't really want to talk about it,' she said. 'I'm in a kind of transition phase.'

'Lucy! There's no need to be rude,' said Rhea, feeling for her new friend, who was only trying to engage Lucy in what she assumed would be a favourite topic.

'I'm not being rude. I'm simply stating a fact. And by the way, don't talk to me like I'm a five year old.'

Rhea opened and shut her mouth, then looked at Eleanor. Would she understand?

'Oh, that's okay, hon,' Eleanor said to Lucy, leaning across the table and patting Lucy's hand. 'I guess new inspiration's needed, huh?'

***

That night Lucy couldn't sleep. The fact that Rhea had looked around the gallery with Eleanor, after refusing to look around it with herself at the beginning of the holiday was galling. Imagining Rhea and Eleanor chatting away over arts and crafts really irritated her, and she felt hurt. Why would Rhea take an interest all of a sudden? Obviously, she and Eleanor got on very well - in fact, *just* like sisters were supposed to. Just like herself and Rhea never had. *Of course she loves you,* her father used to say, *you're just different, that's all.*

Then a thought struck her, like a slap in the face. Why am I bothering? she asked herself. To fulfil Dad's wish? Well, I've tried my hardest, haven't I? And what exactly has *she* done? Well, on the jetty, she'd finally come up with a plan to address it, and only Sadik knew the details. She didn't have anything to lose now.

She switched on her light and grabbed Hasim's book in the hope that it would lull her to sleep.

***

Meanwhile Rhea wasn't getting much sleep either. Lucy's cold shoulder routine was a new development and she wasn't sure how to handle it. She'd asked her what was wrong with little response. Just tired, she said. This, from Lucy, was unprecedented. Lucy, who always said exactly what was on her mind, who was always analysing herself and everyone else within a five mile radius.

She felt some itching on her lower legs. She switched on her light and threw back the cotton sheet. There were some blotches around her ankles and calves, blemishing her smooth tanned skin like red ink blots on parchment.

'I've been bitten!' she exclaimed, fingering the swollen areas.

Lucy roused herself to have a look. She peered at Rhea's legs. 'Didn't you spray yourself today?'

'Yes, of course I did. But you keep opening the balcony doors.'

'Oh, so it's my fault, is it?'

'Well, what else can it be?'

'Wasn't your cigarette smoke supposed to keep them away?'

Rhea glared at Lucy.

'Maybe you got them by the river,' Lucy continued. 'Maybe they wanted to suck your blood, regardless of the spray. You were always a bit more susceptible to bites, like Mum was. Remember those midge bites you both used to get, every time we went to Scotland? Something similar in your blood, Dad used to say.'

'I don't think so. I don't remember that.'

'No. You don't remember anything, do you?'

Rhea tried to ignore the sarcasm. 'Well, never mind that. Have we got anything for bites?'

'No. That was one thing I *didn't* get when I was getting in *our* supplies. I suppose you could go and ask at reception.'

Rhea fell silent. She didn't relish going down to reception in her thin silky wrap which barely covered her, and with no make-up on, in case Hasim was there. And it didn't look as if Lucy would do her any favours right now. Her tone had been decidedly malevolent - another distinctly new development.

Suddenly, Lucy sighed, jumped out of bed and threw a

bottle of talcum powder at Rhea. It landed with a thud on her mattress. 'Here. That might help.'

'Thanks,' Rhea replied tersely, sprinkling the powder over her legs and rubbing it in.

It was, however, of little use, and the throbbing itches kept her awake until the early hours. She remembered what Hasim had said to them about mosquito bites, how they were like *little kisses in the night*. If only, she groaned. She'd just started to deepen her doze, when the prayer song of the Imam jerked her awake. Her immediate repulsion was like the shocked response to the crude insistence of a vintage alarm clock, with a twin-belled rattling ringtone, screaming out a new day has begun.

***

Lucy and Rhea didn't have much to say to each other at breakfast, after another night of poor sleep, and there was no sign of Hasim or Sadik to relieve the monotony of mood. Rhea asked the waiter, and was told Hasim had gone on a business trip and wouldn't be back until Tuesday night.

Also afflicted were June and Brian at their usual table. It looked all round as if the rot was setting into the holiday, like spots of mould in pots of preserved apricots, where the juicy succulence is laced with poison. Lucy waved at June, and she waved back, but June carried on eating her Turkish sausage and boiled eggs with a tight-lipped grinding. Brian was slouched by the breakfast bar, while a member of staff was making him his third omelette.

There were two days to go before Tuesday's jeep trip, so Rhea and Lucy discussed what they intended to do. Rhea declared she was happy to spend time shopping with Eleanor and sunbathing at her villa - it was the kind of relaxing holiday she'd originally had in mind. Lucy stated that it wasn't exactly in the spirit of the holiday, which was for them to do things together, and that they were in danger of losing the plot.

Rhea squirmed in her seat. 'But we have plenty of time left, and we probably need a break from each other after the sailing trip, don't you think?'

'I suppose so,' Lucy replied in clipped tones, as she poured herself another coffee. She didn't offer Rhea one. 'Well, we'll have the whole of Tuesday together. So, in the meantime, I'll go to the beach, swim and snorkel. But we should still meet up for dinner.'

'Yes, of course.'

Just then, June and Brian passed by their table to leave the terrace. June was wearing three gold chains around her neck, including the one that she'd bought at the gold centre, which looped down under the neckline of her dress. She fondled it where it was exposed on her reedy neck. Her thin mouth twisted into a sneer at Rhea, then she jerked her head and twitched her curls at Lucy.

'Hello, pet. Still enjoying the holiday, I hope?'

'Yes, thanks. You?'

Brian had walked off as June lingered. 'Oh yes, luv! Of course! Best we've ever been on, this.'

Rhea shook her head as she watched June stalk after Brian. 'You know, if anyone's got the evil eye around here, it's that woman!'

The next two days passed as planned and the activities were entered on Rhea's timetable. This document was becoming recorded proof of their holiday and their sisterly efforts, in case there were any future allegations of doubt. Rhea said she'd send Lucy a copy when they got home.

On the Monday, Rhea and Eleanor shopped together, taking a day trip to Fethiye on the dolmus. They needed new stimulation, which they were quite sure thorough retail research would provide.

Lucy used the public boat from the riverside to enjoy the trip through the reed beds to the turtle beach at the western end. She had lunch, then sauntered down the beach to the east end and its headland, where she found rocks to snorkel around and more fish to follow. After exhausting the fish, she got the bus back to Dalyan, picked up Sadik for a walk to her special jetty, where she had a glass of wine before dinner. She repeated the exact same activities the following day.

On both evenings, they decided to have take-out by the pool at Eleanor's villa. Under the cover of darkness and its pinpricking of stars, the pool lights turned the water into the midnight blue of a sea cave, flooded by the low rays of the moon. Since swimming in the hotel pool after dark was forbidden, Lucy made the most of this opportunity, gliding silently underwater with her fins on, like a manta ray confined in an aquarium, while Rhea and Eleanor gossiped, prattled and debated the night away. The sisters made their way back to the hotel at around 10pm with little communication between them.

It was now Monday night, the night before the jeep trip into the hills and down to Asi Bay. Despite packing up their bags for the next day, and agreeing together what to take with them, including two 2.5 L bottles of water, just in case they ran into any difficulties, the tension between them was as taut as over-stretched warp threads on a loom, threatening to snap.

Rhea felt a little nauseous after her doner kebab and Lucy said she was shattered after all her swimming, which rankled as she'd assumed she was pretty fit.

'Well, you're obviously not as fit as you thought you were,' Rhea said, from the balcony, her mouth setting hard around her last cigarette of the day.

'Well, I'm a dammed sight fitter than you!' Lucy replied, slamming the balcony door shut on Rhea, to stop the smoke getting into the room.

But the stale miasma of the smoke lingered and hung over them, like the lack of trust that had developed between them since the sailing trip. It had sunk into their pores and each could smell it on the other.

***

While Lucy had her shower, Rhea settled herself in bed for some more reading. But she decided to take a break from *Pride and Passion*, so that she could relish reading the ending on the flight home. It would be a reward for having got through the holiday, together with some quality items from duty free.

Feeling tense about getting through another night, and the day to come, which she refused to think about right now, she noticed the book on Dalyan that Lucy had left on the side table between the two beds. She reached for it, and started flicking through the pages back and forth, idly browsing the content as if it was an out of date women's magazine from a doctor's surgery, rather than a rare socio-cultural work of reference, which Lucy was treating it as - as if its dilapidated state deserved cotton glove handling in a library archive. A piece of torn paper wafted to the floor and she realised she'd probably lost Lucy's place. She tutted, thinking she'd pick it up in a minute and insert it near the middle somewhere.

Searching for something to capture her attention, she ignored the history of Kaunos and aerial pictures of the reed beds of the estuary, wandering on to further ignore the fishing and farming. She halted when she came to the mud baths by Köyceğiz lake, staring at the pictures of people turned to clay by a full body dipping, and considered whether she wanted to bake herself in slurry to benefit from the mud's restorative mineral power. It was more Lucy's thing, but it might be worth considering for its anti-aging properties. She inspected the superstitions, what the evil eye really meant. She thought again of June, who certainly looked as if she had bad spirits lurking behind her glassy eyes, and decided, whether she believed in it or not, she might as well get herself a small evil eye pendant to bounce the badness back to its source.

Then she came to the back of the book and a double-spread aerial picture of the turtle beach.

But something unfamiliar caught her eye - totally out of context.

In a calm area of sea, something was hand written in large deliberate rounded loops, the kind of handwriting Rhea had never liked, the kind some clerical assistants use to persuade of unequivocal simplicity in life when we all know it certainly isn't. The big letters added insult to the content's injury: 'Hasim was a stallion last night'. Then a score was written alongside, expressed as a fraction: '10 out of 10'.

Rhea gasped. She felt a gripping in her stomach, that squeezed its way up to her heart, and before she could stop herself she shrieked out loud. Her eyes wavered, but she held the book rigid. There was more to come.

Below the first comment, there was another, in another's hand, careless and irregular compared to the first, as if the writer had been a little tipsy or worse for wear : 'I'd say more 9 out of 10.'

Rhea's breath hitched in her throat. She tried to turn herself to ice by producing an ironic laugh, thinking that perhaps their judgment was impaired at the time?

But there were more comments, more scores.

Bitter disappointment flooded through her, and before she could stop herself, hot tears scalded her cheeks. How could she have been so stupid? She was just like all the rest. Actually, she was worse. By beginning to take him seriously, by beginning to think there might be real affection as well as attraction. At least those women had just used him, as he used them. But, oh no. She had to think that she might be special. That she just might stand out from all the rest. He was a serial womaniser, just like the Greek in *Shirley Valentine*, seeing it as his mission to make women feel good about themselves. But now women played that game too - this book confirmed it. A book that was passed around from room to room, that had put itself about, just like him. This book was his ploy to be an engaging host. Was it some kind of selection tool? His accomplice? But if so, didn't he know what was written in the back? Even in these days of sexual equality, surely it would be likely to put the reader off. Well, wouldn't it?

She hurled the book to the floor, just before Lucy emerged from the bathroom in a cloud of steam.

'Did you say something? I thought I heard you,' she said, tugging on her wrap over her slip nightdress.

'No,' Rhea scowled at her, drawing her knees up to her chest under the cotton cover.

Lucy spotted the book spread-eagled on the floor between their beds, with the torn piece of paper alongside. 'What have you been doing? You've lost my place! That's just like you. No consideration at all!'

She bent down to pick it up.

Rhea sprang out of bed, shot out her arm, and snatched the book away from Lucy's grasp. One side of its hard cover was tightly clamped in her hand. The other side hung loose.

'What the hell are you doing? I'm reading that!' Lucy cried. 'It's mine! You've taken no interest in it whatsoever. Now you've had your little token look, give it back to me!'

'No!'

What do you mean, *no*? It's mine!'

Lucy grabbed hold of the loose side of the book, and tried to pull it out of Rhea's grip.

They both tugged hard.

'What's the matter with you? I can't believe you're doing this!' Lucy shouted. 'Give it to me!'

Rhea kept on pulling. The fragile spine started to split.

'Look what you're doing!' cried Lucy.

'I don't care about this stupid book,' Rhea panted.

'What the hell is the matter?'

There was a thumping on the wall from the adjacent

room and both sisters looked to where it was coming from, then at each other.

Rhea let go of the book. The thumping sound made her feel like a naughty child. Their father had sometimes done this when she and Lucy had shared a room, and Lucy had woken her up with her bell, when all hell broke loose in the middle of the night. 'It's right at the back,' she said, slumping onto her bed.

'What is?'

'You'll see.'

Lucy turned the pages, then gazed at the back cover. Her eyes widened as she read.

'Oh God!'

'Exactly.'

Lucy perched herself cross-legged on her bed opposite Rhea, with the book open in her lap. Here comes the analysis, thought Rhea.

'Well, it's not necessarily true - what it implies, I mean,' Lucy said, with open handed emphasis. 'It could have been made up.'

'I doubt it.'

'Well, let's say it's true. Why would he lend the book around with this written in the back?'

'Because he's got no idea it's there. Obviously.'

'Well, I still think it could be made up. It's not proof.'

'I think it is.'

'Well, even if it is, you said on the boat to Trish that you were under no illusions. That it could work both ways.'

'I know I did. I don't need the bloody reminder.'

'You really like him, don't you?'

'I don't know. But I don't like been played.'

'Well, he's not back until Tuesday night, so you can think about it. You could show him the book,' Lucy said earnestly.

'What? You must be joking!'

'Well, I'll show him, then. See what he says.'

'Don't be ridiculous, Lucy. Don't you dare! What's he supposed to say? He'll just deny it. Now, get rid of the thing. Take it back to reception, where it can help pick up another woman with a dodgy marriage.'

'But it's not the book's fault. I'm still reading it.'

'Oh no, you're not! I want that out of this room.'

'Oh, come on. That's just being silly.'

Rhea flinched at Lucy's accusation and a hot temper overcame her. She leapt to her feet, seized the book from Lucy's lap, stamped over to the balcony and yanked the door open. Stepping into the hot air, she flung the book out over the railing, where it fluttered its wings, trying to fly like a startled pheasant, then crashing through the trees and into the shrubs below.

'Rhea!' cried Lucy.

'There! It's out of the room and it's not coming back.'

There was a renewal of the thumping on the wall with the muffled cry, 'Cut it out, or we'll bloody well complain!'

After standing and staring at each other, with their hands thrust on their hips, they lapsed into silence.

Then Lucy said, 'Try to get some sleep. We've got a long day tomorrow and you need to forget about this for now.'

'I'm really not in the mood for a jeep trip now!'

'What?' Lucy's voice had an edge of hysteria. 'You've got to!'

Rhea made no reply.

Lucy calmed her tone. 'Look. We've not got long to go after that, just another four days after tomorrow, with Ephesus and the village life trips paid for. And this trip is booked and paid for and we have to go. It's what we've arranged and agreed on. This thing with Hasim can't get in the way of that. Not in the way of our holiday. Right?'

Rhea was silent, as she stared at the wall opposite.

'Right?' Lucy repeated, her voice rising again.

'Oh, for God's sake! Rhea sighed. 'I suppose so. But

right now, I'm having a glass of wine.' She stalked over to the minibar and pulled out a half-full bottle of white wine, tipping its contents into a large water beaker from the bathroom.

'Right,' Lucy said, slipping her feet into her sandals. 'I'm going to find the book and hand it in. We can't leave it sprawled all over the side of the swimming pool.'

***

Lucy quietly tiptoed downstairs in her wrap, and gliding through the back doors, she made her way outside to the pool area. Under the gaze of the moon, she found the book amongst the verbena bushes. Its spine was broken and it had fallen apart. She carefully picked up all the fragments, hard covers and bundles of pages, handling them with the respect she felt such a book that had survived for so long was due. She decided it would be insulting to leave it at reception in such a state, with no-one there at the moment to hand it to, or to receive sincere apologies. And anyway, she thought wryly, there were still some sections in it she could read when Rhea wasn't around. So she piled the remains together into a bundle and pressed them against her stomach beneath her wrap, intending to smuggle them into her side of their bedroom and hide them under her bed. All she had to do was accomplish this without Rhea noticing.

***

Meanwhile, Lucy's absence, and her working her way through the half-bottle of wine, had got Rhea thinking more clearly, or so it felt. This holiday had been a disaster. It had been a stupid idea from start to finish. The internal strain upon her, and the resistance she'd needed to maintain in the onslaught of Lucy's questions, had been intolerable, and she simply didn't deserve it. She had been loyal to her father, she had done her best, and she was still keeping their secret. But she'd had enough of Lucy, despite family supposedly being *everything*. The only thing that had refreshed her was Hasim. And now that was tainted, and she felt ridiculous not to have seen it coming. She'd made a complete fool of herself, and even worse, she'd shown herself up in front of Lucy. So, she'd had enough and she wanted to go home. Right now. She missed Rob, she needed to see him. She needed the familiar. She needed her work. She needed to get back to normal.

Rinsing out her wine beaker, she pulled on her wrap and crept downstairs to reception. It was as she hoped. No-one was there to notice her, and the guest computer terminal, situated in a discreet corner of the lobby, was vacant. Internet access was a free perk at the Onur, and Rhea decided to use it. If Lucy came by with the offending book, she'd say she was looking at images of Asi Bay, to try to get into the mood for tomorrow's trip.

Swiftly seating herself in front of the screen, and tucking her legs under the chair, she clicked onto the English language option and searched for flights from Dalaman to Newcastle, eventually finding an afternoon flight for the very next day. She sighed in relief. If she took it, there would be no jeep trip alone all day with Lucy, no more sharing a room, and she'd never have to see Hasim again. She could be the one that got away.

But as her fingers hovered over the keyboard like restless spiders, she was assailed by a countering batch of thoughts. She'd have to tell Lucy she was going home. There would be no jeep trip, and she'd have to tell her. Lucy would blow her top, she would huff and puff and blow the house down. She would tell everyone. She would say that, she, Rhea, had welched on their deal. She would blab. She would tell Seda and Trish. She'd probably tell June. She'd be sure to tell Eleanor. What would they all think? She cringed as she imagined their looks of shock, their shaking heads, their sorrowful looks of sympathy. Sympathy for Lucy. And for ever after, Lucy could say that, she, Rhea, was the one who didn't follow through their promise to their father. The holiday was the evidence Lucy could cite. Well, she couldn't have any of that. She wouldn't have any of that! And if that wasn't enough, she certainly would never stand a chance of getting her ring back.

She peeled her thighs off the sticky vinyl seat covering, glancing around for any signs of life, then retreated back upstairs, gritting her teeth as she contemplated the ordeal of a whole day of Lucy driving her around in the hills. But it had to be done. To rule out any difficult situations with Hasim, she would simply avoid him. He wasn't due back until tomorrow night. Apart from tomorrow morning, she'd purposely miss breakfast. Lucy could bring her some bread and jam, and handle any other practicalities that came up. After tomorrow, there would only be three more days, then the flight back home on Saturday. Collapsing back into bed, she turned off her bedside light. Her limbs ached with tiredness, and she hoped she could get to sleep by thinking of the flight home. She'd think of Newcastle from the air, as she'd last seen it - the sun setting on a circuit board layout of housing estates, factories and shopping centres, with the silver wire of the Tyne looping between. And the glint of millions of parked car roofs, like hers in a long-stay car park, ready, like electrons, to be sparked into life and pulse through the network of roads. This was the civilisation she needed. Safe inside her silver Ford Focus and on the way home to Leicester.

***

As Lucy made her way through the back door and across the marble foyer, she glanced over to reception, glad to see no-one was there. But she spotted a figure hunched in the

209

corner by the guest computer. Although the face was hidden, she recognised the blonde hair, the blue robe, enough visual clues to work out it was Rhea. She darted behind a large potted palm, luckily being able to see through the slats of the leaves. What was Rhea up to?

Lucy waited, watching Rhea bang the keys, tut to herself, and tug her fingers through her hair. Then she finally smiled. But why? As the minutes passed, Lucy felt silly for being in hiding, as if she was the bumbling Inspector Clouseau in a Pink Panther film. The theme tune suddenly popped into her head and she had to clamp her hand to her mouth to stifle a giggle.

Eventually, Rhea left. Lucy crept over to the computer, switched the internet back on and found the history button. She was expecting Rhea to have been checking her emails, something she'd already suspected her of doing over the last few days. But when she saw the page of flight times, her heart began to thump and pump, hard and fast. Had Rhea booked to go home early? Tomorrow? Was she going to wreck the holiday because of Hasim? As far as Lucy was concerned, that would destroy any future chance of them fulfilling their dad's wish. Back at home they would be sure to revert to the old avoidance routine. And more than that, this new development would destroy any chance that she might have of finding out what Rhea was hiding.

She sank into the computer chair to think, clutching the wrecked guide to Dalyan to her breast. Her fear now turned to a sweating anger as she thought of all her own efforts and tolerances with Rhea: a sister who preferred to look around a gallery with an American woman she hardly knew, rather than her own sister; who would talk and confide in this American rather than her own sister; Rhea, her sister, who had clearly never wanted a sister. Their dad would have to be disappointed, she vowed, wherever he was. She'd had enough. But the jeep trip must happen, she decided. Finding out the truth would be an important achievement. At least some sort of outcome for this holiday.

She climbed back upstairs, gently pushed the door open, and listened. She could only hear faint breathing noises. She quickly passed Rhea's bed and nudged the bundle of book fragments under her own bed with her foot, then she went into the bathroom.

Washing her hands with the worn slick of soap, she caught sight of herself in the mirror - dark hair hanging over her face, a sunken look under her eyes. Look what she's doing to me, she said to herself. No decent sleep for days, because of *her*. All the questions she needed to ask Rhea had been swimming around her head, like they had when she was snorkelling around the boat. They'd been keeping her awake as she'd been trying to get them into some kind of order. And then there was June's remark that had bred more doubts: *That's all you know. Well, I'll leave that with you, then*, she said. And even if June was a total fake, the seeds of doubt within Lucy's mind, somehow beneath the surface of her awareness since their father died, were now thoroughly planted, and she needed to tackle Rhea. But she needed an image to cling to in the meantime, images worked best because she was an artist. So, she saw the Lord of Valour in her mind, and she saw herself driving in the stake.

But how was she going to do that if Rhea got a flight home tomorrow? She narrowed her eyes in the bathroom mirror. You're not going to be defeated, she told herself, flicking back her hair. You'll track her to the airport and stop her, you'll make her tell you. Until you know what she's up to, you'll play it cool. Until you know what's she's going to do, stick to the plan.

She tiptoed back to bed, already knowing she still wouldn't sleep.

***

In the early hours of the morning, Rhea and Lucy were woken by the call to prayer. They shifted in their beds, too exhausted to react in their usual way. But an hour's reprieve later, a dog in a back street started barking. With relentless insistence, its deep cries alerted the inhabitants of Dalyan to coming dangers, like a drumbeat, its signal dragging the sisters into consciousness and out of bed to face the day.

PART THREE

12

Into The Hills

The jeep was red, not white as depicted in the brochure.

And when Lucy saw it, she felt a rising panic that things were not going to go according to plan. If this one detail wasn't right, what else could go wrong? But she gave herself a swift inner shake and recovered the strength of spirit she knew she was going to need for the day. It was 8am in the morning, she was frayed around the edges after another terrible night's sleep, but she'd improve later on and all would be well. Ever the optimist, Charlie always said. And what was wrong with that?

She and Rhea arranged their bags on the back seat, placing the two 2.5 L water bottles on the floor, and climbed into the front seats, Lucy behind the steering wheel on the left, Rhea on the right, clutching the map.

'Okay! Lucy said, her excitement mounting. 'Off we go!'

'Just take a few minutes to familiarise yourself with the controls, will you?' Rhea said, her back as rigid as a ramrod.

'I have done. And the most important thing is we have a full tank!'

She revved the gas, let out the clutch, and the jeep shot forward, throwing herself and Rhea into the snap of their seat belts. Rhea glared at her and Lucy suppressed a laugh. Then finding second gear, she eased the jeep slowly away from the Onur and down through the quiet street. Crossing a small roundabout, they headed south on the road to Iztuzu beach, on the first part of the journey to Asi Bay.

The air rippled as they began their ascent, passing villas with landscaped gardens and gleaming swimming pools, then local homesteads with their more disordered growth of vegetables and fruit trees. The road clung to a hillside of rocks, pines and scree on their left, with a view down to Dalyan on their right, which lay in the river valley in a haze of heat. As Dalyan simmered down below, in their open top jeep, Lucy and Rhea were buffeted by warm breezes blowing inland from the Mediterranean. Lucy had to keep holding onto her hat with the pink roses to avoid it being blown clean off.

Rhea clearly disapproved. 'Why did you choose to wear that?'

'It's my favourite.'

'It looks ridiculous in the jeep and it's not practical. You can't keep taking your hand off the steering wheel like that. We'll have an accident.'

'Okay,' Lucy said, whipping her hat off and tucking it under her seat. 'But I wish I had a long silk scarf to flutter out behind me.' She tossed her hair loose into the breeze.

'What? Like you're on the French Riviera, I suppose. Like some Hollywood starlet?'

Lucy grinned.

'Honestly, Lucy, you're so fanciful. Anyway, remember what happened to Isadora Duncan?'

'Well, that's so typically practical of you, isn't it? And look what you're wearing - combat trousers and a cap. Very practical, but you're not heading into the jungle you know. And you're no Demi Moore either. I mean, what are you expecting exactly? An ambush?' (But given the nature of what was going to happen, the irony of her own words did not escape her.)

'I'm *expecting* mosquitoes!' was Rhea's terse reply.

As they rose higher and picked up speed, the road hugged the cliffside of Sulungur Lake, and the magenta oleander bushes glowed in picture postcard harmony with the emerald green pines against a backdrop of saturated blue.

Lucy was feeling in control now and was enjoying the

wind beating through her hair. She found the jeep easy handling and was unfazed by on-coming vehicles passing her on the left with just inches to spare - she was also undeterred by Rhea's sharp intakes of breath. She kept leaning towards Rhea to glance down at the view of the lake, wishing she could stop to take photographs. And urged by the beauty of the scene below, she felt like being whimsical again and knew it would irritate Rhea.

'The pink oleanders were in bloom,' she said wistfully. 'Sounds like the first line of a novel, doesn't it?'

Rhea said nothing.

'Don't you think?'

'None like I've ever read.'

'Well, maybe Daphne du Maurier, then?'

Rhea was silent.

'Actually, I was going to ask you if I could borrow your *Pride and Passion,* to see what you like reading.'

'It's not your kind of thing.'

'Why not?'

'Too romantic.'

'I don't mind a bit of romance.'

Rhea turned and looked at Lucy. 'Look, you've made it pretty clear that you consider my reading material beneath you.'

'Well, I want to know what you like about it. How you can take it seriously.' Lucy switched into third gear with a flourish of her wrist and accelerated up another incline.

'I don't take it seriously. It's just a form of distraction.'

'Right. You don't enjoy it, then!' Lucy looked at Rhea over the top of her sunglasses. 'I'm sorry, but reading romance must mean you hanker after romance yourself.'

'Not necessarily.'

'But what about Hasim? If the comments in the Dalyan book are true, as you believe, look how you can't be dispassionate about it. You can't just see him as a bit of a good time, like those other women. It affects you emotionally, you obviously need it to mean something -

that's romance.'

Rhea reddened and scowled at her. 'Don't you start analyzing me! And leave that man out of it!' she snapped.

Just then, as Lucy was feeling a little flushed with guilt at the look of fury on Rhea's face, a beaten-up truck came around the corner in the middle of the road. Lucy veered sharply to the right, and a scatter of stones skittered down the hillside.

Rhea, who was closest to the edge, shrieked. 'Keep your eyes on the bloody road!'

'Okay, okay. Sorry!'

In the next ten minutes or so, as she took it steady, staying well on the right, and feeling confident with the gear changes, *and* as Rhea seemed to be relatively relaxed, Lucy started humming to herself The Pink Panther tune, which had stuck in her head from the previous evening. She was determined to enjoy what she could and everything was going well so far.

***

Rhea consulted the map again. She wasn't impressed by it. It was a black and white photocopy of a map of Köyceğiz Lake and the coastal area south of Dalyan, showing minor roads, tracks and contours, with hand-written locations scribbled on it. But she did manage to work out where they were.

'You need to ignore the next left turn which goes to Gökbel, stay on the beach road, then take a left onto a hairpin bend to get into the hills,' Rhea said, frowning at the map. 'You know, these tracks in the hills might not be drivable all the way. They go into dotted lines.'

'Oh, Rhea! That's why we're in a jeep! It's exciting!'

Rhea was feeling edgy as she reached for the small water bottle in her bag. Her legs ached, her head ached, her heart felt hammered by a series of blows, and the heaviest had been discovering the true nature of Hasim.

Lucy was winding her up, as if on purpose, and she had no idea why. Again, there was that slightly malevolent tone to her voice.

After she'd taken some deep gulps of tepid water which left a metallic aftertaste in her mouth, she heard the unmistakable sound of cicada beetles rehearsing their symphony in the trees by the roadside. She groaned, as she imagined them sucking on sap with their long proboscises and vibrating their disgusting little abdomens. What was it Trish had said? Symbols of resurrection and ecstasy? Well, she didn't believe in that. And of course it was the males that made all the noise, that got under your skin, just after they've shed their own skins. It was just typical.

The soft bodies of flies occasionally bashed against her cheeks, reorientating themselves to continue their flight, but many more unfortunates were hitting the windscreen and coming to a grisly end. Lucy's attempts to clean it by switching on the wiper blades resulted in them being smeared across the glass like spits of mucous.

'Just leave them alone. You're making it worse,' Rhea said.

'Okay, okay.'

The road snaked higher, and they came to a junction and took the left fork into a steep hairpin bend, followed by more twists and turns. They were travelling across country now, through denser pine and oak woodland, on a narrow tarmac road. There was no other traffic in sight.

Rhea found that the numerous cups of coffee she'd had at breakfast to try to wake herself up were taking their revenge, as she desperately needed to go to the loo. The burning was becoming unbearable. She cursed herself for not taking it into consideration.

'I need a pee,' she said.

'Oh well, I could do with one too,' Lucy replied. 'I'll pull over somewhere.'

'What? Out here?'

'Where else do you suggest? There's no-one around. Just go behind a tree. That's why they call it the call of nature.' She paused and glanced at Rhea. 'It's nice, anyway.'

'What do you mean - nice?'

'It's nice, *au naturel*, don't you think?'

'Well, I wouldn't know. I'm not in the habit of it.'

'No, I suppose not. I suppose you're a townie where you live, with plenty of public toilets in your landscaped parks.'

Rhea stared at Lucy. 'Well, you must be a country bumpkin, then. Does that mean you go anywhere you fancy? In any field or hedgerow you're passing? You just pull your knickers down and get on with it?'

Lucy pulled off the road, bringing the jeep to a halt in red dusty earth and scratchy roadside grasses. 'Oh, never mind. Just try it.'

As Rhea traipsed her way through the trees, carefully avoiding clumps of thistles, she was heartened to discover this was a cicada-free zone. There was the spicy smell of pine needles as she crushed them underfoot and an overhead canopy of branches dappled with cones, which provided some cooling shade. After selecting a tree and checking around it for snakes, she did the deed rather nervously, then stood up, took off her cap, and stared around her.

The trees disappeared into a thickness of quiet. Beams of stray sunlight filtered down between the slender trunks, holding tiny motes of life in suspension. It was such a contrast to the confines of the jeep and the roar of its engine. It was so peaceful here, just the piping of some songbirds, counterpointed by the low caws of crows, finally softening to make way for the solo drumming of a distant woodpecker, drilling its beak into a hollow trunk. Rhea wanted to follow that sound, to find the bird, to look up and see it winkling insects from the bark, then to hear the beat of its wings before settling for another feed, on another tree, to tap out its presence in the forest all over again.

But a different sound called to her, a shrill insistent tone that drove out all the rest. 'Rhea? Where *are* you?'

She sighed. Here she was in a special place, where she was just managing to forget about the trials of this holiday, and Lucy was going to drag her back to a dusty jeep gathering dead flies on the windscreen, to rough it on a remote bay with zero facilities. Why couldn't she be left in peace?

She strode towards the voice and came out on the road into the eye of the sun, tugging her cap back on.

'You shouldn't go wandering off,' Lucy said, clambering into the driving seat, sounding like a tyrannical teacher on a school nature trip. Then her mood shifted and she looked at Rhea. 'I take it you enjoyed the call of nature?'

'The woodland, yes.'

' It's beautiful, isn't it?' Lucy breathed, her hands poised on the steering wheel and gazing ahead. I think I'm going to have to stop to take pictures, you know.'

'If you must.'

'Yes, I must. I really must,' Lucy said dreamily.

***

The next hour was hard going. More uphill bends, and lots of clutch and low gear work for Lucy, with nothing to see but road, trees and sky. Lucy was inwardly worried that progress was too slow, that she'd miscalculated the timings, but when the jeep emerged onto a hilltop, she was able to relax. The woodland had given way to an arid chaparral landscape, speckled with snap-dry shrubs with the ultramarine blue of the sea beyond.

And Lucy had never seen anything like it before. She felt excitement pulse through her veins and she pulled over. She tried to sound nonchalant, not wanting to share her passion with Rhea and make herself vulnerable. 'It's downhill to the bay from here,' she said, 'but we should stop to appreciate this view.'

'There's supposed to be a radar station near here,' Rhea said squinting at the map. 'I think it was that dirt track to the right we passed just now. The view might be even better from there.'

'No, we'd better not,' Lucy said checking her watch. 'It's around eleven already. We need to get on.'

She had a few swallows of water, refilled her small bottle, then stood by the jeep, peering into the distance.

'What are you going to do now?' Rhea asked, with an edge of irritation.

The question pestered Lucy like a troublesome fly. 'I'm just looking,' she murmured, mentally swatting the fly away.

Something about this landscape felt so right. This struggling, stony land, where any plant she glanced at looked strange. She wandered into its twisted and stippled forms. Its heat hit the back of her throat and it felt as if it was drying out her lungs. She was pleased when she recognized the gnarled trunks of juniper trees, the glossy oval leaves of myrtle, and the solitary spent stems of mullein thrusting up their spears from the crevices in-between the rocks. But it was the overall sense of the unfamiliar that held her. The grey-green growth in the red sandy soil, the bleached and pitted bone of exposed rock, the broken twigs, and the trackways of animals meandering into the distance. All these features piled up inside her, and pulled at her. Like the desert landscapes she'd seen in travel magazines. She wanted to trek through it all and never come back.

She strode to the jeep and pulled her camera from her bag. 'I won't be long,' she said to Rhea.

Rhea opened her mouth, then she clamped it shut. She delved behind her seat, and snatched her novel out of her bag. She opened the pages of *Pride and Passion* with an emphatic thrust and hunched herself deeper into her seat.

Lucy took lots of pictures - standing, then crouching, drawn to the colour contrasts and rock textures. She tested the sharpness of spiny leaves against her finger tips, she crushed others to release a pungent herby aroma, that reminded her of sage, or was it marjoram? She scooped up a handful of soil, then let it fall like powdered pigment between her fingers back to earth. Then finally, she settled herself on her haunches on a rock, her elbows resting on her knees. All thoughts of Rhea and her mission leached away like drops of water into the parched soil at her feet. First the surf, and the colours of Dalyan, then the snorkelling, and now this. She was starting to feel inspired again. Inspired to paint. But was it possible she could overcome her demons?

Her line of thought swerved suddenly. Would Mum have liked this place? she wondered. But in remembering her mother, she was reminded of her plan and her stomach tightened. She turned to look at the jeep parked by the roadside. Rhea was reading that slushy book of hers again. The calm before the storm, she chanted to herself as she hurried back. Rhea had no idea what she was in for. For once, she, Lucy, was in control of events between them.

They continued over the summit, and started their descent, where the road became a rutted dirt track. Lucy felt no inclination to make it comfortable by slowing down to avoid the pits and troughs and she enjoyed hearing Rhea tut and swear as they were jolted around in their seats.

'Can't you take it easy?' cried Rhea, gripping the edge of her door.

'But it's a bit of off-roading. It's fun!' Lucy said as she steered into another bend at speed.

'For the driver, perhaps,' Rhea shouted above the engine. 'Are you doing this on purpose to wind me up?'

'No. Of course not,' Lucy said, skidding into the scrub

and narrowly avoiding a boulder.

'I think I should drive now. You're driving erratically.'

'You can't. You're not the named driver.'

'Since when do you care about the rules.'

'I'm just as responsible as you are.'

'Well, for God's sake slow down, then!'

Finally, they joined the main road that skirted around the foot of the hill, and they continued down to the coast, passing through more woodland. Lucy pointed to some remote dwellings of goat herding families, and to some goats foraging amongst spindly vegetation up on the hillside. But Rhea barely glanced at them.

After Lucy had sent a few more stones ricocheting down slopes, and after one more jack-knife bend, they finally emerged down onto Asi Bay. She brought the jeep to a bumping stop in the crudely signed parking area, alongside some worn-out portaloos with their doors hanging open as if they were gagging from over-use. She was pleased to discover there were no other vehicles in the vicinity. They unloaded their bags and trudged onto the empty shingle beach. Finally, they were here, just as she'd imagined.

***

Rhea let her bag flop down onto the shingle. Her knees felt wobbly, as if she'd just got out of a dodgem car at a fairground, but at least the ride was over now and she was able to reflect. Lucy had been behaving atrociously. Why? There was the edge of sarcasm to her voice now and again, that was very disturbing; there was her sitting in the middle of nowhere for over half an hour, without a word of apology; then the dangerous driving, which Rhea felt certain was designed to antagonize her. She decided she must play it cool, not react. Keep it light. As light as a feather, as light as cappuccino foam. That was the best way of getting through this day. Then she'd be free. There was just one more trip, and she'd be on her own for that. Of course there was the Turkish night, but she could invite Eleanor. Today was the only day left where she had to be all alone with Lucy.

She surveyed the beach. Lucy was standing alongside her. It was a tiny bay, its calm waters sheltered by tree-lined cliffs of jagged rock. To the right was a tall cliff face, shading the sea on that side. To the left, at sea level, was a shelving of rocks like rows of sharks teeth. Some had been eroded into stumps, and they were in the full heat of the sun.

'Let's go over there.' Lucy pointed to the sharks teeth. 'We can lower ourselves in from there.'

'I'm not swimming,' Rhea said, feeling back in control. 'I'm just sunbathing, and I'd prefer the shingle to hard rock, thank you.'

'But...' Lucy faltered.

Rhea took off her combats and cotton top, folded them up and put them in her bag. She was wearing her turquoise bikini underneath.

'I'm going to settle down here. You can do what you like.'

She flapped out her towel and set about securing the corners with her bag and some large stones.

But just then, she heard a whining sound, varying in pitch and volume like a frustrated wasp in a quiet room, then another one joined in. She knew what it was. Motorbikes. She and Lucy squinted towards the road. Two black Honda bikes came around the corner and did an well-practiced skid to a halt in the parking area, raising a cloud of dust. Two leather-clad, middle-aged men dismounted, had a stretch, then strode straight towards the sisters. Their boots scrunched heavily and scattered the shingle. Their weathered leathers bore the vestigial remains of hand-painted skulls and flickering flames, but so faded that they'd lost their power of intimidation.

Rhea saw Lucy's face fall.

'Is this it? No bar or anything. Is this all there is?' the tall one with a ponytail, said to the portly one with a goatee.

'Must be, mate,' the portly one replied, mopping his brow with the back of his hairy hand.

'Hi,' the tall one said to Lucy and Rhea, sweat beading on his forehead. 'Is it okay to swim 'ere?'

Rhea averted her gaze, feeling self-conscious standing there in her bikini. Lucy could deal with the questions. She had it coming.

Lucy hesitated. 'Well, I think I can see quite a few rocks out there,' she said, pointing into the bay. 'It might be a bit dangerous.'

'Oi, Pete. We haven't got any trunks with us,' the portly one said, his goatee bobbing up and down. 'Just our underpants, like.'

'Well, we can still go in, can't we? We can go in the buff. That might be more brisk. I'm sure these girlies won't mind,' Pete said, winking at Lucy. 'We can always borrow a towel, can't we, love?'

Rhea flinched. The idea of two men wading into the sea in the nude, splashing around, and making grunted exclamations, while she struggled to relax and top up her tan was anathema to her, let alone them wiping their sweaty crotches on her and Lucy's towels.

She looked at Lucy, who seemed to be dumbstruck. It was obvious she wasn't going to be of any use.

She turned around to face the bikers. 'Jellyfish,' she said. 'Don't you remember, Lucy? We were warned there were loads of them.'

Lucy peered into the sea for a moment, looking puzzled. Then she grinned. 'Oh yes, that's right. Loads of them. Floating out there, waiting to sting. Especially soft vulnerable parts.'

The bikers raised their eyebrows.

'Yeah? Well maybe you're just saying that to have the place to yourselves?' Pete said. 'What do you think, Rod?'

'Yeah, I reckon so, Pete.'

' Think we'll stick around, if you girlies don't mind,' said Pete. 'We've come all the way from the Blue Lagoon and you don't own this bay.'

'Yeah, we'll stick around,' Rod added for emphasis.

They both started pulling off their boots.

'Please yourselves,' Rhea said to them, 'but you've been warned.' She turned away. 'Come on, Lucy, we'll go over to the rocks.'

***

After refilling their water bottles from the 2.5L ones in the jeep, Lucy and Rhea climbed over the sharks teeth in their flip flops to arrange themselves on a suitably flatter tooth, half way out into the crescent of the bay. Just what Lucy wanted. There was good access to the water from here, and it was a beautiful spot. Sun-baked rock, a slight breeze stirring the branches of a backdrop of small pines and shrubs, with a ceramic blue sky pressing down on them. Rhea lay on her towel with her head resting on her bag and started reading her novel again, while Lucy sat cross-legged in her black swimsuit with the pink trim. Her snorkelling gear was beside her, but at the moment she was monitoring the bikers' movements. They were standing in their underpants by the water's edge, and looked like they were having an argument.

Her victory of getting Rhea into a suitable position was hollow, when she realized she wouldn't be able to carry out her next move in examining the underwater terrain. How could she snorkel in the bay if it was supposed to be full of jellyfish? The bikers would see her and know for certain they'd been lied to. Then they'd stick around. She pointed this out to Rhea, who murmured that she shouldn't have mentioned 'vulnerable parts', because it was then that it became obvious they were probably lying. And even if the bikers considered that they might be telling the truth, she said, they'd still have to go in to prove their fearlessness. That was men for you. Lucy would have to be patient.

But Lucy couldn't be patient. It was vital they were alone, and her stomach was tightening up again. 'But a boat might come in later,' Lucy said.

'So?' Rhea put down her book and looked sharply at Lucy over her sunglasses.

'Well...it'll spoil the peace, that's all,' she replied, urging herself to be careful.

Along with the tension in her stomach, she felt it grumbling with hunger. She rooted around in her bag and checked her watch. It was around 1pm. Still plenty of time.

'It's lunchtime,' she said.

'Okay. I must say, Lucy, you're being very organised today.'

Lucy opened the prepacked slices of cheese and ham, and slapped them between four torn-open bread buns. The cheese looked and tasted like melting plastic, while the ham just tasted of salt. They refreshed themselves further from their tepid water bottles.

As she munched on this engineered food, Lucy nervously kept her eye on the bikers. They waded in slowly, muttering to each other. Maybe the shingle was sharp? That would help. Of course, they knew they were being watched, and they kept glancing over at herself and Rhea. When the water reached his groin, Pete dived in with a crashing splash, and started a frenzied front crawl, thrashing around in the water, showing what he was made of. But as soon as he'd begun, he floundered, and his arms began to jerk around his body. He yelled something. She couldn't make it out. But Rod turned around and waded back to the shore and Pete swiftly followed. His hunched stature and clenched fists made his anger obvious. Had he been stung by something? Or was he just being jittery, his ego as deflated as a popped balloon?

They both hung around on the shore for a while, gesticulating towards the water, then started pulling on their leathers like old skins. They'd been defeated.

When they were ready to leave, they called across to the sisters, and getting both of their attention, they made a show of giving them the finger. Then they paced over to the jeep.

'We've made them feel stupid,' Rhea said. 'You've not left the keys in the ignition?'

'No, of course not. What do you think I am?'

'What if they slash a tyre?'

Lucy didn't reply, but her breath caught in the throat. A slashed tire wouldn't do.

They both stared at the bikers, who had grabbed hold of the sisters' bottles of water, unscrewed the caps, and now their heads were tipped back, gulping down the sisters' precious supply. They had their fill, then replaced the caps and tossed the bottles into the back seat.

'Oh, no!' Rhea said. 'What if they haven't left us any? It could be dangerous.'

'I'll check, when they've gone,' Lucy replied.

She watched the bikers use the portaloos, faintly impressed that they had obviously restrained themselves in the sea. Then they straddled their machines and after some heavy throttle they departed up the hill, revving their engines and stirring up a dust trail behind them like a departing posse. Soon they were gone, and she and Rhea were alone again.

I've got to get going now, Lucy said to herself.

She clambered over the rocks as deftly as a goat, and went to check the water supply. She found they still had about three litres left between them.

She waved over to Rhea. 'It's fine,' she yelled. And even if it hadn't been, she reflected, nothing must interfere now.

When she got back to the rocks, Rhea had resumed her reading. She quickly put on her mask, snorkel, and fins and lowered herself into the azure water, which was slapping against the side of the rock about two feet down. The sea felt so cool on her body, the impact gave her a shivery thrill. She felt in control again. Excited, even. She circled around the base of sharks teeth, then further out into the bay, ignoring the shoals of tiny fish that flickered around her like drops of mercury. She noted the underwater layout of the shoreline, and the sandy areas further out - where it was deeper. Satisfied, she returned to the rock.

'That was quick,' Rhea said, as Lucy settled herself back on her towel to dry off.

Lucy fixed her gaze on the blurring ripples two feet below her and clutched hold of the edge of her towel. She twisted it in her grip.

It had to be now.

She swallowed hard.

'I have to talk to you,' she turned and looked at Rhea. Rhea's face was hidden behind her book. 'I need to ask you some questions.'

There was silence. Rhea didn't move.

'I mean it, Rhea. I want to know things about the past. About Mum. Things you seem foggy about. Things you won't discuss.'

Rhea slammed her book down on the rock and pulled off her shades. Her eyes burned into Lucy's. 'I've been through this before. I don't want to talk about anything! I've had enough of your probing and wittering on. There's nothing to know. Nothing to talk about.'

Lucy flinched from Rhea's anger, and the old insulting term of 'wittering' pierced her. This was the moment she had to get through. She mustn't back down.

'I think there is plenty to talk about. I have lots of questions, and you're going to answer them now - right here.'

Rhea arched her eyebrows and slowly got to her feet. She knotted her sarong around her bikini top and thrust her feet into her flip flops, then she looked straight at Lucy. 'Oh no, I'm not. You can't force me to do anything.'

She packed up her towel and shoved the book in her bag. 'You can get stuffed. I've had more than enough of this. Now piss off and leave me alone!'

But she was forced to make her way gingerly between the sharks teeth, into the crevices, then onto the peaks, while holding on to her bag. She scraped her shins a couple of times and swore.

Lucy followed behind, jumping from stone to stone with her long legs and swinging her bag wildly.

' No, I won't leave you alone!' she cried.

Rhea made it to the beach and stalked ahead towards the shady cliff, her flip flops slithering around in the sharp stones and impeding her progress.

Lucy followed. She must stop Rhea before she tried to leave the bay.

She caught hold of her arm and twisted Rhea around to face her.

'You're not leaving this time, like you did on turtle beach. I have these questions, and you're going to answer them.'

She'd rehearsed this moment for days. She'd gone over her questions, like rehearsed lines in a play. She felt strangely detached as she asked them now. Out loud.

'Why did our relationship get worse after Mum died? You deny it, but it's true. I always felt as if you and Dad shut me out, you never talked about Mum.' She paused. 'Why not?'

Rhea's eyes widened. She struggled to pull her arm from Lucy's grasp.

Lucy dug her fingernails into Rhea's flesh. She knew she was hurting Rhea, but she didn't care. This wasn't a rehearsal anymore. This was real. 'No!' she cried. 'There's more, and you're going to hear it!'

The questions started jostling for position. Like angry people, exhausted with waiting in a long queue, and deciding to dispense with cultural norms for the sake of a civilised society and barge their way to the front. It turned into an disorderly free-for-all.

'Why have you repeatedly implied that Mum didn't take her art seriously? I mean, did she enjoy it or not? Was she successful or not? Why did Dad say Auntie Kathy had been given her paintings, when all that time, for over 30 years, they were buried away in his attic? I mean, why hide them?'

Rhea finally shook her arm free. She looked hard at Lucy.

There was a twisted expression on her face that Lucy couldn't read.

More questions forced Lucy on. Having reached the base of the cliff, there was nowhere else for them to go.

'And then into the now of this holiday,' she said. 'This 'oh so' sisterly holiday, where you prefer the company of an American woman you've barely known five minutes, whose sole aim in life seems to be spending as much of her husband's money as she can, before she divorces him.' She found herself blurting this out, completely out of the blue. Couldn't she even manage to stick to the point? She told herself to get a grip.

'She's got her own money,' Rhea rasped, her eyes as steely as nailheads.

Lucy recoiled. She'd never seen Rhea look like this before. It was almost frightening. But she drew herself up straighter.

'Whatever,' she replied. 'Back to the point. Why were you so upset at the sight of that necklace June bought on the bus trip, that looked like the one Mum used to have? You must remember it, you can't just deny it. She wore it all the time.' She paused for breath. 'And you've implied she wasn't happy either. When I talked to June, she made me realise –'

'I'm not interested in what that woman thinks,' Rhea hissed. 'She's a – '

'She made me realise that you might be hiding something. And she asked me about Mum's death. And I realised I didn't know much at all, because you and Dad would never talk about it.'

Lucy came to a halt. There were only a couple of questions left, but they didn't seem to fit right now.

'Is that it? Are you finished?' Rhea asked.

'More or less.'

'Well, I'm not answering any of them. You can't force me to tell you anything.'

Lucy had anticipated this moment. And she had her next move ready.

Rhea looked weary now. Her mouth went slack. 'I'm not going on with this. I'm getting out of here. Give me the keys to the jeep. It's up to you whether you come as well. Right now, I don't give a damn.'

Lucy grinned. 'But you're not the named driver. And even if you suddenly don't care about following the rules, you're not getting them until you answer the questions. I'm not giving them to you until then.'

'For Christ's sake, Lucy. Stop behaving like a silly little idiot.'

Rhea started digging around in the outer compartment of her bag. She tutted, then thumped it down onto the shingle. She squatted down and emptied out all the contents of all the compartments, spreading them out: make-up bag, clothes, cap, towel, her novel, some tissues, a packet of paracetamol, a small water bottle, her purse, Trish's map, a couple of pens and a notebook. She kept turning the things over, and she checked through her empty compartments again. Her jaw was clenched, and her hands were trembling.

'What are you looking for?' Lucy hovered over Rhea. She felt a sense of elation that her plan was working, but it was pricked by a dawning sense of horror at her own behaviour.

'What do you think?'

'Your mobile.' She just couldn't keep the sound of victory out of her voice. The elation was winning. 'To ring Trish to arrange something. Or to ring Dalyan for a taxi. You've got a load of local numbers stored on it.'

Rhea stood up and stared at her, wide-eyed.

Lucy could tell from Rhea's face that she was working it out, bit by bit. She started to feel nervous under her scrutiny. Just how badly was she going to react?

'So *you've* got it?' Rhea asked.

'No.'

Rhea's eyebrows shot up. 'No!' she whispered, looking at Lucy. She stepped back for a moment, staring out to sea. Then she turned and lunged at Lucy, grasping her by the shoulders and shaking her back and forth. 'No!' she shouted. 'Where the hell is it, then? Where is it?'

'Get off me!' Lucy shook herself free. 'It's back at the hotel. I put it in the safety deposit box.'

'You stole it from me, then left it behind?' Rhea shrieked at her. 'But we're in the middle of nowhere! What if something happens to us? What do we do then? You silly little idiot!'

'Don't call me that again, do you hear? I've had enough of it.'

'You are silly! You're bloody silly, playing these stupid little silly games.'

Being called stupid and silly over and over again made Lucy's hackles rise so much she wanted to slap Rhea hard across the face. But she forced her right arm, which was tensing up, to hang loose. She must stick to the plan.

'Whatever,' she replied, trying to sound haughty. 'The fact is you can't call anyone to get out of this situation. The only way back is in the jeep and I've got the keys. You have to answer my questions. As for stupid games, you gave me no choice.' She paused, 'You weren't even supposed to bring the mobile with you on this holiday anyway. We agreed.'

'Oh, not that again! You never pack it in, do you? You

never pack anything in. Look how you're behaving over your art - should I, shouldn't I? You won't let it go. Oh, no! That would be too simple for you, wouldn't it? You have to have something to chew over. Something to analyse to death.'

Lucy took a step backwards. 'That has got nothing to do with this!' she gasped. 'Nothing at all. And you're a bitch to even bring it up.'

She couldn't believe that Rhea was using this against her. Sisters were supposed to be supportive. But hers was been as vindictive as a spiteful schoolgirl. A spiteful schoolgirl betraying a confidence from a new girl, trying to make friends, to her pack of cronies in the school playground. What had she ever done to Rhea that was so awful to deserve this? Well, I'm going to find out, she thought. This is it. Right now.

She turned around and began marching along the beach towards the sharks teeth. 'If you want the keys, you're going to have to take them off me,' she called over her shoulder.

Rhea stuffed all the contents of her bag back inside it and stamped after Lucy. She followed her back over the rocks, scratching her legs again and panting in the glare of the sun. Cicadas in the trees above the rocks had started their mating call and now the hot air was swollen with the static surround sound of the beetles. Rhea's face was red and pinched as she kept glancing towards the branches. Her hair hung loose, plastered around her cheeks and neck.

Lucy stood on the same rock that they'd been sunbathing on. She stood with her legs apart and one hand on her hip. With her other hand she pulled out the car keys from the side pocket of her bag and she dangled them over the side of the rock, right above the foaming seawater. This was the moment she knew would come. This was the critical bit.

'Tell me!' she insisted to Rhea.

'You won't do it,' Rhea rasped.

'Fine. If that's how you want it.'

Lucy did a strong overarm throw. The keys soared up into the air, flashing silver as they caught the light. Then they fell down into the ocean with a soft plop.

The sound felt so satisfying to Lucy, a defining moment. At last, she had some bargaining power. She peered out to where they'd gone in, realising they'd gone a bit wide of where she'd intended. But whether recovering them from a sand bed, or from between rocks, she was still confident she could get them back. She had to be.

'If you answer the questions, I'll go in and get them with my snorkelling gear, and we can get out of here,' she said to Rhea.

Rhea had been looking where the keys had entered the sea. Her mouth was contorted into a grimace, her eyes wide open and glassy.

She's so afraid, Lucy thought. But of what?

They looked at each other, straight into one another's eyes, unflinching, during seconds of stretched silence. Only the sounds of surf and cicada competed with each other for their attention.

Then Rhea drew herself up. There was a cold look in her eyes now and Lucy felt a snake of fear slither down her spine.

'Okay! You win!' Rhea cried. 'You want to know? You really want to know? Then I'll tell you! Are you ready? Are you sure you're ready?'

Lucy felt the need to nod like a child who knew it was in trouble, and had to go through any possible show of contrition. But she managed to restrain herself. 'Just say it,' she said breathlessly.

'Our mother, who you've placed on a bloody pedestal all these years didn't drown by accident. She did it on purpose. She killed herself!'

Lucy staggered back as if Rhea had punched her in the

stomach. Her mouth hung open. Her mind and emotions felt paralysed by Rhea's last three words.

'So, if you'd kindly get those fucking keys, I want to get out of here.'

Rhea turned her back on Lucy and started making her way back to the beach.

13

Promises Broken

Rhea's heart thudded in her chest as she picked her way through the rocks, heading once more for the beach. New agonies burned inside her. What had she done? What would her father say?

Her lower legs were oozing blood from the scratches on her shins and ankles. She glanced at the tiny red beads in horror. There were so many. So many to heal.

'You can't leave it at that!' Lucy screamed behind her from the rock.

Rhea hit the shingle hard and tried to run to the shaded side of the beach beneath the cliff. The heat pressed down on her, and sweat was dripping off her forehead as she slipped around in the stones. If she could just get to the cool, get away from the beetles.

She collapsed onto her towel and jarred her shoulder blades as she propped herself up against the cliff face. Retrieving her water bottle from her bag, she gulped down the last of its contents.

She moaned when she saw Lucy heading straight for her, with a look of outrage on her face. No more, she begged. Please, no more. But of course she knew there would be. This was only the beginning. She'd told the secret.

Lucy stamped around in front of her, glaring at her. 'You're a liar!' she shouted. 'That's a lie. I can't believe you're saying this. She didn't…she wouldn't…Why are you saying this?' she yelled, clenching her hands into fists.

'Because you pushed me into it! You wanted to know. You wouldn't leave it alone. You wittered on!' Rhea struggled to her feet. There was no way she was going to be a sitting target.

'You're lying. She fell into the pond when she was reaching for some magnolia blossom for a still life.'

'Oh yes, the Edith Holden story. Magnolia blossom over the pond in Springfield Cottage garden, rather than chestnut buds over the Thames.' Rhea hated the sarcasm in her voice, but she'd built up so much resentment behind the dam she'd been forced to construct inside herself, it was too late now - the dam had been blasted apart. Lucy had done it and Lucy had it coming.

'Dad thought that story would make it easier for people, easier for the family,' she continued. 'The idea of a tragic accident. But you have to get it into your head that she did it on purpose, with the help of some tablets and booze. She killed herself.' She couldn't keep the disgust out of her voice.

Lucy's forehead was knotted in concentration. With Rhea's last words, her eyes narrowed and she shook her head slowly.

'No!'

'Yes. It's true. That's the big secret. That's what you've been protected from all these years - 32 to be exact. The big secret was kept.'

Her own words rang in her ears. The secret kept until now, she thought. Now, I've broken my promise to Dad. What would he say? Would he forgive me?

She felt this ache inside, it throbbed into a sharp pain, pricking tears into her eyes. The old hurt. She shifted her gaze from Lucy, up into the sky, but there were no birds, so she lowered her eyes to the horizon, then followed the waves in as they advanced upon the shore. Was the tide rising? She could swear it was, but it wasn't supposed to do that in the Mediterranean because of it almost being a landlocked sea. She looked back at Lucy and trembled.

Lucy was clutching the sides of her head and pacing around. 'No, it can't be true. She was happy. She was fulfilled! A happy marriage. The two of us. And her art. Her art made her happy!' Then she grabbed Rhea's arm.

'Why would she kill herself? Why?' Lucy yelled full into her face, jerking her arm. 'Tell me why! It must be a lie. How do you know she killed herself? How?'

She shoved Rhea backwards against the cliff. The impact of the knobbly rock against Rhea's shoulder blades made her cry out in pain and she lunged at Lucy. She · pushed her and pushed her, back and back, away from the cliff and into the full force of the sun.

Lucy teetered, clutched hold of Rhea, and then they both tumbled down onto the grey, cinder-hot shingle.

As their limbs thrust and wrestled, Lucy snatched a fistful of Rhea's hair and twisted it against her scalp. 'You bitch!' she spat in her face.

The pain urged Rhea on, and she clawed at Lucy's cheek. Lucy deflected the full force of Rhea's hand with the back of her forearm, but she still caught a nasty scratch. They rolled over the hotbed like a couple of scrapping cats feuding over their territory.

'Spoilt brat,' hissed Rhea, tugging at a hank of Lucy's hair.

'Leave me alone!' yelled Lucy, trying to knock her away.

'You started it!'

Just then, Rhea took another scrape on her elbow from the scorching stones. She felt the searing pain and cried out. She also became aware of the burning on her knees and her torn sarong. Enough was enough.

Rolling herself off Lucy, she sat with her legs bent in front of her, and stared into her lap. What the hell were they doing? How had it got to this?

Lucy adopted the same pose, her limbs covered in grit. She began to sob. 'For Christ's sake, Rhea,' she said, shaking her head, and sobbing harder.

Rhea felt the enormity of having told Lucy the secret press into her, squeezing the breath out of her. She'd made a mistake. She'd betrayed her father. And look how she'd told Lucy. So scathing, so vengeful. What had happened to her that she could behave and feel like this?

But she knew why.

And as she remembered, she felt her shoulders heaving and tears began rolling down her face.

And this spiral of emotion, unwinding faster, as she sobbed more and more to get it out. Not recognising herself at all. Outside of herself, and the sounds she was making - the whimperings and wailings of a wounded animal.

All that hurt coming out, inside out, from so deep a place, but now at the surface and pouring out.

No control.

She heard Lucy stop crying and could feel her scrutiny, but still no control. She picked with her fingers at tiny pieces of shingle. They blurred in and out of focus. On and on she cried, until she had nothing left, and her tears dried up in the heat.

Lucy broke the silence first. 'Rhea! What is it all about?'

***

As they sat together on their towels in the shade of the cliff, beneath the crying of a seagull, the waves lapped against the shoreline like a ticking clock. Lucy was waiting for Rhea to compose herself, for her sniffles to stop, for her to become the Rhea she was more familiar with. The reliable pragmatic Rhea, instead of this emotional one - though she never thought she'd have ever have wished for that. She groped into her bag for the last of her water and swallowed it down. She felt impatient, she needed to know. Right now.

'Tell me,' she said. 'Tell me what happened? Why was I never told?'

'There's a lot to tell,' Rhea said, her voice breaking. 'So much.'

'Just start somewhere.' Lucy felt like shouting it at her, but managed to restrain herself.

'Okay,' Rhea looked at Lucy. 'I'll try. But don't keep butting in until I'm finished.'

Lucy nodded, relieved to see Rhea back in charge. But how much could there be to tell?

'She wasn't happy with Dad. She'd been having an affair for about three years. Another artist. A sculptor, her life drawing tutor - '

'Oh, my God!' Lucy cut in. 'But that's such a cliché. I mean - '

'Let me get on with it!' Rhea snapped. 'He died in a car crash. He was married, so she couldn't go to the funeral. Anyway, afterwards, she became depressed.'

'What about Dad? Did he know about him?'

'He found out a couple of years into the affair. The usual signs, I suppose. Snatched phone calls, staying late at the art class, her suddenly saying she had to go and see a girlfriend over the weekend, there was even a week's life drawing course down South somewhere. And naturally, *he'd* have been there too. She kept promising to break it off, but she couldn't do it. And Dad was desperate. He let her carry on seeing him, hoping she'd see sense, or that it would burn itself out. But she told Dad it was love. That this man was the love of her life. Then a year later the sculptor died.'

Lucy felt a shiver flush through her body. 'Oh, no. She must have felt terrible.'

'Oh, for crying out loud, Lucy! That's just typical of you. What about Dad?' Rhea gave Lucy a stricken look. 'What about his suffering? I mean, can you imagine what he went through…what he - '.

'Okay, I'm sorry! Go on.'

Rhea reached into her bag for a tissue and blew her nose hard. 'Well, Dad said after he died, Mum got more and more depressed, and was prescribed some antidepressants.' She paused and looked at Lucy again. 'You must have noticed that. She wasn't really herself that last year. She slept in a lot, didn't do much cooking or cleaning, didn't meet up with her friends, she just kept to her studio all the time, not going out.'

'No, not really. I just thought she was working hard.' Lucy wracked her brains to remember. But all she remembered was a rapid succession of fresh flowers in vases and checked cloths with still life arrangements. Her mother's bright smile. Fish fingers for tea. No packets of pills. But looking back, perhaps she was over-bright? Was all that flurry of activity a diversion from her grief? I didn't see anything wrong, Lucy thought. I really didn't. Why didn't I see?

As if answering Lucy's inner thoughts, Rhea continued. 'Oh well, you were only eleven, too young to notice, I suppose. I noticed. But I didn't know what was going on.'

'Did you talk to her?'

'I tried once. I found a bottle of pills in her underwear drawer, so I asked her what they were for. She said they were nothing, just something homeopathic she was trying for period pain. She denied there was anything else wrong.'

'Just once? You tried just once?' Then she saw Rhea's face. 'Okay, sorry. What happened next?' she urged.

'Right, well basically, one fine summer day,' Rhea said coldly, 'that last year, she went down to the pond at the bottom of the garden, with too much vodka inside her, mixed with pills. She drowned herself. It was intentional.'

Lucy shivered again. How could she do that? How could *anyone* do that? Deliberately let their lungs fill with water, without the choking reflex to fight back? Was it actually possible?

'It's not possible is it? It must have been an accident. It must have been!'

'It is possible, if you're semi-conscious in the first place, apparently.'

'But weren't the pills picked up...you know, in her system? How could it have been recorded as accidental?'

'I'll get to that.'

'Just a minute! Dad found her there. He found her. How did he know it wasn't an accident?'

Rhea hesitated. 'Because there was a note. She left it for him on his desk.'

Lucy suddenly felt nauseous and her stomach slowly turned over. Bitter saliva flooded her mouth, but she swallowed it back down. 'I can't believe we're having this conversation. It's not real! Tell me it's not real!' she moaned, looking wildly at Rhea. Rhea, who was so calmly coming out with this *stuff*. This hidden drama. Just like the secret stories of *other* people's lives, *their* skeletons, bursting out of *their* cupboards. But surely not the Allen family's. 'You've got to be lying!' she cried.

Rhea gaped at her. 'How could I lie about something like this! Tell me!' She faltered, then her voice shook. 'Now that I'm telling it, I need to be believed, Lucy. I'm the only one left. I need to be believed!' She clutched at Lucy's arm, her voice rising.

Lucy felt frightened by Rhea's desperation. How much worse was this going to get? How did Rhea know all this? Just keep her on track, she told herself, keep calm.

'Okay, okay. Carry on. She drowned, and there was a note.'

Rhea sighed and hunched her shoulders, twisting her hands in her lap. 'I missed a bit out. Now it's the complicated bit. It'll be hard to tell you. It's been so long. Just listen. Don't butt in.'

Lucy glanced at her watch, and as she did so, she was struck by astonishment at her own ability to be practical at a time like this. As if this was all some kind of macabre matinee performance and they were running out of time. It was already around 3pm. She looked over to the other side of the bay. A few clouds were puffing across the sky. The car keys were on the seabed. But this was critical stuff and the usual rules just didn't apply. Time would have to wait.

'Go on,' she said. 'I won't interrupt.'

325

***

As Rhea started speaking again, she relaxed her spine against the cliff, yielding to the discomfort. She was determined to get this right. And it was too late to turn back now.

She swallowed hard.

'I found her, Lucy. It was me who found her.'

'You!' she heard Lucy gasp, as if from far away.

'I came back from school early that afternoon. It was a Friday and I bunked off double physics. It was the only time I ever did that, I just couldn't face it that day. I hated physics. Anyway, you were still at school and Dad was teaching. When I got home, I looked into Dad's study. I don't know why. Habit, I suppose. And I saw this cream envelope propped up against the phone. I went and looked at it, and it was Mum's writing on the front. 'George', it said. Well, I knew something was up with them both, because they'd been arguing a lot. But I didn't know anything else at that point. But to find a letter there was odd, like maybe she'd left him or something, so I started looking for her. First her studio, then through the house, then into the garden, past those huge sunflowers she liked to grow. I thought maybe she was outside painting. I went right down to the pond area, where she liked to go. It was a gorgeous day, really bright sunshine, really hot. I could smell those tall lilies we had in the border - their sickly sweet smell hanging in the air. I've hated the smell ever since.

'I went down to the edge of the pond - the place where she liked to sit. It was the grassy shallow end nearest the garden, not the high bank with the magnolia trees at the deep end, where Dad said she'd drowned. Well, at first I couldn't see anything. Just that sunhat of hers, with the floppy brim, lying in the rushes.'

Now it comes, she thought, and she glanced at Lucy,

who was staring at her with a twisted expression of both dread and rapt attention, her face so ashen and drawn.

'Well, I stepped closer. And then I saw her. At least, I saw that dress of hers first. The Laura Ashley one she used to wear on special occasions. Long sleeves, tight embroidered bodice, long skirt.'

'The chintzy one, with the frill at the bottom. Her favourite,' Lucy muttered under her breath.

'Yes. Well, it was wet and billowing near the edge of the pond. And I thought what's her dress doing in the pond? Then I saw her hair. It was drifting in the pondweed, and then I knew. It was her. She was floating…face down.'

'Oh God,' Lucy breathed.

'So, I crashed in. And I turned her over. It was so hard to do. I didn't want to do it. Her eyes were closed. I was glad her eyes were closed. I pulled her up into the rushes. She was so heavy. All dragged down with wetness. Mud was everywhere. All over that dress, all over me. And I saw the bent rushes where she must have waded in.'

She turned to Lucy, surprised to find herself reaching out to the sister who she'd loathed so much for so long. Lucy held her gaze. 'Then, I just sat with her head in my lap, looking at her, pulling the pondweed out of her hair. She did look peaceful. That part was right. She was beautiful, wasn't she?'

'Yes, she was.' Lucy's voice wobbled. 'You took after her for looks, you know.'

'Just for eye and hair colour…nothing much else.' Rhea smiled weakly and turned away. 'Then I thought I should check her breathing. I put my ear to her chest, but there was no movement. Her skin was so cold. She smelled all musky, like the pondweed. And she was wearing that locket on the chain necklace you were on about. It flashed in the sun. And the chain *was* like the one the prune on sticks bought.'

'So that's why you didn't want to recognise it.'

327

'I suppose so.' She hesitated and chewed at her lip. 'Well, you know how we always used to like looking in it?'

'Yes. There was a picture of the four of us in it, a tiny copy of a portrait we had done at the posh photographers in Hexham.'

'Yes. Well, I opened it up. It was still around her neck. I looked inside, expecting to see that picture.'

'Right?'

Rhea's mouth felt like sandpaper. 'Well, it wasn't us, it was a picture of him - the sculptor. And her. Both together. A Woolworths photo booth type of picture. You know the sort, with the blue pleated curtain at the back. The picture was cut into an oval, the two of them together, cheeks pressed together, smiling. It was loose in the locket, so I pulled it out. Our picture was underneath.'

'Oh God. She must have had it so bad.'

Rhea felt numb. She'd noticed changes in her mother, sleeping in, instead of making the breakfast, those faraway looks, not answering questions. But she hadn't asked her about it, hadn't done anything. She was too wrapped up in her own life, not thinking of her mother at all. In fact, her mother used to irritate the hell out of her at the time. But afterwards, Dad had said it was his fault, not hers.

Lucy was silent for a moment, her brow set hard. 'What did he look like? What was his name?'

Rhea groaned. 'Oh, I knew you'd get around to that! Was he irresistible? Was he some sort of perfect man in all respects? And if he was, would that make the betrayal okay?'

Lucy looked at her with tears in her eyes. 'No. No, I suppose it wouldn't.'

'Well, it hardly matters, but if you must know, in the picture he looked a bit like George Harrison, with some grey in his moustache and long hair. And as for his character, Dad said he was an arrogant selfish bastard - a womaniser who exploited the women who went to his life drawing class.'

'What else did he tell you?'

'Nothing else. That's all he would ever say.'

'What was his name?'

'John was his name. That's all I know.'

'Did you ever try to find out more about him?'

Rhea grimaced at Lucy. 'No, I bloody well didn't. Dad would have hated that. And I didn't want to know.' And Dad would hate what I'm doing right now, she thought.

She glanced at the tide again, glad to see it was lapping against the same jutting out rock embedded in the shingle that she'd judged it by previously. Time seemed to be standing still. But she knew it wasn't.

'So,' she continued, 'Mum did a kind of Ophelia act, in her own way. Just like the painting she had a print of in her studio. It must have been intentional. Artist to the last.' She hated how she sounded so caustic, but Lucy didn't seem to be noticing.

'You know, I always wanted to see her death something like that,' Lucy said. 'She loved that painting.'

'Right, well I'm glad it suits you, then,' she said tersely. 'Look, Lucy, I can't stand much more of this, I've got to get to the end. And we need to get back.'

But as she carried on speaking, and as Lucy stopped interrupting, her detached mood shifted, and she felt sucked back into the past, to what she'd tried so hard to forget, but the memories were still waiting to bind her - to Springfield Cottage, the 10th of July, 1978 - to the panic of that afternoon, the shock, the confusion. And finally, her dad telling her how things were going to be.

With the tiny oval picture squeezed tightly in her hand, she left her mother, went into the house, into the kitchen, and phoned her father's school. It took so long for him to come to the phone, she thought she'd been forgotten about. Her tension coiled up and tightened inside her and she broke into a shivering sweat. It was such a relief when he finally answered. So much so, she suddenly felt calm. She didn't know how to prepare him, so she just blurted out the words. 'Mum's dead,' she said. 'She's drowned in the pond, Dad.' This was all she could manage to say. But the calm continued, as if someone else was doing the talking. Like a stranger was pulling her strings.

He drove home in about ten minutes, brushed past Rhea in the kitchen and ran out to the pond. When he came back, just a few minutes later, his trousers were dripping water on the tiles and his shoes were pasting mud all over the floor. His face was waxy and pinched, and she suddenly knew what it meant when someone was said to look as if the blood had drained out of them. Her dad looked like that and it scared her. He was standing there, all limp, looking so much smaller, and shaking his head. She caught hold of the frayed sleeve of his tweed jacket, which he always insisted on wearing during the summer, and tugged him silently into the study. She pointed to the letter by the phone on his desk. He collapsed into his carver chair, and with his thumb, he slowly edged his way along the seal, prying it open. He pulled the small sheet of paper out and unfolded it. It shook in his grasp. Reading it, he started to cry. This frightened her again. She'd never seen him cry before. The strangled sobs, the sharp intakes of breath, the juddering shoulders. He released the letter, and it fluttered to the floor, crawling with Helen's handwriting.

She placed her hand on his shoulder; he put his arm around her waist.

When he was finally quiet, she asked, 'Can I read it, Dad?'

'No, love,' he said. 'Best not.'

That was when she felt angry. She stepped back and then felt the photo scrunched in her fist. She opened her hand and thrust it at him.

'Who is this?' she asked. 'It was in her locket, on top of *our* picture. Was she…was she having an affair, Dad?'

He snatched it off her to look at it, grimaced, then tore it up into pieces. The tiny fragments wafted down onto the carpet like confetti.

'Yes, she was,' he said, tightening his grip on the arm of his chair.

Then he looked up at her and she saw the strain in his eyes. And the fear. It frightened her. It was catching. He was always the strong one, the one who always knew what to do.

'Tell me the truth, Dad. Please! She's killed herself, hasn't she?'

So he reached down and handed her the letter. 'I suppose you know enough now. But please don't judge her too harshly, love…' His voice broke and he put his head in his hands. 'She threatened it before, but I didn't think she was serious. Why didn't I listen? Oh, Rhea, why didn't I listen?'

It was strange to see her mother's writing, all the loops making up sentences, one after the other, crammed onto too small a piece of paper. All she'd ever seen were quick scribbles on shopping lists or phone messages. It had taken effort too. It was covered in swollen patches, so she must have been crying. The ink was from a biro, so it hadn't bled. Planning, or good luck? In any case, the content made its mark.

George,

I'm so sorry, but I just can't go on. The light has gone out and I can't get it back. Art means nothing to me now - without him. I'm sorry to let you and the girls down, but I have tried so hard. The pills aren't working, and how can they be expected to? The way is clear now. Thank you for being a loyal and caring husband and I know you'll be a loving father to the girls. Please don't ever tell Lucy about my taking my own life. I don't think she'd handle it well and I don't want her to think badly of me. I know it's a lot to ask, but will you please scatter my ashes at Housesteads.

Yours,

Helen

Rhea had felt a sharp pain deep in her breast by the time she got to the end of the letter. She could still feel hurt like that back then.

'Why Lucy?' she asked her father. 'Why did she choose *her* not to be told? What about me?'

Her father looked up in alarm, a flash of recognition lighting up in him. 'No, no, Rhea! She wasn't thinking straight. It doesn't mean anything. She's presuming you'd be more likely to understand in time, that's all. And she's presuming *I'd* find her, not you!'

Then he paused, straightened himself and glanced up and down at her. 'We'll talk it over later, love,' he said hurriedly. 'I must ring the police now. Go and change out of those wet things, put on a fresh uniform, it would be best for everyone if they think I found her, as she intended. I want them to think *I* found her, do you understand? And it would be best for everyone if they think it was an accident. Better for her memory. Better for the whole family.'

And as Rhea slowly walked away through the study doorway, she turned back for a few moments, to see him striking one of the matches from the box that always lay next to his pipe and tobacco on the fireplace mantel. The orange flame licked the corner of the letter, its tongue curled, and it swallowed the letter up. As she ran upstairs to change, in her mind's eye, she saw the flames consuming the words of her mother's last request - *Scatter my ashes at Housesteads.*

In the days to come, she was to know they never were.

***

'So that's why you've resented me all these years,' Lucy said quietly, after Rhea fell silent. 'I suppose it all makes sense now.'

But the letter implied all sorts of things to Lucy's mind. A few words that could be taken to mean so many different things about what her mother might have thought and felt, and Lucy was nothing if not analytical. It implied that she, Lucy, was her mother's favourite. That, she, Lucy, was the one her mother really cared about. That Rhea could take care of herself and that she wasn't concerned about Rhea thinking badly of her. But it also implied something else, that made Lucy wince. It was pretty clear that her mother assumed that Lucy wouldn't be able to handle it. Like she was the sensitive one. And she suddenly felt furious with her mother. No wonder her relationship with Rhea had changed after that. It had practically been programmed to. They'd never stood a chance. But then, Rhea was never supposed to have found the note. It was supposed to have been just between her mother and father. So then what?

She frowned. They divided us up, she thought. Her mother knew their dad would look after Rhea, because Rhea was his favourite, and she knew Rhea would be there for him. I'd supposedly be protected best by not knowing the truth. But it hadn't quite worked out like that. It had brought her dad and Rhea closer together, and despite her father's best efforts, she'd been left out in the cold.

And what about the ashes? They weren't even where she thought they were! She'd always thought they'd been scattered at the top of Brook Farm near where they lived, a place where they all used to go on a Sunday walk. That was what her father had told her. He hadn't wanted Lucy there at the time, as it might be too upsetting. Instead, her mother's spirit was floating around Hadrian's Wall at

Housesteads, on a barren moorland. Why? They'd only visited the place as a family a couple of times. She groaned and shook her head. Did it really matter where her mother's ashes were? Now, after all this time?

Lucy felt burning bile rise into her throat again. Enough was enough.

'You can tell me the rest later on,' she said, springing to her feet, and gathering up her towel. She looked at her watch. 'It's four o'clock now, we've got to make a move.'

Without looking at Rhea, she turned, hoisted her bag onto her shoulder, and made her way over to the other side of the beach. She wanted action, not talking, not thinking. She, Lucy, was the one going to get them home - home, being Dalyan for the present.

'Are you sure?' Rhea asked incredulously, struggling to keep up with her, her torn sarong flapping around her legs. 'There's still a lot more, you know! How Dad wanted it known and reported to everyone as an accident…and how I had to promise not to tell you. Not to tell anyone. There's - '

'You can tell me later!'

Rhea's jaw dropped. 'So you're going to get the car keys now?' Her tone was clipped and accusing.

'After I've had a drink.'

'Right. Well I need one too.'

They strode over to the jeep and Lucy reached into the back for the 2.5 L bottles they'd been using to top up their smaller containers. What she saw made her gasp. A dark stain on the floor, with one of the plastic bottles completely empty. She picked up the empty bottle, and held it up for their inspection. The screw cap hadn't been put back on properly and the water had slowly leaked out. She'd never noticed this calamity earlier.

'How much is in the other one?' Rhea cried. She shoved Lucy out of the way and reached for the other bottle. She swished the water around in it - their remaining water supply looked to be only about one and a half litres.

Lucy looked at it in dismay. She knew she was responsible. She'd been the one that went to check on the water after the bikers left, but her mind had been on other things.

'No mobile, and now no water, thanks to you! You should have noticed the cap wasn't on properly! That's just typical of you!'

'Oh, shut up, Rhea! There's some left. We'll half it between us.'

By the time they'd carefully transferred the remaining contents to their small bottles, with Lucy wishing she had the use of a measuring cylinder to keep Rhea happy, they both took a hefty swig each, and soon realised they had very little to get them back to Dalyan.

By Lucy's reckoning it had taken them about four and a half hours to get to Asi Bay. She kept this to herself for the moment, hoping that if they didn't make any stops on the return journey, they'd get back in about three and a half.

They clambered over to the flattened rock where Lucy had left her snorkelling gear. The cicada were hushed and the ceramic blue sky bore down on them. The sea was calm - dead calm.

Lucy looked out for a few moments, trying to remember exactly where the keys had gone down. She broke into a sweat. What if she'd got it wrong? What if a current had moved them?

With her fingers trembling, she spat on her mask to stop it fogging up, then stretched it over her head with the snorkel attached. She lowered herself into the sea. She shuddered. It felt colder than before. Rhea handed down her fins - one at a time.

Adjusting her mask, she turned onto her stomach and floated into the coolness, out towards where she thought the shallow sandy bed was, where she'd tried to aim the keys. It all looked uncomfortably vague.

Minutes passed, as she circled around the sandy area,

seeing nothing but shafts of light holding floating motes and the shimmer of tiny fish darting over the seabed. So she decided to widen her search to the rocks that skirted the shoreline, thinking that the keys must have gone more to the left, but hoping they were nowhere near the domed boulders suckered with seaweed. She was about six metres out from the flattened rock now.

Just as she drifted above some rocks encrusted with lichens, which were about two and a half metres down, she thought she spotted the keys, a glimpse of silver in a small crevice between the rocks. Her heartbeat quickened. She raised her head out of the water and waved to Rhea, who was squatting and peering in her direction.

Then she took a deep breath, and thrust her upper body downwards to do a handstand dive, just as she'd practiced. It was perfection. She swooped towards the stones, dolphin kicking behind her. She felt like a mermaid again. She reached out with both hands, grasping onto one of the rocks to try to hold herself down. The lichen was rough and scratchy but it gave her a reasonable hold. Freeing her right hand, she groped for the keys in the gravelly crevice, breathing out a few air bubbles that rose to the surface - her vital signs. I'm going to get them, she thought. I'm going to do it. Her fingers caught hold of the black key fob, she tugged at it, and then her fingers closed around the keys. A rush of relief flooded her and she arched her back upwards to ascend.

But as she did so, her legs swung down and the fin of her right leg sliced through the gap between the rocks and became jammed in the crevice. Frantically, she tried to push the sea down and away, like she had before, but this time she couldn't move.

More air bubbles escaped as she floundered. In her panic, she unclenched her jaws and lost her grip on the mouthpiece. It was of little matter, as there was no available air. She tried to pull her foot free of the fin, but it was caught too deep.

Then she froze, looking up at the surface blue and searching for the sun. Almost within her reach, but not quite. If it wasn't for the fact that she wanted to take a breath of air and couldn't, she could have appreciated the beauty in the stillness around her.

But she realised that this time, she wasn't going to rise to meet the sky.

This time, she was stuck.

***

Rhea saw the first few bubbles break on the surface, just like they had before on the sailing trip. She felt a surge of relief, thinking it meant Lucy had found the keys and they were going to get out of here. They'd be back in Dalyan in a few hours and she was looking forward to a glass of wine and a cigarette on the balcony. She'd get her phone back and text Rob.

A few more seconds ticked by. A few more bubbles.

Come on, she thought, we have to get a move on. 'Come on!' she shouted at the bubbles.

She waited for more.

But, after a few more seconds, there was only one or two, then none.

Then it hit her. Fast.

The empty alone feeling. Miles of ocean and miles of sky. And right now, it felt like she was the only one alive in the whole bay. While there were bubbles, Lucy was with her. But now they were gone, where was she?

'Lucy!' she screamed, jerking to her feet. 'Lucy, get back here!'

Nothing.

'Lucy!' she screeched again.

Then suddenly, an ironic realisation. That push off the diving board had been some kind of rehearsal. And she wasn't going to go through that worry again. She wasn't going to lose Lucy. Not her mother, her father, *and* Lucy.

She remembered her mother's words that she'd resented for so long after her death: *you're the sensible one, you need to look after her sometimes.* Words that had made her feel like doing the exact opposite, back then. But this was different, this was now.

Time swelled and became shapeless. The minute or so since Lucy dived down felt like an hour and she knew that if she didn't act right now, Lucy could die.

Shifting her bottom onto the edge of the rock, she let her body drop into the sea, giving a sharp intake of breath as the coldness shocked her skin. She found a slippery foothold for a few moments and her sarong clouded around her, obscuring her view. She ripped it off , then struck out towards where the bubbles had been - doing her breaststroke with her head out of the water. Salt stung her eyes and she wretched on a mouthful of seawater.

Approaching the spot, sooner than she even thought possible, she drifted on her stomach, with her face in the water, looking down, taking the occasional breath on the surface and kicking her feet as if she was snorkelling. At least this way she could see where she was going.

She saw a flash of bright yellow a few feet below her. She recognised it as the shaft of Lucy's snorkel and she dipped her body downwards to see more. She saw Lucy's hair fanning out, then the black costume with the pink trim. The long legs. Lucy was suspended vertically. Rhea's breath hitched in her throat. She remembered her recurring dream, where she was drowning and trying to scream. Then the pain, and her mother's face.

But then she saw the figure move a little.

Still alive? Or the movement of currents?

And in the clear Mediterranean waters, she saw Lucy's hand pointing downwards. But maybe it was just an illusion, like Captain Ahab, in *Moby-Dick*, beckoning his men to follow - dead, but still alive?

Now treading water directly above Lucy, with no seconds to spare, Rhea thrust herself down. But she immediately bobbed back up like a life buoy. Then she remembered Lucy's handstand practices. She tried to copy her. She tipped her body right down, her legs vertical, and she found herself descending. But then there was no more movement and she was rising again. More momentum needed.

Back on the surface, she took just a little breath, so she wouldn't have so much air inside her, then she repeated the dive. And this time she did an underwater breaststroke to get right down, kicking away the water.

Reaching Lucy's legs, she grabbed hold and followed the line of them to Lucy's right foot, where she found it trapped. She pulled hard on her ankle, but there was no movement. So she folded back the rubber of the fin at the back of the foot and tugged at Lucy's heel. Her foot slid out.

Now, struggling for breath, she pushed at Lucy's bottom to get her rising, and thrust herself upwards.

They rose to the surface together.

As their heads cleared the water, she gasped and filled her lungs with air. Then she looked at Lucy. Her eyes were closed behind her mask, and she felt lifeless in Rhea's arms. She has to be alive, Rhea thought. She has to be! She started to shake her. How long had it been? Surely no longer than five minutes, but her sense of time was irretrievably skewed.

Lucy's eyes flicked opened. She was magnified into life behind the thick plastic of her mask. She opened her mouth and tried to say something, but no sound came out.

With her heart crashing against her ribcage, Rhea began to thump Lucy on the back, over and over.

After time stretched wide again, a jet of water finally spewed out of Lucy's mouth. She coughed, she spluttered, she blinked hard. But she still made no movements with her limbs and there was no talking - a bad sign to Rhea.

So, Rhea now did what she hadn't done for thirty years or more. Not since those forced lessons at the local swimming pool. She started doing a life saving sidestroke, with her arm around Lucy's neck, to take her back to the rock. But then she realised Lucy might not have the strength to get herself out of the water, so she craned her neck towards the beach. The whole scale of things shifted in her vision. It was scary. They were so small, the two of them. Two heads bobbing in the sea, suspended on a curved horizon. All she could do was make for the shore. So she slowly began to swim for it, fighting the current, over and over, slowly edging on, using all the strength she had, hearing the odd gasp from Lucy, confirming she was still alive. Finally, she felt the currents moving in their favour. Then she felt rocks beneath her feet and felt Lucy finally moving and shifting her position to help.

Choking on a few shoreline swells, they managed to beach themselves up on the shingle, crawling on their hands and knees, gathering more grazes. Then they lay there on their backs, coughing and panting, like two creatures from the deep that had just acquired lungs and didn't know how to use them.

'I nearly drowned,' Lucy gasped. 'Jesus, Rhea!'

'I know.'

'That was very brave of you,' Lucy panted.

'I know. We're very lucky you didn't need mouth to mouth, because I haven't a clue how to do that!'

Then Rhea groaned.

'What?'

'I forgot to look for the bloody keys!'

'Oh, yes.'

Lucy propped herself weakly on her elbow and looked at Rhea. Then she opened up the fist of her right hand. The keys fell out and chinked onto the pebbles.

'We've got them,' she said. 'We did it. Now, let's get out of here.'

14

Under A Gum Tree

Two hours later, they were accelerating up the track that lead to the summit of the hill, where Lucy had stopped to admire the chaparral. Leaving a dust-bowl fog of dirt behind them, the jeep bumped and skidded its way, this way and that, to avoid the troughs and rocks. It was a good bit of driving on Lucy's part and Rhea had made no complaints. Road, trees and sky began to give way to the more open desert terrain.

There had been little communication between them, as they'd soon found that shouting over the roar of the engine in low gear made them thirsty again. An undesirable outcome, as they'd drank all their water after their exertions in the salt waters of the bay.

Lucy said the more circular route via Gökbel might be faster and more roadworthy, but Rhea had been adamant they should go back the way they came.

But it proved to be a fateful decision.

They'd just met the tarmac road that would take them over the crest of the hill, when the front passenger wheel suddenly thumped down into a deep pot hole. They were both jolted downwards at a steep angle, strapped into their seatbelts.

Lucy revved the engine in first gear, trying to inch the wheel up and out. But it was stuck fast. Then Rhea got out, and tried to push from the back, to gain some momentum, while Lucy tried again - but it was too heavy a vehicle for this to make any impact. Lucy revved the engine in reverse and they tried the same technique from the front.

But the jeep was going nowhere. Listing to one side, it was a sorry sight - like an abandoned ship stuck on a reef.

Pacing around the jeep in her combat trousers and cap,

Rhea looked the part to come up with a proactive and practical solution. Lucy, on the other hand, determined to wear her sunhat with the pink roses on, did not. But as they both stood there with their hands on their hips, glaring at the jeep, they turned on each other instead.

'You should have been looking where you were going! What the hell are we supposed to do now?' Rhea yelled. 'No mobile - thanks to you! No water - thanks to you! I want to get back. I need.. I need...'

'You need a fag and a glass of wine,' Lucy shouted back. 'That's what you need. Well, so do I! Especially after nearly drowning.'

'Yes, well I had to jump in and save you. That was a bit of a strain, you know! Now just get the stuff out of the jeep. We'll have to walk,' Rhea snapped.

'We can't! Its miles away!'

'What the hell else do you suggest? Maybe a car might come along. I don't know, but we can't stay here. And it'll be your fault if we die out here.'

'Oh, don't be so dramatic.'

'I'm not being dramatic, that's your domain. I'm simply stating a fact.'

They lapsed into silence, as they gathered their belongings - in Lucy's case, inclusive of one fin, rather than two.

They trudged along the sweltering road over the rise of the hill, with their matted stringy hair and their bulging beach bags cutting into their shoulders, while the sun stretched their ink-black shadows out in front of them. It was around 7pm now. Lucy's silhouette was distinctly feminine with her soft-brimmed sunhat and her loose skirt flapping around her legs. Rhea's cap and combat trousers made her look altogether different, like a veteran hiker or a soldier on patrol. If it hadn't being for her wedge sandals, it might just have been convincing.

Rhea sniffed. 'I'm knackered. I'm sweating. My feet are

hurting, and I'm covered in scratches and bruises.'

'So am I.'

'I want to get back.'

'So do I.'

'Oh, shut up.'

'You shut up.'

After a few more minutes of traipsing in silence, Lucy began to kick a stone down the road. Skittering over the tarmac, it rolled and bounded along with them, until Rhea made a pass, intercepting it and directing it into the scrub.

They were on their own again, and with Lucy robbed of her diversion, her thoughts inevitably turned to their mother's death.

'You know, Dad should never have put you in that position,' she said. 'Promising never to tell anyone. It's ridiculous. I should have been told. And what about Grandma and Granda?'

'Yes, well, it was done for your sake. It was done for everyone's sake. You could at least be grateful. I'll probably end up back on Prozac now.'

'What? You what?' Lucy's tone was incredulous. 'You've been on antidepressants?'

'I thought you didn't want to talk about it anymore for now,' Rhea said sarcastically.

'Yes, well, maybe we should. Maybe we should pick it up - right here.'

Rhea stopped in her tracks and glared at Lucy. 'Well, what if I've had enough for now? After all, there are other things to worry about, don't you think?' She flung her arms out wide. 'Like being stranded in the middle of nowhere in this heat. Like been thirsty again. I mean, we haven't actually got any water,' she said, her voice rising. 'We could get dehydrated, we could get heatstroke - '

'I know. But we have to try to have a little faith.'

'Faith?' Rhea screeched. 'In what exactly?'

Lucy shrugged her shoulders, exasperatedly. 'I don't know, but we have to. And if we pass the time talking this through to the end, then it can only be a good thing.'

'A good thing! It doesn't feel like a good thing. It feels lousy! And we're in the middle of nowhere! It's ludicrous talking about it under these conditions. We could die out here.'

'Yes, well, you've had lots of opportunities to tell me, in the comfort of a hotel room, by a pool. It's your fault that you wouldn't. So, it might as well be here, before we die,' Lucy said sarcastically. 'Anyway, you know you need to get it out, and I need to hear it, whether I like it or not.' Lucy looked around. 'Look, there's a tree over there. We can sit under it and cool off a bit, while you tell me the rest.'

'Oh, I don't believe this. First, on a raging hot beach. Now under a gum tree?' But Rhea sagged her shoulders and traipsed over to the tree. 'I need a rest now, anyway.'

Sitting on their bags under the spindly branches of the small gum tree, the shade was minimal due to its spidery clusters of narrow leaves. But it was the only tree by the roadside, so they made the best of it and propped their backs up against the striped satin bark.

Lucy suddenly cried out, 'The apples! I forgot the apples!'

She started ransacking her bag, pulling out a paper packet containing two shiny red apples, that she'd bought back in Dalyan as dessert for their lunch. 'They'll give us some moisture,' she said, dropping one into Rhea's lap.

'So, let's get it over with,' she said. 'Tell me why Dad covered it up.'

Rhea looked hard at Lucy and shook her head in disgust. Then she took a bite of her apple and began to munch and speak at the same time. 'It wasn't as cold and deliberate as you make it sound. It wasn't some big contrived 'cover-up'. He was very upset. He didn't want me interviewed by the doctor, or the police. He wanted to spare me that, so it made sense for him to say *he* found Mum. To be honest, Lucy,' she said, swallowing hard, 'I felt relieved, and anyway, that's what dads do isn't it? Protect their kids. It was all about that - for you too. And he protected the family from knowing the truth - he thought it would be an unnecessarily painful thing to bear. To do that, he had to burn the note. He had to. *Why spread the hurt around*, he said. It was bad enough that she'd died, and an accident was something people might be able to cope with better. It would be better for us at school as well.'

'Yes, I can see what he thought,' Lucy said drily, nibbling at the glistening flesh of her apple. 'But tell me what happened after he destroyed the vital evidence.'

'Oh, for goodness' sake, Lucy. There's no need to use the language of a crime thriller. You make it sound so cheap, so calculating. It wasn't like that. You can't think of him like that!' She glared at Lucy.

'Okay, okay. Just get on and tell me.'

***

As Lucy listened to Rhea, the juiciness of the apple did nothing to dispel the rising poison she felt in her gut. So many on the spot decisions that had a detrimental impact over the next 32 years, right up until today. And all because their dad thought he was doing the right thing. The right thing at the time, maybe, but not the right thing forever. She visualised the actions and reactions within the scenes that Rhea described in detail, as if she was an invisible spirit, drifting from room to room - there, but not there. Putting together a crime report for posterity in the ether. Her way of trying to be objective, she supposed. Or maybe it was just shock numbing her as she listened.

While Rhea went upstairs to change into a fresh school blouse and skirt, George phoned the police, stating that he'd found his wife dead in the pond. When they arrived, they went and examined Helen's body to check there were no signs of life. Then they contacted the local doctors' surgery, who told them that Dr. MacDonald was on call and would be around as soon as possible.

Then they talked to George. He told them how he'd been worried about his wife, who'd been depressed lately. He'd phoned home earlier at lunchtime to see how she was, and had got no reply. It was very unusual for her to be out at that time, so he'd felt worried and had driven home during an afternoon break to check on her. That's when he'd found her.

Just then, Rhea entered the kitchen in a clean school uniform with her school bag hitched over her shoulder. She tried very hard to look surprised, as if she'd just come back home from school to find police cars there. George introduced her, then explained that his other daughter, Lucy, would probably be walking back from school right now, but often visited a friend of hers on the way. The police ushered Rhea and George into the front room, so that he and Rhea could have some quiet time together. They suggested that perhaps he should explain events to her now. The earlier the better, in their experience. They would send Lucy in if she arrived home soon.

Meanwhile, while waiting for the doctor to arrive, the police examined the pond area, then talked privately to George again, requiring a few more details about how he had found his wife. He told Rhea later what he'd said. He explained he had discovered her drifting, face down, near the middle of the pond. He'd waded in and dragged her up onto the shallow bank, where she now lay.

The police conducted a search. In Helen's studio they found some punched-out plastic remains of a packet of antidepressants next to a half empty bottle of vodka and a drained pink-tinted tumbler. George told them his wife had been depressed for months, and that unfortunately, she'd been in the habit of having a drink in the afternoon. All of this was apparently true.

Then the police asked George if she'd left any kind of

communication, a note perhaps. He pretended to be distressed at the implication. What gave them that idea? What were they suggesting? Standard procedure, they said. So he searched and the police helped, with Rhea sticking close to George. His hands shook, while he searched and Rhea said nothing. Both father and daughter were judged as being in shock.

No note was found.

Next, the doctor arrived. Euan MacDonald was a friend of the family, and had been treating Helen for years. George sagged into his carver chair in the study, and sank his head into his hands, as the doctor went off to investigate. After examining Helen's body, and checking over the Anafranil supply, and taking into consideration the vodka, Dr. MacDonald reached his conclusions. He talked to the police while George and Rhea waited in the study.

It was safe to say that Dr. MacDonald saved the day for George and Rhea, if such a day could be said to be saved at all.

Helen's death was certified by the GP as 'accidental'. She had been depressed, yes. But in his view, only mildly. Yes, she had probably taken a higher dose of Anafranil than she should, but it was common for people to do this by mistake, in his experience. That, combined with the alcohol, could easily have made her woozy enough to fall unconscious into the pond. In such a state, one could easily drown in relatively shallow water. But there were no suspicious circumstances. There was no suicide note.

The police trusted the GP's judgment and called for an ambulance, while Dr. MacDonald signed the death certificate. In the doctor's considered opinion, there was no need for an inquest. George told Rhea afterwards that he believed the doctor suspected the truth having known about Helen's situation and their marital troubles.

As the doctor was leaving he suggested some counselling might help. There was someone he could recommend. Then, pausing at the front door, he touched George's arm. 'I'm so sorry for your loss,' he said, looking at George and then at Rhea.

Lucy now shivered as she remembered that phrase being repeated in her hearing for days and weeks after her mother's death. She heard it way past the point where it had been emptied out of all its meaning. Just sounds coming from mouths. But she shook herself - she wanted to concentrate on Rhea's story, and a 'story' was what it felt like.

'Yes, but what about where her hat was lying in the rushes, and the bent grasses?' she asked Rhea. 'Didn't the police notice?'

Rhea looked at Lucy incredulously. 'Well, what about them! Dad must have sorted it. The main thing is we got through it. Dad and me.'

'Yes. You got away with it! And it was all about Dad and you. And the whole funeral was a lie. And what about Auntie Kathy, and Granda and Grandma? Didn't they have a right to know?'

'Dad said Granda and Grandma were better off not knowing, they'd never be able to understand. Mum had never felt they understood her anyway. They'd have been angry, disgusted, Dad said. They would have been mortified with shame and tortured by what their friends might think. He said they would feel tainted by what they would see as her weakness.'

'But that's just one way of looking at it, isn't it?'

Rhea flung her apple core behind her into the scrub. 'Oh, here we go again! Always having to see things differently, differently on purpose. It's just typical of you! And any way you look at it, Lucy, it was selfish of her.'

'Yes. I know it was. And even if you take the depression into account, Dad, you and me, were obviously not enough for her.' Then she muttered, 'Neither was her art for that matter.'

348

Rhea groaned. 'Oh, not art again!'

Lucy fell quiet, contemplating the day she lost her mother. All she could remember was getting back from Hazel's, her friend down the road, where they'd been watching Hazel's black and white rabbit, Patches, nibble at the lettuces with his pink twitching nose, until Hazel's mother snatched him up and put him back into his hutch, giving the girls a scolding. As soon as Lucy had got home, her dad beckoned her into the study. He looked so serious. She'd gone in nervously expecting to be told off for coming home late, or maybe Hazel's Mum had phoned about her leading her daughter astray?

But, of course, it was so much worse. Her father telling her of her mother's death. His wobbling voice, his drawing her to his side. His worried blue eyes, his swollen lids. *Your mothers gone, Lu. She's gone to heaven, she'll be looked after there. It was a tragic accident, love. She drowned in the pond. It looks as if she must have been reaching for some magnolia blossom. They found a few cut stems on the bank. Painting was her passion, you know? Do you understand, Lu?* he said, holding her by the shoulders and looking into her face. *She's gone.*

She'd pulled away. And with her heart hammering, she'd run into the studio, but all that was there were her mother's paintings. Then she ran into all the rooms of the house, calling for her mother. Then up to the attic. Then into the garden. Then down to the pond. 'Mummy!' she screamed. 'Mummy! Where are you? Mummy!' But there was no answer. No answer anywhere. She never forgot the chilling weight of the silence.

And Rhea standing at the foot of the stairs. Long face, cold eyes. With her backcombed Debbie Harry bob and her smudged mascara. 'Stop it,' she said. 'Just stop it.'

Then Lucy had screwed up her face and burst into tears.

And now tears came again at the memory. She sniffed and wiped her nose on the sleeve of her shirt. A faint breeze shook the shaggy leaves of the gum tree and she revived a little. But the thirst was building again and her shirt was sticking to her back. She looked at Rhea, slumped against the tree trunk, eyes shiny with wetness. She looked so defeated, so emptied out. She'd never seen her look like this before.

'So, what about the counselling? Did you and Dad do that?'

'He made me go, he didn't go himself.' Rhea sounded sullen. 'After school on a Wednesday, when you thought I was at the tennis club.'

'Did you tell the counsellor the truth?'

'Yes. Dad said I should.'

'What did they think?'

'Well, she helped me see the bigger picture, how Dad probably had the best intentions for everyone, and that it would certainly have been easier for relatives to grieve over an accident rather than a suicide. And she told me that the reason for my nightmares were because I had been through an awful ordeal. We worked through that, and it did help. But in regard to covering up the truth, she thought there was no right or wrong way to have responded. You know how it goes. They don't judge.'

'No, I suppose they're not allowed to. But did she agree with you keeping the secret from *me*?'

Rhea was slow to reply, flicking a mosquito away from her scratched ankle. 'Well, she could see how I would resent you, because Mum had chosen you not to be told, rather than both of us. It was natural to feel hurt, to feel it was unfair. And at the end of the day, she suggested, it was my choice whether to tell you, not Dad's.

'And?'

'Well, Dad kept saying *why spread the hurt around*. You were better off not knowing, you were too young to understand. So I left it alone. For him. I promised him.

350

And no-one in the family knew about the affair either. Dad said, *why tarnish her memory?* But it used to be so hard when you sang Mum's praises, making out she was the perfect mother, or when you were older, going through that poetry phase. I remember you chanting that saying about her: 'Those whom the gods love die young'. It made me sick. All I felt was furious with her.'

'Was that when you were on antidepressants?'

'God, no! Rhea said, staring at Lucy. 'I had my life to get on with. I wanted to get away from home as soon as possible. It was really why I went down South to go to college. And then I met Chris... I put it out of my mind altogether and got on with my career.'

'So, when did you take the Prozac?'

Rhea sighed. 'We really do have to get out of here, you know. I'm parched, and I'm feeling dizzy now. This is a serious situation. And it's all your fault.'

'Stop trying to change the subject. When did you take it!'

'Oh, for crying out loud, Lucy! I took it after Dad's funeral for a couple of months. Okay?'

'Why?'

'Because…' Rhea hesitated, fiddling with the strap of her bag.

'Why? Lucy cried.

'Because when we visited him at the hospital, that last time together, just before he died, when I asked you to get some water, I asked him if I could tell you the truth about Mum, if I needed to.'

'Oh, yes. I remember you getting me out of the room. It felt odd. So, what did he say?'

Rhea flinched, then a few tears trailed down her cheeks. She looked at Lucy. 'He…'

Lucy grabbed Rhea by the shoulders. 'What did he say?'

Rhea shook herself free. 'He didn't say yes, and he didn't say no. He fell asleep. And the next day, he died.

So, you see...' her voice rose, as she looked piercingly into Lucy's eyes, 'I never got his permission! He didn't say it was fine to tell you. And now, I've betrayed him. I've betrayed him and I feel terrible.' She started to sob.

When Lucy put her arm around Rhea's heaving shoulders, she was surprised to find Rhea didn't shake her off. They stayed like that for a few moments, Rhea's sobs slowly ebbing. But then she felt a stab of annoyance. Things should never have been covered up. Far better, things out in the open, even if the truth was ugly and everyone hated it.

'He shouldn't have put you in that position back then, and then expecting you to keep it secret for so long - it was wrong, Rhea. Don't you see? It was too much of a burden and he wrecked our relationship. It was wrong.'

'But he thought he was right, and he was our dad! What he said made sense!'

'He made a mistake.' Lucy felt a hard stone form in her heart, something she'd never felt for her father before.

'Oh, you were always finding fault with him. I knew that would be your attitude. I just knew it.'

'And you were always idolising him. Like I did with Mum, I suppose. Don't you see?'

***

Rhea didn't reply. Her tongue felt as dry as blotting paper and she had a pounding headache. She felt the need to move, so she cast off Lucy's arm - it had lingered on her shoulders for too long. She was tired of Lucy's amateur psychoanalysis and she was tired of talking.

She got to her feet and swayed a little as she picked up her bag. Her heart fluttered against her ribcage.

'Look, we can't stay here. We'll get ill. I think I'm already getting dehydrated.'

'Yes, I know, I'm dripping with sweat. I can't believe there's been no sign of a car, or a truck. It's almost eight

352

o'clock now.'

'We'll have to carry on walking. Maybe we'll find some shelter - a corrugated shack or something. Come on,' she said, as she saw Lucy beginning to twist and coil her hair again with more intensity than usual. 'I'm not going to die under a gum tree.'

'Okay,' Lucy said, with resignation. 'We're all talked out for now anyway.'

Back on the road and going downhill, their shadows stretched further - so spindly thin. Like enfeebled aliens struggling to survive Earth's atmosphere. Across the desert land, to the west, the burning sun was preparing to sink and quench itself in the ocean.

All that water and not a single drop to drink, thought Rhea, as she peered out to sea. Thank God they weren't still at the beach, she would probably have felt compelled to drink mouthfuls of saltwater.

And as she watched the sun, it seemed as if time was accelerating. Moment by moment, faster and faster, the sun was slipping down. And she had the growing conviction that they must get back to Dalyan before sunset or something dreadful would happen. Something evil. She glanced over her shoulder, to check they weren't being followed. By whom or what, she didn't know. They were in a foreign country, in the middle of nowhere. Anything could happen, she thought, trying to keep her breathing regular - absolutely anything. And a scene from *Bram Stoker's Dracula* came to mind, where the count is chasing the setting sun to his castle to rise from his coffin once more - to drink blood, to…

She tried to shake away the nonsense of her drift, worried she was becoming delirious.

Lucy's change of mood didn't help. 'It's kind of an adventure, don't you think?' she asked Rhea, shifting her bag to her other shoulder to ease the strain.

Despite her own imaginings, Rhea threw Lucy her best rolling eye look, that she reserved for complete idiots, whose notions weren't even worth responding to.

But Lucy was not to be deterred. 'No, honestly! That's the best way to look at it. Here we are. No food. No water. No human contact. Suffering from heat exhaustion and dehydration, we walk on. Trying to survive in a hot land. Lost in -'

'We're not lost! We've got the map. And don't you think we've had enough drama for one day?'

'Oh, come on, Rhea! Try pretending. It'll take your mind off things.' Lucy insisted. 'Lost,' she continued. 'Lost in a strange land, full of strange fruits and strange trees. Wildlife lurking in the scrub and in the woods. Two lost travellers, trying to find a shelter for the night. Against all the odds, we must carry on, step by step, our lips cracked by the sun, our blistering feet dragging across the ground, we -'

'Hang on!' Rhea hissed and grabbed hold of Lucy's arm. She couldn't believe what she was seeing. 'Look! Down there! To the left.'

There were two motorbikes. Two sets of wheels, parked up under some pine trees on their kick stands at a dirt road junction.

'It's that track to the radar station,' she said. 'It must be.'

They stumbled down the road, glancing all around for signs of life.

But there were none.

Rhea examined the bikes. And they were unmistakable. Two black Honda Deaville 650cc tourer bikes. One with a worn leather jacket draped across the seat, pasted with faded skulls and flames. They were the bikes of Rod and Pete, the two morons that had drunk their water, then not put the cap back on properly. Her eyes travelled to the fixed panniers on either side of the pillion seats. Then she noticed that one of the bikers had left his key in the ignition. Both helmets were perched on the fuel tanks.

'Do you recognise them?' she asked Lucy, who was

examining the jacket.

'Yes. But where *are* they?'

'Maybe they've gone up the track to see the view from the station. It's in a lot of the brochures. You can see the whole of the turtle beach.'

'But why leave the bikes here?'

'To save the suspension or something, I suppose. Bikers can be very precious.'

'Not exactly hells angels, then. And it'll be a long hot walk there and back. I bet they've underestimated the time it'll take. And where are they on their way to, anyway? They're heading in the opposite direction of the Blue Lagoon.'

'Maybe they decided to try a little nightlife in Marmaris. They'll be cutting it fine now though.'

Rhea fumbled with one of the panniers. As she opened it, she pounced on what she found inside.

A full 75cL bottle of water.

She yanked it out, unscrewed the cap, and took a deep swallow of the warm water, that slid down her dry socket of a mouth, like water running in a parched channel of earth, barely touching the sides. Then another swallow, and another.

Lucy snatched the bottle off her and did the same.

By the time the bottle had been grabbed back and forth, Rhea was surprised they managed to share it pretty evenly. Maybe some childhood sibling training must have survived, she reflected. How weird was that?

'Let's check the rest,' she told Lucy, wiping her mouth with the back of her hand.

Lucy emptied the contents of the other panniers, and held up another bottle of water. 'We'll have to leave them this, they might not have taken any with them.'

'Sod them,' Rhea said, feeling no sympathy for the bikers whatsoever. Not after the day she'd had. But she didn't stop Lucy putting the water back with the bikers things.

355

Feeling a little more refreshed, and gazing at the key in the ignition of the lead bike, Rhea had a wild idea. The very wildness of it surprised her, and her spine tingled with the shock of it. Suddenly, anything felt possible.

'I take it you're not happy with the idea of asking for a lift back with them,' she said to Lucy, shuddering at the thought herself.

'No way. That would be like out of the frying pan and into the fire.'

'Exactly. But Lucy, we can get back by ourselves. She darted a look up the track. Still no sign. 'We'll have to be quick though.'

'What do you mean?'

'I can just about remember how to ride a bike,' Rhea said. 'You can ride pillion. We can leave them the bike without the key, they must have the key with them.'

'We can't just steal one of their bikes,' Lucy said incredulously.

'Oh yes we can! We can leave them a note,' Rhea said, grappling with the contents of her bag. 'Come on, get a helmet on! We're doing it. Quick, before they come back.'

Lucy's eyes widened. 'But can we really do it? It might be dangerous, Rhea. We might have an accident. I've never been on a bike before.'

'Oh, right! Where's your sense of adventure now?' Rhea stamped up to Lucy and looked her straight in the face. 'No argument. No discussion. We're doing it!'

Rhea felt determined that for once, Lucy would do what she was told. The older sister was taking control now, even though she'd only tried riding a bike twice under Chris's instruction on the Lancashire Moors - and that was back in the eighties.

She thrust a helmet into Lucy's hands, and scrabbled for her notebook and pen. 'Empty out their stuff, and get our bags into these panniers. They should fit in fine. I'm going to write our lovely Rod and Pete a nice little letter.'

As she penned the note, her decisive stabbing action

with the biro became shaky with nerves.

Boys,

*Our jeep is stuck in a hole way back and we're stranded.
We need to take your bike to get back to Dalyan and don't
fancy a lift with you.
We've helped ourselves to the water you owe us. We could
have died out here without it.
You can pick up your bike from the Onur Hotel.*

Cheers,

The Girlies.

Then, she ripped it out of her notebook and handed it
to Lucy. 'Tuck it under the pannier strap'. Lucy read it first
and giggled. 'Oh God, they're not going to like this.'

'Come on! Get your helmet on. We've got to hurry! I'll
get it started and tell you when to get on. Hold onto the
bar on the back. Lean in to the bends with me, that's the
most important thing. You *must* do that, and make no
sudden movements. Do you understand?' She reached
down and flipped out the pillion foot pedals.

Lucy was fiddling with her helmet strap and didn't
appear to be listening.

'Do you understand!' repeated Rhea, fear starting to
prick her now.

'Yes!' Lucy made a mock salute.

Rhea tied on her own helmet and mounted the bike.
She stared at the handlebars, the instrument panel and the
switches. It all looked so different from Chris's old
Triumph. She reminded herself of the left and right handle
functions, left for clutch and signals, right for throttle and
front braking, just as she had seen Hasim using on his
Suzuki. She glanced down by her left foot at the shift lever
for changing gear and by her right foot, the rear brake

pedal. But breaking out into a sweat stopped her in her tracks. Could she do this? Should she do this?

'Hurry up. Get the engine going,' Lucy urged, glancing up the path to the viewpoint.

'I don't know about this,' Rhea said, her voice wobbling.

'What?'

'No, really. It's not very responsible. What about all those hairpin bends? What if we get injured?'

'Oh come on, Rhea. Adventure, remember? We've decided now. Just take the bends slow. You'll be fine! *We'll* be fine!'

Lucy's eyes flashed determination through the slat of her open visor, which served to pump some fuel into Rhea's resolve. She turned the ignition key to the right, and flicked the engine cut off switch to the on position. The engine started. A churning throbbing irregular pulse. Rhea felt adrenalin firing through her veins to keep pace with it. With her right hand, she squeezed the front brake in, and with her left, she held the clutch in.

'Get ready!' she shouted above the engine noise to Lucy, who hitched up her skirt.

Rhea rocked the bike forward a little, and the kickstand sprung free. 'Now!' she cried, pushing down the gear shift with her left foot. The bike started to creep forward, so she tightened her grip on the brake, while Lucy mounted the pillion seat, perched her feet on the pedals, and took a firm hold of the hand bar behind her back.

'Ready?' Rhea shouted, glancing up the track again.

She gasped when she saw two leather-tubed pairs of legs lumbering down towards them, picking up their pace into a run.

Taking a deep breath to steady herself, she remembered to release the clutch slowly to avoid stalling, and the bike rolled away - away from the running legs. She pulled back on the throttle, and after directing her attention to changing gear and picking up speed, she turned her head just in time to see Lucy give the bikers the finger.

'Bye bye, boys!' Lucy shouted.

As the engine sound rose into a high-pitched whine, and the road was swallowed up in a blur, Rhea felt her heart thudding with both elation and terror. She'd done it! She'd really done it. And not only that, she was doing it. Riding a bike. All that engine power. But could she control it? And it felt dangerous being on the opposite side of the road. Lucy was squealing now and again, as the road twisted this way and that, but they soon settled into a rhythm of leaning one way then the other, as they started to descend the hill down to Dalyan.

Rhea took the first hairpin bends slowly, in first or second gear, stalling the engine now and again until she got used to keeping the revs high. Then she became more confident, and by the time they turned right onto the turtle beach road, she was astonished to find she was enjoying herself.

She pulled back on the throttle and the bike shot forward, picking up speed to around 50mph. The sun was setting now, burnishing the hillside treetops in a golden glow, but the light was fading fast. She searched for the headlight switch and flicked it on. It was exciting to see the beams flare out into the dusk. With the rush of air against her face, the buffeting of her clothing against her body, and the race of the engine, she felt an exhilaration she hadn't felt for so many years. Lucy whooped in her ear and Rhea grinned as they leaned into another snaking curve. She felt as if she wanted the ride to go on forever, all around the lake and beyond - to leave that part of herself she couldn't resolve, way behind, another Rhea, falling exhausted to her knees in the dust.

Half an hour later, Lucy pointed down to the left. The lights of Dalyan spangled in the darkness. But to Rhea, the sparks of civilisation meant inevitable responsibilities, and she felt sick at heart that her escape was going to end.

As she parked the bike on the forecourt of the Onur, a weight settled on her again and exhaustion finally asserted itself. Even if Hasim had been at reception, she wouldn't have cared one way or the other.

***

That evening, after leaving a message for the car hire company at the desk, as to the approximate whereabouts of the jeep, and after Lucy returning Rhea's mobile from the deposit box, they drank all the bottled water they had left in their room. At around 10pm, they decided it was too late to eat, so they showered and changed into their nighties. They massaged antiseptic cream into their cuts and grazes, then sat together, slouched in the white plastic chairs on the balcony. Lucy tolerated Rhea's cigarette smoke wafting into her face, despite Rhea's attempts to blow it in the opposite direction, whilst they recuperated with a bottle of red wine.

After a few sighs of relief at having survived the day from hell, which they both managed to agree it had been, they soon fell quiet, staring down into the pool and occasionally casting each other surreptitious glances.

Lucy broke the silence first.

'I know we've both been through a lot today, but I still want to go on my trip tomorrow.'

Rhea gaped at her. 'What?'

'I know. And I am shattered. But I don't want to be with you. I want to have the day to myself. To think.'

'But you won't have that in the middle of a Turkish village! And I thought you'd want us to talk tomorrow. There's still a few things to -'

'It's all too soon for me, Rhea. I've hardly absorbed it. But I need to be doing something, so I want to go on the trip. Why don't you go to Ephesus? You might as well, as it's booked and paid for.'

Rhea was quiet for a few moments, then she groaned,

'Oh, please yourself.'

15

Lucky Fields

Lucy never saw Rhea the next morning. She'd had an early pick-up at 6.45am for her long bus trip west to Ephesus, and had left Lucy lying in a stupor in bed. So, on the breakfast terrace Lucy crammed into her mouth as much bread, honey and coffee as she could manage, feeling starved after the previous day's trials, while wondering what on earth Rhea had done for some food.

She traipsed down to reception at around 8.30 in a loose cotton maxi dress and her walking sandals, for her own pick-up. Her bag was loaded with more bottled water, her camera, and the tattered remains of the Dalyan book. Hasim was on duty, as she'd anticipated. About to attend to some boringly practical issues, she felt the stone in her heart that had developed yesterday, aiding her with some hardened resignation.

She checked that the car hire company had the jeep's collection in hand and it was all apparently covered in the insurance. Hasim told her that she and Rhea could pay the bill for the petrol when the vehicle had been recovered. He smilingly enquired as to Rhea's whereabouts, but the warmth went out of his eyes when Lucy told him she'd caught an early bus to Ephesus and would be gone all day. His smile slid away and he changed the subject.

'How did you get back last night?' he asked.

'We stole a motorbike and Rhea got us back on it,' Lucy said.

His eyebrows shot up and Lucy felt an unfamiliar flash of pride in her sister. 'Yes, she drove it back, or is the term rode it back?'

Hasim looked confused.

But Lucy had more in store for him, as she rustled

363

around in her bag. Having decided to act according to her principles, and not feeling disposed to employ her usual sensibilities, she simply thrust the tattered remains of *Dalyan: The Land, The Sea, The People* into his hands.

'You should look at the back cover,' she said. 'I don't know what you're playing at, or if you're playing at anything, but she's seen it.'

She turned on her heels, leaving Hasim leafing through the loose pages, with a deeply cracked brow.

Entering the forecourt, to wait for the tour bus into the Taurus mountains, she noticed, with some relief, that the stolen Honda was no longer there.

But June and Brian Walker were.

Of course, she thought. They just would be. Well, she was in no mood for them today.

'Ooo pet, you look like you've been in the wars. Doesn't she, Brian? You've got some bad sunburn there, and how did you get that scratch on your face?' June's puppet smile seemed even more turned up at the corners today, her eyes shrunk into two tiny black holes. And her celery stick neck was wound around with ever increasing circles of gold chains. More than Lucy had ever seen her wear. One twist and a pull on them might very well snap her neck.

Responding to June's comment, Lucy couldn't help touching her cheek at the memory of Rhea's lashing out at her during their fight at the bay. ' Oh, I just tripped on the shingle beach where we were the other day.'

'Well, you look exhausted, luv. Your aura's less bright today. You should take it easy, mind.'

Lucy surveyed them both. June was wearing a blousy bright yellow chiffon dress, her tiny feet at the end of her peg legs showing off pink nail-varnished toes in gold strap sandals. Brian was wearing a Hawaiian-style shirt over his huge khaki shorts and his trainers were still Persil white. Hardly suitable attire for visiting a Turkish mountain village. All flashy and westernised. And looking at them

364

both actually hurt her eyes. How was she to make it clear she didn't have any desire for their company today?

'Well, yes, I'm shattered actually.' A useful extension of June's own comments might work very well, she decided. 'So, I just want to be by myself today. Things to think about. You understand?' Damn, she thought, why did I say things to think about?

June's nose seemed to twitch, as if she could smell something had changed. 'What things, luv? You know you can always tell me anything, if you need to.'

'Nothing in particular,' she tried to say airily. 'So, you won't be offended if I keep myself to myself?'

June and Brian exchanged an unreadable look, then they both stared at her. Their joint scrutiny felt unnerving, as if they knew she was hiding something - something new, something big. Well, she was, and it had to stay that way - at least from them. She returned their scrutiny with her own.

June looked edgy all of a sudden, as if she'd made a wrong move in a game of chess, but was trying not to show it. 'Oh, well pet, that's a shame,' she muttered.

Brian was less sensitive. 'That time of the month, is it?' he said, raising his eyebrows.

Before Lucy could react to the blatant sexism in her usual way - like a well-oiled trigger ready to fire off, a minibus pulled up and Seda's head emerged from the doorway with her long plait swinging over her shoulder.

'Good morning,' she smiled. 'Another hot day, yes?'

And Lucy felt a surge of relief at the very sight of her.

An hour later they were travelling south east on a main road, en route to a village in the western Taurus mountains. Ediz was once again the driver, and an evil eye swung from the rear view mirror again, along with a grinning purple monkey hanging from one arm. Lucy was sitting near Seda on the front left side of the bus. Having learned her lesson from the previous excursion, she'd let

June and Brian get on first and they were seated near the back.

Seda explained the day's itinerary to the group of eight people on board. They would be travelling east to the coastal resort of Kalkan, then they'd be transferring into two jeeps and heading north, up a winding road into the mountains, to visit a farming family living in the village of Şanslı Alanlar, which meant lucky fields. It was a yayla, which was the Turkish word for a beautiful high mountain valley. They would have lunch in the family home, trying some traditional Turkish bread called gözleme which came with a variety of fillings, then they'd be able to walk around the village or enjoy a donkey ride.

As Seda delivered another monologue about the lifestyle of the farmers in these summer villages, Lucy rested her bony elbow awkwardly on the narrow window ledge and stared blankly from behind her sunglasses at the passing chaparral. The freckling of arid scrubland, the dry-brush edgings of stands of conifers on the hillsides, and the misted mountain peaks beyond, did nothing to stir her artist's soul. Her mind was deep in the past, with no anticipation or care about what the day might have in store. It was as if her mind was stuck like a fly to flypaper, an unwelcome state of mind that she was very familiar with. And today, she'd been expecting it, she wanted it, even though she felt it might somehow kill her in the process.

And of course it was all about her mother. Her mother, whose spirit she now visualised drifting around Housesteads instead of Brook Farm. Why did her father lie? She resolved to ask Rhea.

But the biggest thing on her mind was why she hadn't noticed anything was the matter with her mother all those years ago? Why hadn't she noticed she was unhappy? She tried to remember those last few years, when her mother would have been having her affair with the sculptor. With John, the George Harrison lookalike. She was struck by the irony of Rhea's comparing him to a different George to their father. According to the timescale Rhea had described, it must have started around 1974, when she, herself, was nine and Rhea would have been eleven, just starting secondary school.

But all she could remember were good times - that's all she'd ever remembered. Beach holidays, picnics, and days out at Blanchland and Edmundbyers in Northumberland, where their dad would be on some kind of history mission, examining the ruins and records in the local churches for some project he was working on. And sometimes she and Rhea would be left in the car with a packet of crisps each, while their mum and dad had a drink at a local inn with their friends. Pubs with gold-lettered names and mantles of Virginia creeper. Of course, she and Rhea bickered as they ate their crisps, but nothing like the vicious sniping that came after their mother died.

And good times at home, with her mother painting, her father studying some Open University courses in his spare time, her mother in the garden, weeding and trimming, while her father mowed the lawns. Then there were Sunday lunches with trifle afterwards, and playing in the back field with her friends from down the road, even sometimes with Rhea and her friends joining in to boss them around, and they made dens out of all sorts of rubbish from a nearby dump. And all that television watching too, all those romantic black and white movies, with Bette Davis, Ava Gardner, Lana Turner, the list was endless. Her mother loved those, just like Aunty Kathy. And then came colour.

And she suddenly remembered something. She was with her mum and Rhea in the living room, in front of the expensive new colour television set. The Nimble advert was on, and she and Rhea were dancing around the room with their mother, pretending to fly like birds, arms out wide and singing the song. Then when it ended, they collapsed into giggles on the couch, and she had vowed to her mother that she was going to be the girl in the balloon one day. And her mother said *You will Lu, I know you will.* 'Me too,' said Rhea, 'I want to, as well.' *Yes, both of you*, her mother replied, hugging them together. And their dad stood in the doorway, shaking his head and smiling.

Her mother, having taken to her heart the flower power of the sixties, was a hippy chic, and she seemed happy. She'd qualified as a primary school teacher, but had dropped it after a couple of years to be a housewife. She said she couldn't control a whole classroom of kids. George was happy with that as long as she was happy. Then, she discovered art and that made her more happy.

So, where did it all go wrong? She had the occasional exhibition, got frustrated sometimes with the lack of success - that old chestnut, Lucy thought. But how had her mother reacted? Usually with renewed zest, as far as she could remember, she'd always seemed to bounce back. Of course, she'd painted portraits of them all. Lucy still had hers, showing a pensive eight year old, with bunches in her hair, in the style of a Matisse - bold features, flattened planes. And that's how she painted her still lifes too.

But why did she have an affair? Why did she put her family at risk? Why was Dad not good enough for her anymore? Was he too boring? Too serious? He certainly didn't go with her to art galleries, he said it wasn't his thing. Yet her mother still went.

Lucy remembered going with her once to the Laing Art Gallery in Newcastle one Saturday, while Rhea had been off shopping in town with a friend. It was a one-off occasion in her memory. A rare treat, where she'd had her mother all to herself. Well, almost.

She remembered staring up at the painting of *Isabella and the Pot of Basil*, by William Holman Hunt. It was a gruesome story, which her mother explained and she'd never forgotten. Isabella, dressed in a white nightgown, was draped over a pot of basil in which she had buried the severed head of her former lover, Lorenzo. He'd been murdered by her brothers. Isabella pined for him at this altar she had made. It made Lucy feel sad, but it was beautifully painted in a style she was to come to love, detailed realism.

But her mother's telling of the story had been interrupted by a tall man approaching them. A tall man with shoulder length hair. Her mother seemed surprised, flustered even. She told Lucy he was just a friend, for her to carry on looking at the painting while she had a word with him - she wouldn't be long. She talked to him in a corner of the room, in hushed tones. Then somehow, they all ended up going to the cafe together. Lucy remembered she had a Dandelion and Burdock, because she hated it and never had another one again. And then she remembered the foam on the man's moustache - he must have had a beer. And her mother laughed at him, pointing it out, and he grinned back at her. Lucy couldn't remember what they talked about. And then they parted company, and she and her mother went home on the bus.

And on the way home, it was odd, because her mum said not to mention that they'd bumped into him.

'But why,' she'd asked.

Because your dad wouldn't like it, Lu.

'But why?'

Just because! Oh Lu, sometimes you ask too many questions. Then she'd looked at her pleadingly. *It'll be our little secret, okay?*

'Okay,' she'd said. She liked secrets back then. And it was special sharing a secret with her mum.

Just a minute, Lucy thought. The man had a moustache, and long hair. And there was the way they'd been with each other. She could see it now, looking back, it was so familiar, like they really knew each other. Surely, it must have been him? John, the sculptor, the George Harrison lookalike. And he looked nothing like George Allen, her father. This man was broad in the shoulders and long in the back, with big hands and a cheeky grin, compared to her own father's short, wiry stature and hesitant smile. And this man was full of himself, she remembered that much, definitely unlike her more reserved father.

'Oh, my God, I met him!' she gasped out loud.

Just then, her thoughts were interrupted by the coach lurching to a halt and Seda announcing it was time to get into the jeeps. Lucy shot a scowl at the two vehicles, waiting at the bottom of a steep hill. She wanted to wander about by herself, and think. She felt trapped by all this transport, and with her thoughts queuing up again, she was last to get off the coach.

'You okay today?' Seda asked her, as Lucy stood by the coach entrance watching the others pile into the jeeps.

'No, not really, Seda.'

And before she could even consider the effect her words were likely to have, and that she certainly hadn't prepared herself to deliver - out they came, regardless. 'Rhea told me yesterday that our mother killed herself. She's known for 32 years. A family secret, Seda. No innocent tragedy, but wilful suicide. We weren't good enough for her. I wasn't good enough for her.'

She felt cold in the heat, and exhaustion dragged at her. She slumped against the side of the coach. But Ediz was revving the engine to depart.

Seda pulled her away, her eyes wide. She darted glances towards the waiting jeeps and their drivers.

'I'm sorry, Lucy. We need to go now! Can you carry on?'

'I can't sit next to June and Brian,' Lucy insisted, looking imploringly at Seda.

'No. You can get in with me at the front. And when we get to the village, after lunch, you can be by yourself, or I can be with you.'

'Thanks, Seda. I just need some space.'

The ride to Şanslı Alanlar was all cloudy and smudged to Lucy, focused as she was upon her introspections and memories. And what she remembered, or what she thought she remembered, seemed to waver in the heat of her scrutiny. Only the bumping up and down of the jeep, painful to her aching muscles and joints after yesterday, sporadically jolted her into the present. That, and taking plenty of swallows of her drinking water.

The scenery became dramatic as they travelled along the dirt roads, with distant chalky limestone crags, shadowed by peaks and columns of rock. And in the valleys beneath, grazing sheep and goats shifted on the pastures. The drivers parked at viewpoints for photo stops, but Lucy remained uninspired. It wasn't in her nature to be dictated to as to what to take pictures of under normal circumstances, let alone during her current turmoil, so her lens cap remained firmly in place. Seda chatted about the valleys being covered in wild flowers in May, and the village where they were going to, usually having fields of red poppies. But as it was late June, they'd all be gone.

'Just typical,' Lucy commented. And she suddenly realised she'd used the same expression that Rhea had been using a lot on this holiday. Well, so what? she thought. I use it too. But it made her squirm inside.

They got to the village of Lucky Fields at around noon. Sprawled out in a flat green valley of trees and patchwork fields at around 700 metres above sea level, it was surrounded by barren mountains on all sides. As they all climbed out of the jeeps and stretched their legs, Lucy cast their surroundings some cursory glances.

They were in a meandering street of white-painted stone houses with overhanging pan tile roofs. A few had upper floor verandas with timber beam supports. Scrambling grapevines, colourful kelims and pots of geraniums spilled from these balconies. There was a grassy square further on, and outside one of the shop fronts, Lucy could make out a group of men sitting in the shade. They were wearing checked shirts and caps and were hunched over a table playing some kind of game. She could also hear the fade in and fade out of tinkling bells that reminded her that donkeys featured on this trip, sure-footed residents that defined a mountain village. Before yesterday, she would have felt enchanted by this sound, but not today.

Seda led them to the end of the street, towards a large house of the same local design, and after changing their shoes for slippers provided at the entrance, she ushered them into a dimly lit interior which smelled of baking bread and spices.

'Lunch,' Seda said, smiling. She introduced them to the farmer's wife, Yazmira, a robust looking woman wearing a patterned headscarf tied under her chin, a white blouse and a long chintzy skirt, like the kind Lucy had seen in the markets. Seated in front of a fire and griddle, she was in the middle of rolling out dough and brushing it with beaten egg. She smiled a greeting.

Soon, they were all seated upon divans covered in cushions, kelims and white lace covers, with a glass of Turkish tea. Seda explained that Yazmira and her husband, Batur, owned fruit orchards and many fields on which their herds of sheep and goats fed, and on which they grew grains and chickpeas. The whole family worked on the farm.

Various fillings were offered for the gözleme breads, to be folded into the circles of pastry dough and cooked on the griddle. Seda translated what Yazmira began to list. There was spiced mince, chopped lamb, mushroom, peppers and a wide range of other vegetables and herbs grown in her garden, as well as Turkish white cheese, called Beyaz peynir, explained Seda, and goats cheese, called Tulum.

'So, can I take the orders, please?' Seda said, pen and clipboard at the ready.

372

'Hasn't she got any chips?' Brian asked.

Lucy felt a wave of disgust flood through her as she saw Seda's look of embarrassment and Yazmira's face wrinkle in miscomprehension. There were a few sniggers from some of the others in the party, and June gave Brian a sharp dig with her elbow into the blubber cushioning his ribs.

Lucy broke the silence first. 'Brian! We're not in a MacDonald's! Have some respect.'

'I'm only asking, like! If you don't ask, you don't get!'

'Well, you could do with a few less chips!' she said, glaring at his belly bulging from underneath the beach parasols of his Hawaiian shirt.

There were more giggles. Seda bit her lip and looked at the floor.

For once, Brian had no retort to make. So with no appetite, and a need to get some air, Lucy dived for an exit, any exit.

Still wearing her slippers, she groped towards some light and found herself in a back garden overlooking an orchard. To escape from the full scrutiny of the sun, she hurried to a vine-covered pergola, sat down on a rickety wooden bench and fixed her gaze ahead, trying to calm the angry turbulence she felt. And it wasn't just about Brian. And the earthly delights of chattering birds, a swarm of bright flower heads, the abundant plantings of herbs and vegetables, and the strut and peck of a foraging hen on the path that led down to the orchard, all did nothing to soothe her. Everything had gone wrong on this holiday. It wasn't the way it was supposed to be. She and Rhea were supposed to be getting to know each other better, fulfilling their father's wish. But that was all based on lies. Why should she bother *now*?

And yet…she had found out what they'd both been hiding. She'd accomplished that, which is what the holiday had become about, for her, and she'd very nearly drowned in the process. But she couldn't dwell on that right now. And there was the irony of June's cards seeming to fit. The hanged man for a new perspective, the moon reversed for past secrets. And what about the empress? Was their mother watching over them? And did she, Lucy, care one way or the other now? And how was she going to handle –'

Her flurry of anxieties was scattered by the sight of a plate with a golden glazed gözleme bread on it.

'Eat,' said the farmer's wife, holding it out to her. She noticed Lucy's look of surprise and said, 'It best to know a few words.'

Seda hurried up behind, carrying Lucy's sandals for her. 'I picked a filling for you.'

'I'm just not hungry. I'm sorry,' Lucy said to Yazmira, looking into her darkly determined eyes. She felt her stomach heave, as if she was going to be sick with her hurting.

Seda spoke to Yazmira in Turkish, a quiet urging tone at first, then sorrowful. Then they both looked at her. Yazmira put the plate down next to her on the bench.

'I hope you not mind,' said Seda. 'But I explain what is making you sad. What happened to your mother. Yazmira's uncle did this many years ago when all his crops failed. She not forget.'

'Oh.'

'In Turkish, it is called intihar, it is a sin to Allah.'

'Yes, well I expect it would be,' Lucy said sarcastically. 'But I'm not sure I believe it is a sin. I've always thought people have a right to do it - it's their life. Or at least, that's what I used to believe. I don't know what I believe now.'

She shoved her feet into her sandals and handed the knitted slippers back to Yazmira.

'What was she like?' Seda asked, sitting next to her.

Yazmira smiled at Lucy. 'Eat,' she said. Then she turned and left them alone.

'I don't really want to talk about her right now,' Lucy replied to Seda. But when she turned and saw Seda's frowning concern, and her fingers nervously fidgeting with the tassel of her plait, she changed her mind.

'She was kind. And funny. She was sensitive, always guessing how we were feeling, she cheered us up. She hated rules though, a bit like me. She'd rant and rave if there was something she didn't agree with, but she wasn't very brave with authority figures like teachers at parents evenings, or maybe she couldn't be bothered, I don't know. She was always driving Rhea mad doing more than one thing at once, like cooking and reading a book at the same time. She used to laugh a lot and sing around the house. She was always bringing plants in from the garden and arranging them, she had a knack for that. And she had some weird friends that descended now and again for the night. Dad didn't like them much. She and Dad were so different, I don't know what they saw in each other in the first place…but they seemed okay…' she trailed off.

But maybe it hadn't been what it seemed, she thought. Maybe they were badly matched. Maybe her mother just wanted to get away from her parents; she was always saying they were snobs. Then George Allen came on the scene at teaching college. These things happen, after all. And she had tried to stick it out. It was obvious she'd tried. But if someone came along under those circumstances, and she'd never really loved their dad in the first place, then she could have fallen in love deeply, passionately…and then she'd have wanted nothing to get in the way. Not even her own children, it would seem.

Lucy felt nauseous again, and her breaths came in long drags, deeper and deeper. She couldn't control it. She bent over double. The hurt swelled up in her, higher and higher. It had to come out or she'd burst. Tears rolled down her cheeks and her ribs shook as she sobbed. 'Such a… long time…I never knew,' she cried. 'I never knew! Why didn't they *tell* me? They should have *told* me! I would have understood, wouldn't I?'

She felt Seda's hand on her shoulder. But where was

Charlie? She needed him. He would know what to say, what to do. And her lovely Poppy, she could never imagine doing to Poppy anything like her mother had done to herself and Rhea. The pain inside her exploded, took her over, and all she could do was cry harder, harder than she'd ever cried before. Seda's hand stayed on her shoulder the whole time, a gentle, but firm pressure.

Eventually, she was spent. She wiped her eyes with the hem of her dress and sat up. She yanked back her hair into a scrunched bun, using the band she kept on her wrist.

'Your mother, she sound like a Ücretsiz Ruh, a free spirit,' Seda said. 'You have to remember the good.'

'Yes, well that's not enough for Rhea,' she sniffed. She's got nothing nice to say about her. They divided us up, you know. She was a daddy's girl and Mum didn't seem worried about Rhea knowing. She seemed to discount her. She was more worried about me knowing, which is kind of insulting to me in a way, like I wouldn't be able to handle it. Well, I might have being able to handle it a lot better than them! And I would have told the truth.'

'And you blame Rhea for not telling you?' Seda asked.

'Yes, I suppose so,' she replied, squinting at Seda through her puffy eyelids. 'But it was both of them. Rhea and Dad. A kind of pact. Started by Dad, because Mum didn't want me to know.'

'But intihar is shame, maybe they want to protect you, protect all the family.'

'Yes, well they did that alright. They had it all sewn up.'

'It not your sister's fault. Think of the heavy weight she carry.'

'I know that,' Lucy looked hard into Seda's eyes. 'I do know. And it wasn't fair of Dad to do that to her. It wrecked our relationship. I'm very angry with him for keeping it from me, and I can't have a go at him about it, because he's dead too. Very convenient, isn't it?'

'Still time to fix you and Rhea. Family is all in Turkey.

376

We look after each other always - no matter what.'

'Even with intihar?'

'Of course,' Seda nodded gravely. Then she passed the plate of gözleme bread to her. 'You eat now?' she urged.

At the first taste of the mixed herbs and goat's cheese filling, Lucy was surprised to find her appetite pricked into life. After relishing the tastes and textures, she sniffed again and looked towards the back door of the house. 'Where is everyone?'

'Donkey rides. But not June and Brian, they went to a local shop to get him a beer. Sometimes, I not like this job, people can be so - '

'Yoo hoo, Lucy!' June's voice suddenly called out.

The sound was as intrusive as a dentist's drill to Lucy, and she saw June trotting towards them around the side of the house, clutching a brown paper bag.

'How are you, luv?' she said, perching herself on the other side of Lucy. She prodded her jewelled fingers into the paper bag. Out came a huge strawberry, and she popped it into her mouth, greased and creased with lipstick. 'Something's wrong, I can tell, she munched. 'You wouldn't normally have snapped at Brian like that. I know he's big, like, but he's sensitive underneath. He says not to mind about it though.'

'Well, that's such a relief to know, June.' Lucy couldn't hold back the sarcasm, but June didn't seem to notice.

'And I have a feeling something has happened with your sister, especially after the tarot reading.'

'Yes, well, June, I don't want to talk about it, but it would appear the cards were right,' Lucy grimaced.

'Oh well, I hope it helped, pet.' Then her wheedling tone changed. 'Ooo, what's that?' asked June, pointing to what appeared to be a brown rock moving slowly down the path towards them.

'It's a tortoise,' said Seda. 'They come into gardens many times. To eat the vegetables.'

They watched it approach. Its blunt head and crinkly neck peeped from under its carapace as it edged forwards on its scaly legs and extended claws, feeling its way on tip toe.

June clamped her legs together and her body stiffened.

The tortoise came closer, nuzzling the ground with its nostrils.

'Get it away from me!' June cried.

The tortoise looked up, as if in response, and started to turn its shell in the direction of the vegetable patch.

'Is it going?' June said, nervously grabbing at another strawberry.

But the fruit escaped her clutches and fell to the ground, rolling close to her pink nail-varnished toes in her open sandals. The tortoise caught sight of the strawberry and headed straight for it. June froze.

Seda and Lucy glanced at each other, then at the tortoise.

It stretched forward its desiccated neck to the plump juiciness of the strawberry and opened its jaws to reveal its thick pink tongue. It tried to take a bite but nudged the fruit right next to June's big toe. Then, it seemed to get confused, and it tried to take a bite of June's big toe, its nail varnish glistening like the strawberry.

June leapt up. She hopped around, her tight curls twitching. 'Get it away! Get it away!'

Seda got to her feet, reached down, picked up the tortoise by its shell and ambled down the path to the orchard.

'What has it done to me?' June cried. She bent right over in front of Lucy, to inspect her toe, wiping off some tortoise saliva.

'Don't be silly, June.'

Welcoming the distraction, Lucy watched June with some amusement as she examined her toe. Then something caught Lucy's eye. A flash of sparkle. June's gold chains had all fallen forward. One of them was longer than the rest and had caught against the yellow scoop neck of her dress, which had a open slash to her cleavage. Then she saw the flash of light again and realised it was coming from something weighted on the end of the chain, flopping against the chiffon. It looked circular.

A private keepsake? wondered Lucy. But that didn't seem right as June was obviously in the habit of showing everything off. And then she saw the chain was the necklace June had bought at the gold centre, the one that looked like her mother's. So what was on the end of it?

With a burst of instinct, while June was still bent over, Lucy plunged her hand into June's neckline. Ignoring the feel of leathery flesh, she grabbed at the bottom of the necklace, wresting it out.

'What the hell are you doing?' June shouted at her, her beady eyes narrowing. 'Let me go!'

Lucy looked at the object in her hand on the end of the chain which was straining around June's scrawny neck as she tried to pull away.

She recognised it immediately. It was Rhea's pink kunzite oval-cut ring. The lost ring, which now turned out to be the stolen ring. Rhea had been right all along.

'You stole it!' Lucy shouted. 'You really stole it! Why did you do it?' What kind of person are you?'

'Let me go! It's not hers, it's mine!' She tried to back away, but Lucy held her fast by the ring on the end of the chain, like a fish on the end of a hook.

Her heart thumping, Lucy tugged at it. 'Give it to me!'

June squealed. 'You're hurting me - it's not hers!'

'Right then. I'll take it!'

Incensed by injustice, and in revolt against being messed around and manipulated, in the present, and the past, and by life in general, holding onto the ring, she gave the necklace around the celery stick neck a sharp jerk. June's puppet face lurched towards her, but the clasp still held. Relieved and emboldened by the fact that June's head hadn't snapped off, the second attempt proved more

379

successful. With another fierce pull and with June howling, the chain broke and slipped away to the ground like a wriggling snake. June staggered backwards and Lucy held in her fist, Rhea's ring.

She saw June opening and closing her mouth like a dummy without its ventriloquist.

She saw Seda standing close by, with a tightness in her eyes.

She saw Brian lumbering towards them. 'What's going on? Sounds like a bleeding cat fight, back here.'

June found her voice. 'She's taken my ring!' she wailed. 'It's not hers.' She glared at Lucy. 'You can't prove nothing!'

Seda stepped forward. She took the ring from Lucy and held it to the light, turning it around and around. 'It is the same ring as Rhea's. Remember, I had a good look on the coach. Same cut, same purple in it, same little scratch in same place. It is Rhea's.' Then she looked at June. 'You are thief. I can report this to the Jandarma now.'

'No...no, you mustn't,' June croaked, her eyes darting to Brian. 'Brian! Do something!' Her face looked tattered like a dried leaf, her thin body shrunken into odd angles as she stuttered out incoherent protests.

Brian stuck out his belly and jutted his chin into his neck, bloating himself up like an angry bullfrog. 'Now, you look here,' he said to Seda and Lucy. 'You can't prove nothing. You can't go accusing my wife, like this. My Juju owns this ring. Paid for it, good and proper.'

'Then you have payment paper for it?' Seda asked, tight-lipped.

'Well, at home, we will, aye!' Brian replied.

'Rhea will have her receipt, she's very thorough about things like that,' Lucy said. 'She'll want to prosecute, I should think.'

Lucy decided this approach might scare June, but at the same time she didn't like the way things were turning. She desperately tried to think of a compromise. One that would work for Rhea.

'Look, June. Just admit you took it and I'll try to get Rhea to drop it, just as long as you leave our hotel. After all, in a strange way, you might have helped us. Of course, Rhea will insist on an apology.' She turned to Seda. 'Does that sound reasonable?'

'It's up to you and your sister.' Seda's expression remained hard.

Lucy looked at June. 'I can only try, mind. I can't promise she'll listen.'

June's eyes became slits and she started to cry. 'Yes, alright, I took it. She looked down on me! I could tell. She's stuck up! I wanted to teach her a lesson, that's all. And I didn't have any kunzite. I needed it!'

'Come on, Juju,' Brian said. 'Let's take the offer, like. I want to change hotels anyway, the bar is bloody tiny.'

June picked up the gold necklace, straightened the neckline of her dress, smoothing down the chiffon. 'All right, we'll do that, then!' She stalked past Lucy and Seda, her snub nose in the air with her puppet's mask back in position.

As they left, Seda sagged onto the bench. 'I think I don't like this job,' she sighed. 'The people can be so rude. And now this. Stealing on a coach tour!'

'Come on, Seda, don't let it get to you. There are still plenty of good people around.'

'I know, but the job is spoilt by the nasty ones. I think I look for something else.' Then she handed Lucy the ring. 'Put it away out of the sun. Remember?'

Lucy grinned and tucked it into the front pocket of her bag.

As they were leaving Yazmira's village home, Seda thanked Yazmira for her hospitality and Lucy felt the need to take some pictures of the façade and the street.

'Can I take your picture?' she asked Yazmira.

Yazmira neatened up the folds of her headscarf, tucked away some stray hair, then posed with practiced ease for

Lucy, sitting squarely on a wooden chair outside her front door with her hands on her knees and grinning. After her photoshoot, she reached into one of her pockets, caught hold of Lucy's hand and pressed something into it. 'I make this,' she said. 'I give you.'

Lucy stared down at the coils of colour in the palm of her hand. Braided, crocheted bands of wool - oranges, turquoises, greens and blues, with blue and white evil eye beads threaded on. It was a wrap bracelet with tasselled ties, and Lucy loved it.

'It's beautiful,' she said. Thank you.'

'It's for luck and protection,' Seda said.

'You come back to Şanslı Alanlar, Lucky Fields?' Yazmira asked.

'I don't know.' Lucy shook her head.

'You come back.' Yazmira smiled, turned around and closed the door.

As the jeeps bounced back down the Taurus mountain tracks, and as the coach wheezed its way back around the bends to the fishing town of Kalkan, the visitors were all very quiet. Seda chatted to Ediz, and threw a few frowns in the direction of June and Brian at the rear of the coach. Ediz shrugged his shoulders and shook his head.

By the time they were on the main road west to Dalyan, Lucy got thinking about something else. How she had nearly drowned yesterday, if Rhea hadn't saved her. And the irony made her feel sick again. And she thought about how it had felt, trying to stay calm, trying not to release any more air bubbles, then the choking feeling, her lungs starting to feel like they were going to burst. The pain. Yet it couldn't have happened like that for her mother. Her mother couldn't have been trapped there in the stillness, like she'd imagined her, whenever the serene image of Ophelia had slipped into horror. Hopefully, she had been in a kind of oblivious state, after all. Oblivion. She liked that word, but what did it mean? Peace? A kind of ease?

And surely it was also about forgetting. But how could a mother want to forget her own children?

Her limbs were stabbing with pains now, and she had a headache. If yesterday hadn't happened, she'd have wanted to go for a swim. Swimming in the sea relaxed her. But would it still be like that, after yesterday? Would she feel the same about what she'd relished on this holiday? Or would she be afraid, or panic, the truth about the past and her own near drowning, wrecking something she'd just discovered she loved? She imagined her lost fin wedged between the seabed rocks for all eternity, like a relic marking the spot of a near death catastrophe, fluffy with algae, studded with barnacles, with a cantankerous lobster living inside the foot. The image made her shudder.

Then, after a few strained moments, she realised what she had to do.

When the coach got back into Dalyan, it was around 3.30pm - right on schedule. Lucy said goodbye to Seda and gave her a tight hug. She dragged her weary legs to the street off the square where the sports shop was and bought a pair of black fins. A little breathlessly returning to the Onur, she asked the boy on reception for the key to the safety deposit box and gently placed the kunzite ring inside, together with her new wrap bracelet.

Trudging up to the room, she quickly changed into her black swimsuit with her shorts and t-shirt on top, then wrote a note for Rhea who wasn't due back until 7.30. As she sat on the edge of the bed, it took a couple of attempts before she was satisfied, screwing up the rejects into crumpled balls and pelting them into the waste basket. She placed the final note on Rhea's pillow, heaved her beach bag onto her shoulder with all her gear inside, and left the room, slamming the door.

As she paced back and forth at the bus stop in the square, she had to wait a few minutes for the next dolmus

- the quickest way to Iztuzu beach. It was around 4.30 now, so she reckoned with a half hour journey to get there, she'd have about two hours at the beach's east end where the rocky seabed was, but she'd have to make sure she got the last bus back to Dalyan at seven. All set then, she thought as she paid her fare to the driver and wedged herself into a window seat.

When she arrived at the beach and trekked into the heat of the sun over the pebble-strewn sand, she suddenly felt strange. As she squinted at the Mediterranean sparkle, as she surveyed the straggle of die-hard sunbathers, prone on their rows of loungers, and heard the recreational screams of those splashing in the shallows, and the strident calls of gulls wheeling overhead, the beach felt like a very different place from the one she had made her own on this holiday. But why? Looking around her, it really was all the same. The tree-lined headland, the shaded sea beneath, further up the beach, the palm trees and cafe. And people were going about their usual activities, tripping down to the shoreline for a paddle, topping up their tan…but not seeing her, not knowing.

Not knowing - that was it.

Not knowing that she was the daughter of a mother who'd killed herself, and that she, herself, almost drowned yesterday, almost drowned like her mother.

Her mouth was dry, so she had a few swallows of water, and struggled to fight the pain that was swelling inside. Standing by the water's edge, the tide not quite reaching her toes, she tried to let the normality of the world wash over her. But a woman, pulling a whining child along by the hand, knocked past her shoulder and barely muttered an apology. Lucy flinched and bristled with anger at the insult.

Her resolve hardened.

She stalked to the quiet area at the base of the headland, where the underwater rocks and fish were more plentiful, and found the spot on the beach she'd

384

previously used, in the shelter of a large rock. She took off her sunhat with the pink roses on it and weighted it down with a stone, though the air was so heavy with stillness, it was hardly necessary. Tugging off her shirt and shorts, she spat on her mask, and was soon ready to swim and snorkel. That was the plan - to 'get back on the horse' - to tackle any fears head on. And not to let what she had found for herself on this holiday be destroyed by its revelations and crises. She had to go home with something of value.

Wearing her mask and snorkel she stepped slowly down to the water's edge. There was a gentle ebb and flow, and further out she could hear the hush of the ocean swell. The glinting lights were sharper in the late afternoon sun, like fragments of mirrored glass.

The coolness of the water numbed her skin as she sat in the shallows, and she trembled. But taking a deep breath, she stuck her snorkel's mouthpiece tightly into her mouth, slid onto her tummy and pushed herself forward with her hands digging into the sand - out into the deeper water - until the sea held her body in its sway. She placed her head in the water and drifted forward, looking down. Her breathing quickened, venting in and out of the snorkel, sounding like a gale blowing through a keyhole. She remembered what it felt like yesterday, not being able to get any air, the blockage, the helplessness, the bursting in her chest, the pending panic. She breathed faster to make sure she could get as much air as she wanted, but it had the opposite effect and she felt as if she was hyperventilating.

She scolded herself and slowed down her breathing. Checking how far she was from the shore, she moved further out. She relaxed a little as she watched the glowing interference patterns of the surface waves glimmer on the seabed and shift over the slabs of rocks - rocks that looked like a landscape of terraces, butts and mesas. She finned over them, seeing steep descents further down into grey-green depths.

And then, she found herself in something familiar, something she'd loved on her scuba diving trip. She was suspended in the neck of a vortex of rays of sunlight, which darted down from the surface blue into green-gold depths to meet at a point beyond sight. She turned to hold her position, while a shoal of tiny fish flashed into silver around her, shifting direction in synchronised union like a flock of starlings at dusk.

But Lucy couldn't enjoy the magic. Neither did she want to dive down into the light, like she'd imagined after the scuba day. Instead, thoughts rose to the surface of her mind and popped like bubbles. Why hadn't her mother's painting sustained her enough through her troubles? It should have, if she'd been serious about it. That's surely how it was with any kind of art. It should have seen her through - her passion, and her family. But then, Lucy had another thought that felt like sacrilege. Something she'd never considered before. Maybe her mother had just been playing at it? Maybe she just liked the idea of being an artist, like many did. And maybe she'd have maintained that she'd lost her muse when her lover died, when in fact, reality simply struck. Lucy didn't believe in all that muse nonsense, you did the art because you had to. But then she felt a pang of guilt. So why aren't I doing mine?

She floated away from the vortex, back to the shoreline rocks, looking up to check her position again, seeing blurring ripples at eye level, the reassuring presence of the beach, and the steep shelter of the headland cliff. She decided she'd just give it just another five minutes, then head back - at least she'd got back on the horse, if nothing else. Finning over rock ledges, fastened with black bundles of sea urchins and green tubular colonies, she glanced around her, spotting some low-lurking fish, too shy to be colourful.

Blurry dark shapes hovered in the distance. Her eyes scanned them. Probably just rocks. Then she saw an irregular oval silhouette. Her gaze wandered past it. Then drifted back to it. She saw it moving. She fixed upon it. As she came closer, she saw it had forelimbs, like wings, beating up and down. Then she saw a head stretching out and the dome of a shell.

Her breath caught in her throat and she gasped for air as she realised what it was.

A Caretta caretta - a loggerhead sea turtle. Such a size too. At least three feet long.

But could she believe her own eyes? Seda and Ray had both told her it was practically impossible for this to happen. That the caretta were only there for a few days a year, and even then, they used the beach at night or very early in the morning.

Yet, here it was.

Unmistakable.

And she wasn't going to miss a second.

She swam slowly after the turtle, not wanting to alarm it.

She watched its graceful motion, its twists and turns as it searched for food. She was swimming above it, seeing the light dapple on its bronzed blotched shell, its amber skin, its splayed flippers. But to see it properly she had to get lower. So, she took a deep breath and kicked back with her fins and pointed her body down. Within seconds she was level with it, where the water was colder and her ears were filling with pressure. She reached out and touched its vast shell. It was surprisingly smooth. It turned its head and glanced at her with its heavy lidded eyes and down-curved mouth. Then, it moved up through the blue towards the surface. She saw its lemon yellow underbelly, ghosted with silver, its gliding motion as it surfaced to breathe.

She needed air too.

And it was just like that. A simple sensation, nothing more.

She rose through the stillness to clear the surface,

taking a few deep breaths. Checking the shoreline position, she went under again, following in the turtle's wake.

And before long, she found herself back in the funnel of light. And the turtle dived down, all too soon disappearing into the depths of glancing strobes.

She waited there on the surface, imagining.

She imagined herself diving down too, finding out, with the turtle, what it was like where the rays of light fused on the ocean floor. Then they'd surface again. Diving and surfacing together, leaving pearly bead trails behind them to mark their passing.

If only.

Doing a strong front crawl, she made her way back to the beach, locating her rock by the tiny spots of pink roses on her sunhat. When she checked her watch, she discovered she only had ten minutes left to get to the bus stop. After a frantic gathering together of her things, and one last glance at the shifting sea, glowing orange in the approaching sunset, she arrived at the bus stop with barely a minute to spare.

On the way back to Dalyan, which now had a sense of home about it, she felt more relaxed in herself than she had done for days. And a few cramps in her stomach told her she was ravenously hungry. She was looking forward to a glass of wine at her riverside jetty amongst the rushes, and some of that spicy mince bread. And Rhea would be back by now. Maybe she would come and join her? But there again, maybe not.

16

Ephesus

Rhea wasn't in the mood for a trip to Ephesus, but it was paid for and she despised waste. And she certainly wasn't going to be left behind in Dalyan for the day. She didn't feel like talking to anyone, not even Eleanor, so maybe she could lose herself on a coach trip? She had plenty of water with her, and she'd grabbed a banana from the fruit on the breakfast bar while it was deserted at 6am in the morning. There was no sign of Hasim, for which she was grateful.

She munched her banana at a table on the hotel forecourt, relieved to be the only one waiting for the bus. All she could hear were a few murmurings and the chinking of cutlery coming from the restaurant opposite. The air was already warm and she was glad she was wearing her loose fitting shorts and her white cheesecloth top, to keep her cool amongst the dusty arches and columns of what she expected would be a oven-hot Ephesus. Her wedge sandals were ruined after yesterday, so she was wearing a pair of cushioned mules, which she'd thrown into her luggage as an afterthought when she was packing. Her hair was tied back in a ponytail and pushed through the back of her combat cap. As she glanced down at herself, she was struck by how unglamorous she looked. No floating dress with strap sandals and floppy brimmed sunhat for posing amongst the ruins, as she'd imagined. But it didn't matter. There wasn't going to be anyone to take a picture, and after yesterday, dressing up would have been a farce.

Yesterday, she thought, feeling a shiver. She'd slept such a deep sleep last night, no dreams, no nightmares, but when she woke up she was assaulted by worries. How could she have let it happen? But Lucy had been so determined, she'd planned a showdown and then nearly drowned in the process. Surely her father would understand she had no choice with that kind of pressure? Or would he be shaking his head right now, or even worse, turning his back on her and walking away?

Her tired eyes started to itch and burn again. At that moment the coach arrived, with the Go Turkey logo on the side, and Trish climbed out with her clipboard clasped to her chest, wearing her tight turquoise sweatshirt and her cream shorts.

'A lovely day again!' she said with her strawberry jam smile. But one look up and down at Rhea and her face crumpled into its walnut shell. 'Are you okay? You've got some bad scratches on your legs.'

'I'm fine,' Rhea replied tersely, swinging her tote bag over her shoulder and stepping onto the bus.

The coach wound its way through Dalyan's streets, picking up other hotel visitors for the trip, and then skirted the lake to hit the road to Mugla. People were called to attention from their early morning lethargy by Trish, with some taster information about Ephesus and the days itinerary, delivered through her microphone from the front of the coach.

'Ephesus is the best preserved classical city in the Eastern Mediterranean,' she enlightened them. 'Dedicated to the goddess Artemis, it became the second largest city in the Roman Empire. The roman name for Artemis is Diana, goddess of the hunt, the moon, wilderness and fertility. Legend also has it that the Virgin Mary travelled there at the end of her life. There is a chapel now on the site where she used to live.'

'When do we stop for breakfast?' an American man called out.

'Just before we go into Ephesus. At around 10am, at a small restaurant in Selcuk,' replied Trish.

'Jeez!'

Unperturbed by this comment, Trish carried on. 'The

ruins include a theatre, agora and baths, and the library of Celsus, but there is so much more to see. The temple of Artemis is one of the seven wonders of the ancient world, although just the foundations remain today. You can buy a map of the whole layout at the entrance and you can cover it by foot in about two hours. I'm sure you'll just love it. Everybody does!'

As the bus picked up speed down the dual carriageway, Rhea stared out of the window at the crash barrier, the low-rise blocks of buildings, and the landscape of scorched brown fields overlooked by a pitiless blue sky. There was nothing to hold her interest, and despite her tiredness, she found she just couldn't nod off. She desperately needed some diversion for this long stage of the journey, so she pulled out *Pride and Passion*.

It felt so long since she was in its world of pirates on the high seas, so she reminded herself what was happening by scanning through the last chapter. While the Sea Sprite lay at anchor off the coast of St Vincent, with no wind to swell its sails, Jacques had fallen into a fever after his arrow wound had become infected. Although it had being cauterised and stitched up by his trusted first mate, his crew could do no more to help their beloved captain and were whispering about being cursed by having a woman on board. But could Madelaine help? Could she face her growing feelings for Jacques, even though he'd been hired to deliver her into the hands of the scoundrel Comte?

Rhea read on.

As Madelaine gazed down at Jacques in his bunk, his white shirt open to his belt buckle, the thin cotton sticking to his moist tanned chest, as she studied his face, his handsome features looking more vulnerably boyish in his delirium, and finally as he muttered her name on his lips, her mood changed. Blood rushed through her veins as she realised she wanted this man. This adventurer, whose crew were so devoted, whose advances she'd rejected because they insulted her pride. But now, she wanted him, with every fibre of her being. She just needed him to stay alive, so he could hold her in his arms, so he could love her and she could give herself to him.

So, she persuaded the suspicious first mate to take her over to the island to find some herbs, and she'd make a poultice for the wound to draw the infection. Her grandmother, on her mother's side, had been a wise woman and had taught her the medicinal arts. After flashing her green eyes and adopting a hands on hips stance, asking what did they have to lose, she was rowed over with four crew members armed with loaded muskets. After firing a couple of shots in the direction of some lurking Caribs, they made their way through the palm trees onto higher ground, clambering through the high grasses and shrubs, the crew following the swish of Madelaine's tattered silk skirts and the locks of her long red hair. She found the feathery foliage of some yarrow, the ripening leaves of the tobacco plant, and she got the crew to dig up some rhizomes of arrowroot. Then they hastened back to the ship.

As Rhea tried to concentrate on Madelaine's preparation of the poultice, the crushing of the leaves in the mortar, the addition of a binder, she became impatient. Just slap it on him! she urged Madelaine. For goodness' sake, get on with it. Wake him up!

She threw the book into her bag and closed her eyes to the haze of tarmac through the window. She tried to doze, her body heavy from the exertions of yesterday. But pictures flitted across her mind's eye - her mother at the pond's edge, her father in his study burning the note, the funeral of downcast faces, faces that never knew the truth. These moments were stuck like barbed burrs in her memory. And telling Lucy had brought them all back again, fresh and raw for re-examination. And now that Lucy knew, things had changed forever. Opening her eyes, she glanced around at other passengers. But they looked oblivious. What was she to do with this new guilt she was now feeling of betraying her father? Would he have understood?

Something else that was disturbing her was that she felt all blurry around the edges, like nothing was holding her together and people could see right inside her, and see her struggling. She could function the same as usual, but it scared her. I'm coming apart at the seams, she thought, feeling her chest tighten and tears threatening again. And it's all Lucy's fault.

She reached into her bag for a tissue. After blowing her nose, she straightened up her blouse, crossed her legs, then unzipped a compartment in her bag and drew out her mobile. Maybe she should ring Rob? It would be so good to hear his voice. But what to say? She decided to text instead. So she punched the keys with a bland enquiry as to how things were going, then forced herself to look at the scenery of threadbare fields. Of course, Lucy would insist he be told the truth. How would he take it? And what about Poppy? And how many others would Lucy insist on telling? She groaned. Maybe she could persuade her that it wouldn't do anyone any good. Oh, why did I have to come on this stupid trip? she asked herself. I'd have been better off with some quiet time by the pool. Now I'm tied to a whole day of people buzzing around me. And she vowed to try to find a quiet corner in Ephesus.

Selcuk was a busy tourist town full of hotels, restaurants and shops, catering for the masses who visited Ephesus. Overlooked by a castellated fortress and a mosque, Trish led the coach party through its bustling streets, to a small restaurant, called the Okyanus, which Trish informed them meant 'oceanic'. Hardly appropriate, thought Rhea, dismissively. They settled themselves at some outdoor tables in the shade of some awnings and ordered their breakfast which came with tea, rather than coffee - much to Rhea's annoyance, as she was desperate for a shot of caffeine. Instead of the traditional Turkish breakfast she was used to at the Onur, she chose a dish called menemen, which consisted of eggs scrambled with diced peppers, tomatoes and spices served in a copper skillet, which you could dip your bread into. She positioned herself in a corner, hoping to be left alone, but found Trish squeezing in next to her and from the way she leaned forward and plaited her legs together, Rhea knew she was zooming in for some chat.

'How are you finding it so far?' Trish asked.

Rhea faltered. What could she say to that? Did Trish mean today? Or the whole holiday? A pile of crap, she thought.

'Good,' she said. 'Very good.'

'You're looking pretty whacked, if you don't mind me saying. Is the room okay?'

'Oh yes. It's just sharing it that's the problem. We're not used to it. We're not getting much sleep.'

Trish's crowfoot eyes squinted at her and she started to giggle. The volume and pitch became higher and higher, and her shoulders started to shake. She clamped her legs together tighter and clutched at Rhea's arm. Heads turned towards them from every direction - from the bewildered looking staff placing more bread on the tables, from those in the coach party, and from passers-by who were threading their way under the wrought iron arches that spanned the road.

Rhea flinched, certain that people could see right into her again. She stabbed her fork into her menemen and took a big mouthful, trying to disappear along with it as she chewed.

Oh, I'm sorry, so sorry,' Trish stuttered, trying to stifle her laughter. 'It's just...well, it's just I'd never ever share a room with a single member of my family! I would never go on holiday with them either.'

'Yes, well. We had our reasons.' Rhea felt defensive. After all, they'd both put a great deal of effort into it. 'We promised our father before he died that we'd try to get on better.'

'Oh.' Trish's giggles dried up and her face shrank into its walnut shell. 'Oh, I'm sorry if I sound flippant, Rhea. That's a different matter, of course. But…still, I just can't imagine doing it.'

'Why?'

'How long is a piece of string?'

So while Rhea ate, Trish went into more depth, while Rhea wished to God she could be by a pool, any pool would do, anywhere but here.

Trish told her about her father, who had always disapproved of her lifestyle, her boyfriends, and most of all her becoming a holiday rep, and how she'd gone for the job to get away from home and the arguments. 'And he treats Mum like a dogsbody,' she said. 'With her doing all the washing, cleaning, cooking, and of course he has to have his roast on Sundays with homemade Yorkshire puddings. And he never agrees to a decent holiday, either. Goes on about being ripped off if you go abroad, how you're better off going to Blackpool. Mum works long hours in the local Coop, and for what?'

As Trish chatted on, Rhea was surprised to find herself listening more intently. Trish was the youngest and seen as the irresponsible one. All her brothers and sisters had now settled down in their semis, paying their mortgage and raising their kids. They all thought she should have done the same by now, most of all her father.

''What security will you have?' he always asks,' she said. 'He's like a broken record. I mean, he's been working for the same brewery as a stock controller for over thirty years! Security is about all that drives him.'

'Sounds like he's just worrying about you, though,' Rhea offered.

'Yes, but it's not for me. Life is for living, don't you

think? And I really enjoy what I do. Anyway, I do save up, I've got quite a bit put by. And I mix and mingle with the expats too. Maybe I'll find a sugar daddy.'

Yes, but you're not in your twenties, are you?'

'Well, cheers! 38 isn't that old!' She tossed her hair back again and grinned. 'Okay, more sugar than daddy, then.'

'But what about love?'

Rhea could hardly believe she was asking this question. She remembered telling Lucy that love was just a temporary infatuation.

'Oh, well…I've had my heart broken a few times. It gets harder to trust, you know? I'd settle for good company these days.'

'But is that really enough? My husband and I have been playing it that way for years now, and I don't think it's enough. Come to think of it, he's not even good company anymore.'

'Then why are you still together?' Trish twisted her legs into the opposite position, her brown eyes boring into Rhea's like pneumatic drills. 'I mean, what's the point?'

Rhea was silent, thinking of a talk she'd had with her father some years ago, when her marriage had first started struggling, back in the mid-nineties. He'd told her the point was the marriage vows they'd made and providing a secure family life for Rob. *We all have to take the rough with the smooth*, he said. But that sounds so bleak, she thought. Is that how it has to be? Is that how he felt about Mum in the end? But one thing she did know, was that it was through his advice she'd stuck with Chris, because she'd always valued her father's opinions above anyone else's, sometimes even her own.

Trish looked at Rhea expectantly, still waiting for a reply.

'Well, you might be right, Trish. Maybe there is no point. My father thought it was the right thing to do. I let him influence me, I suppose.'

Trish snorted. 'Well, they don't know everything, do

they?'

'No. I'm beginning to realise that.' Rhea stirred her tea round and round with the spoon, feeling a pang of guilt that she'd let her father's halo slip sideways. 'But back to you. Why don't you visit home just for your mother's sake?'

'I know, I should. I do miss her. We do write, and she tells me what's going on in the family. But to be honest, the trouble with family visits is trying to remember what I'm supposed to know, and what I'm not, because Mum gives me all the gossip behind their backs. They all go to her with their troubles, you see. And of course, she keeps them all from Dad. He'd go ape.'

'What kind of troubles?'

'Oh, like which one of my sisters has been spending out on designer gear behind her husband's back, knocking up a big credit card bill. Like which one of my brothers has an alcohol problem. Like which one of my sisters or brothers or their husbands and wives has had an affair, who knows, who doesn't. Things like that. And I haven't got much time for secrets. I mean, what's the point? They always comes out in the end, don't they?'

There was no quiet corner in Ephesus. People thronged through its time-worn streets, dabs of shifting colour amongst its bleached-out truncated columns and sculpted relics, shuffling their feet like pilgrims through the dustings of stone, while the sun rose higher. Not a breath of breeze to cool sweated brows. The coach party had entered by the eastern Magnesian Gate, so that they could take advantage of walking downhill through the ancient city. Trish instructed everyone to meet at the Celsus Library steps at 2pm so she could escort them to Ricci's restaurant at the exit gates to have lunch. There were souvenir shops there too. They had two and a half hours to explore the ruins by themselves. 'Enjoy!' she said, as if they were about to feast themselves.

As Rhea made her way down the road of stone slabs and straggly shrubs, towards the main attractions, she felt numb inside, and her calves and feet were sore from all the walking she'd done yesterday. The snippets of conversation and exclamations of wonder around her seemed so utterly trivial in comparison to the burden she carried, that she felt furious at the world's indifference and its banal normality. She wanted to stop walking and just stand stock-still - a protest against carrying on regardless - but to do so would be to stand out, and then what? So, she allowed herself to be sucked into the stream of people heading for what she presumed was classed as the centre - the famous Library of Celsus. But what was she to do with herself? All that time before the coach party rendezvous stretched out before her like a wasteland with no comfort to find. And then the long bus journey back to Dalyan. Her eyes filled with tears again as she felt her pain. Was this what it was going to be like from now on? This guilt - this aching guilt?

She forced herself to look up as the stream of people flooded into the entrance courtyard of the library ruin. The front façade soared above her - three entrances, with two tall tiers of dappled marble columns surmounted by entablatures. Female statues gathered the folds of their garments about them in niches on the ground floor - personifications of the virtues of the Roman senator, Celsus, for whom the library was built. 12,000 scrolls had once been stored within its walls. Plinths, scrolled carvings, inscriptions, and arched pediments were piled high on a crumbling edifice that looked like a puff of wind would topple it.

But Rhea didn't want to read about the history in the leaflet scrunched in her hand. All she wanted was the shade the ruins offered. Climbing up the steps, she headed towards the right corner at the top, finding a cool spot in the shadow of a wide column, under the headless gaze of the virtue - Knowledge. Looking up, she saw one of

Episteme's legs provocatively outlined beneath her robe. A good bit of carving, in Rhea's opinion, just a shame about Episteme missing her head. But maybe she was more comfortable like that, after all she couldn't do much thinking, could she? Her own mind felt like it had been put through a mincing machine, jumbled thoughts not connecting, just like the eroded, indecipherable inscriptions around her. Craning her neck, she looked up higher, right up inside what remained of a coffered ceiling, on top of which appeared to be wafer-thin seams of concrete and rubble holding up the upper storey like layers of puff pastry. It all looked so fragile, tilting around in her vision, so she sank down, sitting herself with her back against the column, as out of sight as she could possibly get.

After gulping down some water, she relaxed a little and examined her fingernails - the pale pink varnish was chipped all over and the edges were jagged. She was in need of a serious manicure after the shingle scuffles on the beach. Then she fingered the scratches on her knees and shins, noticing at the same time that her legs would soon need re-waxing. Female body maintenance, she thought angrily, it's so relentless. Men are better off. And finally, she massaged the place where the kunzite ring used to be. It seemed like a lifetime ago now, since it encircled the third finger of her right hand. Her gift to herself for her losses, though she couldn't have named them precisely. Lulled by the mumblings of gaggles of tourists in the courtyard below, she found herself musing on what Trish had said about secrets always coming out in the end.

She remembered that awful moment, standing by her father's hospital bed, when she realised he was really going to die. The full reality of it - he would be gone and she'd be on her own. Then asking him if she could tell what they'd kept to themselves for 32 years. Where had it come from after all that time? What had prompted her to ask him for that vital permission? She remembered being taken aback by this tiny hope she'd suddenly felt pricking inside, when she realised he was going to die. That feeling of a chance, a chance for ...what?

But it wasn't to be. He hadn't said yes. And then she'd spent weeks reliving the past in her dreams, not being able to concentrate at work, and relying on Prozac to blot it out, so she could get on and grieve for her father. But of course it was all interconnected. Her bereavement was like being in a jungle of tangled, knotted roots and creepers, ensnaring her every time she struggled to get clear of its dense canopy, into the light and space of the plains.

She closed her eyes. She allowed herself to imagine, as she had when she was young, but not for many years now, what it might have been like if she had told. She used to feel the freedom in that possibility, freedom like she'd felt for a little while riding that motorbike yesterday. Freedom, but for what? What else could there have been?

Well, for a start, she'd never done what Auntie Kathy had told her to do with men. *With your looks, you'll get plenty of offers. Just you keep them dangling like puppets on a string, until you find the right one.* But she hadn't. She'd gone for the first man who she'd fancied, the first man who made her feel special, and she had tied herself to him to escape from home - and just look at how that had turned out. But she could never regret having Rob. He was everything to her.

Swings and roundabouts, the rough with the smooth, the grass is always greener - all these clichés came into her head.

Then another thought fluttered into her mind, its touch as light as a butterfly. What if, as Lucy had suggested, her father *had* made a mistake? What if he should never have covered up her mother's death? And mulling this over, for the first time in her life, she felt a flash of anger towards him. A sacrilegious feeling that rocked her core.

So, all too soon she brushed the butterfly away and the ache of guilt in her breast returned. He did the best he could under the circumstances. He wanted to protect the family. That was all there was to it.

She hauled herself to her feet, glanced at the headless figure of Episteme, then faced the glare of the sun, looking out to the low hillsides patched with stunted trees and shrubs. Then her gaze dropped and landed on the pathway by which she'd come. It was then she saw someone frantically waving. Someone with red hair, turquoise top, cream shorts. She recognised Trish immediately, and that the waving was directed at her. But what to do? She decided not to wave back. She wanted to be alone.

The next few moments were slowed down in time. Just as she was edging behind the pillar, she saw the figure of a man approach Trish. Faded denims, dark blue t-shirt. There was something familiar about his profile, the look of an Arab, his dark hair, and the way he was standing easy, with his thumbs hooked into his pockets. Then she realised, with sudden shock, that it was Hasim. Her heart started to race, thumping in her chest, her thoughts casting around wildly for an explanation. What was he doing here? Why was he here? Then she saw Trish pointing towards the library, right where she was. He started striding straight over in her direction. Her legs wanted to run, but she couldn't move, like when she was caught in the act of doing something very wrong as a child. As he sprinted up the steps, she just managed to arm herself with some anger, to gain some control. Remembering the comments in the book helped considerably.

She came out to face him.

He came to an abrupt halt in front of her, his face all sweaty and dusty. With his urgency stemmed so suddenly, he still managed to resume his relaxed stance.

Impressive, thought Rhea.

'There you are. I've been looking all around for you,' he said, with a small smile that searched her eyes. 'I am pleased I found you. I remembered I had Trish's mobile number at the hotel.'

They examined each other. He tried to grin at her, but when he read her expression, he frowned. He ran his fingers through his hair and started rubbing his chin.

Rhea crossed her arms in front of her. 'Why are you here?'

'To see you. To give you a lift back to hotel - on my bike, you understand? I came on my bike.'

'No, I don't. Why would you come all the way out here for that? For just another score in your book?'

She finally found her feet and turned to leave him, but he caught hold of her wrist. He looked hard at her. 'No. That is wrong. They make it up.'

'Of course. Well, you would say that, wouldn't you?'

Rhea tried to loosen his grip, but he tightened it. She surprised herself by finding she liked it.

He gave her a pained look. 'I need to tell you -'

'Don't bother!'

'No, I need you to understand. Let me explain. Then you can do as you will.' He let go of her arm and started pacing around, muttering to himself in Turkish. Then he delivered his explanation. 'I have had a few girlfriends that were here on holiday, that is true, but only a few over many years. But also, I have had lots of them trying to…you know…when I wasn't interested. You see? They must have put the marks in the book.'

'Well, you were bound to come up with that, weren't you!'

A spark of anger flashed in Hasim's eyes. 'Look, Rhea. I am a single man, I not like to marry, but I don't just sleep with any woman. I have to like her a lot. And I like you a lot. I came to say sorry for the book and to give you a lift home, instead of you getting bus back. I can show you villages, a nicer way back. Okay? I think…' he hesitated, 'I think, maybe it's up to you now.' He stooped down and sat on the top of the library steps, his shoulders hunched, with his chin propped in his hand, staring down the steps.

When Rhea saw him looking moody, like she hadn't seen him before, she had the thought that he just might be telling the truth. And one thing was for certain, whether he was or he wasn't, he had no ties. Well, none she was aware of. And he did look upset.

Still feeling the ghost of the grip of his hand, and imagining it gripping her elsewhere, her attitude changed. It was pretty simple, if she didn't think too much about it. And she didn't want to think too much about it. She liked him. He liked her. And he had ridden all the way from Dalyan to Ephesus to find her. Around 240 kilometres was the distance, Trish had mentioned earlier on. That had to count for something. In fact, it could be considered romantic, if she chose to forget about that book.

Then something occurred to her. 'How did you find out about the book?' she asked, sitting down next to him. 'I thought Lucy handed it in to the night staff.'

'No. She gave me it this morning. I was at my cousin's all yesterday, talking about starting a hotel shop, like he is running, and I came back to Lucy telling me you were gone for the day, and giving me the book all in pieces, telling me to look at the back. She good sister to you, I think.'

'Oh,' Rhea replied, thinking this was the sort of thing her feisty good friend, Vicky, would do. Of course, Lucy was one for confronting the truth - she knew that all too well. But this time, she had to admit, Lucy may have done her a favour.

'And you rode a Honda back from radar station?' Hasim asked.

Rhea nodded.

He grinned at her.

And Rhea, once more charmed by him, grinned back.

'You coming back with me on the bike, or you taking bus?'

'With you,' she said. 'But I need a bite to eat first.'

After explaining her travelling plans to a goggle-eyed Trish, she and Hasim settled themselves in the dark interior of Ricci's restaurant, well away from the prying eyes of Trish and the coach party. Hasim told her more about himself, about his upbringing, his time in England, and about his current plans for a gift shop in the hotel, while Rhea listened, fascinated, and she couldn't help giving him a few tips on merchandise display. After Hasim paid the bill, they left, with Rhea reflecting that she still felt fuzzy around the edges, but deciding that right now, she simply didn't care.

Accelerating east down the duel carriageway, they cut off south into the hills on Hasim's Suzuki, stirring up dust on road tracks through villages that Hasim shouted out the names of. Oblivious to most of this, with her hands on Hasim's hips, Rhea rested against him, feeling the curve of his back against her cheek. There was a familiarity about him now which she liked - the feel of him, the scent of him.

They stopped for a break at an ancient hilltop acropolis called Alinda. Hasim told her this was where Queen Ada ruled over all of Caria, after she'd triumphed over Alexander the Great during her exile here.

Rhea listened to the tale, seeing the passion of storytelling animate Hasim, like she'd not seen him before, and she realised she was enjoying discovering new things about this man. He wasn't just a good looking Turk with a motorbike, and a penchant for blondes. But there again, remembering *Shirley Valentine*, she knew it was probably wishful thinking.

But as they stood by a thick wall of stone, looking down over the fertile plains of the town of Karpuzlu, rich with olive trees, and further out still, to the ripples of mountain ranges on the horizon, Hasim held Rhea's hand in a firm grip, while he pointed to the distant peaks, naming them for her. And Rhea knew, no matter what this man was about, it felt right, and that was all she cared about for the moment. And as she looked out to the skyline she had the feeling that maybe it was possible to get out from her jungle into the plains after all.

When they arrived back at the Onur in Dalyan at around 6.30, Rhea said she wanted to shower and change, managing to avoid saying 'to slip into something a little more comfortable', but thinking it all the same. And astonished at herself, she had to suppress a giggle. He suggested they meet on the terrace for a drink in about half an hour.

'That's fine,' she said.

When she got to her and Lucy's room, she wondered whether Lucy would be there, or if she'd gone off somewhere after her trip. She wanted to thank her for confronting Hasim with the book. Let's face it, she thought, if Lucy hadn't done anything, Hasim would never have gone all the way to Ephesus to find her.

But when she saw the empty room, her heart sank a little. She spotted the folded piece of white paper on her pillow. A knot tied itself in her stomach. Had Lucy gone? Had she left Dalyan in a fit of disgust or changed hotels maybe? With trembling fingers she opened the note, and couldn't believe what she read.

Rhea,

Well, you were right.

The prune on sticks had your ring, after all. I'm sorry I doubted you.

She was wearing it on the end of the chain she bought, tucked down her front. I spotted it and took it off her. Seda has identified it as definitely yours from a small scratch on what she called the crown. I've put it in the deposit box for you.

Off to the turtle beach now, have to get back on the horse, then I think I'll go to my jetty. If you fancy joining me for a drink, it's along the river path, past the Calypso, a small jetty opposite the Bayram hotel.

Lucy

PS I don't think June can really see auras.

Rhea sat on the edge of the bed re-reading the letter.

A flush of warmth slowly crept through her and she smiled. She leapt to her feet and scrambled for the door. Running down the stairs, she caught hold of herself and slowed to a sedate pace as she entered reception. The young man at the desk was surprised at her barking instructions at him for the key to the deposit box for room 23.

She fumbled with the key in the lock. Then as she opened the box, and saw the pale pink gemstone ring winking at her, she heaved a sigh of relief. She held it in her palm, examining it, turning it around and around. It was just the same. Giving it a good rubbing with the hem of her shirt, to try to get rid of all traces of June, she slipped it onto her finger - where it belonged. Then she noticed the wrap bracelet, sitting on top of the passports, and wondered where it had come from. Must be Lucy's she decided, so much her style. She wondered what Lucy was feeling right now, and she wanted to thank her. But then she remembered Hasim, and her thoughts were taken over by the urgent matter of what she was going to wear.

Half an hour later, after showering and changing, she was behind time, but ready. She gave herself a quick glance over in the dressing table mirror. Hair down, tousled from a towel drying, but not too bad. Makeup retouched. Tan holding up. And she'd chosen her salmon pink dress which showed off her curves, accessorized with a simple diamante drop pendant necklace. She was wearing a pair of gold strap sandals which were her reserve pair for special occasions on this holiday, and which gave her that all important extra couple of inches. Her nails had been given a quick filing to remove the scratchy edges.

As she examined her fingers, she noticed her wedding ring. And the enormity of what she was planning to do struck her. She was about to commit adultery. But it was more of a tap on the shoulder, than a smack to bring her to her senses. She leaned in toward the mirror, looking into her face to find some guilt, or sign of regret, perhaps. But all she saw was the excitement in her eyes. When was the last time, she'd seen that? So, she grasped the wedding band, and with some determined squeezing and pulling, she twisted it off. It bounced onto the glass top of the dressing table, shimmying with harsh vibrations in the silent room, as if it was trying to get her to change her mind. But she gazed at her pink kunzite ring on her other hand, smiled, and headed for the door.

When she got to the terrace, Hasim was waiting. He looked cool and refreshed in a white shirt and dark blue jeans. And they were all alone.

'You got this far, then?' he grinned, handing her a glass of white wine, and lighting himself a cigarette. His eyes narrowed as he inhaled.

'Are those Turkish?' she said, glancing at his cigarette, and taking a sip of wine.' Do you mind if I try one?'

'You smoke?'

'Just now and again,' she replied.

They settled themselves on the same leather sofa as before, rather than the low bed recliners that Rhea had found so full of suggestive possibilities. The sofa already had acquired a sense of familiarity about it and its musky skin was warmed by the low angle of the sun. She was surprised to find the cigarette quite mild, with a scented flavour that she liked. As they replenished their glasses, Hasim talked about what it was like living in Dalyan in the winter months. Lots of rain was the main feature, so there was a lot of work done indoors. It was a quiet time, when businesses caught up with their marketing, updated their websites and made plans for the next tourist season. That would be when he sorted out the hotel shop.

Then he fell silent and slid his arm around her. She relaxed into his shoulder.

He looked into her eyes. 'You sure this okay? I know you are married.'

Rhea felt no trace of tension, no vibrating wire of warning. She wanted this man, the same way Madelaine wanted Jacques in *Pride and Passion*. Maybe not forever, of course, no sailing off in to the sunset, but certainly for now - and she was going to get there before Madelaine.

'It's over,' she said simply, returning his gaze. 'And I don't want to talk about it. I'm sick of talking.'

'So, we can enjoy?'

'Yes, we can enjoy.'

A few minutes later, Rhea's edges blurred more, and then dissolved altogether as Hasim led her into his room. Her senses registered the dark furniture, the luxurious fabrics, and the exotic aroma of incense. It was all she could have imagined his room to be - masculinity, full of eastern promise. And once more images of the harem filled her mind.

'I really want you, Rhea,' he said.

There it was again. That way he had of looking at her with his dark eyes, that way he had of saying her name.

He gripped her around her hips, pulling her into him, pressing her so close she could feel his hardness. He pushed her hair away from her face, and tilted her chin upwards. She closed her eyes as his lips met hers. The scraping of his stubble sent shivers through her body from head to foot, intensifying as he began to plant small kisses on her neck. Then she felt him unzipping her dress, slowly and gently, and just as she melted, he pushed the door shut behind her with a thud, that sounded as if it was sealing her fate. And as they sank onto his bed and started to make love, she slipped into a kind of bliss. And it was all so much more than she could have possibly hoped for. It was…well…

Two hours later, as Rhea sauntered down the river path, she felt like that second self she'd become a couple of times previously on the holiday. She responded to the invasive enquiries of restaurant staff fishing for customers, with serenely dismissive smiles rather than her customary flickers of annoyance. Darkness had set in, and the lights of the cafes and bars gleamed on the water, while the empty boats shifted restlessly in their moorings. When she found the jetty of the Bayram hotel at around a quarter to ten, Lucy was just getting up, ready to leave.

'Oh, hi!' Lucy said, looking startled. 'Where have you been? Did you get back late from Ephesus? I've already eaten.'

'I'm sorry, Lucy,' Rhea said, clambering down the wooden steps. 'But have we still got time for a drink?'

Lucy's eyes searched Rhea's. 'I expect so. White wine?'

Rhea nodded as Lucy disappeared off the jetty and through the trees, re-emerging a few minutes later. 'Drinks ordered,' she announced, flopping herself back down on her cushion.

'What have you been up to since your trip? Where have you been all this time? Did you get your ring?' asked Lucy.

Rhea grinned at the characteristic barrage of questions - one at a time was never enough for Lucy. She'd taken advantage of this in the past by just answering one of them and ignoring the others she was uncomfortable with. But tonight, she didn't mind. 'Well, thanks to you showing Hasim the back of that book, I've been with him. He came to Ephesus to give me a ride back. And, yes, thanks to you again, I have my ring back.' She wiggled her hand in front of Lucy's face, so she could see. 'Thank you, Lucy. Thanks for all that. After all that's happened...I don't know if I would have done the same for you.'

Lucy stared at her. 'No. I don't think you would.' She paused. 'You look different.' Her tone became suspicious. 'What do you mean, you've *been* with Hasim?'

Rhea was silent, determined to keep the specifics to herself, determined not to let Lucy winkle the facts out of her. But a smile crept stealthily across her face, so much against her will that her cheeks ached.

Lucy's mouth dropped open. 'You've been with him, haven't you?' She tugged her cotton skirt tight around her knees, her voice rising. 'You have, haven't you?'

'Yes, okay, okay! But I don't want to talk about it. That would spoil it.' She couldn't carry on looking at Lucy, so she started examining her ring, turning it so the ambient lamps stirred its latent fire.

'Was it good?' Lucy asked.

'What do you expect me to say? Give him marks out of ten, like the others?'

'Do you believe in the others in the book?'

Rhea shrugged. 'I don't know. He vows they were just making it up, says he gets pestered a lot.' She looked out into the blackness of the river. 'I don't really think it matters. He is what he is, I am what I am.'

'Very profound,' Lucy giggled. 'Okay, of course you should keep it to yourself. Then it stays special.' She faltered. 'But what about Chris?'

'I'm certainly not talking about him.'

After their drinks arrived, with a couple of packets of crisps that Lucy had asked for, Rhea fell into a comfortable state of repletion, sipping her wine, and munching, with no desire for a cigarette, as she listened to Lucy's long description of her day. How she tackled June to get the ring back, about the hope that June would apologise to Rhea, so Rhea would take it no further, as long as the couple changed their hotel. That was the arrangement they'd made. Then how delighted she'd been with the present from the farmer's wife, how she'd like to go back to the village one day. Then, about how she'd got back into the sea at the beach and finally swam with a caretta turtle! Against all the odds, she said. Lucy's depth of feeling made her eyes shine, and for once Rhea reflected, she could identify with that sense of excitement and passion. That stirring feeling in the blood. As she listened, she studied her ring, thoughts forming and fading, then reforming, like reflections in a lake disturbed by a playful breeze.

Lucy noticed her pensiveness. 'What are you thinking about?'

Oh, nothing much.' She changed the subject. 'What should we do tomorrow? We've got the Turkish Night in the evening. But you can choose what we do with the day.'

'Well, we still have a lot of talking to do, you know, about - '

'Yes, I know we do.' Rhea looked hard at Lucy. 'But where? I don't fancy staying in our room tomorrow, but you can choose where we go, as long as it's relatively private.'

Well…' Lucy hesitated. 'We could go to Kaunos again, and then maybe climb up to the rock tombs. There must be such a good view from there.'

Rhea stared at her. 'Can we get up there?'

'I think so, if we're careful.'

'For God's sake, Lucy.'

I know, *just typical*, isn't it?

17

Kaunos

The next morning the sisters had a much needed lie-in, followed by some essential personal grooming after sea, sand, shingle and travel had taken their toll over the last two days. By the time they arrived on the breakfast terrace, it was around 10am and deserted. But the smile that Hasim gave Rhea, as she and Lucy settled themselves at their usual table, signalled to the sisters that their late arrival wasn't an issue this morning.

'Just help yourself at the breakfast bar, and the chef can still do you omelettes if you like. I go to get some food supplies. I see you later?' Hasim said to Rhea, as he poured their coffee.

Rhea looked at Lucy and hesitated. 'Well…to be honest, Hasim, I should probably spend the day with Lucy. There are things we need to sort out before we go back.'

'Okay. It's no problem. But I see you here, at the Turkish night?'

'Yes, see you then,' Rhea smiled.

'You like to dance?'

'I love to dance.' Then she looked at Lucy. 'We both do, don't we?'

Lucy raised her eyebrows. 'Yes. But it's been a long time since we did anything like that together.'

Hasim looked at them both, then made a flourishing bow worthy of a cavalier. 'Okay! Later, we dance.'

He turned to go, then reeled around, with a frown on his face. 'Oh, I nearly forget. Trish is bringing a car for to take the Walkers to another hotel. I do not know what happened exactly.'

Rhea quickly explained to him and showed him the

ring on her finger.

He nodded thoughtfully. 'I understand.' Then he took her hand and kissed it. 'I see you later.'

As Hasim left, Lucy leaned towards Rhea, perching her elbows on the table. 'He's very nice,' she whispered, 'but what are you going to do about him? We've only got today, tomorrow, and some of Saturday, then we go home.'

'I don't know yet. I haven't had time to think.'

Lucy dropped back in her chair and shook her head. 'Oh well, I suppose a lot can happen in three days. Look what's happened already.'

After Rhea had locked her ring away, the sisters emerged onto the forecourt with their packed tote bags, about to leave for Kaunos. But they paused in the doorway when they saw a taxi pulling up. Trish got out of the front passenger seat. Then they saw two figures standing up from a cafe table, suitcases by their sides. They were thrown into shadow by the angle of the sun, but their silhouettes were unmistakable. It was June and Brian, and June was smoking a cigarette.

'Here's her chance to apologise,' Lucy muttered to Rhea.

She marched across the forecourt to June. 'Haven't you forgotten something?'

June's mouth set hard like concrete around her cigarette, and her embellished fingers sparkled with their mystical powers. She shot a glance at Rhea, coming up behind Lucy. 'No. I don't think so.'

Then she tilted her chin in the air, looking defiantly at them both. Her makeup was thicker than usual this morning, like greasepaint on an aging diva, making her final curtain call.

'What do you mean, no!' Lucy cried. 'You agreed! If you don't apologise to Rhea, we'll go to the police and report you.'

414

Brian shifted his bulk from side to side, like an emperor penguin out of his natural element. 'Come on, Juju. We don't want any more bother.'

June tried to kill his interference with a toxic look, but he held his ground. 'Come on, lass. Then we can get shot of them.'

Trish stepped forward, her face crumpled. 'I really think you should apologise, Mrs Walker. It is a serious matter.'

'Okay, okay!' June swung around and stared at Rhea. Her black eyes glittered like gimlets. She cast her cigarette onto the ground and stamped the life out of it. She twisted her puppet mouth, working it from side to side, then she pulled her stick-like frame into a line as rigid as a ramrod. 'Sorry,' she said, spitting the word at Rhea.

Rhea flinched, as a few drops of saliva hit her in the face. But wiping them away with the back of her hand, she turned around to leave. 'I can't be bothered with this,' she said to Lucy. 'They're not worth it. Let's go.'

'But that was hardly an apology!' Lucy said, looking from Rhea to June. 'More like an assault.' She glared at June. 'What is the matter with you? You steal rings. You make up crap about auras and star signs and reckon you can do tarot readings. And you can't even see when you're in the wrong. Is there anything authentic about you at all?'

'Now, hang on a minute, like!' Brian said. 'There's no need to be - '

'I helped you! You know I did!' June cried at Lucy, her tight curls shaking. 'I helped you both!'

Rhea got hold of Lucy's arm. 'Let her go. It's not worth it. Maybe she did help us somehow. You're just angry she manipulated you. Just let her go.'

Lucy looked at Rhea, in open-mouthed silence. Then she clenched her jaw. 'Fine! If that's what you want. I suppose it's your decision.'

Brian dragged June to the waiting taxi. As it pulled away, June and Brian had their faces pointed forward, noses high. There were no swivels of the neck. They were done with their prey.

As the taxi drove down the street and turned a corner, Trish's face brightened with sudden force. 'Okay, that's hopefully that, then. Seda told me all about it, by the way. I've arranged alternative accommodation for them at a new build right across the other side of town. They shouldn't be bothering you again.'

Rhea and Lucy nodded numbly.

'I hope you manage to have a good day,' Trish said. Then she hesitated. 'Seda and me are off duty tomorrow and wondered if you fancied a picnic on turtle beach. We don't normally consort with the punters, but we'd like to in your case. That's if you like? For your last full day?'

The sisters looked at each other.

Rhea frowned.

Lucy sighed.

'Can we let you know later on?' asked Rhea.

The two sisters sat in silence, squashed together like two squeezed lemons, in the prow of a small blue rowing boat. Opposite them, a plump Turkish lady wielded the oars for their crossing of the Dalyan river for 3 lire each. The water was an avocado green in the morning light, but Lucy was not disposed to trail her hand in it.

Their mood was pensive, compared to the previous evening's calm after the storm, as they began trudging along the concrete path to Kaunos. They were both wearing cargo trousers, cotton tops and caps, with their sunglasses already in position for what was promising to be another roasting day. Lucy had her camera slung around her neck, but so far hadn't taken any pictures, and this time she didn't stop to examine the spiky grasses and sweet scented shrubs, sizzling with crickets.

Rhea, on the other hand, paused to gaze at a cobbled together wooden footbridge and gate, which led into the back garden of a white-washed house. It was a well-tended garden, green with ornamental palms and trees bursting with ripe oranges, and a sweet smell hung in the air. A thick tangle of pink geraniums, unchecked by any annual frosts in this Mediterranean climate, scrambled over the fence like an unruly hedge. Curled up asleep, and nestled in the foliage was a sleek golden-haired cat. It sensed Rhea's presence by stretching out one paw, then retracting it.

'Don't you think we should take a picture?' she called to Lucy, who was striding on ahead.

'If you like it, you take one!' Lucy called over her shoulder.

So Rhea grabbed her small compact and snapped away for a few seconds. Then she caught up with Lucy.

'What's the matter?' she asked Lucy, catching hold of her arm.

'What's the matter?' Lucy turned to face her. 'We're supposed to be talking. That's what the matter is! And what about June? Why did you let her off the hook?'

Rhea pulled her to the edge of the path to let two walkers with backpacks trek past, their strides matching each other with serious intent.

Rhea looked piercingly at Lucy. 'Firstly, June is not worth bothering about. I've got the ring back now. I just don't care about her anymore. Okay? We'll never see them again. Isn't that a good enough result?'

'But she played us.'

'She played you, not me.'

'Oh thanks!'

'She probably just guessed the star signs.'

'Yes. but - '

'And as for the tarot reading, well maybe the cards helped, maybe they didn't. But somehow that talk with her helped. It helped you to force me to tell you about Mum. So maybe we should both just let it go.'

Lucy started to twist a strand of her hair, while she stared back down the path. 'I suppose so.' Then she hesitated and turned to look straight at Rhea. 'And are you glad you've told me about Mum?'

Rhea drew in a breath and stepped back, her eyes still meeting Lucy's. 'Well, yes...yes, I think so,' she stammered. Then she drew herself up. 'Are you glad you know?'

Lucy pressed her lips together into a grimace. 'It's always important to know the truth.'

'Yes, but are you glad?'

'Well, glad isn't exactly the word,' Lucy snorted. 'More like shocked, disgusted, conflicted. You've had years to get your head around it. I've got a couple of days before we go home and then I'll not see you for months.'

'Yes, I know,' Rhea said. 'But here we are, talking, like you wanted. Where do think we should start?'

Lucy groaned. 'I've got so many questions, but they're going around and around in my head.'

'Right. Well, let's go to the amphitheatre again, and try to sort them out.'

Lucy faltered. 'I think I need to be by myself first. I feel very confused right now. I have to sort out what the priorities should be.'

'Well, snap to that,' Rhea replied.

After hiking slowly up the rocky slope to the ruins of the ancient city, the sisters had a sit down outside the refreshment van. The heat was rising and the morning air was thickening with the chirping of beetles and crickets. They sipped at their diet cokes watching the movements of a newly arrived troop of tourists jostling for prime position at the information board. Amongst them was a beanpole of a man in a white panama hat who Lucy mentioned she was sure she'd seen before, but couldn't remember where. Rhea gave him a brief glance, but was none the wiser. As the tourists scattered to become grains of colour amongst the earthy archaeological remains, the sisters still had little to say to one another. The marshes of the estuary below, lay sluggish in their stillness, and the sea beyond was a vaporised blur.

'Right,' Lucy said, getting up and stretching herself. 'I think I'll go over there, to the bathhouse.' She pointed to her right. 'Shall I come and find you at the amphitheatre in about an hour?'

'Yes, okay,' Rhea replied, squeezing her empty can and tossing it into the nearby bin.

***

Lucy plodded over to the network of interconnecting collapsed walls, sunken floors, and archways built from huge slabs of stone. The bathhouse's position afforded a view right out over the green hillsides to the blue of the bay and Rhodes beyond. Originally a place of pampered prestige, today a flock of sheep dozed in the shadows of the ancient building blocks from the fourth century BC. The sleepers stirred themselves at Lucy's approaching footsteps, but judging her as harmless, they soon resumed their napping. With struggling trees anchored into the ruins, once again visions of an Arcadian wilderness inhabited by shepherds jumped into Lucy's mind. But rather than explore this place further, to fuel her usual fancies, she sat down heavily on a dusty wall. She had priorities to sort out.

But what were they?

The first thing to slide into her mind was art. And she knew that this, rightly or wrongly, was number one. That slippery chimera, that kept changing shape and voice according to the times and the whims of the day, just as she thought she'd grasped hold of it and moulded it into what *she* wanted it to be. But what was her relationship to it now? Would she able to go into her studio and paint again when she got home? It wasn't a problem of inspiration. That was always there, and there'd been plenty on this holiday. It was more a question of faith in the doing of it, despite her cynicisms. Would having seen the turtle make a difference to her, as she'd felt it had yesterday? Or had finding out about her mother wrecked her chances for good? After all, art had not sustained her mother. If it had, she'd never have opted out of life, no matter how despairing over the death of her lover she'd become, no matter how depressed. She could have used her art as a catharsis of a kind. That was surely one of its functions. But no, her mother's relationship with art was not what she'd thought it was. It wasn't as committed as she'd imagined all these years - passion and drive spurring her on, an attitude of mind that Lucy had used to spur herself on, to follow in her mother's footsteps. Maybe her mother wasn't even the person she'd remembered all these years, but an ideal she'd conceived from photographs and recollections of family moments, all painted by a rosy palette and the mutable eye of a selective memory.

She felt an ache in her chest, that twisted itself around. She had to find out more of the truth from Rhea, even if it hurt.

And then there was her mother's killing herself. Suicide. The taking of one's own life. Self murder. Something she'd read about in tragic novels, and the stuff of myths and legends. Even Kaunos had it in its creation story, which she'd read about in Hasim's book. The city was founded by the Greek King Kaunos, who had a twin sister called Byblis. She fell in love with him. He ran away in disgust and finally settled here to build Kaunos, while she wore herself out with grief and finally hung herself with her girdle. Suicide. Romanticised far back into time. Done on impulse, or carefully planned. The end for misunderstood poets and artists of delicate sensibilities. For those shamed by life, or guilt-ridden. For those preserving their honour. Or for those simply in deep despair or mental anguish. For those with no meaning. And that was the crux, she realised - her mother had no meaning left. Not even her own children could supply it.

And that was what hurt Lucy the most. And the image of Ophelia floating in her river, a willing victim of her own despair - this disgusted Lucy now. Ophelia was a stupid girl, who let a man twist her mind around, play with it, a man who didn't seem to give a toss about her. How ironic, she thought, that quite unknowingly, she'd chosen this very image to romanticise her mother's drowning. And yet, it had been nearer the truth after all. And her mother had probably used the painting as inspiration - her final inspiration. But there again, there was her wanting her ashes scattered at Housesteads for some other notion which their dad felt the need to cover up. It was just so sickening. So selfish. Where was her mother's strength? Where were thoughts of her family?

Then Lucy came to a decision and the ache in her chest eased a little. She could no longer sentimentalise her mother's death, or indeed her mother.

And this - was new.

***

Rhea wandered into the amphitheatre, relieved to get some time to herself. She headed straight for her olive tree, sat in its shadow, and took off her sunglasses to stare out beyond the toppled stones of the stage to the marshes.

She tried to think of priorities, but found she couldn't think of anything at all. The heat was making her feel drowsy, the crickets were resting their wings, and she felt like lying along the seat, with her bag for a pillow, to bask in the memory of her recent lovemaking with Hasim.

She gave herself a shake. She couldn't succumb to temptation and have Lucy find her asleep and not working on their problem. So she scrabbled around in her bag for her novel, deciding that when Lucy arrived, she could always say she'd just this minute picked it up. Once again, she'd packed her book and her mobile phone without Lucy noticing, the difference being that this time, she *did* feel guilty about it. This was an unusual feeling where Lucy was concerned and she wasn't sure what it meant.

When she found her place in the book, she could see there wasn't much of the story left to go. But she wavered. Should she savour the ending now, or leave it for the flight home? The caressing of a balmy breeze on her skin, and the fact that this ancient place of comedy and tragedy seemed a fitting place to escape into fiction, persuaded her. Far better than in a draughty airport or on a crowded plane. So she lowered her eyes to the task.

Madeleine's poultice turned out to be efficacious for Jacques. It drew out the infection, the red streaks around the wound disappeared and his fever broke. The first mate told the crew and they celebrated his recovery with plenty of rum.

When Jacques regained consciousness, he found Madelaine by his bunk, sleeping in his captain's chair. She'd obviously been watching over him, and he wondered why. He gazed long and hard at her lustrous lashes, resting on her flushed cheeks, the tilt of her nose, the sweet fullness of her lips, the long locks of her auburn hair drifting over her bare shoulders to her waist. What was it about this woman? She, before all others. He wasn't accustomed to such deep desire on his part, or to such resistance on hers. And she was trouble for him, wasn't she? He'd already decided not to deliver her to the Comte, but what was he to do about her uncle and the transaction he'd made, the profit from which currently swelled his coffers? What was he to do with Madelaine?

When she opened her eyes, there was the spark of defiance he was used to, but then it changed to a warm glow that he'd never seen before. She smiled at him. He found himself smiling back. And in this moment everything changed.

'You've come back to me,' she said.

'Come here,' he said.

And she did.

They kissed, and fell into one another's arms.

She made love with a haunting intensity that he'd never experienced before. He wanted to possess her, over and over, forever. He wanted to look after her. Their hearts were as one.

Oh, for crying out loud, Rhea thought. Wasn't there any more explicit detail than this? Is this what she'd been waiting for? What a waste! But she read on.

After the consummation of their love, as Madeleine curved her body around Jacques's and nestled her head into his shoulder, they made plans. Madeleine was adamant. She wouldn't be his mistress and she wouldn't marry a pirate, not even a privateer. His status must change. But she didn't want to stem his spirit of adventuring. In fact, she believed she had a hankering for adventure herself. So she'd been thinking…

At this point Jacques felt his hackles rise. A thinking woman could be a dangerous thing. Was she already trying to take him in charge? How dare she? But he waited. He was curious.

What about settling in South Africa? she suggested. The Cape of Good Hope. Though the colony was administered by the Dutch, there were French Huguenot refugees homesteading there. She and Jacques could change their names and learn Dutch. Maybe they could set up a trading company, with their own shipping line?

Jacques was surprised. This was actually a good idea, an exciting challenge, though fraught with political tensions. He grinned. He was now ready to reveal the truth of his lineage to her, and he savoured the shock on Madelaine's face when he told her he was actually the son of a French noble, with an inheritance he could put to good use. Times were changing in the Caribbean, and he knew the age of the privateers was nearing its demise. And he thought of the wide open territories of Africa, the game that ranged across its pasturelands, and he'd still be able to go to sea - there were so many uncharted territories to explore. He'd get word later to his family of his new life with Madelaine.

As they talked through this idea over the next two days, the air stirred itself into a gentle breeze. On the morning of the third day, when Jacques was quite recovered, they put their plans to a bewildered crew. They could either join Madeleine and Jacques in their new enterprise, or they could be set down in a safe harbour and sign up with another ship. There were a few malcontents, who vowed Madeleine had cast a spell over Jacques with her potion, but the rest said 'Aye'. So they changed the name of the ship to Far Horizons, unfurled its sails, and set off for Africa, while the setting sun burned upon a haze of ocean.

Rhea read on eagerly.

A few days later, a severe storm swept through the Caribbean, great walls of sea advanced upon the coastlines of the islands, many ships foundered and sank. When the Sea Sprite didn't come into port at Martinique, she was assumed to be one of these unlucky ships, and all souls aboard were presumed lost. Fate was on the couple's side.

On the very last page of the book, Madelaine stood with Jacques on the quarterdeck, his arms tightly around her. Buffeted by a fortuitous tailwind, which urged the ship onwards, they both looked to the dawn of a new horizon. They knew there would be rougher seas ahead, but for now, all was well, and all was as it should be.

Rhea was disgusted when she found herself in tears. Romantic drivel, she thought. But she glanced at the back cover to see if there was a sequel. She felt a sting of disappointment that there wasn't.

As the afterglow of the novel's ending slowly faded within her, she was struck by two things. One. In no way had she ever been able to cast her husband, Chris, in the role of a romantic hero, not even in her fantasies. This felt like a fundamental error. And two. She'd never really ventured into a private business enterprise of her own, like she'd imagined at college all those years ago. Her father had warned her against it, in favour of job security.

She glanced at her watch. Lucy was late and it would soon be lunchtime. Maybe they could get back to Dalyan and have their chat over lunch? Then she noticed some movements in the corner of her eye. Shifting her gaze to the left, to the bottom of the amphitheatre seating, she saw blotches of grey, moving around the circumference of the arena towards the shady nooks of the stage. Looking more closely, she saw three small tortoises shuffling, plodding, heads bobbing, under the burden of their backpacks.

And as she watched them, something struck her. That's what Dad did, she thought, security always first. *Slow and steady wins the race*, she could remember him saying. And that was what she'd done. She'd worked her way up to the top of her game in the retail world, a senior position, salary of 45K per year. Job description: maximising profits, minimising losses, merchandising, promotions, human resources, marketing, logistics, customer service and finance. And meetings, endless meetings, and having to follow market trends, monitoring the competition, always having to be on form. Plod, plod, shuffle, shuffle.

And time had passed by, with the only thing now on her horizon being the menopause. And she was wary of that. She's seen her secretary, Clare, go through it. The embarrassing hot flushes, the panicky feelings, where she would suddenly rush out of the room, the lack of concentration. 'It's so awful!' Clare had kept repeating. 'You've no idea!' Rhea had been understanding, but had inwardly vowed there was no way she was going to have it happen to her. She'd done the research already, she'd planned her attack. Despite the warnings, HRT was the best option, and she really had no choice. If the menopause got her in its grip, Kevin, her assistant manager, who was already straining at the leash for her job, would run at her heels and trip her up. She'd lose her form. And then what?

And anyway - where was the glamour and colour in her job? She'd been struck by these things during this holiday, especially at the market. Back home, all those grey and black office suits, all that following of trends back in the store. Plod, plod, shuffle, shuffle. Where was the spontaneity, like in *Pride and Passion*? Where was the enterprise?

But then she flinched, as if a hand had struck her. Enterprise. That was what Chris, her husband, was all about. *Speculate to accumulate*, he said. And he was always *exploring new avenues*, had some *interesting opportunities opening up, something in the leisure industry*. Yet, even though he was in finance, and should know about investing, he did it so badly: he always hit a sticky patch, or he was let down, or something had just fallen through. And it had changed him for the worst. He wasn't the Chris she'd married. Perhaps enterprise just didn't work, and all your hard-won cash got flushed away? Perhaps there were no new horizons? And after all, no-one ever asks what happens *after* you sail off into the sunset. Maybe her father was right about not taking risks. But in that moment, a surge of energy mounted inside her and her heart crashed around inside her ribcage. One thing she was sure of was that her dad had been wrong about Chris.

And before she could calm down and talk herself out of it, she yanked out her mobile and stabbed at the keys until she got a signal. Finding Chris in her contacts, she blinked at the text screen and her fingertips shook. How to phrase it. Her thoughts jerked from phrase to phrase, but in the end the words were simple.

'I want a divorce. Don't bother replying. There's no point. You knew it was coming. I'll tell Rob.'

When the message was sent with a curt beep that sounded like a full stop on her marriage, she leaned back against the stone and breathed out long and slow. She knew he'd get the message, as he was always on his phone, and for once this was a distinct advantage. And she knew he wouldn't tell Rob, because he was too much of a coward. Of course, he'd fight for his share of their assets. Well, bring it on, she thought. The fear of this had held her back for too long, and hadn't she made some provisions already? Made enquiries? The tension in her leached away, like the last few drops of water going down a plughole.

And when she heard Lucy calling from the high ground above - she found herself smiling.

Lucy scrambled down the steps and sat next to her. 'I need to ask you some questions about Mum,' Lucy said. 'How did *you* get on?'

'What do you mean?'

'What do you mean, *'what do I mean*?'' Lucy said, her voice rising. 'We're supposed to be sorting out our priorities for when we get home. How did you get on?'

Rhea grinned at Lucy. 'Well, I've sorted one thing out. I've texted Chris for a divorce.'

Lucy's mouth sagged open like a gate on a broken hinge. The look of shock on her face made Rhea feel a quiver of doubt, so she stiffened her back.

'It feels so good, Lucy. I should have done it ages ago.' She managed to keep her smile firmly in place.

'But…but…couldn't you have waited until we go home?' Lucy garbled.

'No. I don't think I could. I had to act in the moment.'

Lucy snatched off her shades and her eyes grew as round as paperweights. 'But you don't do that kind of thing!'

Rhea felt a lightning strike of fear flash through her. Lucy was right.

Then Lucy groaned. 'It's not that you believe you're in love with Hasim, is it?'

Now, anger grumbled around inside Rhea like thunder. 'Of course not! Don't be silly.'

'Then he's got nothing to do with this?'

427

Rhea considered for a moment, trying to calm herself, while Lucy glared at her. 'Well...I can't pretend knowing him hasn't made a difference. It's made me realise what I've been missing. You only get one life, don't you?'

Lucy's eyebrows shot up again. 'You don't say things like that! You never say things like that!'

'Well, it's true, isn't it?' Rhea demanded.

Lucy frowned. Rhea felt uneasy, sensing a shift.

'Well, I suppose so,' Lucy said. 'But there may be other possibilities.'

Rhea rose to her feet, lowered her sunglasses onto her nose and angled some emphasis across the top of them at Lucy. 'Don't start talking about reincarnation and karma. That would be just typical of you. We need to keep things simple. We need to concentrate on this life. And right now, I'm hungry. Can't we go back to town and talk over lunch?'

'No!'

Rhea drew back at Lucy's angry tone. 'What's the matter?'

'I want us to climb up to the rock tombs. Remember? You're not getting out of it, you agreed. We can talk there.'

'Alright! We'll talk there. *Then* can we have something to eat?'

***

As she stood with Rhea at the bottom of the hillside, Lucy felt a mass of irritation seething within her like wriggling maggots. This, together with the sickening drag of habit. Here she was again, imposing conditions, setting a scene for herself which she'd imagined in some detail. Rhea and herself were to talk about what to do when they got home, and for that, she'd decided last night, they must be looking out over Dalyan from the rock tombs - to give them some perspective. Yet Rhea had already got some perspective and done some deciding - and it made Lucy feel angry, short-changed, and much to her inner disgust, actually jealous. The solution to her art problem wasn't as simple as sending a text.

The stony path up to the tombs looked like an assault course, winding up through a tumble of boulders, stunted trees and sharp shrubs. At the top, the pitted brow of the cliff face overlooked the temple fronts of the tombs, their dark open niches resembling empty eye sockets. Grizzled and ravaged, the cliff with its inset tombs looked forbidding and Lucy instinctively sensed Rhea hanging back.

'Come on,' said Lucy sharply. She set off on the path, kicking up dust with her sandals.

Rhea called after her. 'This isn't going to turn into another trial, is it? Don't you think we've had enough of those?'

Lucy turned and looked at Rhea who was standing there with her hands on her hips. It was so predictable, but at least more like the Rhea she knew. Lucy adopted her usual persuasive tactics. 'We've got the right footwear on. The view will be amazing and it might help with some perspective. Come on, let's try.'

Rhea shrugged her shoulders. 'Oh, all right.' She trudged up to Lucy. 'But we have to be careful, the ground looks dangerous.'

'I'll stay just in front of you. I won't go charging up.'

Lucy was annoyed to find that the going was indeed difficult. The soles of their sandals kept slipping in the scree, loosening stones that playfully bounced down to the bottom making skittering sounds. She and Rhea were soon glistening with sweat and couldn't talk much for panting. There were big boulders to step up onto, putting the strength of their thigh muscles and knees to the test. Lucy found her balance and agility were her assets, and noticed that Rhea's muscle strength was hers, with the result that more than once she caught hold of Rhea to stop her falling over, while Rhea was able to take the lead over the boulders and help her up. With grunts and gasps and frequent pauses to share a bottle of water, Lucy was too wrapped up in her thoughts and focused on the task of getting to the top, to properly appreciate this clasping of hands teamwork between them. Glancing down, the path to Kaunos disappeared as the sky came to meet them. They stopped occasionally to let other visitors to the tombs pass by on the descent of the escarpment.

'It's going to be harder going down, you know,' Rhea commented, watching a couple of walkers stop at every boulder to discuss and negotiate the twists and turns.

This characteristic negativity of Rhea's and her not being able to be in the moment, irritated Lucy. 'We're not even at the top yet! We'll get to that later.'

'I was just saying!'

As they neared the top, it was tricky for Lucy to decide where exactly the top was. But the base of the nearest temple front came into view and, for Lucy, it was a sight for sore eyes. Here she was, standing beneath one of the tombs she had seen from the boat on the day of the turtle watch. She eagerly surveyed it. Riddled with cracks and nibbled at by time, the golden stone of the ancient edifice looked like a desiccated wood carving about to crumble into dust. Yet here it stood, with its classical pediment, entablature and ionic columns, although one of the columns had collapsed from the base, leaving behind a stalactite of stone clinging precariously to the roof. Inside the temple front, a black hole had been stoved into the stone door, and she knew what that meant from Hasim's book. Desecrations had taken place by robbers determined to steal the gold intended to accompany the royal nobles into their afterlife. Staring into the blackness was compelling. Then she noticed a tall slit of darkness to one side. It was another entrance into the tomb, its sides as smooth and striated as a wind and water channel in a canyon rock face, inviting of exploration.

Lucy turned to Rhea. 'It said in Hasim's book, that it

was believed that a winged creature would carry the dead into the afterworld and that's why the tombs were built on high cliffs. Isn't that fascinating?'

'I suppose so. But where are we going to sit?' Rhea replied.

Lucy scrutinized the base of the temple. 'I think we should sit outside the tomb. We can climb up and sit on one of those big steps underneath the columns.'

Rhea looked where Lucy was indicating and frowned. 'It's too dangerous, Lucy. What if that broken one comes crashing down?'

Lucy brushed away Rhea's objection by flicking her hair over her shoulder and starting to make for the entrance. 'It's not going to come down just because we happen to be sitting underneath it on the 1st of July, 2010.'

'No! I'm not having it, Lucy. It's too dangerous. It's high up and slippery. You've already nearly drowned on this holiday, and now you want to tempt fate again? Think of Charlie and Poppy.'

Lucy stopped in her tracks at Rhea's words hit their target. Irresponsible. That's what she was being. Under other circumstances, it could be classed as being adventurous. But not today. Today, they were up here to talk about what to do when they got home. And she was finding it so difficult to know where to start, she was going off on a tangent and procrastinating.

She slumped her shoulders. 'You're right,' she said to a red-faced Rhea. She glanced around. 'Look. There's a nice flat rock we can sit on and we still see the view.'

They settled themselves on the rock, wiping their brows and flicking off a few flies sticking to their shirts. Staring out at the panorama, beneath the peaks of their caps, Lucy felt familiar with it from the pictures and descriptions in Hasim's book. She tried hard to enjoy it.

The Dalyan river slid through the fertile valley plains, where olives, walnuts, oranges and lemon trees were cultivated in the shelter of hills on the horizon. The town, built up along the eastern bank, was an expanse of terracotta roofs, and whitewashed walls, with turquoise puddles of swimming pools marking the hotels and private villas. Cypress trees rose to touch the sky like the shining white minaret of the mosque. River boats were trailing south towards the delta and the open sea, or north to Köyceğiz lake and its revitalising mud spas. The rest nosed against the long harbour, waiting for customers. Further south, the reed beds lay, slowing the progress of the boats, with their wavy-edged contours, the patterns of which looked to Lucy like an exploded giant jigsaw puzzle. And it was here, in these lazy marshes, that she'd read the caretta turtles came to breed, before laying their eggs on Iztuzu beach. To Lucy's mind, that sounded just a little too convenient a use of the marsh when they migrated through the open seas. It was probably just another romantic notion - and she was finding she was going off them these days.

'It's so beautiful, isn't it?' Rhea said.

Lucy cringed. Everything was wrong. That was supposed to be her feeling, not Rhea's. But the wriggling maggots inside her were ruining her appreciation. 'Yes,' she replied, lamely. Thoughts and questions jostled for position, elbowing each other out of the way. She was rendered speechless.

'I'm glad you made us come up here. Thanks, Lucy.'

Lucy barely heard her.

Rhea shot her a sideways look. 'You said you had some questions about Mum. What do you want to know?'

Lucy's heart started pounding. 'I don't know where to start.'

'What do you want to know about Mum? Start there. Start anywhere,' Rhea said with a hint of irritation.

Lucy stared at the sky, then looked down the hillside, and an image popped into her mind, something she'd remembered the previous day. A girl in a yellow suit, suspended from a hot air balloon - as close to flying as you

432

could get, back then in the seventies. 'Yesterday, I was remembering the Nimble advert we used to watch with Mum. We used to dance around the room, pretending to fly.' She turned sharply to Rhea. 'You do remember that, don't you?'

Rhea nodded. 'Yes. It was before things started to go wrong.'

Lucy went on to describe her memory in detail: the flying, the giggles, them both wanting to be the girl in the balloon. Their mother telling them one day they both would be. Their dad smiling.

'He didn't have much of a sense of adventure, though. I realise that now,' Rhea said.

'But he'd had loved it up here.'

'Oh yes. But he wouldn't have gone clambering into the tombs by himself. He'd have wanted a safe guided tour by a noted archaeologist, followed by a lecture.'

Lucy surprised herself by managing a laugh. 'Do you think that's what went wrong? Mum needing more adventure than he could give?'

'Maybe.'

Then Lucy found the courage to ask what she needed to know. 'I always saw Mum that way, free in that balloon, doing her own thing. Happy being an artist. But she couldn't have been. I don't think she was who I thought she was.' She turned and looked hard at Rhea. 'How did you see it? Was she a proper artist? Where did she exhibit? Did she sell much?'

Rhea held Lucy's gaze, then shook her head. 'No, I don't think she was really. She didn't sell much. She was a member of a local group, she exhibited with them. She had a couple of solo exhibitions at the town hall, I think. She seemed happy for a while.' Then she paused. 'Like I told you before, she didn't take it as seriously as you. She dabbled with it. And she tried all sorts of different subjects, never settling on anything for long.' She searched Lucy's face. 'Why is this so important?'

Tears burned in Lucy's eyes as she looked at Rhea. 'Because I thought I was following in her footsteps. I thought it was her vocation and I wanted it to be mine! To be close to her memory somehow. And now it's all trashed. If she felt about art, the way I feel about it, if it had given her real meaning, she'd never have taken her own life. She'd have wanted to carry on regardless.'

Rhea put a hand on Lucy's arm. 'Okay, so it wasn't a vocation for her. But it is to you - that's obvious. Don't bother comparing yourself to her any more. Just get on with your own art. It's *your* vocation. *Your* passion.' She hesitated. 'And…you've even seen a caretta like you wanted.'

At the mention of the turtle, Lucy recoiled and turned away. She felt so utterly ridiculous. What had she been thinking? Romantic, fanciful nonsense about a sea turtle helping to heal her creativity. How could it make any difference with the art market the way it was? And yet a part of her felt she was betraying the turtle. She groaned. 'But I'm so disillusioned with the art world and the self marketing you have to do. I have to keep my feelings from Poppy too, in case I upset her. I just want it to be like it used to be. Me doing what I love and being able to share it.'

'If you love it, then you have to do it, come what may. Separate doing the business from doing the art.' Rhea batted a mosquito on her shirt with the back of her hand.

'It's not that easy!'

Rhea frowned. 'Maybe you just need someone to help you with the marketing? A kind of agent. You can't be the only one that goes through this. Lots of artists are probably terrible self-promoters.'

Lucy scowled. 'I suppose so, but I don't know. It could be expensive.'

Rhea was silent for a few moments as she gazed down at the view. Then, still staring at the bends in the river, she said, 'Maybe I could help you. You could vet what I do and take over when you're ready.'

Lucy turned to look at Rhea, shock caught in her throat like a fish hook. 'Really?' she croaked.

'I don't see why not. I can be more objective. That should work better, shouldn't it?'

'Yes,' Lucy managed to reply. She didn't doubt Rhea's capabilities, but the idea of them working together was something she just couldn't conceive of. What was going on? But not wanting to immediately reject Rhea's offer, or indeed to upset her, she said, 'I'll think about it.'

Then she felt a twinge of guilt, remembering something she'd completely overlooked. She knew it was probably intentional, as the very idea of being indebted to Rhea was unthinkable. She straightened herself up and twisted her hair into a bun.

She turned to Rhea. 'I've never thanked you,' she said, not quite able to hold Rhea's gaze.

'For what?'

'For saving my life,' Lucy replied. 'Thanks.' Then she hesitated. 'It took a lot of guts for you to go underwater like that.'

Rhea shuddered. 'Don't remind me.' Then she looked at Lucy. 'I didn't want to be the only one of us left,' she said in clipped tones. 'Can we go for lunch *now*?'

***

As they picked their way down the escarpment, Rhea felt puzzled as to why Lucy kept looking back at the rock tombs and she asked her about it.

'It just seems symbolic somehow,' Lucy said. 'Kind of like leaving the dead behind. After all, life is for the living, isn't it?'

Rhea nodded. But she felt distinctly dazed with what was happening to her this afternoon. She'd told Chris she wanted a divorce; she hadn't checked her messages; and now she'd offered to be Lucy's agent. Maybe the heat was getting to her? But she was so hungry, she determined to put these things from her mind and follow Lucy's suggestion of having something to eat at the cafe on the jetty. Then they could cross the river back to town.

Sitting at a rough wooden table covered in a red and white checked cloth, in the shade of some mature oak trees, only the sound of the river sucking at the posts of the jetty and a few rowing boats rocking in the river's swell disturbed the quiet. The menu was limited to honey and banana pancakes, so that's what they chose, together with fresh watermelon juice to wash them down with.

Watching the boats on the river, travelling to and fro, and not being able to see them arrive anywhere, made Rhea feel queasy and she wished the talking could be over. She had the seed of an idea growing, that she just couldn't get rid of. She needed to examine it, but to do that she had to make sure she and Lucy were as resolved as they could be for the present.

'Oh!' Lucy exclaimed. 'I nearly forgot!'

Rhea braced herself. 'What?'

'Well, not only was Mum not quite *who* I thought she was. She wasn't even *where* I thought she was! Her ashes weren't scattered up at the ridge near Brook Farm. I mean, I used to go and talk to her there sometimes. How could Dad have lied to me like that? To us all? You said in the note she asked to be at Housesteads? Why there?' Lucy threw down her knife and fork, making a clattering sound.

Rhea saw the lady cafe owner, who was dressed in black in the shadows behind the bar, stare over at them. She scowled at them through the furrows of her shrunken face. Rhea shivered, wondering if she was giving them the evil eye, and wishing she'd got herself a protection charm like she'd planned. She leaned in close to Lucy. 'The owner thinks you don't like her pancakes!'

'Oh, for goodness' sake!' Lucy turned around and gave the woman a wave and a broad smile.

The woman's scowl eased and Rhea felt better.

'Well, come on! Why Housesteads?' Lucy insisted.

'I was going to tell you about that the other day,' Rhea said, 'but you wouldn't let me go on. She *was* scattered by the sycamore trees near Brook Farm - not at Housesteads.'

'What? Lucy shrieked. She flung down her knife and fork again and began to rise to her feet.

Rhea got hold of Lucy's arms and yanked her down, feeling the woman's eye upon them again. She sighed. 'Dad betrayed Mum in the end. He didn't want to scatter her at Housesteads, because he knew that the sculptor was scattered there. And he also knew it was where they used to meet.'

Lucy fell back in her seat, her eyes narrowing. 'Oh, very romantic,' she said. 'Very Cathy and Heathcliff meeting on the moors.'

'Exactly,' Rhea said, going on to explain that their father said he just couldn't do it. He couldn't reunite them.

'Do you think he was justified?' Lucy said, with a curious look.

In her mind's eye, Rhea saw her mother's note burning in her father's hands, her very last request turning to cinders. She'd never forgotten it. 'Well, it has preyed on my mind sometimes,' she found herself admitting. 'But yes, I think he was justified. Tit for tat, I suppose. What do you think?'

Lucy shook her head. 'It was asking a lot.' Then she fell silent, chewing thoughtfully as she finished off her pancakes.

Rhea watched a group of four tourists enter the shady cafe and select a table close to the bar. The owner came from the shadows to take their order. As Rhea examined them more closely, she recognised the man in the white panama who'd been at the information plaque at Kaunos earlier. When she looked at the woman sitting next to him, fiddling with her handbag in her lap, a penny dropped and she drew in a sharp intake of breath. It was the man Lucy had the argument with on the day of the coach trip -

about Trish's job *at her age*, about pensions, about order, the man who had wound up Lucy about personal fulfilment not being a very responsible attitude.

Rhea decided not to point him out to Lucy, as she had her back to his table. They just didn't need any aggravation right now.

'Oh...by the way,' Lucy said, munching, then swallowing hard. 'I meant to tell you. I think I met John, the sculptor, once.'

'What? Rhea said sharply, her eyes boring into Lucy's. 'You can't have!'

'I'm pretty sure I did, though I wouldn't say he looked much like George Harrison. He was much taller, and - '

'How did you meet him? When? And how do you know it was him?' Rhea's heart was racing and she was trying to restrain herself from shouting. She felt incensed at the possibility of Lucy having met her mother's boyfriend, when all these years she'd only been able to imagine him.

But Lucy's reply was interrupted by some loud squawking in the vicinity. All heads turned to see five white geese strutting across the bare earth floor between the tables, stretching their necks, then bobbing their heads down to hunt for scraps. Assuming them to be domestic, conversations were resumed.

'Well!' Rhea said to Lucy. 'Go on!'

So Lucy described the day her mother had taken her to the gallery in Newcastle, and how they'd bumped into this man, how her mother said he was just a friend, but she'd seemed very different with him. All giggly and shining. How he seemed to think a lot of himself - well compared to their dad, anyway. How, afterwards, her mother had asked her to not mention meeting him. It was a secret, she said, just between herself and Lucy, because George might not like it.

Rhea sprang to her feet and glared at Lucy. 'Another secret?' She broke out in a cold sweat. All these years she'd assumed she knew everything there was to know.

The geese made their way to the sisters' table.

'And you kept it? You kept her secret?' she asked accusingly.

'Well, of course!' Lucy said, scattering some bits of pancake onto the ground for the geese. 'It was a special day,' she mused. 'It was just her and me.'

'And him!'

'Well, I didn't know any better, did I?' Lucy's voice became indignant as she stared back at Rhea. 'I must have only been around nine or ten. I didn't know she was having an affair with him!'

Rhea sprang up from the table and began to pace around, hands on hips, unable to gather any coherent thoughts. Lucy joined her, but the geese scuttled after her and began to hiss. Marching legs and raised voices from the sisters, together with hissing beaks and thrashing wings from the geese, attracted the attention of the owner and the group of tourists, who all gawped at them.

'And how do you feel about it now?' Rhea demanded, looking squarely at Lucy.

'Well, she'd have known children like secrets, wouldn't she?' Lucy garbled. 'She knew I'd keep it. I suppose I feel manipulated…disappointed in her.' Lucy grabbed some more pancake pieces and threw them down for the geese. They honked louder and dived for the scraps, shouldering each other out of the way.

Then, both sisters froze on the spot in the middle of this mayhem as the owner sprang from the shadows. She sped towards them like a ghost on castors, in widow's weeds, with a deadly grudge carved into her face. One moment behind the bar, the next, close-facing them. So close, Rhea could see fury blazing in her ink-drop eyes.

Both she and Lucy staggered back a few steps.

The woman in black pointed at a sign at the entrance, with a crooked finger. Rhea could see plainly that it stated 'Do Not Feed The Geese.'

'You not feed them!' she rasped. 'You upset them. They angry now! You no good, you go now!'

At first Rhea quaked, aghast at the scene they were making. The occupants of the other table were peering over and the man with the white panama had a smug look on his face. Then she looked at the angry old woman, making a fuss about nothing. After all, she and Lucy *were* customers, and the geese were roaming around freely.

'Go! Shoo!' shouted the old woman, making a sweeping action with her arms as if she was wielding a broom. Then she turned her attention to the geese in the same manner.

While her attention was distracted, Lucy tugged at Rhea's arm. 'We haven't paid yet. What should we do?'

'Well, we're going. I don't care about paying. She can forget that!'

Rhea stalked towards the exit, which meant passing the table of tourists, two couples sitting together, including the man in the panama. Lucy followed.

But the woman in black hadn't finished yet, and she rolled after them.

The geese had stopped honking and were swaying their way nonchalantly out of the cafe grounds, as if on a Mediterranean evening stroll.

The man in the white panama started laughing, a snuffling, snorting sound, which Rhea decided sounded just like a pig at a trough. Now if they could only get past his table and get away.

'I want money! You pay first!' demanded the owner, who'd caught up with them.

Rhea turned on her heels to face her. To stare down the demon with the evil eye. Instead of fear, she was surprised to feel rage.

Lucy tugged her arm again. 'Let's pay her, Rhea. Please!' she urged, and she began to root around in her bag.

'Well, look who it is!' The man in the panama said

sarcastically. 'The aaartist! Does what she pleases and hang the rest of us!'

'Shut up!' Rhea snapped at him.

'I want my money!' the woman in black repeated, not moving an inch.

Lucy stuffed a 10 lire note into Rhea's hand. 'Pay her, and don't take any notice of him. 'He's not worth the bother,' she said loudly.

Rhea stabbed the note into the woman's knobbly palm. She looked fiercely into her shrivelled face. 'That's all you're getting! It's a bit short, but your treatment of customers is appalling. Now leave us alone!' she shouted.

The woman in black stood motionless. Then to Rhea's surprise, she slowly slid backwards on her castors into the shadows behind the bar.

The man in the white panama guffawed. 'Oh, I say! You really put on a show, don't you! Must be the influence of the aaartist!

Lucy coloured and said nothing.

Rhea turned to look at him. She saw his heavy jowls, his large proboscis of a nose, and his down-turned mouth all forming a sneering expression to rival Somerset Maughan's, and she felt a pounding in her ears. Her temper was rising again. She remembered the disagreement on the coach trip - Trish's job being put down, Lucy's defending her, defending personal fulfilment, and him coming out with a need for order, for taking responsibility. Well, Lucy's instincts about this man had been spot on. He needed putting in his place, and she was in the mood to do it. She'd pick up where the argument had left off.

'And what exactly do you do for living?'

'None of your damned business! Anyway, I'm retired now.'

'Okay, well what are you retired from?'

The man stared back at her, but said nothing.

His wife was peering down into her handbag on her

441

lap, but her body twitched.

The couple they were with began to squirm in their seats.

'Come on! You're pretty quick to criticise others,' Rhea said.

His wife looked up. 'Why don't you just tell her, Malcolm.'

He pointed at his wife. 'You stay out of this.'

His wife thumped her bag onto the ground and looked at Rhea. 'He worked for HM Revenue and Customs, National Insurance.'

Malcolm pointed at his wife again. 'Shut up, Brenda, I'm warning you!'

Right,' Rhea said. 'So, you had a nice safe job for life, pushing papers around, squeezing people for a pension they don't even know they're going to get if things carry on as they are.'

Malcolm stood up, as tall and lanky as a giant stick insect and leaned over them. He waggled his finger at Lucy. 'I bet *she* doesn't pay anything. This arty farty lot won't go out and get proper jobs, so they can properly contribute for services. They live in cloud cuckoo land instead.'

Lucy gasped. 'That is such a stereotypical attitude! And I do pay my contributions, actually.'

But Rhea and Malcolm both ignored her.

'Excuse me!' Rhea replied. '*She* is my sister, Lucy. She is a talented artist, and it takes a lot of determination to be one. Not to mention doing the work with a lot of-self belief and motivation required, and then having to open yourself up to criticism. I bet you can't take much criticism, can you, Malcolm?'

Malcolm rolled his eyes. 'Oh, for God's sake! What *exactly* is your point?'

Rhea felt fuelled with fury looking into his supercilious expression as he shrugged his shoulders at the others around the table, trying to recover some ground. But her

442

persistent seed of an idea had suddenly sprouted a tiny shoot, and as if there was a connection, she found herself firing on all cylinders.

'My point is, that not everyone wants to slog away at a boring job for life! Some people want to take chances, be enterprising, get some personal fulfilment in this life, which as far as we know we only get one of.'

She shot a look at Lucy to keep her reincarnation theories to herself.

Malcolm folded his spindly insect arms across his chest. 'And what exactly do *you* do, may I ask?'

'I'm the manager of a department store. Worked my way up, using *your* mindset. Plenty of order, plenty of responsibility, a job for life if I want it. And do you know what? I'm sick of it. Didn't you ever get sick of your job? Didn't you ever have any dreams, Malcolm?'

Malcolm's jaw dropped.

His wife unfolded herself from her seat and stood as stiff as starched linen. 'I don't think he ever did. As soon as he retired, all he's done is play golf.'

Malcolm glared at her. 'Shut up, Brenda. I've just about had enough of you!'

'I had dreams, though,' Brenda carried on, looking at Rhea. 'I wanted to join an amateur dramatic society, but he always used to put me off. First for the children when they were young, and then after they'd gone, he kept saying it was for nincompoops who wanted to strut around a stage. Did I want to be a nincompoop?'

She turned to look at Malcolm. 'Well, I've had enough of you too, Malcolm. You're a bully and you're always picking on people. And when I get home, I'm going to join the local group.'

The other couple at the table glanced at each other and sidled out of their chairs. They stealthily approached the bar to settle up quietly as if they might just be the next targets.

Lucy pulled at Rhea's arm. 'Time to go,' she hissed.

Brenda's interjection had stalled Rhea, and the couple had rounded on each other.

She turned around and began to deliberately amble away with the intention of conveying she wouldn't be rushed. Then they picked up the path through the trees to the rowing boat pier. Brenda's and Malcolm's voices could still be heard shouting at each other.

'Do you think this is a turning point for Brenda?' Lucy asked her.

Rhea smiled. 'Maybe? But old habits die hard,' she said, thinking of herself and Chris.

As they stood on the rickety wooden pier waiting for the boat to be rowed from the other side, Rhea sensed Lucy studying her.

'What is it?' she asked.

'Well…' Lucy hesitated. 'I was wondering what got into you back there. Defending art, defending me - you've never done it before.'

Rhea felt a flush of embarrassment. She knew it wasn't just about Lucy and her art. It was also about enterprise and taking risks. And her seed had sprouted so many shoots now, and they felt like sparks of excitement and fear in her gut. She couldn't control it.

She tried to look calm as she replied to Lucy. 'I was just going from what you've told me, and about the conflicts. It's no big deal or anything.'

***

But to Lucy's mind, it had meant a very great deal - and it had stirred her. She didn't quite know how and decided to think about it later.

As they were being rowed back over the river, she was surprised to find she felt lighter in herself. They had both tackled some serious issues today. All they had to do before going home was to work out who to tell the truth about their mother's death. And they could decide that

444

tomorrow, on their last full day. Of course, she suspected Rhea might have totally different opinions on the matter, but they must agree before they went home. For now though, despite their traumas, she felt they deserved some fun, and the forthcoming Turkish night at the Onur was sure to provide it.

She glanced at her watch. It was around 3.30pm. That gave herself and Rhea three hours of free time. She decided she would go to the Pomegranate gallery to buy some presents. She'd ignore the vampire owner and buy some of those lovely Iznik tiles for Charlie, and there was sure to be some jewellery for Poppy. She told her plans to Rhea.

What will *you* do? she asked Rhea, who was being very quiet.

'Oh, I think I'll go and see Trish…I can ask her if there are spaces left for the Turkish evening, for inviting Eleanor.' She hesitated. 'And I can ask Eleanor if she wants to come to the beach picnic tomorrow.'

Lucy frowned. They hadn't actually agreed to the picnic. What had happened to consulting each other? But she decided to let it go, as she loved the idea of spending their last full day on the turtle beach, as long as they got some time to themselves to sort the remaining things before they went home.

'Right,' she replied. 'But we will get some time to ourselves, won't we? We'll have to, you know.'

Oh, yes,' Rhea replied. 'Of course - we will have to.'

***

The evening was well planned. The roof terrace of the Onur was converted into a magical stage for oriental dancing. Fairy lights and candle-lit tables were arranged around a cleared space that served as the dance floor. The breakfast bar groaned under the weight of a buffet of Turkish delights: platters of meze starters to share, spiced lamb pilau, chicken kebabs, pide breads with a choice of toppings, with desserts of baklava and rose cream and raspberry jellies. And the wine was ready to flow. Hasim was now concentrating on receiving the dancers and sorting out where the musicians were to go.

But the sisters were not so well prepared. When Lucy got back to their hotel room after buying her purchases, she found Rhea missing. After ten minutes passed, during which Lucy was struggling to decide what to wear, Rhea arrived, panting from running up the staircase.

'Took longer than I thought,' she muttered in answer to Lucy's querying look. 'But everything's sorted, Eleanor's coming.'

When they finally arrived on the terrace, it was already full of people. Hasim came over to greet them, looking very clean-cut in a dark suit and a pressed white shirt.

He gazed at Rhea first, who was wearing a full-skirted white dress with a plunging neckline and a nipped in waist. Her pink kunzite ring and the filigree necklace she had bought from the gallery flashed in the candlelight.

He took her hand. 'You look beautiful,' he said, while Lucy stared at them.

Rhea smiled in reply as he led them both to their table, where Trish, Seda and Eleanor were waiting. Lucy's attire was particularly admired by Seda, which consisted of a purple multi-layered gypsy skirt, which she wore with an embroidered tie front blouse showing off her midrib. She was wearing the wrap around bracelet Yazmira had given her.

As the evening got underway, the throbbing beat of the hand drums and cymbals and the haunting tones of the oud and clarinet drifted over the rooftops of Dalyan - to mesmerise and charm the night. Louder and louder became the music, as the dancers swirled and twirled, in a blur of chiffon, sequin and veil, arms reaching, beckoning, snaking. Hips dropping, lifting, twisting and circling, moving around the floor, shimmying with torso's glistening.

Rhea asked Seda about the bedlah costumes, Lucy asked her about the moves. The chatter at the table rose with the music, glasses chinked, cutlery clinked, until they were reduced to fits of giggles. And when the time came to join in - they all did. Hasim danced with Rhea, Lucy with the others, with Seda showing her some techniques. Now and again, Lucy and Rhea danced together, trying out the head slides. Coloured lights pulsed on the floor and the beat went on until around midnight.

As the company dispersed like champagne bubbles, Rhea disappeared to spend some time with Hasim, while Lucy skipped and lilted her way to bed, still drifting with the music. It would seem, that against all odds, it had turned out to be a good day and the evening a fitting culmination for the holiday. Who would have believed it?

18

Back On Turtle Beach

High in the blue, a white-tailed eagle drifted on warm thermals along the arc of Iztuzu beach. In effortless flight, it headed towards the eastern end and its pine-crested mountain, the ocean lying below like softly shifting silk. Resting, as it floated through space, alone on suspended wing, the eagle was content - it had plucked a fish from the foam and its belly was full.

Far below, flecks of colour scuttled on the sand. Then closer, at the edge of the sea, four women could be seen. Struggling with a gentle breeze, they were trying to lay down a picnic rug. The group comprised of: a lean redhead in a red bikini; a black-haired girl with a long plait, discreetly wearing a sarong over a one-piece; a curvy blonde wearing a white bikini; and a leggy brunette in a dark blue halter neck costume, cut in a retro style - on her head, a straw hat with pink roses.

Securing the corners of the rug with some stones, they settled themselves into easy poses and fell upon a pile of Tupperware, paper plates and cutlery, and unscrewed the cap of a bottle of white wine, letting the golden fizz splash into four plastic cups. During these manoeuvres, fresh peaches rolled around on the cloth like bowling balls.

'This is the life,' said Trish, raising her cup to the others. 'Sun, sea and sand!' she exclaimed. 'Cheers!'

Seda smiled and picked up her cup. 'Şerefe!'

Lucy grinned, toasted the others in both languages and took a sip.

Rhea repeated the gesture, then stared into the bubbles. 'It was good of Hasim to let us have the leftovers from last night, wasn't it? And he got the chef to make us the sandwiches this morning.'

'He's a nice bloke,' replied Trish, 'but he's not the committing type.'

Rhea's mouth tightened. 'I know, he's told me. I'm not looking for that from anyone these days.'

Trish's face shrank into its creases. 'Oh, I'm sorry, no offence.' Then she brightened. 'Although that bike ride to Ephesus was quite something.'

Seda looked earnestly at Rhea. 'I have not heard anyone speak bad about him.'

Rhea nodded and spooned some bulgur wheat salad onto her plate.

'Well, it hardly matters now,' Lucy said to Rhea. 'You won't be here.'

Trish giggled and nervously grabbed a spam and egg sandwich.

Seda bit into a pide bread.

Lucy looked at their three munching faces and changed the subject. 'When did you say Eleanor is coming?' she asked Rhea.

'Around three,' she replied. 'She has things to do. She's trying to get an earlier flight home.'

Lucy looked puzzled.

'Her husband has apparently been missing her and wants to give their relationship another go,' said Rhea. 'She says they're as bad as each other, so she's willing to give it another try.'

'Hmm,' Lucy said. 'Has it made you have any second thoughts?'

'No.' Rhea scowled. 'There's no connection whatsoever.'

Trish bit into a peach and juice began to trickle down her chin. She caught the drops in her cupped hand. 'It's been quite a holiday for you two, hasn't it?' she said, managing to smile and eat at the same time.

There was a sudden silence, and Trish's comment hung in the air like a speech bubble with no response.

Seda looked at Lucy and gave her a tiny sympathetic smile.

Rhea looked daggers at Trish, who bit her lip.

Lucy looked sharply at Rhea, then turned to Trish. 'What do you mean exactly?'

Trish reddened and fidgeted with the edge of the picnic rug. 'Oh…well…' She glanced at Rhea. 'Well, I only mean you've been up to a lot, haven't you…and what with the Brian and June thing.'

Rhea, Lucy and Seda all grimaced.

Trish looked flustered. 'Anyway, they've gone now. They paid for an earlier flight.'

'Good!' said Seda, so viciously that all three women stared at her. She noticed their amazement. 'I'm getting sick of my job and this is only my first season.' Her eyes misted over. 'I always thought it was what I wanted to do - it was my dream job. But some of the people…' She shook her head. 'But how are you supposed to know?'

'Don't feel too bad, Seda,' Lucy said. 'Sometimes you just don't know until you try something out. What do you think you want to do instead?'

'What about a job at the airport? They're always advertising!' Trish said.

'But you've still got the tourist people problem there,' observed Rhea, munching on some baklava.

'I don't know…I will have to think,' Seda replied. She peered out to sea as if to find the answer amongst the waves.

After half an hour or so, while Seda was describing to an inquisitive Lucy how to properly de-seed a pomegranate, Rhea caught Trish's eye and gave her a pointed look.

Trish nodded. 'Seda, why don't we go for a paddle?'

Seda stared at her. 'But I was going to go snorkelling for shells.'

'That's all right,' said Lucy quickly. 'Rhea and I need to talk, anyway. There's a nice sheltered spot where we can go, up by the lake.' She pointed vaguely behind her and up the beach. 'You stay here with the picnic and do what you fancy.'

Trish nodded.

Seda looked troubled.

'It's nothing,' Lucy said to Seda. 'Just something we need to sort out before we go home.'

Yes,' said Rhea. 'Let's go and do that now, then.' She grasped the second bottle of wine and two cups, glanced at Trish, then turned to follow Lucy up the beach.

Trish tittered nervously again, as she watched the sisters leave.

Seda stared at her wonderingly. 'What is wrong?'

'Oh, nothing...nothing yet, anyway.' She turned and smiled at Seda. 'Best get on with your snorkelling.'

***

As Rhea followed Lucy up the beach, she desperately needed a pee. Nerves were now getting the upper hand and she knew exactly why. When she emerged from the toilet block, she found Lucy patiently waiting. Here we go, she thought.

Lucy led the way to the muddy edge of a stagnant lake, then to the shade of an old pine tree, its trunk curving to the ground and just right for sitting on. Pink-bloomed stems of foliage trembled in the breeze and she could hear the shushing sound of the ocean. A faint chorus of cicada began their song in the invisible distance, but for some reason they didn't bother her. It was a secluded place where they would not be interrupted. Lucy was suitably adept at picking such locations, she thought wryly.

She took a couple of gulps of wine and tried to begin. 'Lucy, there's something I need to discuss - '

'Yes, I know.' Lucy flicked her hair back.

Rhea shot her a glance. 'What? You know already?' Her heart started to hammer in her chest. How could Lucy know her plans? And if she did, why was she being so calm?

'Of course I do. Now that we are going home, we have to agree on who to tell about Mum's death.'

Rhea felt her stomach lurch. That wasn't it. That wasn't it at all. 'But can't we just keep it between ourselves?' She noticed the pleading tone in her voice and resented it.

'Well, it's not that relevant, but Seda knows already - I was upset on the village life trip, she was there to talk to. She was very supportive, actually.'

'Seda knows,' repeated Rhea mechanically, trying to take it in. Then reality struck. 'But at home, nobody needs to know!'

Lucy gasped. 'Of course they do! I'll have to tell Charlie, I tell him everything! And then there's Poppy and what about Auntie Kathy?'

'But Poppy and Rob never knew Mum! What's the point? And as for Auntie Kathy, well there's no need to upset her. It was so long ago. Why bother?' She shook her head. This was not what they were supposed to be talking about. Trust Lucy. And trust Lucy to tell a tour guide. No matter how lovely a person Seda was, it was their own private business.

'But the truth is always important!'

'For who exactly? For whose benefit? I told you because you wouldn't let it go. You pushed and pushed…'

'Well, you're glad I pushed, aren't you?' Lucy looked at her fiercely.

Rhea shrank under her gaze. 'Yes…'

'And why?' Lucy sounded like a schoolteacher drilling a pupil for a right answer. 'Why are you glad?'

Rhea gave her what she wanted. 'Because I held it in for too long. Because Dad was probably wrong about keeping it secret - at least from you.' Then she resisted. 'But I don't know what good it would do for anyone else to know!'

Lucy stood up and began pacing about. 'But you

suffered, keeping it to yourself. Sharing it makes it easier to cope with. You've passed it to me, now I have to pass it on.'

Rhea groaned. This was taking too long. 'It's not like passing on a baton in a relay race, is it? It doesn't have to be passed on at all.' Then she saw the steely determination in Lucy's eyes and caved in. She didn't have time for this. 'Who do you suggest we tell, then?'

'Well, how about you tell Rob, for your own sake, so that you're not hiding anything from him? And I'll tell Charlie and Poppy for the same reasons.' Lucy frowned. 'I guess we can leave Auntie Kathy with her romantic illusions - I know all too well how comforting they can be.' She looked hard at Rhea. 'How does that sound?'

'Fine! Yes, that's fine,' she said in a rush. 'I can tell Chris, I suppose, though it doesn't matter one way or the other now.' She swallowed hard. 'Right. There's something I need - '

'So, is Dad off the pedestal you've had him on all this time?'

'Oh, for God's sake, Lucy! Yes, okay? Yes!' she yelled. 'Are you happy now?'

'Well happy isn't exactly - '

'And if we're going down this road, is Mum off your pedestal?'

Lucy flinched. 'Yes.'

Rhea saw the desolation in her face. Lucy was right, it was a lot to get your head around when you hadn't known all these years. And she was soon in for another shock.

The wind shook the leaves of the shrubs, and some pink petals fluttered down. Rhea dug her toes into the sand, feeling the warmth. As she scanned the sky between the overhanging pine branches, she saw a few gulls circling overhead. Their screeching urged her on.

She turned to look at her sister, who was sitting next to her again, looking a little defeated. 'Lucy,' she said gently.

'There's something I need to tell you.' She hesitated. 'I won't be - '

'You know what you said the other day about being a kind of agent for me?'

Rhea groaned. Was she ever going to be able to say the words she'd been practicing all last night? 'Yes, of course. And I meant it. I'm good at marketing.'

Lucy gave her a small smile. 'I know that. But I've decided to do it myself.'

'Are you sure? Can't I at least help?' Rhea felt desperate. She needed to do something to help Lucy. She owed her that much with what she was about to tell her. 'Please. I want to.'

Lucy looked surprised. 'Well, okay, if you feel strongly about it. Maybe I can use you to check things with. But I'll have a good stab at it myself. I just have to change my attitude,' she said pensively.

'Right. Good. Now, there's something I need to tell you.' She forced herself to ignore Lucy's plaintive tone. Her mouth was dry, so she took a swig of wine. She poured some into a cup for Lucy and handed it to her.

Lucy took it and frowned. 'What kind of something? What else is there? You have told me everything. You haven't kept - '

'Shut up!' Rhea snapped. 'Shut up and listen!'

'Okay! Keep your hair on!'

'It's about going home.'

'Well, what about it? You know, when we go home, we'll have to make an effort to keep in touch from now on - proper visits.'

This is it, thought Rhea, say it now. She could feel Lucy's eyes upon her. Say it now!

She turned to face her. 'I'm not going home.'

Rhea waited. Waited for a reaction, her own words reverberating in her skull.

Lucy's eyes slowly widened. Then her mouth dropped open. She stood up and backed away a little. Her wondering expression slowly changed, into what Rhea perceived as on the cusp of a scream in a Hammer House of Horror film. Rhea shuddered. She would never forget this look.

'What?' Lucy whispered. 'What do you mean?' Then her voice rose. 'What the hell are you talking about?'

Rhea gulped. Now it was time for the explanation. And in some ways this was even harder. To say the words would crystallise her plans, and they were so fragile, she was frightened they would shatter.

'Well?' Lucy insisted. 'What are you talking about? We have a flight home tomorrow. How are you *not* going to be on it?'

All the facts Rhea had researched since the walk to Kaunos came tumbling out. 'I checked with Trish yesterday. We came in on a visa, right? Well, it lasts for three months. After that I can apply for a resident's permit, then later, if I can sort out some work, I can get a work permit. And of course I'll need a Turkish bank account and somewhere to live. I talked to Eleanor and she is contacting her friend, Susie, to see if I can stay at the villa while I sort myself out. I want to try and - '

'Have you gone mad?'

Lucy's tone was quiet and preternaturally restrained. It shook Rhea and she broke out in a sweat. Still standing in the same spot, Rhea felt Lucy scrutinising her, looking at her as if she was a brand new species that she just couldn't make sense of.

Maybe I have gone mad, Rhea thought. She barely recognised herself any more. All she knew was that there was a space inside her where a lump used to be, a hard lump of something which, in the last few days, had slowly dissolved like a compound swirled around in a solvent, like in chemistry class at school. She felt easier, more free, and she had this picture in her mind of sailing off into her own sunset. Madness, or not.

'Why do you want to stay here?' Lucy's voice insisted.

Then a look of panic flashed across her face. 'You are alright, aren't you? What's going on, Rhea? You're scaring me.'

'I'm fine! Better than I have been for months actually. I want to see if I can live here and run a business.'

'You want to live here,' Lucy repeated, 'and run a business?' She gaped at Rhea, the moments swelling and tightening, while the pine branches rustled overhead. She tipped all of the wine in her cup down her throat, then as soon as she'd swallowed, questions started haemorrhaging out.

'What are you going to live on? What business are you talking about? How are you going to get divorced if you're here?'

Rhea took a deep breath. This was better. This was Lucy starting to recover.

'What about the store? What about your friends?' A pause. 'This isn't about Hasim, is it?'

'No,' Rhea replied curtly. Just an added bonus, she thought, at least for a while.

'But most of all - what about Rob?'

And this was the question Rhea had been asking herself in the dark of the night, and when the Imam chanted his call in the early hours of the morning. This was her Achilles heel, which could break her.

'I don't know…' she mumbled. 'I just hope he'll understand.'

Lucy threw her cup down, grabbed hold of Rhea, and turned her around. Their faces were just a few inches apart. 'Rhea! Are you really serious about this?'

'Yes.'

***

When Lucy saw the look on Rhea's face and the tears in her eyes, she knew she meant it. Lucy's breath hitched in her throat and shock tingled down her spine.

'I need…' she said, 'I need to think.'

She jumped up and started making long strides away from their spot by the pond and down to the beach. She needed to get away from Rhea, the picnic, everything. She could hear Rhea panting, running after her.

'Lucy!' Rhea called. 'Don't go off. Please don't go off! I need to explain!'

'What is there to explain?' Lucy shouted back at her. 'You've made your mind up. You've plotted with others behind my back. Stuff me and everyone at home!'

Rhea fell back, and Lucy marched on - through the sunbathers simmering on recliners, through the inane cries of teenagers tossing a stupid ball around, she stumbled on through the stifling hot air - sights, sounds and heat suddenly so alien. A beach in Turkey, miles away from home, with a foreign sky stretching as far as the eye could see. She wanted Charlie. He would know what to say to Rhea. Blindly stalking along the water's edge towards the cliff face, she halted when she found herself in the same spot she had gone swimming from, after the village trip into the hills. She sat down on a rock and propped her head in her hands. But riddled with confusions, she found she just couldn't think straight. So, she allowed a numbness to descend upon her like a thick fog, screening off her mind and hiding herself from view. It was far more comfortable like that.

After what seemed like a long while, she looked out at the ocean. Not thinking of anything at first, just absorbing the visual. She was drawn to the flickering water, silver dazzle on ultramarine blue, and the texture of the rocks on the shoreline, a chiaroscuro of bright highlights and dark shadows. She remembered swimming with the turtle, and being suspended in the glowing vortex of rays. How wonderful it had been. How lucky she had been to experience it. How she had wanted to see a caretta on this holiday, swimming free, and how she had done so - absolutely regardless of everything else. And how she had even touched the turtle. Then she looked down at the pebbles cast around her feet by the play of the tides - charcoal, ivory white, and terracotta, scribbled and scored with veins of pigment. Painting methods popped into her mind - how she would go about painting all these textures around her. She knew she had a way of seeing that only artists have.

And she thought to herself, I never want to lose this. Not ever.

And in that moment, she felt certain that no matter what, she had to go on painting. And this was what she'd felt yesterday, slowly starting to renew itself in her, like adding drops of water to something dried out and desiccated. Even after finding out about her mother. And through talking about her art issues to Rhea, and Rhea actually defending her to that pompous Malcolm, some simple facts pumped into her heart and brought her to life. Facts that had marched into this holiday with all its ups and downs. Do the work because it was her passion, do the work and love her creative life more than her self-imposed oppressions. Use some of her dad's inheritance to get by. And as for the garden centre, get a manager to run it to free up Charlie and herself, as Rhea had suggested. Her heart kept pumping. No more comparing herself to others, or to her mother, and not to let the art market decide what she should paint. And with her eyes firmly fixed on the horizon, she vowed to herself that the first set of paintings she would do when she got home would be of this beach.

Feeling thirsty, she let the fog lift and she reached for her water. After she'd drained the bottle, she looked along the beach, scanning the bodies, suddenly feeling guilty that she hadn't been thinking about Rhea. She saw Trish sunbathing on a recliner, but there was no sign of Seda. Then she spotted a woman in a white bikini, trudging through the sand towards her.

As Rhea approached, Lucy saw the worried look on her

face, the despair in her stooped shoulders. And once again, Lucy saw that Rhea was absolutely serious. She gave her a small smile and decided that with her own resolutions in place - admittedly for the time being - then the least she could do would be to listen to Rhea.

Rhea sat herself down on a jagged piece of the same boulder Lucy was sitting on. She said nothing and just stared at her feet.

'I'm sorry I marched off,' Lucy said.

'It's alright. I can hardly believe it myself.'

'Tell me what you want to do. And by the way, I'm angry that Trish and Eleanor got to know before me.'

Rhea straightened up. 'Yes, well I had to find out if it was feasible, didn't I?'

'Well, okay, I can see that. But how long have you been planning it?'

'Believe it or not, the idea only came to me yesterday.'

'Yesterday! What are you thinking?'

'Yes, I know. I know how it sounds. But I was thinking how Dad always used to play safe, always prioritise security, and because I consulted him over problems, he got me doing the same. I've followed his advice all my life, no room for spontaneity because of the risks. And Mum - well, look what yearning dreams and spontaneity did to her in the end. She wasn't a good example, was she?' She sighed heavily. 'Well, I'm tired of my life, Lucy. I'm tired of my job and I'm tired of Chris. And I have to do something about it.'

Lucy felt an aftershock ripple through her. 'Well, you've told me about Chris, and I can't say I blame you. And not that it's relevant, but I never liked him much. But are you really tired of your job? You came out with that yesterday to that stupid Malcolm, but I thought it was just bluster for effect.'

'No. When I said it, it struck me - I mean it. It's too competitive, too much paperwork, too many meetings, too much following trends and always being answerable to others, instead of me being answerable to me.'

'Well…naturally, I can understand that,' Lucy said hesitatingly.

'I want to work for myself. I wanted to years ago, but played safe instead.'

Rhea sounded so emphatic, Lucy looked hard at her.

'And for some reason,' Rhea continued, 'I want to do it here. Despite all we've been through, I find myself loving this place.'

'I can't say I noticed,' Lucy said, trying to keep the sarcasm out of her voice. 'Apart from the market maybe, and the food - oh, and of course the pool and the Turkish baths.' She paused, thinking also of Hasim, but she was desperate to think of something negative. 'What about the cicadas?' she said with a sense of triumph. 'How will you put up with them?'

Rhea frowned. 'I'll just have to get used to them, won't I?'

Lucy felt dumbfounded. 'But are these things enough?'

Rhea paused and wrinkled her forehead. 'Well, there's also the climate, the culture, the landscape…'

Lucy raised her eyebrows. 'I thought it was me that fell in love with the landscape…you haven't seemed bothered.'

Rhea grimaced. 'No, not at all! I like the lake, the riverside, and the countryside I saw on the way back from Ephesus, and I really like Dalyan.' Then her face softened. 'But it was the market that got to me - the fabrics, the jewellery, such beautiful designs, and the belly dancing skirts. They just switched something on in me.'

Lucy became intrigued. Was this really her sister talking?

And Rhea went on to explain her vision of a retail business, stocking filigree artisan jewellery, gemstone rings -

'Rings again?' Lucy interrupted. 'What is it about rings?'

'Yes, rings,' Rhea said, as she continued wistfully describing her vision. She would source gemstones from all over Turkey, have a craftsman make the most beautiful jewellery, and she would stock Turkish fabrics, weaves, satins, chiffons and even maybe have a dressmaker make up some belly dancing costumes with full bedlah, for local dancers and tourists, and she would stock rugs, and pottery…and whatever other beautiful things she came across. Interiors, crafts and fashion, she said finally with emphasis.

The glowing light in Rhea's eyes was infectious to Lucy. And despite her objections she found she could see it: interconnecting rooms, white-washed walls, dark tables of wares, cabinets of jewellery, walls hung with oriental rugs, and the textile and costume area, racks of exotic confabulations. How exciting it would be to make those - maybe she could help with the designs? But she checked herself, she was a painter now. No distractions.

'Will there be paintings?' she asked.

Rhea's expression changed. 'I'm not sure,' she said. 'From what you've told me, I might be better off not engaging in it. But, of course I can display some of yours.'

Lucy managed a laugh. Then suddenly she was struck by the rooms she'd being imagining. She'd been in this space yesterday - the gallery where she got her tiles - and the owner wanted to sell up to get back to her husband, now that the dog had died.

'Remember I told you the owner of the Pomegranate gallery wanted to sell? At least that's what Trish told me. It's a lovely interior.'

Rhea raised her eyebrows. 'No, I don't remember you saying.'

'Well, you weren't taking much notice of me at the time.'

'Don't start.' Rhea paused. 'Oh well, I could make some enquiries. I'm not interested in the cafe. But maybe it's run separately, or could be, anyway.'

They looked at each other.

'I can't believe we're having this conversation,' Lucy said.

'Neither can I.'

'How will you fund it?' Lucy asked, but she knew the answer as soon as the words were out of her mouth.

'Dad's money I suppose, plus I have some back-up savings.'

'Do you think he'd approve?'

Rhea sighed. 'I don't know. I hope so, if it works out.'

Lucy was struck by incredulity again. 'Rhea, are you really sure about all this?'

Rhea sighed. 'I'm as sure as I can be. But it will be an experiment. I don't know - it just feels right.'

'Feels right!' Lucy exclaimed. 'But this is what bothers me. You don't say things like this. You weigh things up, you assess things, you pick over the details, and here you are, not having even worked out costs or a business plan, ready to plough your inheritance into something you thought up yesterday. It's as if you've had a personality transplant.'

Rhea bit her lip and her eyes narrowed. 'I know... I really do. I can't explain it. But I've got the feeling that I have to do it here and now. If I go home, I'm scared I'll get sucked back into work at the store again, and all the rest of the routine...don't you see? I'd go back into secure mode. I'm frightened this feeling will vanish. And I just can't let it. All I am worried about is Rob. I'll explain the basics to him, but will you visit him and talk to him? Please, Lucy? Will you?'

Lucy saw the pain in Rhea's face, the tears now rolling down her reddened cheeks. It was a rare sight and she was moved by it.

'It's got to be now,' Rhea said, wiping her face. 'I want a fresh start - and after all, we're not getting any younger.'

Lucy stared out to sea. 'That's true. Maybe it's a mid-life thing.' She turned to look at Rhea. 'But if it doesn't work out, you will come home, won't you?'

Rhea nodded. 'I promise. And I'll visit as soon as I can.' She hesitated. 'So you'll explain to Rob?'

'Yes. Don't worry, I'll explain it well.'

'I know. That's why I'm asking you.'

A silence fell. Lucy became conscious of the noise of holiday makers further down the beach, splashing around in the shallows. Having fun.

'Let's go for a swim,' she said. 'We can talk about the rest tonight. Let's just enjoy the rest of the day.'

Rhea looked up, surprised. 'Can we do that?'

'We can try.'

Lucy plunged into the water, determined to have no remaining nerves about swimming ever again after her recent scare. She swam out of her depth and flipped onto her back, gazing at the sky. Rhea swam, head out of the water, in the shallows. And after they had cooled off, they waded back to shore, their shins blotched with fading mosquito bites - less desirable souvenirs of their holiday. Lucy stumbled over a hidden rock and Rhea's arm shot out to steady her. They paddled along the waterline to find Trish and Seda. It was a nice feeling, paddling together, Lucy reflected - it felt right.

**

When the sisters spotted the picnic area, they could see that Trish and Seda were there. But there was also a flamboyantly dressed woman waving at them and making her way over with a camera. Eleanor drifted towards them like a steamer in full sail, wearing a huge floppy-brimmed white sunhat on top of her loose red hair, with a kaftan of flowers fluttering around her curves.

'Hi guys!' she cried. 'Stay right there! I've just gotta take your picture.'

They halted on the edge of the sea foam as it churned around their ankles, while Eleanor moved in on them.

464

They glanced at each other, moved a bit closer together, then smiled for the camera.

'Real nice!' Eleanor said, clicking the shutter, then clutching at her hat, as it attempted an unscheduled take off in a gust of sea breeze.

In the months to come, both sisters had a copy of this picture to mark their holiday. Of symbolic significance of course, but it has to be said, the lighting was also most flattering, for which they were both very grateful.

The women finished off their picnic, with another cup of wine to celebrate Rhea staying on. Ripples of laughter flowed between them, with an occasional sudden silence from Lucy, lost in thought.

Seda's astonishment at the reveal of Rhea's plans was a wonder to see, comprising of a sequence of film stills from a jaw dropping 'No!', to blank incomprehension, to smiling curiosity, and these were repeated in the same order when Rhea told her there might be a job for her if she was interested.

Eleanor's friend, Susie, had agreed to let Rhea stay rent free at the Villa Vita, until she had sorted herself out. Rhea was visibly thrilled, while Lucy was visibly relieved.

Trish had an announcement to make which she had withheld until now. After all, timing was everything, she said. At the end of the season she was going home for a winter break.

'My sister wants me to be Godmother to her new baby girl. They're going to wait for me to be there for the christening. I can't believe she's asked me.'

Rhea smiled. 'That's great, Trish. And you might get along better than in the past, you know - with your Dad. People change.'

'Well, I don't know about that, but I'll give it a shot,' Trish replied.

They remained on the beach until they'd all had their fill of sun, sea and sand, then as the others were packing up, Rhea and Lucy walked a little way along the shore together for one last look at the turtle beach.

'The other day, I was remembering those portraits Mum did of us,' Lucy said. 'Do you remember? I had bunches in my hair, and you had long blonde hair, before you went punk.'

'Yes. I kept my picture, actually.'

'Did you?' Lucy sounded surprised. 'Why? Considering how you must have felt.'

'I don't know...I wanted to throw it away. But I suppose I liked it... and it was a connection of a kind. I kept it at the back of the wardrobe.'

'Oh well, at least we both have those, and I'll sort out the rest from Dad's attic - okay?'

'Okay.'

Lucy turned reflective again, as she picked up a shell and examined its contours - another memento to add to her collection of pebbles. 'Do you remember Mum saying to us *The world is your oyster*?'

Rhea smiled. 'Yes.'

'Maybe it's apt now?'

'Maybe it is.' Rhea nodded.

'But what about Dad? What would he say?'

Rhea frowned. 'Well, he'd say *The grass is always greener,* wouldn't he?'

Lucy laughed, then became serious. 'How do you really feel about him now?'

Rhea sighed. 'Well...put it this way, if I hadn't told you about Mum, I know I would still be going home tomorrow.' She hesitated. 'But by breaking the promise - well, we've kind of kept the one about us getting along. I think that'll have to do.'

The next afternoon, Hasim drove them both to the airport so Rhea could see Lucy off. Sadik accompanied them, curled on the floor at Lucy's feet. Inside the car they were all very quiet, so Hasim turned on the radio and they listened to upbeat Turkish pop songs.

A couple of hours later, Lucy and Rhea stood together in the departure lounge to say goodbye. Hasim gave Lucy a kiss on each cheek and respectfully withdrew.

'You'll let me know you get back safely?' Rhea said.

'Of course.'

They studied each other.

There didn't seem to be anything else to say, as they'd discussed all the details already and each had made a long list of things to attend to.

'Look after yourself,' Lucy said, on the verge of tears.

'You too,' replied Rhea.

Then Lucy gave Rhea a hug, and Rhea hugged her back.

Reaching into her bag, Lucy gave Rhea a small folded packet. 'I got you this. It might come in handy.'

Rhea opened the packet and drew out a bright turquoise evil eye on a silver chain. Nice quality, nice design. She grinned. 'It's perfect, Lucy.'

'Good.'

'Oh, I nearly forgot,' said Rhea. She delved into her bag and brought out some folded papers. 'It's the log of the holiday. I thought you might like to have it. I've filled it all in.'

Lucy smiled. 'Thanks. It seems like a long time ago since we started this.'

Rhea nodded. 'Yes, a very long time.'

After one more hug, Lucy joined a queue of people, giving Rhea a final wave before leaving to board the plane.

***

From the observation lounge, Rhea watched the plane as it lifted its mass gracefully into the air, slowly becoming a glimmering speck and vanishing into a hazy sky, taking her sister home. Her mind stretched out and away down a runway of its own, leading to a place deep within herself,

467

through that jungle, rotted and matted with bereavement and the practicalities of life. It led to the girl she used to be, now blossoming inside. Now, with Lucy's help, she'd cleared the way and she could be that self again. This was a new beginning, and she had Lucy on her side, for which she was very grateful. She smiled, then turned and pushed her way upstream through the flow of tourists to find Hasim and return to Dalyan.

Meanwhile, Lucy tried to distract herself from the relentless tinny beats and shuffles coming from the music player plugged into the teenager nearby, and from her feelings and thoughts tumbling and scumbling in confusion, and from the razor-edged fact at the centre of it all that she was going home without her sister. She avoided eye contact with the empty seat next to her, and couldn't bear to watch the landmass of Turkey disappearing below, giving way to miles of ocean. So she studied the airline magazine on her lap, open at the world's flight paths. The white line trajectories were criss-crossing, interlocking and knotting into a tight bundle of threads - the sort she was familiar with from when her sewing machine needle at home kept going over the same stitch when the material was too thick.

She sank back into her seat, sighed, and closed her eyes. Just focus on seeing Charlie, she thought. She'd missed him so much. And she was desperate to see Poppy again, with a new resolution of setting her a good example in her approach to art. Lots of conversations, lots of encouragement. And focus on the fact that in the next day or two, she'd be driving down to Leicester, to talk to Rob, to somehow avoid Chris who had not yet responded to Rhea's text, and to bring home Suki. Suki was Rhea's long-haired pedigree Persian house cat, who was now going to have to relocate to live in the country, with fields to explore and mice to disembowel, and who'd somehow have to get along with Laddie, the border collie.

Then her mood shifted, as she visualised Suki in her

new terrain and she opened her eyes and began to twist a stray strand of her hair. It was change all around then, and change was good.

Epilogue

Rhea poured herself a gin and tonic, and slid a slice of lemon into the chilled glass.

The phone in the living room rang. She took her drink and sat down to answer it.

'Rhea?'

'Lucy?'

'Well, it's finally happened.'

'What?'

'A decent exhibition. At the Laing Art Gallery in Newcastle, of all places, where I met Mum's lover all those years ago. They're doing a series on contemporary regional art and I'm next on the agenda - they like my traditional style. Plus they want a couple of Poppy's paintings too, as a mother and daughter connection.'

'That's great.' Rhea said. 'I'll come over for the preview.'

'Lovely. And I've got some other galleries further afield wanting work too. Looks like the marketing is working after all.'

'Will there be some sea paintings?'

'Yes. I've saved the ones of turtle beach. Why?'

'Oh, because I want one for my bedroom here. I need blues and whites.'

'Oh, do you now? Well I expect I can accommodate you.' Then Lucy paused. 'How are things going at Pomegranate Designs?'

'Good. Better than I expected. After all, it's only been a year. The tourists and the local dancers are loving the oriental dance costumes and the textiles. And try stopping women buying jewellery and scarves. Seda's travelling all over the South looking for quality stock. She's got a really good eye for gemstones, and we're using her knowledge about the properties of the stones as a selling point.'

'Sounds great.' Lucy hesitated again. 'And how's the divorce coming along?'

Rhea sighed. 'Well, he's been very difficult, but we seem to be reaching an agreement now. He says I can sell the house and keep the proceeds, if he can have the endowment - and he wants a few thousand for some new business plans. So I've agreed to that to end it.'

'Right...well that's good news, then. And what about Hasim?'

'What about him?'

'Well, are you two officially together now?'

Rhea hesitated. 'I wouldn't say that exactly. We suit each other, we help each other out with the business side of things, and enjoy each other's company - that's it. It is what it is.'

Lucy giggled. 'It is what it is, and you are what you are.' Then her tone changed. 'You know, Rhea...'

'What?'

'Well, I've been thinking...'

'What about? You do an awful lot of it.'

'Yes, I know.' Lucy faltered. 'But I'm being drawn to a new creative direction.'

'What? But what about your painting? You've made a name for yourself now. Wasn't that what you wanted?'

Yes...and it has been great. But the thing is, now I know what it's like to be properly successful, well it just isn't what you think, Rhea. You have to do commissions all the time, so you don't have much freedom to paint what you want, and when you want. And the art world is still posturing and pretentious, that hasn't changed and I don't like playing their games.'

'Well, what are you getting at?' Rhea sounded irritated.

'And do you remember what Grandma Allen used to say - *be careful what you wish for, otherwise you might get it?*'

'Yes,' Rhea replied impatiently.

'Well, I think it's true. I think it must be more about the

journey. Anyway, what I'm getting at is, I fancy moving into something else, but where I can still paint.'

'Like what?'

'Well, maybe some kind of freelance travel writing, for part of the year. I could write about the land, the people, but from a cultural art and craft slant, so that I can delve into art techniques and art history. And of course the photography will come in handy. I really want to visit different landscapes now, and that would give the travelling a purpose. I could still paint my impressions of places, which could be themed exhibitions at home. Who knows, it might even all end up in a book. There's no rule in life that says you can only do one thing, is there? Dad always told me I should find a way of channelling my energies, and I think this is it.'

'But what about Charlie?'

Oh, well that's the thing. He likes the idea. He wants us to go together. He's due some time off, and he can take it now that the new manager is working out well. He wants to get back to his ceramics and he can get some ideas from other cultures. And Poppy's okay with it, she's busy with her own life now. But she says she'll look after Laddie and Suki.' She paused. 'So, what do you think…'

Rhea was silent for a few moments. 'Well…it sounds as if you've both made up your minds, sounds like you've thought it through. Why are you asking me?'

Lucy hesitated. 'I suppose I wanted to know what you thought.'

'Well, go for it, then.'

'Okay. Well, I'd better not stay on the line any longer.' Bye for now.'

'Bye.'

***

Rhea put the phone down and she shook her head thinking about Lucy. Lucy had always been irrepressible

473

and full of ideas. She'd hated her for it for so long. But she had to acknowledge their lives had moved on because of it.

She took her gin and tonic out onto the balcony of her new villa, which was conveniently situated opposite Pomegranate Designs. Money was very tight, but she'd desperately wanted a place of her own. Once the tourist season was over, the takings from the business would go down and she'd have to find some other avenues. But certainly not like Chris's doomed ventures. She had to admit, sailing off into the sunset had its flaws. And she thought of her father. Well, Dad, she said to herself, the grass *is* greener, and I'm going to make sure it flickers in the sunshine for as long as possible.

She smiled. Rob and his new girlfriend were flying over tomorrow for a visit and she couldn't wait to show them around the shop and around town. So, she was concentrating on the present. And after all, her dad had also told her to play things by ear. So she sipped her drink, she listened to the cicada chorus vibrating in the pomegranate trees below, and watched the orange yolk of the sun sink behind the violet hills of Dalyan. As the Imam started to chant the call to prayer over the pan tile roofs, she spotted a bird of prey circling and gliding on outstretched wings. She watched it, as it angled itself towards the horizon, as it became a tiny speck and disappeared.

***

Lucy put the phone down and went back to her canvas. As she started blending the clouds in her sky with a fan brush, she felt annoyed, because, as usual Rhea had managed to make her feel silly. Why shouldn't she ask her sister about her plans? She got up, too tense to paint for the moment. Oh well, she sighed, it was probably expecting a bit much after all they'd been through, and it wasn't as if she needed Rhea's approval - but there again, Rhea had needed it from her to stay in Dalyan. She groaned; being *real* sisters was complicated. She was still plagued by a few lingering questions about her mother and father, but Rhea wasn't interested. So there was nowhere to take them, no one to take them to, and it probably wasn't worth the bother anyway. Enough had to be enough, life was for the living…and many other clichés sprang to mind, for which she had now grown a new respect for.

She stroked Suki, who was pegged out on her back on top of the painting table, all floppy limbs and curled paws, without a care in the world. Lucy smiled, Suki was pretty good company for a cat. She glanced at Laddie snoozing in the corner – he wasn't getting so many runs these days.

In the next moment she suddenly realised she hadn't mentioned to Rhea that she'd spotted June and Brian in the Metrocentre, while she and Poppy were having coffee in a cafe. They didn't see her, so she was able to watch them - Brian shuffling in June's wake, loaded down with bags, while June strutted ahead, barking instructions at him over her shoulder, and flashing just as many rings and gold chains as she could accumulate on her personage. Lucy had felt very little except wry amusement at the sight of them. But she decided now that Rhea probably wouldn't have welcomed the reminder.

Wandering over to the studio windowsill, she trailed her hand over the pebbles from turtle beach which she had used for numerous still lifes. Then she examined the potted-on spider plants, which were doing well. Their spiky leaves reminded her of the chaparral landscape she'd felt so attracted to on the day of the jeep trip into the hills. This was going to be her new subject matter, and she and Charlie had talked about going to a few of the national parks in North America: Death Valley, Arizona, the Mojave Desert, and the Grand Canyon. There was so much to see, so much to explore. But for now, she settled herself back at her canvas and continued blending the sky, thinking of bleached rocks, sandy soils, Joshua trees, and lots and lots of sagebrush on big lands with big skies. The world was her oyster, that's what her mother had said. And as her thoughts drifted and she worked her brush, the hours once more sank beneath the surface of the day.

ABOUT THE AUTHOR

A writer who is passionate about plunging the depths of human nature, who is an artist, a nature lover, and who shares her life with her soul mate and a cat. Lynne writes literary fiction to explore how we can work through our inner conflicts to come to a place of wisdom and wellbeing.

On Turtle Beach is her first novel, inspired by her fascination with the nature of sibling bonds and by a love of the natural world, where the novel's setting of Dalyan in Turkey became a special place in her heart.

After Black is Lynne's second novel, set in 1990 in Cheltenham, and it spans four decades prior. Janet, a dark and embittered widow, returns to her beloved job at the store, only to find her future peace and happiness soon shattered by a feisty young co-worker she loathes. The mutual antagonism between the two women leads to Janet revealing a terrible secret which soon escalates into her dark and unhappy past being dragged into the light of the present.

Thank you for taking the time to read On Turtle Beach. If you enjoyed it, please consider telling your friends and posting a short review on Amazon. Reviews help independent authors by helping other readers to find their book, by boosting a book's visibility, and by providing useful feedback. It doesn't have to be long, just one or two sentences will do. Many thanks from Lynne.

You can find Lynne at:

Writer's Blog: lynnefisher.wordpress.com

www.facebook.com/lynnefisherheadtoheadhearttoheart

Newsletter sign up for forthcoming books:
http://eepurl.com/gF6ilr

Printed in Great Britain
by Amazon

23037803R00273